The SEAWEED CAGE

DOROTHY BRUCE

Twinlaw

First Published in Great Britain 2014
by Twinlaw Publishing
Kirkcairn, Westruther, Gordon
Scottish Borders TD3 6NE

A CIP catalogue record for this title is available
from the British Library

Paperback ISBN: 978-0-9575913-5-6

www.twinlawpublishing.co.uk

For Russell
- hope you and others
enjoy the story

About the author

Dorothy Bruce has been involved with the restoration of a Victorian pier, the running of an annual festival, curating an exhibition, organisation of a one-off literary award and a multi-agency destination development project. A number of her short stories have been published, she has written restaurant reviews, and one of her plays *See them rats* toured the Scottish Borders in late 2012 as part of a double bill.

An interest in politics was part of her family life, as politics in Scotland during her lifetime has rarely been dull, often strident, a rollercoaster of celebration and drowned sorrows that pulled people into enthusiastic for or against camps. So, not surprisingly, she has occasionally been drawn into active involvement.

She finds the manipulative world of politics fascinating as well as appalling, especially the effect it can have on people, and in her writing creates stories of those who found themselves overtaken by events, often forced into actions, or making decisions they never expected to make.

Dorothy writes a regular blog at -
http://jingsandthings.wordpress.com

Also by Dorothy Bruce
In the Wake of the Coup
Alexander Reid and the Japanese Influence: Art, ships and plants.

Contents

Contents (cont.)

Is Caledon Scotland?

Is Caledon Scotland?

Political machinations and intrigue are common to all counties, especially at times of potential change, whether that be an election, a referendum, or any event that is viewed as a threat to the status quo.

The carrot of success, both party and personal, is dangled tantalisingly at such times, and the desire to bite from it is spurred by the nightmare of being knocked from the political pedestal and having the carrot swung beyond immediate grasp.

The Seaweed Cage takes place in Caledon, a country similar to Scotland, one which is governed from a parliament in another country to which it is attached.

The similarities end there, though the political situation described may lead some readers to conclude Caledon is indeed Scotland. However, that decision could only be reached by accepting the existence of a political party whose members and adherents would stoop to the most noir of black deeds to achieve their ends.

Surely that doesn't sound like Scotland.

Scotland is a country of many personas, of many names — Scotland, Scotia, Alba, Caledonia. Caledon, in this second book where I have used the name, is based on all these and on none of them. So just pour another glass of wine and enjoy the story.

1 - Dirty rats not golden boys

The oxygen of recklessness pumps through his veins, and eggs him to do something crazy, something mad, whatever idiocy he wants. His fate no longer lies in his own hands. He doesn't pause to query who now guides it, nor in what direction this new guiding hand might lead him. Instead he feels as if he is riding a spout of freedom, buoyed up in the air, the grip of the regulatory world falling away, the restraints imposed by convention blown off by the winds that circle, skittish with bubbles of exuberance.

To him and those who know his habits, his sense of release is obvious from his actions this morning, a Friday. His usual routine is exploded by anticipation of the weekend ahead, intensified like fizz in a shaken drinks can. He flags the change by leaving the outside door to the building wide open instead of closing it. 'A wee concession to liberty,' he tells himself, 'but one that indicates changes afoot.' He grins. To ensure the door is closed against all marauders is second nature in the protection of his privacy, his safety, and he rails at the few neighbours who are careless about shutting out all those not invited to enter via the door buzzer.

He abandons his usual caution in crossing the street to reach his car. He waits, energy canned, until the road is busy with traffic. Lorries edge forward, air brakes huff, cars and cyclists weave, then he plays chicken, and slaloms between vehicles. Horns honk, fingers gesticulate, from car windows comments are catapulted, shredded by the surrounding noise. 'Same to you, mate,' he shouts. 'Merry Christmas to you too.' He bows mockingly. Heads shake. Another nutcase druggie – someone should do something about the bastards.

From a window that overlooks his car, reflected light pinpoints the lens of a camera as angle and focus are altered to continue shooting. 'Right bloody nutter, this one,' says the photographer to his companion who balances on a canvas stool. His fingernail chisels between two teeth while eyes gorge on a photo in a men's magazine, top shelf variety. 'No difficulties with him. Look at him. Look. This one'll be dead easy.'

'You said that before.'

'Aye, well, nothin' at his home, but...'

'He'll lead us right to his stash, y' think?'

'Bound to.'

'Wouldnae be so sure.'

'Why's that?'

'Political involvement's made him a slippy bugger. Besides, I'm no sure drugs're his thing.'

'You think we're wastin' our time?'

'Could be.'

'You reckon there's a bit of old pals' chicanery at work?'

'What d'you think?'

'Whatever, tell them he's off.' The surveillance photographer's hand feels the table behind him for a sandwich. He glares at the filling. Cheese and tomato. His grunts, sound like a Saddleback pig. 'No imagination, my wife, no bloody imagination.' A slice of tomato waltzes down the front of his sweatshirt.

Once behind the steering wheel the guy revs the engine and shoots out into the train of traffic. Feet thump brakes to avoid metal enmeshing with metal. Horns blare like rutting deer in defence of their patch.

The avoidance of contact with other vehicles by a hair's breadth enlivens him. 'Hasta la vista,' he shouts to his surroundings. 'So long you stony-hearted bastards.' He boosts his mood further by retuning the radio to a station that thunders out pop music, turns the volume up and opens the window, replicating the actions of those he usually dismisses as poseurs. Into fourth gear with no intention of changing down. As he runs red lights, his heart leaps. Whooping with elation he accelerates past traffic cameras, and, like a fox in a hencoop, scatters pedestrians on crossings. Euphoric at his superior strength, he charges along bus lanes in front of bus drivers livid at his insolence, and parks on double yellow lines while he shops for nothing in particular, swaggering in a cloak of nonchalance. 'Stick two fingers up at the world. Goad, this is the way to live.'

Then onto the dual carriageway, where he belts along a stretch, topping ninety, and induces several heart attacks by driving the wrong way along the carriageway. A few near misses as he spins the wheel, hauls it from side to side, slews into shifting spaces, and cuts across lanes. The sport is exhilarating, yet tiring too, so as he approaches the next slip road he swings into a nifty U-turn, using the additional road width to manoeuvre, one hand on the steering wheel while he flaps the other through the window at drivers around him, gobsmacked by his actions. 'Ach, lighten up, you creeps. Get a life.'

As a glance at the gauge warns he is low on fuel, he squeals off at the next exit. The wee red light flickers, indecisive whether there's a gallon or a few spoonfuls tickling its elderly sensor. With a whirl of the steering wheel, he swings alongside a pump in a shiny petrol station, all tubes and dials like a hospital intensive care unit. After filling he replaces the cap on the car's tank, flips shut the door it hides behind, and debates with himself whether he should play the conventional game and queue to pay in the kiosk, or whether he should slide with nonchalance into the seat of his old Vauxhall and zoom off. 'Should I? Shouldn't I?' He stands, hand on the handle of the driver's door, and debates with himself. 'Would be fun. Sure would. No doubt about it. No doubt at all.'

Reduction of the oil company's profits by the cost of his tank of petrol appeals to him. A small gesture, but a gesture nonetheless. 'Maybe I could encourage others to join in,' he muses. 'A mass non-payment protest at petrol stations across the country. Fill up and fuck off. Think about it, Vauxy.' He thuds the car roof with his fist. 'A rank and file protest against the capitalists who bleed the family man and his car dry. And what do those capitalists make their millions from? Not from the manufacture of something new or monumental like ships or engines. Not from forging greatness and world renown through use of the knowledge of generations, the hands of careworn workers like my old Dad. No siree! They make their sodding fortunes from sucking goo from the ground. Pump it up and pipe it around. Sticky black goo. And from that the profits flow. And flow. Year after sodding year.'

He opens the car door. 'Though, if we're honest with ourselves, Vauxy,' he continues his dialogue with himself, bringing in his car, 'we have to admit there's skill and expertise involved in that too. Those lads who work offshore, I take my invisible hat off to them. Tough work – no doubt about it. Relentless. And the living conditions and surroundings – well they're as unforgiving and dreary as only cold oceans can be.' He thuds the roof again.

A car draws up at the opposite side of the pump. A young guy gets out, wearing jeans and a sleeveless black T-shirt, gold chains around his neck and his wrists. The guy looks at him as he stands there, talking to himself. Shrugs. Reaches for the nozzle, inserts it into his car's petrol tank and stares. 'You see all sorts...' he mutters with a flick of his head with its shorn hair. Sleeveless T-shirt replaces nozzle and exits towards kiosk.

'Mining coal, mining oil. What's worse?' the man asks the car. A clunk of response resonates from beneath the bonnet. 'Aye, spot on, absolutely right, Vauxy. We'll never forget how Hatcheter fisted the miners. Trampled them underfoot. Ground them to coal dust. They weren't part of her circle, were they? Weren't integral to her grocer's world. Dirty rats, not golden boys. Their industry wasn't going to bail out the country. The opposite – it was government-owned mines that needed bailing out. The difference between mining coal and mining oil comes down to money. Nothing more, nothing less. Filthy money.' His fist hits the roof again. A squirm of complaint escapes from the car's rusty bodywork, but he continues his lecture as if addressing the Trades Union Congress. 'Profits. Profits for private oil companies, not for the benefit of the working man. In the end every bloody thing comes down to that. Money. So,' he sighs, 'I suppose we should show solidarity with the oil workers and pay our bill. What d'you think, Vauxy?' No response from the car. 'After all, it's not their fault the bloody fuel costs so much.'

His eyes swivel to watch a car pull in at the pump next to that occupied by sleeveless T-shirt. He needs to make a move. His inaction will attract attention. With a tug he pulls a length of paper towel from the container alongside his pump, wets it by scooshing water on this windscreen and scrubs an accumulation of dust and insect parts from it. 'What gets my goat is the tax governments load onto it while grinning to split their sonsie faces. All these poor buggers that fill the tanks of their family cars have bent the knee to governments. Kept them afloat, the country afloat. Paid for Hatcheter's millions of unemployed too. And the returns are still being frittered away. It's them and their family cars — the workers — who pay the price of existence, siphoned dry for others to enjoy the profits, the bonuses, the good life.'

Sleeveless T-shirt guy returns from the kiosk, shakes his head as he pockets his credit card. He slides into his driving seat and roars off in an explosion of fumes.

'So we'll pay our petrol bill, Vauxy. Not for the supergiant that owns the petrol station, nah, cos its crushing grip now controls almost every aspect of our lives. Not for the oil companies that keep the world they pollute moving. But for the toilers of the world. We'll pay our bill to support them. One worker and his faithful car looking out for another and his four-wheeled mate. That's the only route to survival, isn't it Vauxy? Besides, if we skedaddle without paying, the forecourt cameras will clock us and our registration. We're all identified by numbers nowadays, never mind names just number us. So we wouldn't get away with it. Not that it really matters. Still.'

Another car rolls in behind. He hears the door click, then a voice says, 'Hello, there. You on the skive, too.'

'Eh?'

'So what's your excuse then?'

It's Carol-Anne from work. Occasionally her short skirt and pillar-drill heels inhabit the office next to his, when her black varnished nails clack across the keyboard like a tap dancer on white-hot coals. Forests of paper burst from the printer to be collated, stapled and the report dug into the papers on Stimpson's desk where it moulders before being discarded, shredded, recycled then reappearing, without a blemish or hint of its previous life, in the paper tray of Carol-Anne's laser printer to await her next foray into authorship. The Ferris wheel of paper employment, load up, experience the highs and lows, drop off, load up…

'Just taking some time off,' he says. 'Didn't take my holiday allocation last year so lost several weeks. The company's gain, my loss, not good, so thought I'd get a head start this year.'

'Dirty weekend?'

'What?' Her question catches him off guard.

She laughs. The diamanté pattern on her black-framed glasses catches the light. 'Don't worry. Just kidding. I noticed your wife's not with you. She's not in the car.'

'No. No, Selina's at home. I'm just off for the day to see a friend.' He feels that sounds convincing. 'Better get on.' He turns and makes for the kiosk as he feels Carol-Anne's appearance leaves him no option but to pay up, though he still thinks he's paying a ransom, that the oil company have him lashed tightly across one of their barrels.

He passes Carol-Anne as he recrosses the concrete to his car. She minces towards the kiosk like a geisha with bound feet, credit card waving in the air. 'Cheer up,' she says, you're off to enjoy yourself.' Her eyes take in his appearance, his scrubbed look. Sandy hair curls from the open neck of his blue shirt, topped by an air of…recklessness she reckons. Not bad looking for a guy his age – if you were into that type. A touch of the George Clooney. Nowhere as good looking, of course. She wonders if he's off to see a woman, if the sly bastard feels the main course has become tasteless with repetition, and is now enjoying mid life crisis petits fours? She wouldn't put it past him. Her gaze interrogates him, but he is intent on pushing on.

He waves his receipt. 'Can't believe the cost of petrol these days. Like buying a share in the bloody oilfield rather than a tankful to be guzzled before the week's out.'

'Know what you mean. Though the company pays for most of mine.' Her questioning look softens to a grin. She pushes open the door and turns to shout, 'Enjoy your dirty weekend.'

Damn women. They fair get under your skin at times, irritate like pesky midgies. Bloodsuckers. Scandalsuckers. Now all the office will know. Carol-Anne will punt it as the latest titbit of gossip. He could have done without meeting her.

As he drives off he checks his rear-view mirror and sees a woman in a red fleece waving at him. His foot hovers like a herring gull between accelerator and brake. Bloody hell, he did pay, didn't he? Yes, of course he did. He waved the receipt at Carol-Anne. He remembers that clearly. The gull dives. His foot hits the brake. The woman jogs alongside and his finger presses the button to lower the window. 'You forgot your can of juice,' she says, handing it to him.

He hadn't bought juice, only the bloody petrol, but he takes the can anyway – a low calorie energy drink – and thanks her. She trills her fingers in a mini wave as he drives off, every little helps in customer service. His foot increases the pressure on the pedal. He ratchets through the gears and gains the outside lane of the dual carriageway, aware of the houses, the fields, the trees, the world hurtle from present to past.

2 - The trouble with flying

The plane bounces like a golf ball on concrete as it drops onto the runway. The breaking motion sucks Lippy against the back of her seat as lights and signs on the grass verge zoom past in a blur of monochrome streaks. Speed lessens and she can make out numbers, letters, words on guides and runway markings. She closes her eyes. Almost there. Almost home.

Dear heavens, she needs to pee. Why do plane journeys have this effect on her? No matter how little she drinks beforehand, how often she visits the Ladies prior to take-off, the need to pee inevitably dominates mind and body for the last fifteen minutes of the flight.

During the flight she eyed up the box that intruded into the cabin like a giant cardboard box, endowed with the grand name of toilet. For much of the airtime a ragged queue snaked along the aisle, people lolled against seats or pushed against knees in an effort to allow the passage of fellow travellers or crew, with or without a trolley loaded with drinks and snacks. Should she risk it? Should she hang on, wriggle a bit more in her seat as if an errant spring causes her discomfort, hope for a speedy exit to head straight to the nearest Ladies in the airport?

Ever since childhood, when expected to utilise — with a flashy show of gratitude — the chemical potty enthroned in the coffin-like corner cupboard of the old caravan, she has hated such places with a passion, avoided them unless absolutely desperate. The press phobia, she calls it. The nose-scouring smell, the cramped space where elbows graze walls as she wriggled her pants up or down, while head and knees pushed against the matchwood door as if in an effort to escape. Overwhelmed by a need to make no noise, she usually held her breath during her entire visit, only an errant squeal escaping her mouth when a cold drip from the roof ventilator dropped on head or neck to swim down her back, and trail cold into her warmth. The rattles of the square plastic contraption, like a scuffed upturned Tupperware box, accompanied groans from the old caravan, while gusts of wind sighed bleakly through the gaps to seek out vulnerable parts of her anatomy.

Then there were the beetles — black and shiny like nuggets of coal — that scuttled around her feet, and gangly spiders that crept up on her, surveying her menacingly from the fissure between wall and roof. As if that wasn't bad enough, to top it off was the embarrassment – dear heavens her father had to empty the container, stand in an ordered queue and wait to disgorge its contents into the allotted tank, privy to the potty's secrets.

The old caravan, bought third, fourth or fifth hand, was a sardine tin with a paper lining, mould-encrusted window seals, cream paintwork dulled by the scouring of age and weather, and scratched plywood furniture. Yet somehow it was her parents' pride and joy. The caravan meant holidays, infrequent and brief occurrences until its appearance, though there had been a couple of soggy ventures up north in a borrowed tent. Midges and rain, infected bites and damp bedding had driven them home to lick their wounds on deck chairs in the garden overlooked by the neighbourhood.

The caravan meant not just an annual jaunt, but weekends away whenever they wanted and the weather obliged. Her mother, like a film star with a new mink coat, never tired of boasting to friends and acquaintances that they were off to the caravan for a few days, off to immerse themselves in the dizzy delights of a pocket hankie stance at the marshy foot of a farmer's field in Prestone Plains or Goreybrig. Out of the orbit of her friends and their weekend treats to cinemas and ice rinks, museums and cafes, Lippy complained it wasn't fair, she was being dragged away from life. But her mother refused to hear and redoubled her efforts to impress others. If only her listeners realised, thought Lippy, but they probably did.

Antagonism to the seating had burnt into her mind and being. The orange covers on cushions deformed by age and user bulk into alien landscapes of hills and craters, gave off a musty, earthy smell, were blotched by areas suspiciously darker, and rent by the occasional trembling lip tear. Once- matching curtains had imparted a cheerless rust glow to the interior. But sun shredded the material and her mother had spent long evenings cursing over her granny's ancient sewing machine while feet rocked the treadle to turn the belt that drove the up and down motion of the needle, as she stitched her bargain length of sale material into new floral curtains for the windows. Everything was now rosy, despite the flimsy new curtains adding little to privacy or the prevention of draughts. As she surveyed her handiwork her mother's grin expanded and piped icing on her boasts.

How she had hated those caravan holidays that stretched, like the worn cushion covers, over the years of her childhood. The interior that, irrespective of the weather, smelt like rotting vegetation in a dank wood that mouldered under a winter downpour. She squirmed at the thought of the endlessly boring games of Ludo or Monopoly (with missing pieces) played with forced parental jollity on wet days and grinding evenings. Then there were the filthy showers in utilitarian toilet blocks, water taps marooned in marshes of mud, the artificial bonhomie of caravan park shops with their near empty shelves of food, but stacks of soft drinks, magazines, plastic toys, pails, spades…and sweets. The memory of it still shoots a wave of loathing through her and excavates scenes painstakingly buried, to dump them again on the surface of her mind. Her hands contract into fists, fingers compressed together, nails gouging her palm, to punch them back to their fetid lair.

As the plane ceases its trundling Lippy's thoughts are dragged back to the present by the complaints of her bladder and the bald guy in the neighbouring seat who grumbles as he pushes himself to his feet and cannons into the aisle to join the melee for luggage from overhead lockers. She wriggles again as a wave of heat sweeps through her and panics her as to whether she will mange to hold out. Her eyes are drawn to the facility box. Too late. She should have dragged herself there twenty minutes ago when she had the opportunity. Now she needs to hang on. Still, not long, hopefully – if the idiots bulldozing their way through fellow passengers to the exit doors would just wait their turn.

First call the Ladies and then a large glass of water. That is the trouble with flying – the dehydration, though how she can feel so thirsty and still have this desperate need to pee is a mystery. She wriggles again, decides to join the melee as movement is required to reassure the one urge and banish the other – or perhaps it's the other way round. Move, run if possible and keep her mind off thoughts of liquid.

Outside now, in the brisk air, with immediate needs attended to and no disasters, she feels more composed. Next, bus stop. In which car park is her old Volvo stashed, and what number of bus will reunite them? She breathes deeply, satisfied the bulk of her research is over, venues visited, backgrounds sketched by associates. Pleasure at her discoveries makes her itch to move information from head and scribbled notes onto a computer document, when she will write new pieces, fill gaps, piece the narrative together in the way that appeals to her. And when finished, she'll go over and over, to refine, hone, edit, so that each word, every nuance, is sharp as a chisel and none are left to dangle or recline beneath the wood shavings. Yet under her shawl of satisfaction lurks…

unease, and if she is honest, fear. The subject is a dangerous one. She knew when she decided on it that it could be risky. But the story drove her, continues to drive her. The story is good and she hopes it will bring her the recognition she has for so long striven.

As she drives from airport to ring road she forces her mind to focus on the highway, traffic lights, speed cameras, signage and other traffic, then as she swings onto the road for the Borderlands she relaxes and cuts her thoughts some slack.

The story is interesting, fascinating, though appalling too. That's what grips her — the everyday allied with overweening ambition careless of others, a disregard that appears limitless. Not entirely a revelation as rumours with teeth have circulated for years, flowed and ebbed according to the political landscape, stories of who was safely ensconced on shore and who had been cut adrift to sink or swim in the shark-infested political sea. Or worse.

Though she feels comfortably warm she shivers. Her researches, limited by steel armour she made no attempt to penetrate, have unearthed no weighty proof to add to rumour, nothing conclusive to take to police or papers. Her finger will not be raised to point at any person in particular. But then that was never her intention. The story is what she wants, not the exposition, and she is fairly certain she has gathered the material she needs. The certainty stokes her impatience to start work. Her researches will not have gone unnoticed but she hopes the limit of her prodding will mitigate the intrusion and that no repercussions will result. The people concerned will not appreciate publicity.

There now remains only one more person to talk to — for her the most important person. As she steers the car down the empty road from Sootra, a full moon silvers the rolling landscape and lightens the black mass of conifers. No qualms about that meeting disturb her pleasure at being back on home ground.

3 - The mollusc wars

Fun, fun, fun. The garage incident is tossed behind him as he again tastes the light-headedness of freedom. But as he drives back along the dual carriageway the adrenalin throttles back and he decides to scale down the audacity of his stunts while he savours their memory, aware little else in his present life is likely to match the buzz of his exploits this spring morning. For the remainder of his journey, apart from a few daring moves to overtake a couple of cars on roads now quiet after the morning rush, he contents himself, and drinks in his surroundings of hills and fields where renewal reinvigorates and splatters with daubs of colour.

Acid green leaves unfurl from branches, each like an exotic butterfly emerging from its chrysalis; shrubs wave paintbrushes of colour against the canvas of the air; while on every verge and field edge spring flowers preen themselves in the sun. The very sight of it, and the warmth and feeling of expectancy that imbues the air rushing through the part-opened window, charges his mood like a battery.

Then there is the smell. A mixture of petrol and diesel fumes trail from traffic he sits behind before he spins past, enlivened by a hint of saltiness, seaweed and rotted shellfish from his proximity to the sea, and a scent of spring, of flowers, a rebirth of the green world that carries a sweet nostalgia at its heart. He is reminded of the perfume worn by a woman he met, strictly on business, on several occasions during the last year or so. Her perfume excites him, for some reason — reaches down and grabs at parts not usually sensitive to such feminine wiles. Not that he feels the trowelling on of charms is meant for him.

'I'm nothing but a drone in a gargantuan hive, Vauxy,' he tells the car, 'just doing what's expected of me, before I no doubt suffer the consequences. Whatever they might be.' Drones die after grappling with the Queen, he thinks. He rather hopes that fate won't be his. But the possibility — he stops short of admitting it is a likelihood — the possibility has in the past pushed his mind to buzz over the problem and the routes open to him.

He thumps the steering wheel. 'Relocating's an option, Vauxy. Disappearance then re-emergence under another guise. The loss of a stone or so in weight, dying my hair and a change of style — that kind of thing. Nothing too drastic.' Could be rather fun, he thinks, to let go of one life and embrace another; to trade in parts you had never liked for more of what appealed; to ditch the dreary in favour of the stimulating. Sounds fine. Deep down though, he understands it wouldn't be so simple. Like everything in life, there would be a price attached, and more often than not that price was hefty. 'I could manage the transformation. But there would be the problem of what to do with you, Vauxy. I can change my image with a cheap bottle of hair dye and a new outfit. But you, old pal, you'd be expensive to revamp. And the question is would you be worth it? Or would I be better to ditch you and pick up another car?' The engine shudders.

'Ach, don't take it so hard.' He pats the steering wheel. 'You see, Vauxy, we have a wee problem here, and it depends on the outcome this weekend just how far you and me might have to go.' Plastic surgery to change his fingerprints or the features of his face – he draws the line at that. Anyway, such drastic steps are only available to the big fish, the ones that swim in the black depths, the ones who know more about the beneath-the-surface world and its ecosystems than is healthy. At this stage in the meanderings of his mind he usually corners his thoughts to drive them towards a neighbourhood with fewer anti-social problems, to a less stressful location. Yes, of course he's considered the relocation option, usually in his darker moments when he plummets through the waves of negativity, occasionally despair, aware of the shrouded shapes piled on the seabed, fairly certain he knows their contents, if not by name then certainly their occupation. They all jumped to the same, or similar master.

'Ach, I'm sure things'll turn out fine, Vauxy. Relocation, reinvention, it's an awfully drastic step. Unless absolutely necessary, that is. The contribution of little old me is so menial I can't really envisage steps being taken to blue flash me like a fly electrocuted by a fly zapper. Besides, if they take action like that against all the drones like me, the population will plummet – as if all the chuckies on the beach are spun into the depths of the sea, to leave the place denuded of interest and character. People like me, Vauxy, add salt to life, enhance its flavour.' Though salt also shrivels slugs, he thinks.

What the hell made him think of slugs on this spring day, he wonders? His father, he remembers, used to disappear, slink out the kitchen door, the red Saxa salt container clutched firmly in his hand — much to his mother's disgust when she found out. Her objection wasn't to the slugs being salted, or assaulted, it was to an item from her kitchen, aseptic, functional and characterless, being taken into the proximity of the slimy molluscs — as if the slugs would contaminate the Saxa and therefore her kitchen by the introduction of some deadly disease from which she and her family would keel over in an instant.

As a youngster, the salting operation was one he loved to watch, not so much the curl and shrivel of the slime-draggers, the vegetable chompers, but he was fascinated by the look of satisfaction that glowed from his father's features at wreaking revenge for his masticated garden produce, nurtured by months of double-digging toil. The salting, eyes riveted on the shrivelling, made his father powerful, a feeling he was unused to. 'Workers like my dad were no more than doormats,' he informs the car, stroking the steering wheel with his hands. 'They worked beneath a power structure. Suffered from its effects when problems occurred in the manufacturing process. And that was pretty damn often. Even when all ran smoothly there could be a national or international material problem, or a world crisis that resulted in component shortages, or some event that pushed demand onto a helter-skelter. Then, the doormats like my old Dad would feel the heel of management descend, and bruise their ordered but powerless world. It was always the same. Of course it was.' If his father's only experience of wielding power was through salting slugs, then to his young self that had seemed a small price for such a large gain.

'Don't suppose my Dad won his battle against the slugs, the mollusc wars. What d'you think, Vauxy?' No reply. 'Nah. I don't remember my dad winning any battles during his life, not even the battle against the illness that carted him off before his allotted time. His three score years and all that. Bit of a looser, my Dad. Still, he was my old man, and I remember some good times with the bastard. Mostly when I was a youngster, mind you.' He leans over to rake in the glove compartment for a packet of sweets and pops one in his mouth. 'As for the mollusc wars, sounds like a sci-fi film or a digital game, doesn't it? The Mollusc Wars, award-winning compulsion. Take on Slug King and his sidekick Sloopy Slime. Beat them at their own game, and save the universe'. He throws back his head and laughs, waves his fist in a pumping action out the window, and shouts Molluscs forever into the wind. 'Nowadays salting is probably forbidden, Vauxy. Almost certainly outlawed by an EU directive, in favour of killing with kindness, and despatching on beery biers to sluggy heaven. My Ma didn't approve of that either, the big saftie that she was'.

Probably it's only the wind gasping and whistling through the slightly open car window, but he reckons he can hear his mother. 'You waste more than enough of our hard earned money pouring beer down your own throat, you neednae think you're gonnae waste another penny pouring it down the throats of them poor slugs.'

And his father, as mild as a banana smoothie replies, 'Fine, Denise. That's fine by me. But you'd better start checkin' out the veg in the local shops, cos the slugs'll have mine so chewed up and riddled wi' holes they'll be inedible. Lettuce, carrots, the lot. Munched and holey like yer dad's string vest. Inedible.'

His mother's expression deflates, the righteous-fuelled annoyance collapses, and her face creases into apology and concern. So his vegetarian mother mutters, as she turns to continue with the chores that give meaning to her life, 'Well, as long as you dinnae use more than you need to.'

Yet even then, his father wouldn't win as the slug's portion would be siphoned off from his own. Always the loser.

His hand thumps the steering wheel in time to a pop song that oozes from the radio. A phrase of notes in the music lodges in his mind. What does it remind him of? The thumps continue as fingers and heel of hand pick out a rhythm, and before the question is answered by his mind, his voice pedals out a version of *Ten green bottles sitting on a wall*. Into the second verse and the words are changed to *Nine black molluscs chewing on the veg*. By the time he is halfway through he is spurting to insert after *accidentally fall* the phrase *into the beer trap*. Struck by his cleverness, he laughs again. The car swerves dangerously near the central barrier in misunderstanding of his actions.

As the traffic dwindles further he slows his speed. The buzz came with being daredevil, but with little traffic the buzz has become dormant, so he slows down, takes in the scenery, and dawdles over reminiscences.

Slugs. The thought slimes into his head that he is the person he is because of slugs. The more he thinks of it, the more certain he feels. 'I'll be damned. Who'd have thought slugs could make such an impression. See, Vauxy, that early lesson of my Dad experiencing power must have seeped into me, infiltrated my bloodstream, stuck fast somewhere in my mind – like chewing gum on my shoe. Influenced the direction of my life. Jeez, just think, my life's been directed by nothing more than slugs.' He shakes his head. 'Bloody slugs.'

He chews over that gristle of revelation as he negotiates a roundabout. 'D'you realise, Vauxy, if that's the case, it probably means the track I'm shuffling along is geared to finding my slug equivalent. The means of experiencing a similar joy to what I saw on my dad's face when he salted them. Imagine that!

Foot hits brake to avoid a car that suddenly stopped. 'Sad to have to admit my life's search has been for a high point of slugs. Molluscs — the pinnacle of my achievement. Yes, Vauxy, what I've ended up doing is nothing more than the slimy equivalent of my Dad salting slugs.' The car engine whines.

4 - Message in a cocoa tin

'Ah, at last.'

'At last?'

'Yes. I've been trying to speak to you since yesterday morning.'

'I've been travelling. Researching actually, and I'm sure—'

'Your phone.'

'What about my phone?' It's clutched in my sticky hand, enabling you to speak to me.'

'The other one, Lippy. Your mobile.'

'Oh, that! I switched it off. You need to when you're flying.'

'When did you switch it off?'

'At the airport. I was hanging around, bored, one eye glued to the overhead screen for the gate number to come up, and I thought then would be a good time to switch it off.'

'At what airport?'

'Edin, of course. I always—'

'Exactly, Lippy. Didn't it occur to you to switch it on again after your flight?'

'Can't say it did, Marsha. Heaps to accomplish in a hostile environment.'

'Hostile environment? Where were you?'

'Power City.'

'Power City! What's hostile about Power City?' A cigarette lighter clicks. Marsha, her publisher, is into patches, gum, lozenges, sprays. She pledged three weeks ago to abandon the weed. So why the click, why the cigarette lighter?

'Mmm. Well, have you tried to cross roads in Power City recently. All that traffic, like herds of manic buffalos.' She hears a definite suck that has more than a hint of desperation in the sound, then a long satisfied exhale. 'It's a challenge and a half for a woman used to the gentility of the Caledon Borders, I can tell you.' A frustrated sigh blasts her ear.

'What is it with you and mobile phones?'

What is it with you and cigarettes? mouths Lippy, as she perches on the edge of an armchair. 'Nothing. I have one. Keep it safe and warm in my handbag.'

'Where you never hear it ring.'

Lippy stretches out her legs, crosses her ankles. 'So, occasionally I miss a call! If it's important the caller will try again.'

'And fail to get a response again.'

Lippy shrugs. 'I've been busy.'

'Lippy, mobile phones were invented precisely to enable busy people to keep in touch with other busy people — and with the world. Thereby making us more efficient and more effective.'

She can almost smell the smoke blasting down the connection. 'If you say so. But allow me to disagree.'

'What's there to disagree with?' Marsha waves her cigarette around, gesticulating. The glowing tip draws patterns in the air.

'Mobile phones were invented to make money for phone companies.' Marsha's snort assaults her ear. 'They con us lemmings into thinking we can't live without them, while they coin in the profits. Do you know what it costs to shack up with some of these contraptions? How much you get charged every month? Dear heavens! What a gullible—'

'Lippy.' The cigarette is stubbed into the ashtray like a pile driver ramming supports into hard earth.

Lippy uncrosses her ankles. All this fuss from Marsha about the blasted mobile. She wishes she had never bought the thing – not that she did buy it, it's on some never-ending contract that binds her hand, foot and bank balance despite its foibles and her dislike of the millstone. But otherwise Marsha would have insisted she drag herself into the modern age with an all-singing, all-dancing, global listening device like the one permanently superglued to her ear.

Life was so much simpler years ago. Nor did people seem any less well connected. Or if they were they didn't seem to mind. Life jogged on with no complaints about the difficulties of getting in touch, twenty four hours a day, with friends, relatives, colleagues or the guy down the road whose dog was barking in the middle of the night. It was accepted that you contacted people by phone when you thought they would be available. Otherwise you wrote to them. Simple.

Communication. She remembers one year at the old caravan when her dad's boss had been parked on the same site. Same site, very different caravan. His was larger, newer, shinier, with all mod cons, tasteful coffee-coloured seat covers and oatmeal curtains. All very restrained, very modern, very Scandinavian. His boss had a daughter of around her own age, and whereas the parents didn't mingle socially even when on holiday, she and Eilidh struck up a friendship. Trouble was, one lot of parents or the other kept dragging her or Eilidh off for the day, here, there, wherever. So bosom pal time was restricted to before breakfast, while the evening meal was under preparation, or for a brief sally in the shower block before bedtime.

Communication problems? Never. She and Eilidh solved that after their first meeting. A hedge around the bins was equidistant from both caravans and near enough to visit without their absence being noticed. An empty cocoa tin provided by Eilidh became their post office where notes from one to the other could be stashed whenever opportunities arose. Fun, secretive and effective. Lippy's face creased into a wan smile at the memory, but she shrugged with the acknowledgement that Marsha would never settle for the odd message in a cocoa tin, no matter where it was stashed.

'Liiii-ppy.'

'Yes, Marsha.' Lippy drags her thoughts back to the present.

'Forget the tirade. I need you this evening.'

'This evening? Too short notice, I'm afraid. I've organised—'

'This evening. No quibbling. And if you want advance notice in future, learn to use your bloody mobile.'

Lippy clenches her teeth. 'This evening.' She quashes a sigh. 'Okay, so what's on?'

'That's what I like to hear.' The cigarette lighter clicks again.

5 - Never let the buggers win

'The secret of life, Brian, is never to let the buggers win.' Mingally Dulse MCP (Member of the Caledon Parliament), pushes forward in his chair, slews a stack of papers across his parliamentary desk, dumps his black shod feet into the cleared space, and angles back into a V for victory sign,

'I thought that was the secret of politics.'

'Same thing. Politics dictates the lives the masses lead. It pulls the strings, shunts the levers. With that control comes power. And power is what this game is all about. Right?

'Right.'

'So to retain power we must stay on top?'

'Of course.'

'And staying on top means we mustn't let the buggers win?'

'Absolutely not.'

'Right. Remember that's the philosophy we live by. Forget it at your peril. Never let the buggers win. The most important thing you'll learn here.'

'Never let the buggers win. It's engraved on my brain.'

'Forget it for one instant, Brian, and you're doomed. Kaput.' Ming's fingers snap to indicate ruin, but in the compact office the sound is more like the handclap of a flea than the mortar-shot of a possible dire consequence.

Two years on from that first day, Brian understands the depth of that philosophy, and the work involved to ensure its delivery. It has become an integral part of him. It has become personal. The buggers mustn't win. Not at any cost.

And the buggers are everyone but him.

'What's jumping today?' Ming asks as he cannonballs into the office, laptop and fat reports nestled in his arms, as if hopeful of them hatching, swaddled in ideas as appealing as fluffy down but with more substance. This is the People's Unionist Party MCP's usual request on his arrival, unless a performance bomb bugs him — a gaffe hooked onto by the media, a howler of him citing facts or figures at variance from those published or expounded by others, or a Twitter faux-pas. Or him rattled by opposition taunts, looking weak, weak as a dead battery. Or his inadequate performance in the Chamber, or on Good Morning Caledon, Newsnight or one of the raft of news or political programmes.

Like many of his kindred spirits in the back stalls, Ming is overlooked by his Party for national outings, but has little control over utterances in his constituency. So the media keep him in their sights, aware that Mingally Dulse is no stranger to the performance bomb. And a performance bomb always provides attention-grabbing headlines. Stirs politicians. Riles a few voters. Prods lethargy in the ribs. With the half way stage of the parliamentary term passed and the next election shaking its black fist, the openings for performance bombs are breeding like rabbits.

This morning however there is no bomb. Ming has kept his head beneath the Party table, and the hierarchy are hunched in their meeting rooms, batting platitudes and innocuous insults while they hold talks about talks on strategy. On certain topics in the Chamber and in media interviews, Ming's brand of fudge has travelled from derision to becoming not just acceptable, but lauded by a growing faction as the clever disposal option for awkward questions to which no answers have as yet been thrashed out. His convoluted explanations, that once provoked hair-tearing despair, are now praised as triumphs, as icebergs that sink journalists on maiden forays, before they can venture into oceans whose depths hide the tentacled grotesques of strategies malformed at birth, and ingenious ideas mangled by attempts to secure agreement.

'The Callyman wants an interview for a piece.'

Ming's shoulders jerk back in interest. His pork chop ears flap, his quarter tomato mouth quivers, 'Who?'

'Jasmine Stane.'

'Who?'

'Their lifestyle correspondent.'

'Lifestyle? You mean politics surely?'

'No. Lifestyle. Haven't you noticed? The Callyman's a comic these days — hasn't covered serious politics for years.

' Ha ha! So this…Jasmine…'

'Jasmine Stane. She's writing a series of articles on how decision makers start their day, what they eat for breakfast, how far they jog, the bath and shower products they favour.'

'Mmm. Decision makers, eh.'

'Uhuh. Perhaps she's researching how to boost their brain power.'

Ming throws him a furrowed brow glance indicative of uncertainty on how he should take Brian's remark. 'Lifestyle choices affect everyone,' he intones.

'Some more than others.'

As he paces the carpet tiles to his office, Ming's mind rotates to digest the information, like soiled garments tossed clockwise then anti-clockwise in a washing machine drum. He dumps the laptop and reports on his desk and shuffles back to quiz Brian. 'Bath and shower products! You're kidding. Tell me your kidding.'

Brian shakes his head, and leashes his mirth. 'She asked all Parties for a name. Mutt volunteered yours.'

'Urgh!'

'You must be well in there, Ming.'

Mutt is the nickname for the Party leader. No reflection on his intelligence, so it is said, merely a dig about his appearance, especially when pressure of work has kept him from his barber. Mutt doesn't do hairdressers, despite the determined efforts of a series of consultants employed to restyle his image.

Ming's normal skin tone morphs to a white shade of grey. 'Right, so not a hole to dig in. Hmm! I'll come up with something.'

'Tea and toast, soap and water. Not acceptable. I suggest you research the topic, see what's viral. Undertake in-store investigation. Try out products. You have plenty time. Three days. Have fun.'

The white shade of grey ripens to puce. 'Three days! Mutt might show more concern for his cohorts. Too much bloody work, too little appreciation, that's this job.'

'Yup.'

'Sandwiched between Mutt and the masses. What a bloody life.'

Brian hands him a folder that bulges with files and papers. Coloured tabs marking relevant passages, edge out from the documents like pedestrians ganging at a street crossing. 'Your schedule and papers for today, the committee and the parliamentary session.'

Ming's concern over cornflakes and toiletries is overlaid by a storm cloud of remembrance on his last performance bomb. He glares at Brian, his mouth twitches, squashing its juicy edges, nostrils quiver like a dog sniffing vomit. 'You absolutely certain it's all here?' His voice sounds as if memory has its pudgy hands around his throat, ready to strangle him. 'I don't want another cock-up like last week.'

Brian nods in reassurance. The previous week Ming discovered he was missing the printed copy of the speech he was to give in the Chamber. He didn't notice until called and on his feet that, in place of printed sheets with words of import, and phrases ripe for emphasis highlighted in apricot, his speech comprised several completely blank pieces of paper. He turned them, flapped them as if wings, shuffled his other papers, gaped at colleagues, as a wash of panic brushed across his features. Fellow MCPs cleared throats, muttered. Brian hid his glee. The ploy turned out better than he had hoped, a fit opening salvo to his campaign. He chortled in silence. Ming's errrhumming was a comedy act worthy of prime time TV. His ensuing comments raised farce to high culture…or low politics. As he watched his boss flail around, like a wasp in a jam jar, Brian became almost hysterical with laughter, especially after a look at Mutt's face, the mask of bonhomie configured for the Chamber, stretched and refashioned into one of furious incredulity. Mutt hissed to his deputy who hurriedly scribbled a note, head bobbing. The Party Leader then moved his attention to flicking through one of the reports piled at his elbow, and removed himself mentally from the fiasco.

Later Brian found it easy to mollify Ming. He took himself off, disappeared. Even switched off his mobile phone. He was unavailable until the following morning when he listed all the coverage Ming had received in the media. Column inches, photographs, comment on news and political programmes along with replays of the footage. What more could a politician ask for, he cajoled?

'But it's coverage of me making a bloody fool…of me not quite on top of my brief. It makes me look…unprepared.'

'You think so? Personally, I thought the exposure was great for your profile. Any publicity is good publicity. So you always tell me.'

'That's when others are caught. Not sure it applies to me. I lean towards positive coverage.'

'Look at it this way, Ming. Delivery of the prepared speech would have netted you no publicity whatsoever. The media would have ignored it. You know what they're like. The hacks slaver after the juicy joints, and leave the dry meat alone.'

'My speech wasn't dry.' He sounded testy.

'No, no, of course not, but your speech took a predictable viewpoint for an MCP in your position. Rightly so. No controversy. You know how a trace of controversy spins our media friends into a frenzy. The smallest whiff of disagreement, dirt, never mind full frontal scandal, sends them to scurry around, sniffing like bloodhounds for a trail, nose-tingling on the scent of a scoop. That's all they appreciate. Yesterday you threw them a bone, not controversy that would haul you up before Mutt, but merely a speech with one or two facts and figures squashed, transposed or not quite pinned down. Put it down to an off day. Caused by overwork. The media will warm to that. Colleagues, too. So a win win situation.'

Ming's lips pursed like a rotting apple. 'Maybe. Maybe not. But do that to me again and you'll be slung out of here so fast you'll have permanent indigestion and be two feet smaller.'

Brian tried to look offended but judged it best to say nothing. His campaign would need toned down, greater deviousness was obviously called for. Had he underestimated Mingally's instinct for survival? No, he didn't think so, but best to play safe.

So today reassurance is required. 'I've double checked. All the papers you need are there.'

'They'd better be, Brian. They'd better be.' Ming marches through to his office, the folder cradled in his arms as if a baby. He fans through it, cooing at its contents.

'Jasmine Stane, the Callyman woman,' Brian shouts, 'wanted to know why you're called Ming.' The MCP lunges to the doorway and hangs through it. 'I told her it was a family name, your granny was one of those evicted from the island.'

'Reaction?'

'Interest. In fact I think you should go big on it in your interview. Maybe we could work your responses into that theme.'

Ming looks as if he is suffering a crossing of the rough ocean to the island speck. 'I fail to see, Brian, what Mingally has to do with breakfast and men's toiletries. The good people there didn't have either, as far as I can recall from stories told to me.'

'I think there's something in this, Ming. A great angle. A fresh perspective for the interview, one that will imbue it with a tantalising slant. It paints you with an aura of mystery, and clocks up a gain for tourism.' The look on Ming's face indicates to Brian that his assessment of Ming's capabilities is probably correct, his perceptiveness last week merely a blip. Or the result of a tip off from a more clued-up colleague. Capabilities – three out of ten. Self preservation instinct – six out of ten, maybe five. No, make it six as you always needed to factor in the survival instinct of the herd as a whole.

'OK. If you think there's an angle to be exploited, work on it. Let me have it before you leave tomorrow. Fully worked out. No bullshit. Remember what I said last week.'

'I'll get on to it after I've cleared this lot.'

Ming disengages himself from the door frame, then reappears. 'Apart from the Callyman piece, is there anything else?'

'Opinion poll coming out tomorrow.'

Ming's eyebrows form a question mark. 'And?'

'Down two points on constituency vote, three on regional.'

'Jeez, that bad! Where's the bloody support off to?'

'Need you ask?'

'Bloody voters. Don't know what's good for them. Right, well, plenty time. The tide will turn in our favour. Anything else?'

'Invitation to a conference, a barrow-load of correspondence, including a questionnaire from the Business and Industry Federation on the effect of government policy on job creation in your constituency. And a tourism group in your patch wants you to attend a seminar on destination development. Your travel to Aberdein on that road fact-finding mission has been booked. The one to the Bahamas has been turned down.'

'Turned down! How can we carry out our jobs effectively without proper backup and information. Ridiculous. Bloody ridiculous. Pity, too, I've never been to the Bahamas. A wee trip would have provided a welcome break from all this drudgery.'

'Yes, but hardly surprising it was turned down. Recollections of the onetime expenses debacle at Westmunster still hang over the government, make it clamp down.'

'But that's totally different, Brian. Totally different. You know that. You know our expenses here are tightly regulated.'

Brian's thoughts dwell on the Bahamas. 'The questionnaire?' he asks.

'Ah, the BIF baffs.' Ming considers it suave to ridicule those who aren't in full agreement with him. For some reason he thinks calling them stupid names diminishes them in the eyes of others. It is all part of a them and us attitude, reverse snobbery. Ming likes to lord it over the poor buggers who can't boast a parliamentary office. He believes the two by three metre space endows him with superiority, with a status beyond that of ordinary mortals, BIF members or otherwise. After two years Brian has begun to feel Ming's level of intelligence is more suited to children's TV than playing with adults in the big world – Peter Ming Pan, out of era, out of touch with reality, he should leave the grown up stuff to others. In the modern world forging relationships is essential for success. And that surely means finally ditching the baggage of tribalism and hiding behind the barricades.

'What about the seminar?'

'Ah, the seminar. How bloody tiresome people can be. They should realise MCPs are dashed off their feet running the country. No time to be at the beck and call of the masses. Get me out of it if you can, Brian. I'm sure there's another engagement you can say I must attend. A mother dying in hospital. A family wedding. There must be some bloody thing.'

'It's some months since you attended a constituency event. Perhaps an appearance could be useful — or I could stand in for you.'

Ming's mouth twists in a grimace. One of Ming's few real attributes is a peculiarly mobile mouth. Of course if he tweaks it in the wrong direction an entirely inappropriate message can be sent, so he needs to take a measure of care. Not an attribute he is noted for. 'You really think I should accept?'

'Up to you. Election's in nineteen months. That's why if you don't want to I could...'

Ming's mouth trips through a range of expressions – a deflated football, air sucked from it, booted around, different parts caved in or pouting. 'I'll give the matter thought. No need for a hasty decision. A reply isn't due for a month or so. Wouldn't like to let the bastards think they had my undivided attention. That would never do.'

To hide his glee, Brian swivels his head, and becomes absorbed in rereading an email on the computer screen. Ming is priceless. A laugh a minute, though he doesn't know it. 'You'd better watch your time.'

'Time?' Ming checks his watch. 'Good lord. The committee will be gathering. Gushing Gerty will be ushering her chicks into their seats and clucking over those of us who haven't yet appeared. Must rush.' He dives through to his office. 'Brian, tell me which of these papers do I need?

6 - The tyranny of the mobile

Lippy thinks her talk has gone reasonably well – apart from a couple…
well, three…interruptions when her phone rang. The first couple of
times she jokes about it, her publisher gets twitchy if she turns it off she
says with a grin. She fiddles with it and hopes the trill has either been
muted or she has bamboozled it into silence. The third time she stares
with a look of helpless frustration. Her mouth twitches at the gadget as it
step-dances around the coffee table in front of her. She is using it to time
her remarks, but now thinks it would be better in her pocket or thrust
into the junky depths of her handbag.

'Can anyone throttle a renegade intrusion in my life?' she asks her
audience of eleven plus the bookshop owner and her assistant who
sit like cardboard figures, faces blank, feet at twelve o'clock, hands
incarcerated on skirt-draped laps. Small audience, though not bad for
a rural bookshop. Most arrived in good time to allow them a wander
round the shop where they prodded spines, slipped the odd book from
a shelf, flicked eyes over blurb, perhaps fanned through a few pages,
before determined fingers return the paperback to its allotted place or
impatiently attempted to wedge it between two books on a shelf at waist
level.

Lippy's eyes search for anyone who wears long wide sleeves —
bellbottom sleeves. At a previous bookshop talk the owner related to her
a story about his shoplifter who, on several occasions, browsed and left
apparently empty handed — with selected books stashed up her sleeves.
But this evening all sleeves are too fitting for such a ploy, and a few
clutch paper bags printed with the shop's logo, containing a purchase.
Good sign or bad, Lippy wonders. With a purchase already made will
they still buy one of her books or sidle out the door once her talk is over?

A wiry woman stashed in the second row of folding chairs pokes her
hand through the sliver of space between two matriarchs in front. 'Let
me see if I can subdue it for you.' The look on her face is sympathetic.

Lippy picks up the phone, and drops it into the woman's hand as if the skin is being burnt from her fingertips. 'I find mobile phones such an intrusion,' she mutters limply. A tentative laugh escapes from her twitching lips. Ripples of agreement encourage her, and before long faces in her audience display unsuspected depths of animation as they recount their mobile phone experiences.

The wiry woman returns her phone. 'Same make as mine. You should have peace now.'

'Thanks. You've earned a discount on my book.' The woman flicks a smile and removes her eyes to contemplate the design of the paper bag on her lap.

The rigid posture of a woman in the front row has wilted with the mobile confessions, and she flaps her hands like young birds attempting flight as she gabbles of her husband, a person of some importance apparently, who can rarely be separated from two constantly ringing mobiles. Lippy nods in understanding while her eyes feast on the talker's necklace, a diver's belt of brown rocks and bright yellow plastic that grind together with a disconcerting crunch.

Lippy grins as the woman stutters to a halt amidst a rattle of other comments. The audience reaction is much better than she dared anticipate when conscripted by Marsha, her publisher, to fill in for an author who had the audacity to fall ill. Instead of a talk on a best selling thriller with a background of Tibet and the Arctic, her band of expectant-faced ladies were subjected to her ramblings on her last book, a genre-melding romance cum mystery cum political thriller cum whatever else she had thrown into the bag. Not her best book — an admission voiced only to those closest to her — though it is selling reasonably well, of course it is, or Marsha would never have considered her for a fill-in slot.

But an audience, even an audience of a dozen, who are buoyed in expectation of a talk by a suave headline-grabbing adventurer, could be forgiven for finding her tale of Patty Porter and her eccentric family a tad less invigorating. However the mobile phone episode has created empathy and added the necessary spice to ensure a decent round of applause. Obviously she is not alone in her resentment of the need to be at the beck and call of an electronic device twenty-four hours a day, irrespective of how she feels or what she is doing. The tyranny of the mobile – maybe an article in that, she muses. Or at least a piece for her blog. Hurriedly she scribbles a note on a scrap of paper dredged from the pocket of her events jacket.

When it comes to signing copies, the bookshop is caught short. The owner does not even have the grace to look abashed that none of her books are stocked, not her current one nor any of her previous works.

'We are a small bookshop,' simpers the owner. 'Small and exclusive, and we cater for our loyal local customers. We aim to stock only the best books to give our customers a breadth of quality literature.' The grey eyes of Claire-Louise, the owner, glint challengingly behind her purple-rimmed spectacles.

'Of course you do. And I trust after my success this evening you will now stock my works.' Claire-Louise opens her mouth as if to protest then snaps it shut like a miser closing his purse. Lippy waves a hand. A gleeful smile curls the corners of her mouth. She has brought along her own supply of books. No point in being an author if you can't shift your bloody books. She sells five, including one to the woman with the rocks around her throat. With a show of ostentatious confidentiality she asks for the book to be dedicated to her dear, always busy, very important husband. Mingally she says his name is, in a voice that bounces off the surrounding bookshelves. Mingally Dulse.

'Mingally Dulse,' repeats Lippy as she writes the dedication. Sounds like some kind of seaweed she thinks as she nods and beams in recognition of a name she has never heard of but whom her purchaser believes as recognisable as George Clooney.

7 - Triumph

Mingally Dulse wasn't Brian's initial choice, in fact he'd known next to nothing about him, when he began to investigate employment opportunities in the Parliament. Ming was one of the successful but the faceless — formless, a waft of cologne and beer, high end tailors and back street bookies, never quite pinned down, occasionally drifting past, blown on the wind when it swirled from a certain direction.

Originally Ming had worked for the MP, Charlie Kintail. Ming's father had been friendly with Charlie, so no-one was too surprised, when a vacancy had arisen a number of years previously, that jobseeker Ming had been taken on as his constituency assistant to arrange the pattern of visits and events favoured every year of his forty year stint as an MP by Charlie. Ming answered the telephone, constituents warmed to his friendly tone but worried about his inability to grasp the nub of their problem. Come along and see Charlie, he would encourage. He'll be here on Friday morning. Charlie will sort it out for you. What a helpful young man, constituents would think. Ming viewed himself as poised to wrest the nomination for the seat after Charlie clattered off his Westmunster bench and was persuaded to retire. He assumed Charlie's retirement would see him replace the old stalwart, the usual pattern of patrimony, so he bought a new car, new to him, though four years old but in good condition. He'd need it for campaigning.

His first shock came when, instead of being a shoo-in, he was told there were other applicants, eighteen other hopefuls for Charlie's Westmunster seat. Charlie commiserated with him, 'You've been a grand worker, so you have. Kept the paperwork in neat piles and charmed the women constituents, sometimes flummoxed the men — but that was often a useful trait.' Ming smirked and made a mental note to spend his savings on a new suit. 'And your enthusiasm, your sincere attempts have been appreciated. Of course they have.' Charlie put his arm round Ming's shoulders. 'And I told the high heid yins that, put in a good word for you. But you know what it's like, Ming, when a vacancy comes up. A bit like diamonds on your front path. There's aye a scramble for them. All kinds of idiots, with egos inflated like airships, think being an MP is ideal for them, and them just the ticket for it. So you can discount many of the contenders as non-starters, no-hopers — though you can never be certain. It depends what contacts they can flaunt, doesn't it? What backing they can count on.' Ming sensed a wind about to blow him off course, and plumped down on his chair like a balloon in the final stages of deflation. 'Sadly, you know, it's not always the best man who wins,' Charlie intoned with a shake of his head. His brains rattled, teeth clacked at the expression of disbelief that had settled on Ming's face. 'Nope, you never can tell. Sometimes it comes down to the guy that's most amenable, bends the knee deepest to those who support him. You know what I mean, Ming. I don't need to spell it out, do I?' he said, as he grasped Ming's flaccid hand in his, knobbly with arthritis like a bagful of chuckies. 'So, you see, though I've had a word with the high heid yins, I can't exactly guarantee you'll get it at the end of the day. Of course I'd like to be more positive, Ming,' he shook his head, 'but, as I say, you can never tell what might happen, what'll be decided, who'll be selected.' He replaced Ming's hand on the desk. 'Remember, this seat of mine is a safe seat, so the bloke selected can expect to remain here, comfortably, without hassle, for years to come. Look at me. I've represented the good folk of this constituency for forty years. Forty unbelievable years. Who would've believed it when I was first selected, all those years ago! Never thought I'd earn as much either, not me, a wee boy from the wrong district of the city. Good pay, and of course the fringe benefits too, always useful, that goes without saying. So there you go, in this life you never can tell. Of course, I'll always be grateful to the Party for the opportunity and the lifestyle it's given me. And I'll be right sorry to give it up. Bloody sorry. Still, I suppose I've had a fair innings, and a nice wee nest egg's stashed away, so the wife and me...we're going to enjoy ourselves, travel, a world cruise maybe. Though I'll still keep in touch. Would never do to let go all the levers, now would it?'

Charlie died seven months later. In the selection process for his seat Ming had to content himself with reaching the shortlist. One year and two weeks later, Jimi Jenkins was returned to Westmunster with a thumping majority, eighteen hundred more than Charlie's usual, an MP in a refurbished Party swept into power, broom at the ready to sweep aside the old, brush in the new, and curry favour with the smart neighbours. Ming considered resigning, sounded out another MP in need of an assistant, but swithered over the move to Westmunster and in the end stayed where he was.

And suddenly, after years of talk and bluster, a Caledon Parliament was in the offing. Hundreds of aspiring candidates travelled the country, jostled, juggled, made speeches, wrote letters — never had the columns of national and local newspapers bristled with so many viewpoints. Hopefuls grasped every opportunity, and fabricated others, to put their names out there, dangling them like Christmas tree baubles in front of the public and the Party faithful. A free-for-all of hopefuls, a fairground carnival, aimed at a constituency, a place on the regional top-up list, and often both — just in case.

Ming's father, a Party stalwart for thirty odd years, gutted that the son of a close friend of Charlie's was passed over for some chancer who'd only been a member for five minutes (so he'd like to know what other lure he had waggled), decided this was the opportunity of a lifetime for his son. Forget Westmunster. This was a New Era. The newly elected People's Union Party had sanctioned devolution and so had Big Donnie. Bloody hell! Just think, his son, Ming, one of the first members of the first Caledon Parliament in three hundred years. That was a dog worth backing to win. He'd get a few pints in the club on the back of that, sure he would.

True, he had fought tooth and nail, twenty years ago, against devolution, believed it was a sideshow, a dangerous sideshow at that, one that would dilute Caledon influence at Westmunster, rain damage north of the border. The whole slippery slope scenario. So he had campaigned against it, locked down the part of his mind that reminded him of the Caledon political giants who had striven for the working classes, who had advocated Home Rule. And on the morning of the first of March, before he went off to work, he had trekked down to the local school, into the matchwood booth and voted No, in his determination breaking the pencil attached by a string to a nail in the flimsy frame of the polling booth. The next day when he saw the result he was jubilant, a majority for those in favour, yes, but not sufficient to clear the forty per cent rule decided by Westmunster. Cheers. There would be no devolved parliament. No bloody stupid sideshow with folk, mainly wee lads with big heads, strutting around an old school building as if they knew what they were doing. What a waste of money that would bloody well have been.

But when celebrating in the pub, a worm, black and barbed, wriggled in his mind, and for a second or two, while he waited for a refill, he wondered what he had done, before swatting the thought from his consciousness. Caledon would be a better place for the stance he and others of his persuasion had taken. A yes vote would have whisked the country away on a single ticket to doom, no doubt about that. And besides, those bloody Callyrats, Tartan Tykes, they were; vermin, sewer-rats, their heads blown up fit to burst with a sludge of ideas, dribbled garbage, their gullets spewed out crap, green and bilious, eyes shot black magic spells, bodies, like their policies, nothing but junk. Yes, the bloody Callyrats had to be put in their place, ordered back to the scrapheap, kicked onto their knees to crawl back to the dank holes they had oozed from, to leave governing to those whose rightful position it was, those with endless years of experience. Ruddy Callyrats! We couldn't let the buggers win.

That was nearly twenty years ago, a third of a lifetime ago for too many Caledon folk — health inequalities their truncated lifespans were put down to — and in the intervening chunk of his life Ming's father and everyone else had endured Hatcheter and her sidekicks knocking them sideways, kicking the stuffing from them, like feather cushions savaged by a feral cat. And when the poll tax was imposed by the knuckledustered fist of the steel she-wolf, and thousands of demonstrators took to the streets, the wee worm wriggled again. 'Maybe if he and his mates had voted for the devolution on offer,' his mind whispered in the depths of the night, 'Caledon might have been better able to resist her onslaught. Hatcheter and her ilk might have had to pay heed to the demands, the entreaties of a parliament, even one as castrated as the beastie on offer.'

In those twenty years Caledon had lost its pride, its manufacturing industries, most of his mates lost their jobs, their kids loafed around on the dole; lost its virility; lost its belief in itself, as the message was rammed home, relentless as a battering ram, that there was no such bloody thing as society, so no friendly support and understanding for the frightened and the suffering and the frail. The woman, plus her handbag, even had the gall to stand on her hind legs at the General Assembly and lecture them. Imagine the nerve of her, insisting she knew what was best for a country she knew damn all about! The world, flat and coloured pink like the Empire on the map, ended at Watford as far as she was concerned. Her tears of grief as she crawled out of Downland Street, kicked out by a party that had regained its senses, if such a thing could ever be said of the Tykes, were matched by the tears of relief and joy that gushed down his cheeks. Unforgettable it was, he'd always savour that, taste it, salty yet sweet and satisfying as a chocolate eclair in his mouth. Millions of others who felt like him celebrated too in their homes, the pubs, the clubs, on the buses and even in the streets. Hatcheter had bitten the concrete of the pavement, could be trodden like a bug underfoot. And though the Tykes had now finally been swept away by an electorate that had regained its senses, in favour of a new regime, it might be just as well to have a pretendy wee parliament in Edin, just in case the buggers were ever resurrected.

Eleventh September 1997 was the date of the referendum. He remembered it clearly. Seventy four per cent voted yes to a parliament, sixty three per cent for it to have tax raising powers. Big Donnie Dewart said there shall be a Caledon Parliament, his night dream voice reminded him, as if he was about to magic it from a top hat like a blue and white rabbit as scraggy as himself. Mind you, that's kind of what he tried to do with the Spanish upturned boats fiasco of a building. But that's another story. The devolution act went through Westmunster the following year and it seemed half of Caledon was minded to stand for the new parliament. Ming's father had his work cut out.

So he drew up his plan of campaign, and dragged a reluctant Ming in behind it. Ming had been taken over along with the other office fixtures by Charlie's replacement, as if the fact had escaped him that one of the items lurking among the desks and files, the fluff and dead flies, was a human being. Ming was reasonably happy where he was. He and the job had grown into one another like a tree that embraces a static fence post within its growing trunk, comforting it, wood melding back into tree. Ming felt this was where he belonged. Here he was part of government without all the hassle. Others dealt with that, and if any issue became troublesome the buck could always be passed to Jimi. After all, he was the elected Member, he was the one earning big bucks.

Jimi brought his wife in one day, a compact package, dressed for an executive post, or perhaps for the position of Jimi's constituency assistant as Jimi jigged around showing her this and that and how the other worked. Told her to try the chair, check out the computer. Navy suit, blood pressure band of a skirt, high heels that would deter any mugger. The kids, two girls, now at school and Cindie wanted to return to work. Not what she did before, she glossed over what that was, but a new challenge. Jimi smirked. A bell rang loudly in Ming's brain. As the happy couple were leaving on a visit to a local factory, Ming's father materialised. At a glance he understood the situation. Ming! Home. Six sharp. I'll tell your mother you'll be there for tea. Stuff needs discussed. It would never do to let the buggers win.

Ming's father started with his union colleagues, the brothers, the brotherhood of the working class. Hatcheter believed they were the Cosa Nostra, to be scraped from British life like shit from the sole of her shoe. Always good at making friends, getting on with people, at networking when that became the buzz word, Ming's father worked his contacts. He persuaded, pressured, made deals, called in favours. The use of thumbscrews wouldn't have been beyond him, so determined were his efforts. He put a small team of people together, appointed himself Ming's campaign manager as well as minder — nursemaid some said — and charted a course of action, the goal being to secure for his son the nomination to stand in the Caledon Parliament equivalent of Charlie's old Westmunster seat.

On a few occasions the suggestion was dropped in his ear, like a stream of hot almond oil, that going for the regional top-up list might be more in Ming's line as competition for constituencies was fierce. Half the country's academics were in line, and a gasometer of favours were stacked for repayment. But Ming's father was adamant. Throughout his life he'd just been a foot soldier, a squaddie, who ploughed on but never achieved much beyond scraping a living; a hand-to-mouth existence, squatting on the sidelines as he watched others forge ahead. This was a chance for him to make his mark, to show he could think, and organise like the best of them, and bring about something worthwhile that would add meaning, Bisto flavouring, to his life. To secure for Ming the chance to stand in the first Caledon Parliament election would be an achievement he could be mightily proud of, and after that would come the big prize, winning the seat. Yes. This would be his triumph as well as his son's.

Charlie maintained you never could tell who would win, wangle, the nomination for a seat, and Ming's father wondered, when Ming was finally selected as the candidate, what Charlie's reaction would have been. The poisonous wee double-dealing, back-stabbing, bastard that he was. Ming's father felt he had got his own back, grown six inches in height, and been given a peerage into the bargain. The first fence had been successfully negotiated, but there was still work to be done, arms to be twisted. He allowed himself a week off before he sat down to plan his son's election campaign.

On 6th May 1999 Caledon voted in its new members of its new parliament. One of them was Mingally Dulse who won with a highly respectable majority. When the Queen appeared for the official opening, her outfit in heather colours of muted purple and green, her hat sprouting pheasant feathers as if to impart a Caledon grouse moor dimension, Ming's father was perched on the edge of his front row seat, on the balcony of the General Assembly building, where Hatcheter had pontificated her sermon on the Mound, and knew it was the most exciting day of his life.

No, Mingally Dulse wasn't the MCP Brian would have chosen to work for, had he a choice. But he didn't. And by then he was desperate to wangle a foot in the Parliamentary door.

Vacancies for parliamentary assistants were either filled internally by a back bench MCP's assistant moving to work for one of those in the front rank; or by constituency office people moving into the parliament; sometimes the lucky ones were acquaintances of the MCP; sometimes word filtered from above that it would be appreciated if this particular person was offered a position because he or she sought experience whilst in waiting for a seat. With his business background that lacked any union affiliation, and a father who was a member of the Cally Party, Brian knew his chances were blighted. His only ace was a vague friend whose older brother knew Ming. He cultivated that opening with flattery and tickets to a big match, football, of course, though it cost him dear, and in the end his persistence paid off as Ming took a liking to him when they met. Though he later admitted it was because Brian seemed less devious, and less of a threat, than others on the short list. And therefore less likely to be after your desk, thought Brian. Stupid bastard!

Since his mid teenage years politics had lurked like a colourful shadow in Brian's mind. The moon pulled the tide of his ambition, increased it, decreased it. He was unable to come to a definite decision as to whether he should work towards standing as an MP. Get some work experience under your belt, advised his father. Politics is prey to the whims of the electorate. A solid business background provides a safety net if, or when, you get chucked out. To Brian that made sense, especially as the economy figured large in the fortunes of administrations and in their electoral performance. Business experience would stand him in good stead. The formation of a parliament in Edin crystallised his thoughts, and heightened his ambition, for now he could stay on home soil, help determine the direction of policies to transform the ailing economy, harry for decent jobs, a fighting chance in life for those who still struggled in the quagmire of the midden. His father saw the Cally Party, with their strident demands for independence, as the solution, but for Brian there was only one Party with the welfare of the working class at its heart. The ruling Party. The People's Union Party. Now he was a cog in that Party's Caledon parliamentary machine. But at Holygood it was no longer the ruling party.

8 - Mixed and set like concrete

Lippy stretches, leans back in her chair and picks up her coffee mug. She cradles it in her hands as she glances out the window. Tree branches remain bare, skeletons against a sky ruffled by skittish clouds, but beneath them daffodils glow alongside the browned wilted heads of snowdrops. Despite the sun, a chill nips the air, blown around by wind gusting from the east that snatches the dry copper leaves from beech hedges and tumbles them with dust from verges, to send them bowling along the narrow road that runs past her cottage.

A good time of year, she thinks, relieved winter is almost over with spring and summer to look forward to. Goodbye heavy snowfalls that isolate and make arrangements to visit and attend events difficult, and postponements or cancellations inevitable. Short days and cold weather make her want to retreat into a well-insulated, centrally heated shell, to hibernate until spring stirs itself. She watches the daffodils, dipping and twirling, their heads held proud. A few would look good in a vase. Bring cheer to the room. When she finishes her coffee she will throw on a jacket and sally forth with her secateurs.

Soon lighter evenings will render journeys more enjoyable, with ice and snow unlikely to disrupt travel until late autumn came round again. Spring flexes its muscles, ready for its big push. It is a time of year she likes, the time of year that had sent her parents into a flap like washing in a breeze, as they made endless phone calls and discussed potential sites for the caravan. Seated at the kitchen table they peered over maps, grubby with querying fingers and coming apart at the folds, and consulted a folder of leaflets accumulated over various holidays and trips. For weeks they geared themselves up to visit the caravan in its winter quarters, in a corner of a joiner's yard trapped between the fringe of the city and its new urban sprawl that washed out over the greenbelt, to estimate the winter's damage, and what needed done before it was moved to its summer pasture. Lippy thought it was like visiting an elderly relative on a life support machine.

For a short time its forlorn, dilapidated look raised her spirits as she hoped, fingers crossed, it might not survive another season. Scoured by winter weather, its paintwork was always dull and dirty, patterned by mud that looked as if it had frothed over it in a raging tsunami. In crevices around windows and in seams in the metalwork, green algae bloomed while the windows were scummed and streaked by dirt. Her Dad would note with a purse of his lips that the chassis showed more rust than the previous year and the tyres were flat so would need pumped up, muttering under his breath that he hoped to be spared the expense of their replacement. Tentatively the door would be levered open, dust and rain having mixed and set like concrete around it, and the six month old stale air billowed out to dissipate in the breeze.

Inside the orange cushion covers felt damp and slimy to the touch while the floral curtains sagged limply in the musty atmosphere, a haven for dead flies and spiders' webs. Her mother and father would look around, forced optimism garlanding their faces. *It'll be fine once it's been cleaned and aired. The cushions and curtains need washed. But it'll be fine. Wait and see.* And Lippy's heart would sink. Another summer in the sardine tin, avoiding the cell in the corner, plagued by carrying water and showering in insect-infested concrete bunkers.

Lippy sips her coffee, drags her eyes back from the garden, and mind from the past to focus again on the computer screen.

Progress has been good. Some days she stares at the screen and wills words to come, pounding out sentences squeezed like toothpaste from her mind, only to chop, change, rearrange. At other times words white-watered along, dipping and diving on a fast-flowing stream of ideas, buoyant and bubbly, the sentences streaming out through her fingers to reappear, static but still full of life, on the screen. Joy, at least till the revisions started.

Write two thousand words a day pundits advocated. Some days she manages a few hundred before leaving them to moulder and going off to tackle a more productive task. Other days progress is steady, even if the writing isn't brilliant. Then there are the times when ideas hit and flower as she climbs out the bath, or drops off to sleep. Towel clutched around her, she grabs the notebook and pen kept handy on her dressing table, and scribbles frantically. If in bed, and the room is cold, and the thought of raising her shoulders above the quilt freezes her mind, then she repeats the key word or phrases to herself as if a mantra. Over and over. Wills herself to remember. Links them to significant objects or thoughts. Word association. Any aide memoire that means she can regurgitate them, or words sufficiently like them, the next morning when she switches on her computer.

As she reads over the last piece she has written a surge of optimism tinged with apprehension sprinkled with fear flows through her. She feels she has succeeded in rounding the work off with an interesting ending. Endings can be difficult; she often tussles with them. So much hangs on an ending — the expectation it will perform the weighty function of drawing the plot to a conclusion. A conclusion which is both satisfactory and... And what? Stimulating? Thought provoking? Unexpected? Tie loose ends, or draw them in but leave a question mark? Hands rub eyes. Shoulders are flexed. Arms stretched. Just the final confirmation of details, a few more reads through, and then...

Her eyes drift to the clock in the corner of the screen. Ten to seven. Ten to— Vinegar sticks! She is supposed to be meeting a friend at seven. Vinegar sticks. Now where did her mind unearthed that exclamation?

It must have dug deep for it was one of Eilidh's. Lippy had never heard it till she hooked up with her that summer and, in imitation of Eilidh and her often grown-up ways, the words would spill from her mouth too. Eilidh was slim, with long wavy hair the colour of the big mahogany wardrobe that had belonged to Lippy's gran, graceful — that's the ballet, she claimed, ballet's good for my posture my Mum says. Almost without realising, she copied the way Eilidh walked, head up, hips swinging, tempering her bull-like charge into a more restrained amble. She would like to have worn clothes like Eilidh's — skirts with frills and dresses in pretty colours — instead of the boyish-looking shorts and T-shirts her mother bought for her. A necklace like the one Eilidh had worn that day at the burn, she'd always fancied a necklace like that. Eilidh gave the impression she knew about a world of things unknown to Lippy. She was like an encyclopaedia, her pages full of new information, her mind quick to absorb and to make connections. Lippy had never met anyone like Eilidh. During the caravan months of that summer a current of air blew through her life, energised it, yet disturbed, twisted and spun aspects of her world.

Until the day the Eilidh phase was dramatically punctured.

Since then she hasn't thought about the words, they have never formed themselves into an uttered exclamation till this moment. Weird. Though perhaps not. The flight on the plane, as always, has dredged walled-up memories from the dustbin in the cellar of her mind.

Vinegar sticks! As weekends and then two weeks in the summer cemented their friendship, treats were added by Eilidh to the notes in the cocoa tin. Lippy could never afford such extravagances. Half her measly pocket money had to be saved – her parents insisted she learn financial rectitude – the remainder went towards occasional indulgences – a comic or an ice cream. But it was not long before Eilidh started to fold her cocoa tin note around a sweet treat – a bar of Fry's Chocolate Cream, a packet of Fruit Pastels, a white chocolate Milky Bar or a handful of assorted caramels and soft centres in bright tinfoil wrappers. Into her pocket they were slipped. If her shorts had no pocket then she clutched them in her hand and on return to the caravan slipped them into the draw-string bag where her night things were stashed during the day. It hung on a hook beside the bench that passed as her bed.

Vinegar sticks! How she looked forward to those treats, accepting that Eilidh had the money to spend on such things because Eilidh's father was her father's boss. The parents steered clear of one another, pleasantly if briefly passed the time of day if their paths crossed, their faces bland masks, but made no effort to seek one another out. Lippy accepted unquestioningly their actions were down to their working relationship. But why was there a need to roll that attitude out over their children's friendship? All she and Eilidh wanted was to share their holiday experiences, chat about where they had been, interesting places seen, stories heard, the joys of paddles or horse rides, the boredom of traipsing round shops, the highs and lows of walks, picnics, sheltering from a downpour.

When Lippy complained about it to her mother, she found no support. Her mother was tight-lipped, reticent to comment beyond saying she didn't know how lucky she was to have somewhere to spend holidays and weekends. Usually her mother enthused over her friends, but where Eilidh was concerned she was mute. It was almost as if Eilidh wasn't liked. Lippy had no idea why.

'Why can't we play more together?' asked Lippy one evening as they brushed their teeth in the toilet block. Unless she was meeting Eilidh there Libby avoided it whenever possible. The sinks had greasy tidemarks, leaves of toilet roll littered the floor and the place smelled somewhere between pee and industrial cleaner with a few squirts of air freshener to mask other odours. 'There's a path though the trees behind the caravans, goes to a wee burn. We could go there tomorrow afternoon. Paddle. Pretend we're at the seaside. Take a picnic even.'

Eilidh shook her head and sprayed saliva and toothpaste into the grease in the sink. 'Can't.'

'Off somewhere?'

'Dunno.'

'So why can't you? It'll be fun. We can—'

'I told you. I'm not supposed to see too much of you.'

'But we hardly see one another at all. Just leave notes.'

'It's all right to see you now and again. Just for a wee while, Mummy says. As there are no other girls of my age here.'

'It's not as if I've got measles or something.'

'No, but your dad—'

'He hasnae got anything infectious either.'

Eilidh busied herself rinsing her toothbrush, and made a show of stowing her bar of pink Camay soap in a pink plastic soap dish. She wrung out her facecloth before folding it neatly into a pocket of her toilet bag. 'Dad says we'll need to look for somewhere better for next year. Somewhere with a bit more class.'

Lippy slung her towel over her shoulder. 'You've forgotten your hairband,' she said.

9 - A bunnet amongst the suits

Luck, Pete says, 'has nothing to do with politics.' Brian disagrees. To him, Pete's usual perceptiveness dive-bombs when he says that. 'The schmuck only regards himself as lucky,' insists Pete, 'because he's been in the right place at the opportune time, because he appears to have benefited from an event, an occurrence that has transformed his chances. But nine times, no, nine point nine times, out of ten,' he insists, 'the guy has benefited because he's been savvy enough to know what needed to be done in the first place. Luck had bugger all to do with it.'

Brian agrees about the necessity for strategic positioning of yourself and your ambitions, that an awareness of persuasive techniques and campaign methodologies is required, as is quashing squeamishness with a firm hand, those are the attributes that matter, and that must be pursued with single-mindedness. However he believes luck lurks in the shadows, and seeks occasional openings, chinks where it can blow in and make a difference when nothing else is effective. Luck, he believes can boost opportunities, and hike chances when the outlook spells dire. Luck. Your fingers should always be crossed that it's on your side. But it's too random to count on. You need strategy and action as well.

Pete and Brian met at Party conference the previous year. Brian heard Pete talk in one of the early debates where the audience was sparse. Elderly women were engrossed in romantic novels, or clicked at their knitting, punched fingers into others to chase errant balls of wool into the aisle, interrupting critical points or spikes of humour. Bald headed men slobbered caramels, eyes closed behind rimless spectacles, heads drooping in the heat like parched flowers. Interest in the proceedings had flown off on a holiday to the sun. Still, Pete managed to make an impact. Made the audience raise their heads, blink their eyes at the mention of a novel political slant or argument for policy change, take notice of his words of passion, if only for a brief period.

Pete then attended a well-publicised fringe meeting, and challenged one of the speakers, a leading Party light, ex-minister intent on sloughing off the skin of demotion and re-emerging as a Party grandee, an elder statesman with an expensive suit and the wisdom of Solomon, but who didn't like his thoughts and beliefs questioned by a bumptious young card carrier. Pete revelled in the confrontation. The more the ex-minister expounded, the more he lost his audience to the land of nod or the tearoom, and the more Pete gathered the thought wanderers into the palm of his hand with its fingers like plump spider's legs, ready to grub and to grasp.

Afterwards, in the bar, Brian wangled his way to Pete's side, the crowds far from dense this early at Conference. 'I enjoyed the pantomime back there. Your performance was good.'

'Just good? Bloody brilliant, I thought. Did you see that twat's face? The tic pounded relentlessly, eyelids hammered away to keep his eyes from launching into deep space. The finger that prodded like a lance — no doubt desperate to impale me, to put an end to my filleting questions. Lord, what a feeling to have him teeter on the edge like that.' He banged the bar counter with his fist. Once, twice, three times. The barman turned his head, lifted an eyebrow and approached to wipe the spills from the surface.

'You handled it well.'

Pete's look developed a sharper edge. Eyes narrowed, a question flickered through them. 'You agree with my viewpoint then?'

'In the main. Though further development of key points is required.'

'Yes? You think so? You've thought about these, have you?'

'Part of my job.'

'Which is?'

'Parliamentary assistant to Mingally Dulse.'

Pete laughed, a twirl of derision laced the sound. 'Shouldn't have believed any deep thought was required for that position.'

'It's surprising. Anyway, between you and me and my beer, I don't intend to stay there much longer. Onwards and upwards, as they say.'

'Hmm! Not an ambition you should spread around. Might get you noticed. Targeted. Anyroads, you're in the dollshouse?'

'If you mean the Parliament, then yes. An insider, privy to the lowdown, the gossip, the scandal. To covert information.' Brian could almost see through the pupils of Pete's grey eyes into his brain where cogs and wheels cranked up at his remark.

Pete scanned him, as if pricing Brian's suit and underwear. 'You obviously know my name, but I'm in the dark as to yours.'

'Brian Coldstream.'

'Hello, Brian.' He held out his hand.

Their paths crossed after most sessions, one coming across the other. Conference is like that. Networking is expected. It enhances the feeling of belonging, of camaraderie, fuels speculation and intrigue. By the time the spectacle jogged over the finishing line, Pete and Brian had covered a considerable amount of private and policy ground, and agreed to keep in touch.

Brian was the one who tipped Pete off about a possible by-election for the Wesmunster parliament. The sitting member was ill. Most people thought his return was imminent, but a whisper was going the rounds that his illness was serious, and there would be no return. Pete stayed in an adjoining constituency, the street formerly in the same constituency until the Electoral Commission played snakes and ladders with boundaries and communities. They met in a pub in Edin to talk it over, listed Pete's plus points, aware of the negatives, mainly the payroll and others like him who itched for a punt. As well as the profile he was building as a young hawk, hard working, yet not afraid to challenge, Pete had one major advantage. His father was a stalwart of the Trades Union movement. High profile. Respected. Solid. Connected. Beside that the negatives began to fade. After that first session Pete went off to sound out his father about standing.

Pete didn't succeed in getting selected. Word came down to him that he lacked experience, needed to dirty his hands with more spadework, and then he might have a chance to prove himself by standing for the Party in a seat where he wouldn't have a hope in hell of election, but which would provide the experience he lacked.

'I suppose that's the format,' Brian reasoned.

'The bastards,' Pete fumed. 'This has bugger all to do with experience and everything to do with that slimy, conniving Carnoustie — the shrivelled shit of an ex-minister I challenged at Conference. He was on the selection panel. The bugger's never forgiven me for making him look an idiot.'

'Surely not.'

'Surely definitely. Wise up, Brian. This game's not about what you know, it's about who you know. Who you curry favour with, bend the bloody knee to.'

'But there's an election in fifteen months. What'll you do?'

Pete's teeth clenched, his features rigid as if set with superglue. 'I either get out or I grovel,' he said.

Pete had been unsuccessful, done over by Carnoustie and his bastards he insisted, but Brian was sceptical about that. Perhaps at times Pete was just a bit too brash, self-assured almost to the point of arrogance. He should warn him about the dangers of being too enthusiastically new broom in a People's Union Party where a majority of members remained welded, joined at the hip, to the traditional ideas and beliefs they had imbibed since birth, and perhaps even before. Still, Brian felt he had learned useful pointers and intelligence from the process — what not to do when he embarked on his attempt to oust Ming and replace him, for Ming's seat had been identified as his best, possibly only, option.

A pushover, he thought at first, easy peasy to malign a nincompoop like Ming and take over the mantle. But now he realised it wasn't going to be the piece of cake he first envisaged. Ming, for some unfathomable reason, was popular, both in his constituency and at Holygood — difficult to believe, but there it was. A character, was how he was viewed, and you need a few of them to lighten the proceedings; one of us rather than a political treatise like some of the others; a bunnet amongst the suits (Brian laughed at that given Ming's penchant for designer labels); a nice bloke, not two-faced, not po-faced like the rest; brought up in the Party, like his father, his old man's a great guy; connections with the islands, so he understands the problems of remote areas; maybe no' quite like faither like son, but his faither's a solid union man, you couldnae get any better.

All bloody tosh, rubbish, bullshit, but people conned themselves, believed the nonsense. Brian wondered if this was a hangover from an earlier age, a hankering after the mores and less complicated life of two generations ago. Did these people truly not understand the world, Caledon included, had moved on? That attitudes were underpinned by professionalism rather than native cunning, that the days of the amateur politician had gone with Harold McMillan? Did Caledon folk still hang on to the past, cling to tattered remnants of glory, of a time when its great industries were in decline but our political giants made themselves heard, raising their voices, expounding theories with appeal to the disadvantaged and the disillusioned? Whatever the reasons behind Ming's popularity, Brian suspected any attempt to oust him would be resisted with every underhand trick in the book. He'd need to refine his strategy. There must be a way to undermine him, to make an MCP who didn't rate high in the intelligence stakes fallible to a challenge.

Ming brandishes a dark green wash bag. He spills the contents of plastic bottles and containers onto Brian's desk. A bar of soap wrapped in paper slides across the surface and halts at his keyboard with a swivel like a dancer on ice. A whiff of something vaguely familiar is liberated by the dunt. Brian can't place what the smell reminds him of. Not carbolic, but some kind of cleaning liquid perhaps.

'Got Karen to have a root around her favourite department store in her lunch break.'

'Always good to utilise the ladies, especially your wife.'

Ming looks smug. 'She's come up trumps, you've got to hand it to Karen. Knew what I wanted, and she's delivered. Look.' He holds up containers, brown like tobacco with gold lettering, one in each of his hands, and thrusts them into Brian's face. 'Look at the name. Look. Kelpie. It has kelp in it. Now how suitable is that for Jasmine of the Callyman.' He is pleased with himself. More than pleased. He gushes like an opened sluice.

Brian opens a bottle and sniffs, gingerly. 'Not bad, not bad.' He squints at the small type. 'In fact pretty damn good. It's made by a company in Barragh, so ticks all the boxes. Well done. Good on Karen.'

'And,' says Ming, as he roots in the inside pocket of his jacket, 'Karen remembered we had some photographs, and managed to find them.' He hands Brian one with a flourish. 'That's my great granny with my granny as a baby.' He points at one large and one small bundle of rags on a bench, a stone wall in the background. A pair of decrepit boots poke from beneath the sackcloth skirt of the larger bundle. The smaller one is merely a wad of tattered cloth. 'We think that was taken after they left Mingally, sometime between 1910 and 1912 probably. They stayed in Barragh for some years before they moved to the mainland. This is one of the old cow, great granny, puffing away at a clay pipe. Just look at the state of the droopy bonnet. Never came from any department store, that's for sure. That photo might actually have been taken on Mingally, though lord knows who might have taken it. The inhabitants were too bloody poor to own cameras, ignorant wee bastards, if you ask me, and visitors were few and far between. Anyone stupid enough to go was likely to be marooned there by the weather. It wasn't unknown for them to be cut off for months on end. For communication they had to resort to messages in bottles in the hope they'd be picked up by a boat. Poor sods. Can't imagine how basic their lives must have been. Pretty crap, if you ask me.'

Brian stares at the small photos, records of a community, impoverished, isolated, yet wanting to cling to the hovels and remote, inhospitable island that was home, the only home and way of life they had ever known. A hundred years on, and the images still carry a poignancy even to those with no personal association or link to the place. 'Typically Caledon,' thinks Brian. 'We romanticise poverty, see the dispossessed as martyrs to be placed on a pedestal as reminders of a Caledon past we shouldn't forget. Well, sod that. That sort of social history is embarrassing, it shouts to be buried along with the past, along with the Gaelic language, haggis and Burns. New technology is now reboosting the country from the position it has slipped to in recent years, that's what we should concentrate on. A future that wipes away the poverty of the past.' He gets a grip on his face muscles lest they twist into a grin. The Mingally stuff is meant to make Ming look a bit of an idiot, not to suffuse him in an aura of the past, perfumed with the nostalgia of romance and rosy days of simple, honest toil in idealised communities. To boost Ming's image was never his intention. Bloody hell, what has he done!

'These are great, Ming. I'm sure Jasmine will drool over them. The toiletries. Fab and well done Karen, but I think you might be better to downplay them slightly. You don't want to look, or smell, too different from the norm. Eccentricity is fine, but it's not your style. You're much more…well, man-of-the-world. Man of the people. That's it. I was going to say you were more sophisticated than the toiletries perhaps indicate. Absolutely nothing wrong with them, though. Nothing at all. It's just you're a man of the world. Member of the Caledon Parliament. So you should perhaps play these down.'

Ming looks downcast, his bubble of enthusiasm deflates like a burst balloon. 'So how do I push them yet play them down? I don't understand what you think I should do. You tell me one thing then you change your mind. Some consistency is required here, Brian.' He sounds petulant.

Brian unscrews a container top and sniffs again. 'How would this do. I'm going to run this idea past you and see what you think. Just remember that journalists should always be kept guessing. Never give them the full story. Always leave them wondering. That way you maintain their interest. Right?'

Ming nods slowly. 'That's always been our way of thinking. Don't tell the bastards anything. Not even the time of day. Don't tell me you want to challenge that?'

'No. No. Definitely not. No. I think you should employ that. Now, if the Jasmine woman asks about your favourite toiletries, you can be reticent about telling her. No upfront answers to her questions. You're an MCP. Keep her in her place. Lowly journalist and all that. Play on the typical Caledon male thing. Strong. Not exactly dour but keeps his own counsel. The silent type. You know the sort of thing.'

Ming's head nods up and down like a yoyo. 'Yup.'

Brian warms to his subject. This is going to be easy. He can use the toiletries thing to get Ming listed in the Jasmine woman's idiot book. 'The modern Caledon man, uses toiletries but doesn't flaunt them, or glut the noses of everyone within smelling distance. Right? You're a twenty first century Caledon male, not an eighteenth century dandy desperate to mask ghastly stenches with an overdose of a pong that's only slightly less objectionable. Ask her to guess what you might use, string her along. Women journalists always like that, to be toyed with. Just a hint of flirtatiousness, do you think? That'll save you telling her what you use, or rather don't use. Then you can drop in the Kelpie products. Say you were given them as a present. A Christmas present from…a great aunt, perhaps. Someone brought up on the stories of the place. Of Mingally. Great to see one of our remoter islands manufacturing such products, you can say. Reminds you of your heritage, your great grandparents. That sort of stuff.'

Ming perches on the edge of Brian's desk, picks up the bar of soap and sniffs it. 'The smell is fairly… pungent. Hmm. I see what you mean. But I can say it's great to see a place like Barragh is into manufacturing and wonderful that it's providing much-needed jobs. We could do with more such enterprises. Yes! That's the tack.' As the beam of a smile fades on Brian's face it grows on Ming's. 'Shows the entrepreneurial spirit alive and well and at work in our rural areas, benefiting from policies we put in place when in government. That's it. Brilliant or what! That way I can turn the trivial into a way of saying something significant. Right?'

'Turn the whole toiletries thing around so that it's brought back to jobs. Yes. That's rather good. Clever,' admits Brian with reluctance.

'And I can promote the product but not endorse it, as it were. Yes, I'm sure that'll work.'

Brian gathers up the containers and stuffs them back in the toilet bag. 'Yup, the jobs aspect is good, Ming'

'Got to keep jobs up there in the headlines, Brian. All else is just window dressing.'

'Absolutely.'

'Though there's positive publicity in it for me, too. Always have to keep re-election in mind.'

'Shouldn't think you need to worry about that, Ming. You'll walk it. But, as you say, good publicity doesn't go amiss.'

As he gets to his feet, Ming consults his watch. 'Good lord, look at the time. Must dash. Want to drop a few words of wisdom into this afternoon's debate. My papers. What did you do with my papers, Brian? On my desk are they? All there? Nothing missing? Sure? Right, I'm off. Speak later.'

Brian relaxes into his chair, and kicks himself mentally. With time to himself he can mull over a meeting this morning, in one of the corridors, with a fellow Parliamentary assistant. Kevin has worked in the Parliament longer than Brian, and despite his laid-back appearance obviously harbours similar ambitions. Not that he said as much — that would be dangerous, asking for trouble. But to one with a similar hunger, the signs are unmistakable, couched between Kevin's words, laced through his ideas, underpinning his actions, glazing every thought in his mind, every word uttered. Even his grey eyes give the game away. Watchful. Determined. Obsessive even. A streak of ruthlessness runs through them like a seam of whinstone, but overlaid with a twinkle of humour to disguise the desire.

'So, how's things?' asked Kevin, propping a shoulder against the wall, and wagging a folder like a tail.

'Jogging along. Like always.'

'That MCP of yours still as third rate as ever?'

Brian laughed. 'What do you think? Much the same as yours, I'd guess.'

'Yup, he grinds on, oblivious to his electorate, to the world.'

'But not for us to criticise. Right? We just do the job asked of us.'

'We do it, and we learn, and we keep our heads down. Then in the privacy of our nights we fulminate against our misfortunes.'

'The privacy of our nights. Huh, I like that! Speak for yourself, Kevin. My nights aren't always that private. Work hard, play hard. A good maxim for politicians. All the ones at Westmunster seem to believe that. Why shouldn't we?'

Kevin has this peculiar way of doing things with his eyebrows instead of smiling or laughing. One hitches itself up almost to his hairline, the other plummets onto his eye. Crocheted chains of sandy hairs that march across his face, and loup around it. His face like a piece of paper, scrunched into a ball, slowly expands, flowers, though never reaches its initial creaseless condition. 'I hear Mutt has dumped Ming into the thorny arms of Jasmine of the Callyman.'

'I wasn't aware Jasmine had thorns. I remember Jasmine as a tender plant with a cloying smell.'

'You obviously haven't met this one yet, mate. Prickly, tough, tongue like the tawse, reaction like a boxer's left hook. According to the grapevine and a couple of MPs whose noses are out of joint. You mess with her at your peril. Straight answers to straight questions. No pussyfooting around, doesn't stand prevarication.'

'Is this the same Jasmine? The Lifestyle slot is usually pretty laid-back, adores the quirky and the unusual for that bulks out the thin into a good story'

'Yup, the same Jasmine. Jasmine Stane. I heard she was after Politics but has to content herself with trivia until a certain person moves on. Hence the approach to MCPs on what is on the surface a Lifestyle issue, but I suspect is all about politics. I'd tell Ming to watch his step, mind his approach. On the other hand, you might not want to warn him. The consequences could be interesting.' Kevin couldn't fail to notice a look of surprise settle on Brian's face. 'Oh, come on, mate. Get real. I suspect you've done the calculations too. Know where the best opportunities lie. And given Ming's former mentor, he's maybe a thick bastard but some of the tricks of the trade will have rubbed off on him. So I'd say you had your work cut out. Not impossible. Nothing ever is. Just means you can't let any opportunity, no matter how trivial it appears, pass you by without exploiting it.'

'Right. Thanks for the tip on Jasmine. I assumed she'd be one of the usual new faces in Lifestyle. Bland. Not worth reading.'

'Well, believe me, mate, since she joined the paper three, four weeks ago her pieces have been a damn sight more political and hard-hitting than the usual commentators. One to be watched, I reckon.'

'Thanks. I'll have a look at what she's done. Ehm, what you said about Ming's former mentor. What did you mean?'

Kevin glanced both ways along the corridor. 'Come on, you must have heard of Ming's mentor. How he employed Ming is beyond reasoning. A favour, no doubt. Still, as I say, stuff rubs off even on the thickest material.'

'Ming used to work for an MP, didn't he? Are you referring to him.'

'Yup. Ming had a spell as a certain MP's constituency assistant.'

'So he was the mentor?'

'Could have been. You mean you really don't know any of this shit?' Brian shook his head. 'Jeez, how long have you been a member of this Party?'

'Long enough. Long enough to land me this job for a start.'

'OK, mate, don't get shirty. I just thought it was common knowledge. Part of Party folklore.'

'You thought what exactly was common knowledge?'

'Ming's mentor was a man of some considerable influence in the Party. And outwith it. In wider Caledon. Beyond even. Westmunster too. Ming's mentor had clout that he could be…lets say…persuaded to wield in certain directions.'

'You surely don't mean Ming's mentor was part of the fabled Party mafia?'

'Keep your voice down, mate. And don't refer to the operation by that name. Not advisable.'

'So what do you call it?'

'Better not to call it anything. Better never to refer to it, as far as I'm concerned. But if you have to, not something I advise, use the name he used.'

'Which was what?'

'The Galley.'

'The Galley!'

'Shh! Aye, The Galley. A space that's narrow, and restricted to the cooks. Cooking things up. Burning things, people most often, opponents in the opposition and, like as not, their own party. It wasn't good for your health or career to get in the sights of The Galley 'Cooks'. Know what I mean? They dealt with problems and inconveniences that cropped up, things that might interfere with what they saw as the Party's best interests.'

'Bloody hell! I'd no idea. Of course I'd heard rumours, side-of-mouth mutters, but never anything definite.'

'It was definite all right. Well organised, too. Some of the 'Cooks' started out in the shipyards, served their apprenticeships there, made names for themselves in the unions, so they used a load of shipping terminology. That's where The Galley came from. And they used to talk of the operation being gimballed. Know what that means?'

Brian shook his head. 'Don't think so.'

'Well stuff on boats, lights and things, galley stoves too, are often on this mechanism that compensates for the boat's rolling and heaving so they stay level. Clever bit of kit actually, Simple but clever. The pans don't slide around and the contents don't spill, so the cooks don't get scalded and instead stay clean, and unsplattered by any fallout.'

'Then The Galley was an apt metaphor for them to use.'

'Absolutely. Of course it also refers to the boat used by the Lords of the Isles and others in days gone by. The long boat with its banks of oars. Used for warfare and piracy as well as trade. Feared for the most part. Anyone with sense kept out of the way, hidden, heads down, when such galleys were in the vicinity. So the name, the branding, works on that front too. Controlling with the cut of their sails, blowing careers out the water with their guns. Simmering, stewing, frying, boiling, roasting. The cooking terminology referred to some of the actions The Galley Cooks got up to so they could control events and people. Aye. The outfit was well named.'

'Bloody hell! And here's me thinking talk of it was just the usual backbiting associated with politics.' Brian fights back a feeling that he's been silly, stupid, that his antics over Ming's speech and the toiletries for the interview were childish. The stuff of student pranks, not the charted manoeuvrings of a political stratagem. Nor had he been half as clever as he thought, underestimating Ming like that. Ming, who'd worked for …for…well, as yet he wasn't certain, but quite possibly he's worked for the MP regarded as the Head Cook. What an idiot he's been. 'I never actually believed there was a real set-up. And now you're saying this was just that. A proper set-up. Jeez! How did it operate? Was it on a favour basis? A cash basis? How do you run a venture like that? The mind boggles at the thought of it.'

'Aye, well, if your mind boggles at the thought of such a set-up it would go into orbit if it knew some of the stuff it was involved with.'

'When did it end?'

'Who says it ended?'

'You mean it's still going on?'

'I've said way too much already.'

'What you have said is mind-blowing.'

'Oh, I haven't said any of this. This conversation was all in your head.'

'Absolutely. Off the record. Unattributable.

'Aye. Mind and remember that.'

'Absolutely. But a longer imaginary chat would be good. How about meeting in a mirage for an illusory pint?'

'Just two apparitions passing in the ether, pausing to quaff a measure of nectar?'

'I'd settle for a pint in the Deacon Brodie.'

'Inhabited by too many humans, especially of the Parliamentary variety. How about the Wabbit Hen? Eight thirty. Tomorrow night.'

'Fine by me.'

'Wear your invisible outfit.'

10 - Want more chocolate?

A quick trundle around with the vacuum cleaner, duster dabbed on visible surfaces and that will need to do. Derek is never fussed by a film of dust, or the untidiness that goes with it. He merely sweeps a pile of clothes or heap of books from a seat and sits down, unconcerned by his mother's home resembling the site of recent twister devastation. Though she is exaggerating…a little. Her writing comes before pernickety housewife stuff. Usually there is only her to see it anyway, unless Sara or another of her friends calls round.

It is Derek's companion that has prompted the dust removal — his new girlfriend, though he has been seeing her for some months, but has not brought her to visit before. Must be serious. So more for her son's sake, and his need to make a favourable impression on Gail, Lippy succumbed to housework. If her dust were to become the reason for a break-up between the two, she would never forgive herself.

As she recuperates from her efforts with a cup of coffee, the empty vase on the window ledge catches her eye. Flowers. She and her secateurs have not yet made it to the garden to cull the daffodils. The vase looks forlorn, squatting there amongst her glass bits and pieces. The weak sun is caught in the stirring branches of the nearby beech tree projecting sad eyes and a drooping mouth onto the vase's lustre surface. The image flickers like old cine film. The movement mesmerises Lippy until the sun disappears behind the stout trunk. She rouses herself, digs out her gardening gloves, stiffened by mud from the autumn garden clearance, and wielding her secateurs like a rapier, goes in search of floral companions for the vase.

Against the house wall trails a thicket of winter jasmine that has flowered on and off throughout short days and heavy snowfalls. Most of the flowers have browned and shrivelled but she snips a few where yellow is still discernible. A variegated shrub survives by the side fence to provide greenery, and though the best of the daffodils are past, she tracks down a patch of later bloomers and cuts a few still at bud stage, wondering if a blast of intense heat from her hairdryer might encourage their opening in the next hour.

Sweet and sour pork is on the menu, followed by rhubarb crumble made with frozen rhubarb from the garden. Last year's, or it may be the previous year's crop, but it will taste fine. As luck would have it, a couple of elderly oranges are melding with the fruit bowl so she can add the rusting zest of one to the crumble and the flesh to the rhubarb to temper its slightly metallic taste. Derek promised to bring a bottle of wine and the table is set, so she is organised. She finishes the glass of wine she poured earlier — her aperitif — and checks the time on the clock on the cooker. Time to run a comb through her hair and drag a smear of lipstick over her lips.

The sight of herself in her dressing table mirror, arm raised with comb held in a threatening attitude above her mop of hair — mousey brown but with definite streaks of grey — drops the thought into her mind that perhaps she should change, wriggle into another jumper or skirt. A new grey and purple dress, bought for Christmas but never worn, is dragged from the wardrobe, held against her as she swivels this way and that in front of the mirror, before she peels off the clothes she wears and thrusts it over her head. Not bad. It makes her look…different. Younger even. Mature, but a young mature. After the lipstick draw and the perfume squirt — hope this girlfriend of Derek's is worth it, she thinks – she feels the neckline needs something to add a final touch. A rummage produces a necklace, a rather pretty amethyst and silver one, bought on holiday in Lucca the year before last and rarely worn. It goes with the dress, goes with the neckline.

As she adjusts it, her fingers spidering over it, their action turns the key to memories. Eilidh wore a necklace the day they went to the burn. It was meant to be fun, their only opportunity to play, the two of them enjoying a day at the burn, but pleasure turned sour like cream in the sun. Little had she thought… Instead of the usual note in the cocoa tin in the hedge, Eilidh had appeared at the caravan, rapped on the door and stepped in onto the worn mud brown carpet, a confident expression glazing her face. Lippy noticed the necklace straight away. So did her mother.

'That's a nice necklace,' her mother said with a steely look in her eye.'

'Vinegar sticks!' Lippy exclaimed. Her mother glared at her.

'It looks expensive. Was it a present?'

'Sort of.' Eilidh smiled, tossed her mahogany curls, and fingered the large amber beads interspersed with smaller gilt ones. It had the look of a necklace for an adult not a child, yet Lippy felt a tinge of envy, of admiration that Eilidh should wear it with such aplomb.

Eilidh's gaze wandered, took in the dated caravan interior, the cratered cushions. The curl of her lips said more than words. Lippy saw scorn track across her eyes before they came to rest on her father. Eilidh posing like a model before a photographer, said her mother wasn't feeling well so had decided to spend a quiet day in the caravan. Her father had gone off to visit a museum on his own so she was free to spend the day with Lippy.

'Well, I don't know…we might be going out,' said her mother quickly before her husband could answer. Her hands wiped vigorously round the mini sink and straightened the kettle on the two ring cooker.'

'Were we?' queried her father, settling back against a battered cushion and rustling his paper onto a new page.

'I thought you said we might—'

'Aw, Mum,' Lippy interrupted. 'Eilidh and I haven't had a whole day to play. Never ever. We can't go off anywhere… not today…not when Eilidh's here.'

'Well, yes, but…'

'Dad, tell Mum we're not going anywhere today. We haven't had a chance to play properly together and it's my holiday as well as yours.'

'That's enough, Lippy.'

'Dad!'

'Of you go till lunch time, then we'll see.'

So they had scampered off, along the path that ran behind the caravan park, in the direction of the burn and the rickety wooden bridge where they could sit and dangle their legs above the syrupy water.

'What's wrong with your Mum?' Lippy asked, as she squirmed to get comfortable on the rotted planks of the bridge. The edge where water had roughened the timber and gouged striated depressions was cutting into her bare legs.

'Dunno.'

'You must know. Has she a sore tummy or head, or does she feel sick?'

Eilidh shrugged. 'She's not feeling well.'

'Sometimes my mum doesn't feel well but she just takes a pill and carries on. Says she has to or nothing would get done.'

'But that's different.'

'How's it different? If mums don't feel well then—'

'Cos it is.'

'So has she something serious wrong with her?' Lippy remembered snatches of overheard conversations, illnesses spoken of in muted voices with pursed lips and slow-shaking heads.

'Never mind.' Eilidh extricated her legs from beneath the wooden rail and with a jump was on her feet and making for the bank.

'The water's full of weeds and green stuff.'

Eilidh peered in. 'No, it's fine.' She flopped down on the long grass and peeled off her socks and shoes. 'I'm going for a paddle. Come on.'

'Is is cold?'

'Not really. There's wee fish skittering about. We could catch some if we had a jar to put them in.'

'Well we don't, so just let them be. Your feet are probably scaring the life out the poor wee things.'

'Nah, they don't seem to mind.' She bent down and swished her hands through the water, stirring up swirling clouds of muddy sediment.

'What did you do that for? You've made the water dirty.'

'Cos I felt like it, that's why.'

As Lippy followed her down from the bridge, she rubbed the backs of her thighs corrugated by the bridge planks and peered into the water. She wandered further along the bank to where the water remained clear, though Eilidh still splashed and thrashed behind her. Socks and shoes discarded she slid gingerly into the burn. Bent double she watched insects hover and dart above the surface of the water, tiny fish flick past her feet. She stooped to pick up small stones whose shape or colour attracted her attention. Most she threw back, the plop as they hit the water accompanied by rippling rings of amber and brown like Eilidh's necklace. The ripples joined the breeze in swaying the more delicate rushes at the burn's edge where they danced this way and that, a bounce up, a dip down. The remaining stones in her hand, the ones she liked and wanted to keep as a souvenir of the day, she put in the pocket of her shorts.

Eilidh waded through the water and appeared beside her, her hands cupped, held in front of her.

'What you got?'

'Look,' she opened her hands to let Lippy see the tiny flapping fish, little more than the length of her index finger.

'Ugh! Put it back. It'll die out of water.'

Eilidh grinned at her, a cold mirthless grin. With a flip of her hand she held the fish between finger and thumb of one hand and with finger and thumb of the other she squeezed from tail down to head, expressing the life out of it.

Lippy hit her hand. 'Stop it. Don't do that. Don't.'

Eilidh dangled the limp corpse in her face. Lippy pushed it away with her hand, lurched a step back. Her foot caught on a raised stone on the bed of the burn, she lost her balance, threw out her arms and toppled backwards into the water. The rushes at the edge of the bank danced a frenetic polka.

Eilidh stood, hands by her side and watched. 'You thought my foot would disturb the pond life. Guess it's had a real shock now.'

Lippy flayed her arms, fought to sit up, get her head above water. She coughed, choked, spat out whatever wriggled in her mouth or was caught in her nose. 'Don't help me!' she spluttered.

'Don't intend to. You're old enough and ugly enough to get up yourself.' Eilidh swished her hands in the water to rid them of bits of fish before she clambered onto the bank and wandered back to sit on the bridge where, unconcerned by her friend's plight, she rhythmically swung her legs above the water.

On all fours, like a wounded animal, Lippy grabbed handfuls of rushes, clawed her way up the bank and threw herself on the grass. Head shaking like a dog with a wet coat, she tried to expel water from her hair, scrunching it in her hands to wring it out, moving her fingers through the sodden locks in an attempt to fluff them up. 'I'll need to go back to the caravan,' she wailed. 'I need to change.'

'Don't be so soppy. You'll soon dry.'

'I'm cold.'

'Come and sit here in the sun.' Eilidh raised her hand, a bar of Cadbury's chocolate clutched in her fingers. 'See what I've got.' She waved the chocolate. 'Come and be nice to me and I might give you a square. Maybe even two.'

Lippy hesitated, annoyance with Eilidh, her senseless killing of the wee fish, her lack of help and cutting words, struggled in her mind with the desire for a piece of chocolate to sweeten her ordeal.

'Fine, if you don't want it...' Eilidh waved her hand again, ripped off the purple wrapper and the silver paper at the end to show the glisten of the chocolate.

Lippy kicked her feet in the grass, picked up her shoes and shuffled towards the bridge, dripping water in a trail behind her.

Three pieces of chocolate later and her annoyance was dissipating as well as the water in her shorts and T-shirt, yet she couldn't rid her mind of the sight of Eilidh as she squeezed the life out a harmless wee fish. It was as if the sight had pressed itself into part of her brain, like a pattern stamped into plasticine. The fish. Eilidh's fingers. The look on her face.

She swung her legs, flapped her arms to move the warm air through the material of her damp clothes. The sun was hot on her face and when she ran her fingers through her hair its strands felt almost dry. The stones she had collected were still in her pocket and she grubbed them out and laid them in a line on the wooden planking beside her to dry in the sun. The rich purples and blues, ochres and nut browns began to fade as they dried. 'Why didn't you help me up?' To her own ears her voice sounded pathetic and whining.

Eilidh shrugged, tossing her mahogany curls. 'Didn't want to.'

'Why not?'

'Because I didn't. See!' She scooped up one of Lippy's line of stones and threw it at a duck that had paddled into the water alongside them.

'Hey, that's my stone!'

'So what. There's plenty more. Want another dip to replace it?'

'You shouldn't throw stones at ducks.'

'Who says?

Lippy felt tears threaten so turned her head away to watch a horse munch its way across a patch of grass in a nearby field. It raised its head as if looking at her. 'Why you being so nasty today?'

'Me? I'm not being nasty.'

'Yes you are.'

'It's just you being a wimp.'

Lippy drew her legs from beneath the wooden bridge rail and got to her feet, pulled on her sandals and made a show of fastening them. 'It must be lunch time. I'm going back to the caravan.'

'Why? This morning you complained we never have enough time together to play. Now you're off to be dragged away somewhere when we could be enjoying ourselves.'

'Mum said to be back for lunch.'

'Scaredy, scaredy custard.'

Lippy began a slow skip along the path, a damp oval left behind where she had sat on the wooden planks of the bridge. She felt confused by Eilidh's treatment of her but no way was she going to let on she had hurt her.

'Want more chocolate? There's some left.' Eilidh waved it. The silver paper caught the sun and glinted.

'Going back for lunch.'

Eilidh scrabbled to her feet, and ran after her. She grabbed her arm, forced her to turn and posted a square of chocolate between her lips.

Lippy allowed herself to be dragged back to sit on the bridge. 'What museum is your Dad visiting?'

'Museum! He's not visiting a museum. They bore him silly.'

'But you said—'

'That was just for your parents.'

Lippy looked at Eilidh, and felt today's friend was different to the friend of previous days. Was this what Eilidh was really like? Had she failed to notice this before? Desperate for friendship had she overlooked the real Eilidh? Or was she having a bad day because something — her mother's illness perhaps — had upset her? 'So where did your Dad go off to?'

'How should I know! Somewhere. He usually stomps off when he and Mummy argue.'

Lippy looked confused. 'But you said… Your Mum's ill though?'

'Not really. Just annoyed. She's always annoyed when they've had a barney. She goes off to bed to mope, and Dad disappears. It'll blow over. Usually does.'

'I'm sorry.'

'What for? I'm used to it. Happens all the time.'

11 - It's a la-la-la-la-lahhhhh, de de de deeee

There is a window. A bay window that looks out over the street from the tenement second floor. A woman stands by the window, arms folded, cuddling herself as she surveys the pavements on either side of the window and across the street. She is looking for someone, her husband, but she has scoured the view from the window for days; days during which time her eyes have darted between each view, left, right and across the street, to a slower survey which is no less anxious or penetrating. With only minor interruptions to the routine she has stood there from the morning of the day after his non-appearance until now, rarely sitting as that limits the view from her eyrie.

Occasionally she waves to a passer-by who looks in her direction and mouths a greeting. 'Hello.' Or, 'Nice day.' The woman in one of the flats across the road points to the books cradled in her arms and mimes, 'Off to change my library books.' The man from upstairs gives a smile and nod of acknowledgement as his eyes survey the parked cars.

Her husband went to work on Friday morning and didn't return. After she returned home from work she had made their tea. Chicken nuggets and chips with sweetcorn. Apple pie for afters, with a dollop of scooshie cream — the stuff you squirt from a can, long-life, economical as it keeps in the fridge. She ate hers on her own. His she put in the fridge, though she doubts if he'll be back to eat it.

During Saturday and Sunday — the whole of her weekend when she wanted to wander round the shops, buy bits and pieces, and today since returning from work — she has stood at her window and watched others scurry to live their lives while hers is on hold. Yet she doesn't feel angry. She is past that. Resignation, that's what she feels. Resignation tinged with anxiety. For despite everything she has been subjected to during their twenty-six years of being together, his safety, his wellbeing still causes her concern. Mostly he is there, if not her anchor then at least the rope that attaches her to the security and safety of the jetty. He laughed when she mentioned that to him. 'So I'm a rope, am I? Well… better than being a rat.' The allusion didn't make sense to her, though at times like this she could well think of him as a rat, a sleekit rodent that steals what is hers by right, chews at her sense of womanhood, gnaws at her self esteem.

Yes, mostly he is here, though he has his evenings out, the odd weekend away. 'I need my own interests, Selina. You haven't got me on a leash. Not yet, anyway.'

'I'm not even sure what your interests are,' she had commented, but never received an answer. 'Why don't you tell me about them? Perhaps we could share one of them.' He shook his head. In the end she guessed, assuming they were connected with the disappearances, like now, but she never actually knew. Her stolid partner, fond of his football, his pint in the pub, his flutter on the horses at the Grand National, hid a secret side that she could never penetrate. Her father had been much the same.

On Saturday she had busied herself with chores, the bay window as her base. The room was vacuumed with a thoroughness that led to every corner, especially those around the window being scoured of fluff and dust. Furniture was polished, though apart from the three-piece suite, a coffee table and the TV there wasn't much to occupy her. Still unsettled, she dragged the stepladders from the cupboard in the hall, filled a bucket with warm water and cleaned the windows and the surrounding woodwork, the sleeves of her jumper rolled up, a pair of pink rubber gloves protecting skin and nail varnish, Number Seven's Rosy Glow. Silently she hummed a tune. It might have been an old pop song, she wasn't sure. Music merely lurks at the edges of her life, though she la-lahed along sometimes in the pub. 'It's a la-la-la-la-lahhhhh, de de de deeee.'

When she glanced down, she seemed even further from the ground than when she stood on the floor, as if she was looking through the wrong end of binoculars. *Bloody hell, better watch my step.* Briefly, she wondered how it felt to look out from the top of a skyscraper. She wouldn't like that, up in the sky, vulnerable, so far off solid ground; the second floor suited her fine. Peculiar, though, the unsettling effect another few feet up a ladder can have.

Outside the light drains from the sky and gathers into a mass in front of her, its concentration heightens its brightness to a neon-like exuberance that pulsates and forms into a downward pointing, arrow that bounces, encouraging her to take the plunge. Downwards. To the welcoming arms of the pavement. She shut her eyes, swivelled her head away from the window. *Careful. Watch your step,* she cautioned herself.

Aware the height of the ladders left her exposed, her whole body separated from the crash to the pavement by only a thin sheet of glass, rippled and flawed, she clung to the curves of the mouldings. With effort, she forced open her eyes, and set her thoughts to the task. She winkled out dead spiders from joints and behind the ropes for the casement windows, *Out of there, you dirty wee pests.* She brushed away the webs with filaments that were sticky, and clung like burrs to her washing cloth.

A fall to an untimely demise held no attractions. Her anxiety over Schaw's non-appearance paralysed her, but should he leave for good, or not return, then she had long since realised her life would trundle on and she would find new interests to plug the gap he left. Wouldn't she? Years ago she made a conscious decision to stick with him as long as he kept his part of the bargain. If he broke it, then she was free to remake her life. His failure to reappear was breaking the bargain.

The glass of the windows remained streaky. Heaven knows when I last washed this lot, she thought. As she turned to descend the ladders, a wave of dizziness made her extra careful of her footing, as she went in search of a newspaper to buff them with. *That's as clean as I'm going to get them. The remaining streaks will need to remain,* she decided when finished. She felt tired and thirsty. So she made coffee and drank it in the bay window, inspecting the results of her cleaning spree. *It's a la-la-la-la-lahhhhh, de de de deeee.*

As Sunday stretched before her she hoped Schaw's reappearance would end her search for tasks to accomplish within the confines of the bay window. *Now let me see. These tops, jeans, I suppose they'd do another turn. Ach, I'll just stick them in the washing machine and then they're clean. And there's stuff to iron.* She carried the ironing board from the kitchen cupboard to the window. Without a nearby point into which to plug the iron, she went in search of the extension cable which Schaw kept in his toolbox. *I'm sure there's one here somewhere. The one that's used for the lights at Christmas.*

To pass the time she forces herself to iron slowly, creases smoothed with the tips of her fingers as if she stroked a baby, the point of the iron poked into every corner and around buttons. *It's a la-la-la-la-lahhhhh, de de de deeee.* Each time she laid the iron on its heel to move the garment to a creased area, she stared through the glass, up the road, down the road, across the road. She willed him to appear.

Okay. Okay. You've had your fun, your freedom. Time to get yourself back here and get on with your life. The sound startled her, until she realised it was her own voice. *Right, and you know what they say about folk who talk to themselves, don't you,* she responded, herself to herself.

Heavens, things are bad, she thought, realising she had spoken that aloud too. The pile of clothes, all bounce and life pressed out of them, was gathered into her arms to be carried through to the bedroom. As she elbowed open the bedroom door, she thinks that perhaps by the time she returns to the window she'll hear his footsteps on the stairs. She listened but heard only silence and the sound of a car in the distance.

A noise. The bang of a door. Her heart started to thud as she heard feet belt up the stairs — a peculiar sound, like a wire brush stroking a cymbal. After all the hours when she stared through the window, she has missed the sight of him stride homewards along the road from wherever he had found a parking space. Footsteps neared the door, stopped, and the knocker rattled. She hesitated, and wondered why Schaw would use the knocker rather than his key. During his high jinks he had lost it, thrown from his trouser pocket as he tossed them across some floor. Difficult, if not impossible. His door key was attached to a key ring with an assortment of other keys. What doors they fitted, what locks in what places unknown to her they might open, she could only guess, but along with them were his car keys. So if his bundle of keys were lost he'd be unable to open or start his car to drive home. The knocker clattered again, puncturing her thoughts. The sound was impatient, authoritarian, demanding attention.

'Eh, hello. Selina, isn't it?'

She nodded. 'You're ... Jut?'

'That's me. I was just wantin' a wee word with Schaw. If it's convenient, that is.'

'Sorry, he's not in.'

'Oh, bummer! He's out, you say. Meeting? Drink at the pub?'

'He's out. Away for...for the weekend. Visiting a friend.'

'That right! Lucky him. So what...he won't be back till tonight? Tomorrow? Afternoon? Evening?'

Selina hadn't liked this character the first time she met him and he hadn't grown on her. The opposite. Her hackles had risen, she closed down, wound down the shutters on information. This guy was too nosey by half and she didn't like folk who poked their noses into her and Schaw's doings. As she wondered how he had gained entry without pressing her door buzzer, she responded, 'He wasn't sure. It depends.'

'Depends on what?' His face had a mean look, the cheeks pinched in, the mouth puckered in permanent disapproval. The Pinocchio nose didn't help, neither did the deep set of the eyes which gave them a blank appearance, unfathomable so unable to confirm whether the curve of his lips was a smile, a leer or a sneer.

'Depends what they decide to do. Walk or fish. Watch football maybe. How the hell should I know! He's just away with a friend. Doing things friends do together.'

The genial mask on Jut's face slipped, and allowed her to glimpse eyes narrowed in speculation, lips pursed into a knot of consideration. Her wariness grew, especially as Jut made no move to leave. The look on his face unnerved her.

Suddenly, as if a switch was flicked, his face relaxed and she wondered if her imagination was playing tricks. 'Too bad he's not here. Yup, too bad.' His eyes shifted away then back. 'Eh, Selina, I'm feelin' awfully thirsty. D'you suppose I could come in and have a wee glass of water?'

Selina felt panic, a rising sickness that sent spurts of acid gouging through her. She didn't want this character in her home, yet couldn't think of an excuse.

'Thanks,' said Jut, and ignoring her hesitation, pushed past her into the hall. 'The kitchen's through here? Right? Won't be a tick.'

She left the door slightly ajar and followed him through to the kitchen where she watched as Jut went to the cupboard where the glasses were kept, took out a tumbler and ran cold water into it. Selina wondered how he knew in which cupboard the glasses were kept. She hadn't told him, and she was unaware of him having been in her home before, although she had met him once or twice when out with Schaw. Her husband didn't have a problem with him, found Jut amusing company, nevertheless he occasionally displayed a wariness that suggested a lack of trust. But if she was honest, Schaw never really trusted anyone. Herself included. Apart from the disappearances that were never fully explained, there were other question marks in their relationship. She had learnt to push them aside and live with them. She supposed Jut might have visited previously, when she was out, but that seemed unlikely. Unease squeezed her heart, fear threw a tourniquet around her lungs, while an unseen hand twisted it tighter and tighter.

He sipped the glass of water, then raised the glass to the light and examined it. 'Used to have great drinking water in this country, but that's changed. Tastes of bloody chemicals now. Makes you wonder if the stuff's even good for you.' He poured the water into the sink. 'Tell you what, how about makin' me a cup of tea? That always masks the taste of the bloody water. Besides, tea would be better at quenchin' my thirst. What about it?'

As if hypnotised, Selina nodded and crossed the room to fill the kettle.

Jut passed her on his way to the door. 'Need a pee. Too much bloody beer. Won't be a tick.'

Selina registered he hadn't asked where the bathroom was. She made tea and poured two mugs, small ones, she didn't want to encourage him to stay. Her stance at the bay window was empty, so she went to check. The bathroom door was slightly open but no light was on, and the sounds her ears pick up come not from the bathroom but from the bedroom. She froze. Thoughts of challenging him galloped through her mind but were dismissed. Better to let the guy root around — she had nothing to hide — then encourage him to leave. Confrontation could turn ugly. This was a guy she couldn't trust, a guy who at this moment was rooting through her bedroom, on the search for something obviously, but what? Gold and diamond jewellery wasn't normally found in two room and kitchen flats in Victorian tenements. Drugs? Way off the mark. Money? What she has is in transit in her current account and this month it approaches red earlier than last month. The purse in her bag clutches only a fiver and some coppers. Hardly a haul if it's money he's after. She can think of no reason why this guy is rummaging through her drawers, has no idea what he hopes to find. She heard him move, the sound of a drawer close, and she retreated back to the kitchen.

'Jut, your tea's getting cold,' she called, hoping her anxiety wasn't obvious in her voice.

He appeared through the door. 'Nice bathroom you've got, Selina. What was that about tea?' He checked his watch. 'Goad. Is that the time. Would you believe it! Need to dash, I'm afraid. Supposed to be somewhere else.'

Relief. Her knees felt wobbly. She followed him to the door. 'I'll tell Schaw you were here. Can I give him a message? Tell him to phone you?'

He turned on the landing. 'What?'

'Will I ask Schaw to phone you when he gets back?'

'Naw, don't bother.' He gave a wave of his hand and bounced down the stairs.

Selina stood by the door until she heard the bang of the close door echo through the building, then, as relief flooded through her, went to the bay window to watch him bound along the pavement and turn the corner onto the main road. After she stared in the direction he had taken for several minutes, she went to the bedroom and looked around, but nothing appeared to be disturbed or missing. Perhaps she imagined it, she thought. But she knew she hadn't. And there had been the glimpse of something long and thin under his jacket as it flapped around him when he bowled down the stairs.

It was when she went to bed that she found it. She took off the cover and folded it, placed it over the back of the chair she puts her clothes on, then she pulled back the quilt, and there it was. It lay where she would lie. Without picking it up she recognised what was on it. When her father was alive she'd seen it occasionally on his papers. But she thought all that was in the past. Forgotten. She stretched out her fingers, not to touch but to hover over it as if for vibes of information, and wondered why it was there, knowing Jut must have placed it there for her to find.

She checks the approaches to the window again. It's now early Monday evening. Schaw has been missing since Friday morning. She had enquired, and he hadn't gone to work. The time approaches when she needs to think about a phone call to the police to report him missing, yet she is filled with reluctance to take that step. Selina knows he has gone missing like this before, more than once, and turned up as if nothing untoward had happened, expecting her to behave as if he had merely popped out for ten minutes or so to buy a pint of milk or a newspaper. If she phones the police he will be annoyed, more than annoyed, furious. 'My life's my own, woman! What I do, when I do it is my business,' he will say. When he returns. Besides, a phone call the police would involve awkward questions, awkward answers, awkward explanations to Schaw when he does return. So better to wait it out.

It's the loneliness. It gets her down. The lack of another human voice. No reason to exercise her own vocal chords by talking. *It's a la-la-la-la-lahhhhh de de de deeee.* Although she doesn't really enjoy her work at the department store, at least there is plenty chat, banter, gossip about celebrities and the cost of petrol, the everyday closeness of others that raises her spirits. She works in the home furnishings department. At first she was disappointed to be sent there as she had fantasised about working in ladies' fashions — the opportunity to try on gowns, mother of the bride outfits. But home furnishings is fine. Quite interesting really. Her staff discount means the flat looks good, better than it would have otherwise, with its expensive cushions, bed linen frothy with frills, springy Egyptian cotton towels in the bathroom, and a range of kitchen accessories as well as nick knacks around the house. She'd soon made friends, so there's always plenty to chat about; Daphne's daughter's baby, Greta's man's illness, Corinne's boyfriends— a right rum lot of males, and what she got up to with them. Still, it was none of her business what the youngster did.

Her own daughter is safely married, no kids and Selina has a feeling there won't be any either. Janice is too fond of the high life. Maybe she should phone her. Use Skype and switch on the video camera so they can see one another. *How you getting on? Been to the beach lately? What've you been doing? Anything interesting?* Her spirits jump, until she realises Schaw's absence couldn't be hidden from her. Janice will suss it out immediately, from her voice, from the look of resignation on her face, from her father not being in although it's tea time.

Besides, Janice never understood. Unlikely as it seems, she sympathises with her father, but can't commiserate with her mother. 'Mum, you really need to stop getting on at Dad. You always criticise him. Try to change him. For heaven's sake why can't you let him be? You need to stop clinging to a relationship that's a farce. Cut Dad loose. Let him live his life as he wants to. Make a new life for yourself.' Try as she might, there is no way she can persuade Janice that her father could have left years ago, but chose to stay. 'Mother, get real,' she would say. 'You're in denial. You're the one who won't let go. You need to pluck up courage and wave him goodbye.' Her daughter doesn't realise that marriage perhaps provides the cloak of respectability her father needs for his life, provides a shield for his other activities. Whatever they are. No, Janice doesn't understand, and steeling herself for her daughter's condemnation is more than she can cope with at present.

The coughing arrival of a van, the slam of its door, rouses her from another dwam that has claimed her, and brings her eyes and mind back to the present. She steps closer to the window and peers below in case Schaw has been given a lift by an acquaintance she doesn't know. She presses close to the glass, and feels the cold smoothness of it like frost-chilled air hitting her face on a winter morning. She can see the name on the van. Campbell. It's the woman downstairs getting her meat delivery for the week. *Some folks can't walk the length of themselves nowadays,* she thinks. *What do they think legs are for? Kicking footballs, no doubt. Or dangling them at men to ogle as if they were toys on elastic, the sort you hang on prams for babies, to keep them amused. Well, that was about the measure of it. Toys for boys.* Mrs Thompson appears on the pavement to supervise the delivery. She looks up, not surprised by the face at the window, and waves. *Hello Mrs Thompson of the meat delivery. From your looks you can't really be considered a toy, can you. That would be stretching matters, stretching the elastic to breaking point, for you're right buxom, and that's putting it mildly. But you obviously think you've something, as you fair chat up any man that's stupid enough to go near you.* She'd watched it with her own eyes. The way the woman opened her eyes wide, batted her lashes as if swatting a fly, licked her lips into the curl of a predator. *Oh, I've seen you all right. I've noticed your antics. And you the wrong side of fifty, maybe even sixty. It's fair disgusting, so it is.*

He'd noticed it too, her husband, Schaw. Surprised her when she saw him give the woman a lift of his eyebrow, an appreciative grin, though Schaw's grins these days looked more like grimaces. There was the time too when they'd passed her on the stair, and Schaw seemed to go out of his way to brush against her arm, plump and padded like a cushion it its floral sleeve with the lace trimming. *At her age. Lace trimming! Well, mutton dressed as lamb was what they used to call it.* But she'd noticed that look on Schaw's face and it had grabbed her. Because simpering young men were the attraction for him — at least so she had figured after devoting endless, twirling thoughts to his disappearances and a number of disturbing phone calls. That was why the whole police thing was so embarrassing.

To report your husband missing was bad enough, but it made her squirm to admit he had disappeared before, a number of times, and turned up safely — presumably after passion and attraction waned. Still, always at the back of her mind, fuelled by the alarming phone calls, was this wee demon that grew bigger as night came on and she felt the dark smother her, as if a black hood had been thrust over her head and she was left to stumble around, unsure where she was going, in dread of what might lie in wait. So she switched on all the lights but didn't turn on the television in case she missed hearing a noise that signalled doom.

As lights come on in houses around her, windows aglow, open to the world as if each is a miniature stage for a specific production, with figures on the move, hands and arms thrown wide in theatrical gestures, her resolve trembles. Schaw is still missing. She tries his mobile. He dislikes her checking up on him, but bouts of desperation are engulfing her, causing her to panic, so she calls his number but gets a robotic voice —the number she is calling is unavailable. *He'll have his phone switched off so I can't berate him, ask when he's coming home. The bastard.* But the panic still attacks her, prods her into action. Maybe she should call the police after all. Risk phoning Janice.

She could put on her coat and visit her mother in the home. The conversation would be stilted and one sided. Her mother wouldn't recall who she was.

'They dinnae feed me here,' she will warble. 'I havenae had ma tea. I telt you they're no' nice to me here, didn't I? An' the folk around — they're all snafflin' visitors, intruders, after ma belongings. Pinch ma jewellery an' steal the food off ma plate, so they do. See that one there, over there by the old bag o' bones, she's one of them, one o' the nickers.'

To her mother, the people around were preying mantises rather than fellow sufferers and care assistants.

After the death of her father, her mother had begun to isolate herself. She cut herself off from friends and acquaintances, from the hectic life she had thrived on for so many years.

'I dinnae like travelling on the bus on my own,' she said, 'or being out in the dark. You never know what's lurkin' these days. Waitin' for you and your pension book.'

She invited friends, then didn't want to open the door to them in case they mugged her, attacked her and left her helpless, on her own, lying injured on the floor, bleeding to death.

Occasionally Selina drove her to visit friends, but her mother was fearful of imposing, taking up their time when they were busy. That slid into criticism of their attitude towards her.

'They laugh at me. Imagine, all those folk I've known for years and years laughin' at me, makin' fun o' me. And, would you believe it, they feed me stewed tea, nasty tarry stuff like cough syrup, and stale biscuits that taste o' sawdust. And all the while they sit there an' taunt me, rakin' up the past, snide comments on me and Charlie, especially Charlie. My goad, you wouldnae believe the things they say about Charlie.'

So the family home had been sold. Her mother was unhappy about that but Schaw had talked her round. A residential home had been found near them — not easy as most had lengthy waiting lists, but Schaw knew someone who pulled a few strings. The idea was sold to her mother. She would be much closer to them. Selina could visit often, take her out, they could enjoy lunches or afternoon teas, go shopping. And if she needed anything then she was only a ten minute journey away. So much better for her to be near Selina and Schaw.

Her mother hadn't settled into the home.

'They were here again the day,' she said one day, as she leaned towards her, eyes darting around.

'Who were here, Ma?'

'Those men. Askin' questions.'

'What men?'

'You know, those men I told you about before. The ones that said they knew your father. But I don't remember them.'

'Friends of Dad's?'

'No…I don't know. I don't remember them. I would know them if they'd been friends o' Charlie's.'

'Maybe not. You didn't pay much attention to Dad's political life.'

'Huh, look who's talkin'! I knew, I knew all right. Knew what was goin' on. He thought I didnae, thought my head was full o' cotton wool an' clouds. Huh, stupid Charlie! He thought women hadnae brains, your

Dad. Thought they were just for sittin' in a chair, like an ornament on the mantelpiece, to look nice, add a bit o' class to the place. He was some man, but he didnae think women had eyes or ears. Or, come to that, brains.'

'The men you say were here...'

'Oh, they were here all right. I know what's what, I'm no' away wi' the fairies yet.'

'Sorry. The men who were here, I wouldn't worry about them coming back. Dad's gone, and now you're beside us, they're not likely to bother you.'

Her mother looked at her with a look that shocked her. Contempt flared from her bleary eyes, contempt and a haunted look. Selina had no idea why. 'Wasn't your dad they were wantin', those men. It was his papers. Burned before I moved here, I said, but I'm no' sure they believed me. The thin one wi' the funny name certainly didnae. Gave me a look like a steel dagger, he did. Said he'd be back. So you see you're haverin' when you say they're no' likely to bother me again. Haverin'.'

The men slipped from her mother's mind, faded from her memory. If they returned her mother forgot to mention it. The care assistants hadn't mentioned any other visitors either.

It isn't as if money is a problem. Selina is aware MPs are well paid, but was surprised at how much her father's assets had amounted to. Just as well, for she couldn't afford the fees for the home, not on what she earned at the department store. And every month the amount shown on the building society statement lurches downwards as the fees to the home are paid. What had seemed such a large amount is now reducing at a dramatic rate as the home fees are hiked up yet again.

The home has a good reputation, calls itself a hotel for the elderly, with comfortable rooms and a tidy garden, a paved area with a seat for residents, two flower beds with rows of pastel bedding plants, nothing garish or discomfiting, certainly nothing straggly or pushy, showered twice a week with a garden hose irrespective of weather, dozed regularly with plant food whether required or not. Her mother is well looked after, but the place depresses Selina — the sight of the inmates, clothes hanging in wrinkles and folds, shuffling, deaf, incoherent, with blank eyes and dribbling mouths, and the smell — old bodies, flowers from the local crematorium, fish fingers and decay.

No, she can't face that in her present state of anxiety. The intervals between her visits are lengthening, but her mother will never know. She has entered a zone where time no longer exists. Neither do people, not even her. Only the care assistants and the manager will tot up the weeks between her appearances, but she no longer gives a damn about that. The person who was her mother left long ago. Only a shell entangled in seaweed remains.

From the wall press beside the fireplace Selina pulls out a photograph album, one she salvaged when they emptied her mother's house. She had stretched out her hand, certain it was on the third shelf from the top, its allotted place in her life, but when fingers were unable to find it her eyes discovered it on the second shelf. Odd. She shrugged, thinking she must have been careless the last time she looked at it. Goodness knows, that was long enough ago!

The album is all that remains of her childhood and life before marriage — a few scuffed photos and a box of stuff that belonged to her father, bits and pieces caught in her memory, nothing of value or importance. She flicks through the pages. Granny as impressive as a full rigged ship in her Edwardian blouse of frills and lace, her hat approaching the size of an osprey's nest, similar in colour, with swathes of feathers and spiked hat pins like beaks. Pa stands behind Granny's chair, weedy in stature, shoulders stooped, moustache drooping, barely taller than his seated wife. She'd been very fond of both. Hard, unyielding lives had unaccountably made them warm, loving, family centred people who were never happier than when their friends and grandchildren surrounded them. Their two surviving children had been Auntie Mamie and her father. In pre-NHS days common childhood illnesses had carried off the others, at least a couple hadn't survived the rigours of birth, without ante-natal care or balanced diets. Auntie Mamie had sailed off to Canada with her new husband, and though letters had been infrequent, her daughter had informed them, about eight years ago Selina thought, of her mother's passing, a card, it was, one sent to all who might have known Mamie, inviting them to the funeral. Needless to say, she hadn't rushed out to book her flight.

She turns more pages. There is her dad, young, with hair brushed into submission, looking skinny in a suit that may have been borrowed as it is several sizes too small even for him, outside the Houses of Parliament. It must have been taken on the first day of his new life, bursting with pride yet with a haunted look in his eyes as if he wondered what the hell he had let himself in for. Her mouth curls into a wan smile. The last time he would have asked himself that, she thinks. Her dad was in his element at Westmunster. He thrived on wheeling and dealing. He bargained and traded as if in an eastern bazaar — as if that's what he was born to do. And she was fairly certain he was bloody good at it. Politics wasn't discussed much at home, though. Her mother wasn't interested, so she'd always assumed, yet she had denied that. Anyway, strange though it now seems, her father's doings as an MP were rarely mentioned, unless Schaw mentioned him. Schaw and her father had always been close. Perhaps closer than she ever realised.

Schaw. The name deposits her back in the present. The album is closed carefully, and she returns it to the cupboard. Reminiscences of the past don't bring her company, a friendly face to talk to about trivia.

She thinks of Louise. Dare she call Louise, she wonders? Louise is a friend, probably her closest friend, but Louise knows there's a problem with Schaw. She'd long suspected it and her suspicions were ticked as right the last time he went off, when she turned up unexpectedly and found her wound up like a spring, like she is this evening. Into the sideboard Louise had gone in search of booze, but all she unearthed was a bottle of Baileys Irish Cream that she'd received as a Christmas present years before. Louise had held the bottle up to the light, shaken it, 'Booze doesn't go off, does it?' she asked as she poured them both a large glass. It couldn't have been the effect of the drink, it must have been the unaccustomed friendship, the closeness of another human being, that caused her to start gushing about her life, about Schaw, and his suspected little problem, though she drew the line at being specific about it. Not that she actually knows what it is, or if he even has a problem. She merely suspects he has. It seems a likely explanation for his disappearances. Whether Louise understood, or only partly grasped the picture, was debatable, and she didn't elucidate. After that evening it was never mentioned. Schaw returned, his usual undemonstrative, though perfectly amiable self, home punctually after work for his meal, then slouched in front of the TV, or off to the pub for an hour, rarely more. So she pretends there is no problem, never has been, and Louise, considerate Louise, refrains from mentioning it.

A car door slams. The sound draws her to the window, but the man walks to the close next door. It is dark now and there are fewer passers-by, just the odd shopper who makes for the off licence on the corner with its bright lights and boards propped outside listing the best buys and the bargains. She watches a group of young people approach and pass, push one another good-naturedly, and make the street ring with noise and snatches of music straight from the Bronx.

Should I phone Louise? Not to mention Schaw, just for a chat. Perhaps arrange to meet in town next Saturday for a wander round the shops — John Lewis and Marks, those sort of places. A cup of coffee somewhere. I can say I want... want what? A present. Something for Janice. A wee wedding minding for a colleague's daughter. Or something for myself.

Heaven knows it's long enough since I last bought myself something new to wear. A skirt for the warmer weather, perhaps. Shoes. I could buy myself shoes to wear once the weather improves and I can ditch the boots and the clunky lace-ups. Loads of items I can list as wanting to buy, or none. Surely it doesn't matter. Most folk don't need a reason to phone a friend, to go shopping with a mate. So why all the reasons, the excuses? But she knows why. An umbrella to hide the cloud of unease and anxiety that hangs over her. The reason, whatever it might be, is her umbrella.

And then there is the thing that was left lying in her bed on Sunday afternoon, left by that moron Jut. Hardly something she can discuss with Louise.

12- Turning into her father

The one upside of the caravan was that it distanced her father from the television in the corner of the living room. And though she missed the occasional pop programme and film she would like to have watched — *don't fret, they'll be shown again in two shakes of a lamb's tail,* said her mother — with his political force-feed tube removed, her father's tea time rants that spilled through the evening, were diminished. True he still read his Callyman newspaper from front to back page, with a news stand of titles surrounding him at weekends, but her mother tended to drag him away from them at the caravan. She was determined they should do something, even if they only sat outside on folding canvas chairs, or went for a walk, or visited somewhere of interest nearby. So less political tripe in, less political garbage out — at least so Lippy thought, and she suspected her mother believed so too. Perhaps to her that was even a major benefit of the caravan.

Sometimes her mother believed politics rather than blood flowed through her husband's veins. A man not easily provoked, little riled him — apart from Mags Hatcheter, nuclear weapons, unemployment, the loss of jobs and industries that had kept heads high, the shenanigans around the first referendum, privatisation. Once he got started she knew better than stop him, indeed found it impossible to turn off the tap of rhetoric. Politics was personal for her husband. Politics touched his life, shook his hand. So she sat and knitted complicated cable patterned jumpers that held her mind while the diatribe rolled over her. Lippy would listen briefly, then let her mind wander, fascinated by the animation of her dad's face, the way his eyebrows squirmed, the flop of his hair across his forehead, the mobility of his lips, the sheen in his eyes, until boredom overcame her and she sneaked off to read or do homework.

Politics, thought the young Libby, was the rubbish of idiots, for idiots, by idiots. Politics was boring. End of story. She lost count of the number of times she was forced to hear her father let rip about this politician or that, about how this party was evil and the other good, the one concerned only with the interests of toffs and bosses, the fortunate who had attended the right schools, those with money; while the other party looked after everyone else – the rejects it seemed to Lippy. The adherents of one party went to the ball in gowns, black ties and fancy cars, danced and drank champagne, laughed and exchanged business cards, phone numbers and intentions to meet up again. The Cinderellas sat by the fire, meagre in the heat it gave out for coal was expensive, rustled their newspapers in indignation, shook their fists and shouted (like her father) at the television screen, with only the occasional get-together in pubs or someone's chilly front room to share opinions.

Of course there were the unions, the bastions of working men (mainly), but political rubbish had done for them. Lippy's father had toyed with the idea of joining the People's Union Party (the PUP, he called it) — the Cinderfolk party — as he considered society was imbalanced, out of kilter. He believed that, as in the fairy-tale, Prince Charmings and Cinderellas should share more equally the pluses and minuses of life. But bar a revolution he didn't see that materialising any time soon, if at all. So why join an organisation to achieve nothing. Born to fail, or at least born without the attributes necessary for success in a country that had, during its history, achieved much through the sweat of Cinderfolk.

Wrong, his wife would screech. *Cinderellas have no say. We're repressed twice over — born the wrong sex, into the wrong backgrounds. You're spouting about Cinderlads, not Cinderlassies.*

Lippy's father would draw in breath as if to sigh or perhaps vehemently disagree, then change his mind, and breath out with a slow whoooh as he rustled his paper and disappeared behind it. Even Lippy, at her young age, was aware of the unuttered comment that hung, clanking like manacles and chains between them, father and mother. *What would you know about it — you're only a woman!*

So in her years of growing up, marriage and producing a family Lippy was switched off to politics, and let the arguments and invective flow over and around her, never bothered by her stance on the bank rather than mid stream, part of the army of disengaged who when called upon could utter a plague on both parties. One's as bad as the other, a ready mantra few were roused to disagree with. And if called upon for an opinion she could always wing it with some inane comment. She had a busy life. Why waste time and effort getting to grips with the facts when she could express an opinion without them?

The devolution debate during the late nineties was the event that flicked her political interest switch. In fact, she could pinpoint the occasion. It was the November day in 1996 when wee Malky Fortythe, the Secretary of State for Caledon — him with the trews and tartan bunnet, a fully paid up member of her Dad's evil Tyke party — paraded behind an open-backed Land Rover across the Border bridge. The vehicle brought the stone birdbath, that purported to be the Goblet of Destiny, back to Caledon. It was the patronising nature of a manipulative decision by politicians, stooping to anything to achieve their ends, that broke through her shell of disinterest. Bread and circuses. With one hand the ringmaster threw the Cinderfolk a treat to mollify and keep them sweetly subservient whilst, with the other hand, he cracked a long, curling whip.

A cynical gesture in a cynical campaign against the Cinderlads and Cinderlassies of Caledon who wanted a degree of control over the affairs of their country, a cynical campaign against democracy. She could hear her father's rant about the previous blatant attempt at gerrymandering when that marbles-in-mouth landowner guy insisted the bill for a Caledon assembly with a limited form of devolution was a bad bill. *Vote no and we will give you something better,* he declared. 'Something better. Huh! And what did we get?' her father would ask, eyes popping and spittle frothing at the corners of his mouth. 'We got downright shafted.'

The sight of the spectacle in Cauldburn that played out on her television screen that day made Lippy angry. Why she didn't know. Granted, the piece of rock had been a focus for many Caledons over the years —a symbol of a proud old nation. But why did it rouse her anger and prod her sense of injustice? Why did the sight bring a lump to her throat, and despite the dismissal of the charade, cause her heart to beat as if it jumped for joy? The Goblet's return was a political ploy, nothing more, to reinforce the message that Caledon didn't need devolution or the offered assembly but should stick with a status quo that after 700 years managed to return a stolen lump of stone resembling a garden ornament, or a giant stone potty.

For several days she attributed her annoyance to a general malaise, to her despondency and feelings of inadequacy in the wake of her divorce, but the grumble persisted. A door long closed in her psyche had been prised open by the sight of a man walking behind a vehicle transporting a bloody great lump of sandstone, filched centuries ago by an alien king. To stop her mind probing further she buried herself in writing, in reading. As she downed a few glasses of wine one evening she contemplated the fact she was turning into her father. Like Dad like daughter. Vinegar sticks!

The sight of the Goblet of Destiny being ceremonially repatriated awakened a long-sleeping thing of interest and frustration. Suddenly she was mesmerised by the machinations of politics, like a sinner who had out of the blue got religion. And her sleeves were rolled up to partake in the fray instead of viewing it from afar as a bystander.

She didn't join a political party, she embraced a healthy scepticism for all, though her background had laid foundations and her beliefs swung her towards one in particular. She certainly never envisaged that she would ever use a fascination with politics, drip fed into her during her childhood, in her writing. Not that she had ever viewed herself as a writer. But as she had given up on teaching — she suspected she wasn't temperamentally suited to a profession that required such patience, such word chewing and forced swallowing — she followed that up with a divorce, fairly amicable but which left her with two young children. While they were at school she did temporary work, whatever she was offered. She wasn't fussy as long as it paid the bills. And in the evenings she took to writing, made a few pounds from stories for magazines but had her sights firmly set on a novel.

Cari, her daughter is into travel — the more out-of-the-way dive the better — occasionally returning with scarves and necklaces, hats and rings and nick knacks for a business venture she might set up someday. Meanwhile she has appropriated the large cupboard in the spare bedroom for her stock. Son Derek sits opposite her now. He looks suave in a casual way, his hair styled, an air of supreme confidence imbuing every action, every gesture. He talks with authority on whatever topic is raised. Lippy studies him, and sees little of the Cinderlad, yet nothing obviously Prince Charming either. Perhaps, drawing on the past, she and others of her generation have spawned a new being, one more capable of forging the future. A Caledonlad or Caledonlassie perhaps.

'How's the writing?' asks Derek, as he critically swirls his wine around the glass.

'Keeping me busy.'

'You into another book?'

'You write books?' questions Gail as if not believing that possible. Lippy wonders if her Cinderlassie side is showing.

'Yes, I've written five to date.'

'Published?'

'Yes, published. In print and e-books — so available to read.' She flicks a smile at her son's girlfriend. When she first met her husband-to-be's mother she had quaked in her shoes, her throat tight with apprehension and awe of the woman who was chair of so many local organisations and who made certain everyone was aware of the fact. Changed days.

The young woman who sits beside her son doesn't look the sort to be overawed by anyone.

'Really! How interesting.'

Derek obviously has failed to fill Gail in on his mother. 'So what's the new book?' he asks.

'Not a book. A play.'

'Oh, you write plays, too! Perhaps I've seen one.'

'Unlikely.' Derek checks his watch, a large, flashy multi-dial on a chunky leather strap. 'Mum's plays haven't made it to the limelight as yet. Just the occasional production by a local theatre company.'

'I was shortlisted for a national competition last year.'

'Were you? I didn't know.'

'Well, I told you. Emailed to ask if you wanted to accompany me to the awards event.'

'Don't remember that.'

'You didn't reply.'

'Been busy at work. Pity you didn't win.'

'I didn't expect to. It was great to be shortlisted, and I made new contacts.'

'Contacts are so important, aren't they?' Gail folds her napkin and checks the nail varnish on her fingernails. Lippy is certain she can see her with an outsize Filofax (do people still use them, she wonders?) in her outsize handbag, and a lengthy address book on her mobile phone, tablet and computer. Gail looks the sort of person who gathers contacts like the Green Shield stamps her father used to collect, and ruthlessly uses them when she wants something. But perhaps she is being less than generous about her. From his soppy glances and hand-stroking Derek obviously thinks the sun circles her.

Derek shrugs in a designer way. 'So what's the play about?'

'Skulduggery and politics.'

'Haven't you already done that pretty thoroughly in your books?'

'Derek, believe me when I say there is no such word as thorough when it comes to politics. Politics is the subject matter that just keeps giving, where fact is so much more unbelievable than fiction.'

Gail exchanges a snide wee smile with Derek, and squeezes his hand.

'Gail's not into politics.'

'Don't like being bored,' explains Gail. 'Not when there's so much else to follow.'

'If you're not interested in politics, then you're not living life to the full. Politics is about life, and the way we're allowed to live our lives, whether in poverty or plenty.' That's my father speaking, thinks Lippy.

The caravan guy's on his soapbox again. Maybe his spirit has taken up residence inside me. Chucked out my own and settled in, like a cuckoo in a nest — a caravan-shaped nest.

Derek laughs. 'Bit over the top there, surely.'

'Why?'

'Politics is so boring.' Gail is dismissive in her glance.

'Boring! Compared to? Shopping and airy-fairy enjoyment, I suppose.'

'Lighten up mother.'

'It's getting late. Perhaps we should go, Derek. I've an early start tomorrow.'

Lippy wonders if she should apologise, promise to talk of anything but politics or her writing, but decides to let them go. Why should her views be unacceptable and Gail's fluffy likes and ideas eminently acceptable? Inwardly she sighs. Politics is a minority sport. Like it or loathe it most people don't really care how the country they live in is run. Oh, they fawn and bluster, praise this and deride that, even sign and advocate online petitions against this or that injustice, but at the end of the day how well informed are they to make decisions on their future? Of course their innocence isn't only down to them. Government plays a significant role, both in lack of information and misinformation. Keeping the electorate in the dark is seen as eminently desirable. No info, nothing to cause unrest. And any facts that have to be placed into the public domain are carefully manipulated, sanitised. Lies she usually calls them.

'Thank you for the meal. The crumble was delicious.'

Lippy dips her head in acknowledgement of the thanks, though in her mind she sees the almost untouched plate of pudding she removed from Gail's place at the table. But, as usual she is too harsh in her judgement of others, too critical of their lifestyles. The choice is theirs, not hers to make for them. Though their choices affect her too. Her opinions owe much to her father's genes and influence, the political rants that seeped into her during her childhood. So little to be done about it but to accept and live with the person she is.

As Derek helps Gail into her faux fur coat, and she winds a long colourful scarf around her neck Lippy dives into a cupboard and returns to thrust a book at her son's girlfriend. Meant as a peace offering.

Gail studies the cover. An eyebrow twitches. 'One of your books. Thank you.' She shoves it towards Derek to put in his coat pocket or otherwise dispose of.

'I hope you enjoy it. Maybe you'll...' In the nick of time Lippy stops herself. She can almost hear Derek suck in his breath in anticipation of her putting her foot in it, saying maybe you'll learn something from it. 'Maybe you'll let me know what you think of it. I'd like that.'

Derek's breath hisses out. 'Always out to make converts, that's my Mum.'

'Just trying to earn a living, Derek my son.'

13- The 'Sorry-but-you-know-how-it-is' syndrome

Most days Ramsay can be seen shuffling along the sand, dragging not raising his feet clad in green Wellington boots. They leave tracks like the skid of skates, jagged parallel lines along the edge of the high water mark, that mirror the blotchy line of seaweed left by the last tide. The net of bladder wrack with its sacks ripe for popping with a fingernail, like plastic wrapping material, is interwoven with kelp and other leathery fronds and straps, or delicate algae with diaphanous or fernlike contours. Their smell assails his nostrils, clean, tangy, and reminds these are not from earth but from the depths of the sea, imbued with its mystery, its strange attraction. From the tangle of seaweeds, shells and feathers poke out rusty tins, bits of crab, polystyrene cups, a dead sea urchin, drink cans, strands of turquoise and orange fishing nets, plastic packaging from foodstuffs, crumpled cigarette packets, broken plates with Victorian designs, the top from a flask, a canvas shoe, chunks of wood (adorned with limpets and bolts) from old piers, polythene bags, pieces of masts, oars, pallets, branches or roots of trees, twisted and gnarled by time, bleached by salt and sun. A museum that tells a story of our lives and what we discard on beaches. And what we jettison at sea for its swell to hurl back to land like a spat grape pip.

Ramsay carries a stick, a long stick that reaches to his shoulder. It's sturdy, too, and takes his weight when he leans on it, unbending when he howks in the seaweed to reveal more of a shape or colour that has caught his eye. He likes to prod the seaweed nests to see what shelters there, safe in their depths, just as his life, once thought so secure, was prodded by others. And look what that revealed! To disturb the seaweed safe-houses is akin to getting his own back, though not on those who engineered his demise, but on harmless plants and trash. That is the coward in him he supposes. He bullies others because he was bullied. He prises open their secrets as that was what was done to him. Lulled into a sense of safety by being one of the boys, his blinkers had kept him from awareness and understanding of plans hatched and in execution. By the time the reality of his position dawned, it was too late to swerve or convincingly lay the blame elsewhere.

Strong but fair, throughout his life that's how he had considered himself. He slew necessary dragons but patted heads too. Blame was laid where he weighed it belonged. Justice was upheld. As far as the job allowed, that was. And perhaps with hindsight he realised the job didn't actually allow much of anything except naked greed and the lust after power. Greed and power, they always gouged the worst from people. His strength and sense of fair play was steamrollered into the ground — the reason he took his downfall so badly. The affair made him look weak, spineless. It undermined his sense of self-worth as he was paraded as nice but naïve. Not in the same league as the big boys.

A plastic bag, liberated by the wind, plays games with sand and spray, and takes off into the sky, soaring and dipping like a kite full of dreams. He straightens and watches it. Perhaps it is an omen, a sign that his life might take a turn for the better, that his stupidity might go the way of the faux pas of others and be forgotten rather than be constantly dragged back into the searing glance of public view. It shouldn't be too much to hope that his bruised and trodden dreams might one day be freed like the plastic bag and again be able to float above the ground. For them to soar would be too much to expect — it shouldn't be, but there you are, that is the way people like him are tied to their past, sent to their graves with a muckle stone chained securely to them lest they ever rise again. No forgiveness can be expected. Despite his knowledge, his experience of the system and the world, the contribution he could still make to so many aspects of life, he will always be excluded, for like others he has played the system, but unlike others, he was selected as the fall guy, the one to be made an example of, the sacrifice to a baying media intent on wringing maximum impact from a minor indiscretion. Perhaps they considered him expendable, who knows. Perhaps he had merely stepped on too many toes and ambitions. More likely he was just a convenient hook on which to hang a story that sold papers.

In his daily life he is still the outcast, the pariah, the parasite that headlines had screamed of at the time. Only on this beach can he feel free from their censure and condemnation. This windswept beach has its dirty secrets washed clean twice a day, scoured raw at times of storm, like a penitent flailing his back with a scourge, and here he feels some of his own guilt and shame cleansed in that tidal process. That is why he walks here every day, irrespective of weather. Spring mornings that hint of summer warmth and abundance see him tour the high tide mark, as do winter mornings, gloomy with rain sheeting down and wind punishing every exposed object. Perhaps he likes those days best, as he feels them more suited to his situation. Retribution, just deserts. The high tide mark reminds him of his own life, the detritus of his hopes and dreams caught like the discard of the sea in the seaweed cage.

His dog slithers over the shingle towards him, tail waving. Nose sniffs and buries itself to follow a scent, a shellfish or some other piece of flotsam with a sharp edge that jags it. It withdraws hurriedly, sniffles. The dog shakes its head, then on it pounds, to seek the reassurance of a pat on the head before it skitters off again, bouncing with the sheer joy of the multitude of smells to be investigated. He was once like that, the man thinks. Perhaps not carefree in the same way, but full of relish for the challenges ahead, always keen to root out new material, different angles to use to his advantage, to gain kudos. Perhaps even to draw his sterling efforts to the attention of those at the top of the heap. But others played the same game, others with rods of steel to stiffen their determination to succeed, bottomless pits from which to dredge the bile, the deviousness and maliciousness to back it up.

No, he had not been the worst, far from it. The one who was, the Prime Instigator, regularly gloats at him from the screen of his television or computer. His beaming face is fatter, pendulously jowly like some slavering dog, from the good life of expensive restaurants and elite social occasions. In unguarded moments, though, his eyes revert to slate despite the smile formed by his lips, reddened by makeup. Lines have chiselled themselves at the outer edges of his eyes, and a furrow like a gorge runs from forehead to the bridge of his nose. Moreover, Ramsay is sure that in recent appearances strands of grey tending to white streaked the sleek brown of his hair. Power is all desirable, but there is no denying that power ages, with power at that level aging more rapidly and dramatically, as if those to whom it is granted are expected to pay a premium over and above the actual price. He wonders if the Prime Instigator sleeps at night, whether his dreams are the usual stuff of them, vague and formless of shape and intention, or if he suffers explicit nightmares that haunt his days, poisoning his pleasures, and chilling the hours of darkness.

Sometimes, if he feels like it, Ramsay sits on a flat shelf on the rocky outcrop at the end of the bay, and stares out over the sea, to watch the waves, the gulls gather and screech in packs overhead or squabble on the sand over a found titbit. It seems to him the sea is aware of his presence. It teases him with its eddies and swirls, drenches him with spray when his attention wanders. At times he even thinks the sea speaks to him in a susurrant voice, that laps his senses into a phoney calm. Or if angry with him it froths and foams, spits its displeasure, and flounces around like an angry woman. Is the sea female, he wonders? We refer to Mother Earth, so is the sea Mother Sea. The French obviously believe so. La mer. To him, not so different from la mère. Mother.

Earth and sea. The one dressed in clothes of green and brown, ochres and russets, while the other dances around in floating garments of green and blue, grey and gold. Isadora Duncan with her floating scarves comes to his mind. Or, in contrast to Mother Earth, to maintain the balance of nature, as it were, should it be Father Sea, provider of water, semen, to enable Mother Earth to bring forth her bounty? But perhaps it is the sky that is male. Le ciel, dominant over earth and sea, the overlord with his brutish winds and mercurial temper redolent of the Roman god Mercury who was herald and messenger, god of eloquence and skill, trading, and thieving. That sounds appropriate, the man thinks. As for the days of sun and warmth…probably an aberration…no, definitely an aberration. Bloody hell, he's becoming cynical. Becoming? No, let's get at least this right. He was fed cynicism in his baby bottle and with his first solids, drip fed it like a poison, and like a poison it has remained with him, until it has become addictive, infecting his view of life.

Och, to hell with such thoughts!

As Ramsay turns his gaze from seaward to the direction of his home, his eyes catch a movement at a vantage point above the bay, the flash of a figure who looks as if settling into or changing position A bird watcher probably. The coast is noted for sea birds. The location can't be ideal as the figure emerges from behind the bush, straightens, and raises binoculars (though he supposes it could also be a camera). The figure ducks again behind the vegetation, and is lost beyond gorse and entangling branches of buckthorn, scrubby willow, and dense tufts of dried grasses. Nothing now to indicate whether the figure still watches, or whether he has gone. Ramsay shrugs. There was a time, a more paranoid time, when such a sighting would have sent him into a tizzy of speculation and fear, thoughts of the Party's fixers pounding his mind, out for further retribution as he has been found guilty in his absence of the utterance of indiscrete words, unwise phrases. But assuaged by the passage of time, he now tends to believe watchers on the cliffs are recording birds and not his movements To watch him would be pointless as his only crime nowadays is to walk the beach.

Today Ramsay isn't going to slump on the rock like some pregnant seal, and talk to the sea. Today he needs to rush back to the house, retreat back into his shell, as he is doubtlessly going to be prodded by his visitor as if he is a tortoise, to open up, expose his thoughts and feelings to more picking over, more investigation. Well, to hell with that. He's had enough. He turns to stand, eyes focussed on the hazy horizon, and wishes he had insisted he wouldn't be in, the meeting was inconvenient, he wasn't feeling well, or he could just have told the truth, that he has gone beyond talking to people about a world he no longer is part of, he just wants to be left alone.

Visitors are rare in his life these days. After his disgrace, former friends and acquaintances steered clear of him, as if contact would contaminate them. Friends? Well, those referred to as friends — though in the political world real friendship is a rare diamond. Everyone (and here he had been one of the exceptions) was too busy guarding their own careers for real friendship to flourish, for if it comes to the bit, to a friendly colleague or yourself being blamed, hung out to dry, then self-preservation takes precedence over friendship every time.

That is why the back-stabbing men and eyelash-fluttering women who were previously eager to adorn his dinner parties or share their hospitality with him, suddenly found their diaries full, families claimed their attention and time, the usual transparent excuses. Though they seemed preferable to being told to his face that they couldn't afford to have any further contact with him. The Sorry-but-you-know-how-it-is syndrome. And of course he does know how it is. In his line of business, or rather his previous line of business, only two things are rated adjacent to treason – failure is one, the other is to be found out, and these two have lead sinkers added if your story is splashed across the media in headline type. Whether true or not becomes immaterial. If the story is sufficiently good and well pitched, it grows legs, grows everything else as well, goes viral. Once it reaches that size, truth and reality, the harm caused and the careers and lives ruined, are forgotten, trampled into Mother Earth, sunk in the depths of Mother Sea, blown to smithereens by Father Sky and his stinking breath. All that matters is that the world revels in the story. And if a few embellishments can be added, to further titillate enjoyment, so much the better. A bit like a woman who adds sparkling earrings and alluring perfume to a skin-tight dress with a neckline that leaves little to the imagination.

His dog bounds up, tail wagging, pleased with itself, something dead in its mouth. 'What's that you've found, Jess? Ugh. Drop it. Good girl. Drop it.' The dog complies. Ramsay scratches behind her ear as one foot buries the thing, a long dead small bird, in the shingle and sand. The dog whines. 'Home, Jess. We need to head home now.' He picks up a stick and throws it for her. The animal bounds after the new plaything, the dead thing forgotten. No agonising, no angst. The plaything is dead, long live the plaything. Jess moves on. How he wishes that option was available to him. Instead he bides his time on the margins of life.

Back along the line of seaweed he scrunches. Half way along he stops to poke a mound with his stick, uncovering a pair of scuffed sunglasses while a small crab scuttles off in search of a new squat. Jess bounds back to see what keeps him. Her tongue lolls like a pink till roll snaking out the machine. He follows the dog up the incline where sand and shingle give way to grass on which a track leads up to the road. A hundred yards up the road an overgrown drive veers off to the left and he takes this to his house, an Edwardian villa, built by a sea captain on his retirement, determined that the land should never completely claim him, and that every morning he would wake with the sight of the sea flirting with his eyes, and the tang of it teasing his nostrils. The telescopes the captain installed in house and garden, to keep watch on vessels, remain, still in regular use as the sea feeds the imagination of those who live beside it, and telescopes add colour to speculation.

The villa is painted white, with doors and window frames a suitably nautical blue. It is skirted by a shingle path whose edges are encroached on by weeds and sedums. Beneath the front windows are flower beds, their edges scalloped with shells like lace on a woman's negligee, bunches of daffodils sprout through the matt of withered snowdrops, while the shoots of hostas, like purple pencils, draw sustenance from the sun. Beside one bay window a flowering currant attracts a buzz of bees, by the other the golden bells of a forsythia ring in the breeze. The style of the house is Edwardian of the late Victorian fashion, so traditional in architecture rather than expressing the exuberances of the later period and its flirtation with Art Deco when the page of the design manual was turned and a new sheet begun.

The dog has run on ahead. Its tail lashes the air, its joy at returning to old smells, old haunts obvious. Round to the back of the house it has bounded, on the grand tour of the extensive garden, emerging from beneath the drooped branches of shrubs to dash off again in an excursion around the drying green where it roots into clumps of grass, and investigates captivating scents. The bushes by the summerhouse rustle, a bird twitters, annoyed by the disturbance, then Jess pelts back towards the door as Ramsay pushes it open. She scuttles along the passage, paws slither on the flagstones, polished to a sheen by a century of buffing feet, shoves the kitchen door open with her nose, then straight to her water bowl where her tongue straightens and curls like a spring to quench her thirst. Droplets of water rain from her chin as she trundles across to Ramsay who has thrown his waterproof jacket over the back of a chair where he now sits to remove his Wellington boots. A scattering of sand grows into molehills beneath them. He tickles behind Jess's ears and pats her back. She snuffles his hand then with a sneeze trots across the floor to her basket, and rotates nose to tail to form a nest before she slumps down. Eyes shut, a sigh of satisfaction churns the air.

On the table is a tray set with the good mugs. His wife matches crockery to events and ranks them in terms of importance and impression to be made. She judged her husband's meeting as meriting the bone china mugs as opposed to the bog standard everyday ones, but not the good cups and saucers which are stashed away for occasions of real importance. It's a long time since the cups were last used. Along with the mugs is a plate on which a plastic box of biscuits awaits last minute decanting, and an empty milk jug to be filled when required.

His wife's strict instructions were to take his guest into the sitting room, not to sit in the kitchen which she considers falls below entertaining standards. It was the kitchen bought with the house, its pine units and Formica topped table, surrounded by scuffed chairs, a blight on his wife's life, as she studies the show kitchens, ideal family kitchens, portrayed in magazines. No indiscrete item or out of kilter accessory sullies their expanses of designer units with granite worktops that gleam like jet. With shoulders sagging, his wife looks around hers with its distressed units littered with cooking accoutrements, books, dog leads, letters (mainly bills), packets of seeds, winter hats and gloves, a broken lamp, CDs in split cases, a torch minus battery, computer cables, phone chargers, the list goes on and on. Sometimes she despairs of finding sufficient space to make a meal. Her husband just shrugs. It is home, it is comfortable, don't fuss, be grateful they have a roof over their heads.

Kat left early, as she does every Monday morning, and won't return until early Friday evening. She wanted to continue to work after they moved, didn't want to leave the office where she has been employed for over twenty years, and where she has always used her maiden name. Useful that — when his was splurged across the papers, she didn't need to own up to being his wife, or claim knowledge of him, beyond the bile pedalled by the media. During the week she stays with Doris, her sister, who is divorced. Doris is the extrovert in the family. She never cares what others think of her (though like Kat she draws the line at public association with him), and is probably a nymphomaniac, always with a scheme or a man in train. Kat is a tempering influence on Doris, at least she was during their childhood, so he was told. He is unsure whether this remains the case, or whether his wife is now swayed by his sister-in-law's lifestyle. The two of them enjoy the flat-sharing arrangement, with a social life that leaves Ramsay with questions he is reluctant to ask, though Kat (short for Katherine, of course and nothing to do with the biscuit) seems happy to return home every Friday.

Ramsay sweeps up the sand and fills the kettle and Jess's water bowl. He is apprehensive, and curses himself again for agreeing to talk to this woman about his past life. Why didn't he refuse, politely but firmly, like he has done on so many previous occasions? He's unsure what the answer is. It may be that a part of him feels the time is overdue for the shame to be acknowledged, aired, the boil lanced. For too long he has hidden out here, and the approach over the phone by this woman perhaps let him see how it might be possible to move on.

'Found you,' says a head, appearing round the edge of the door. 'I rang the front door bell but no response, so came to investigate.'

'The door bell doesn't work. Hasn't done as long as we've lived here. There's no need for it, visitors do what you've done.'

Jess opens one eye, cocks one ear. No apparent threat. Eye closes, ear swivels like a periscope, twitches then flops.

The woman smiles. 'Glad to know I've made the right approach.' Her whole body enters the kitchen, and walks across to Ramsay, hand extended. 'Hello, you must be Ramsay. I'm Lippy. Lippy Nevis. Thank you for agreeing to see me.'

Her directness appeals to Ramsay, makes him feel less apprehensive. 'Lippy. Unusual name.'

'Short for Philippa, but friends from my earliest years thought it appropriate, given that I tend to say what I think, straight out. Word punch.'

A smile flickers on Ramsay's face. 'I'd ask you to take a seat, but I've been given strict instructions to take you to the sitting room.'

'Instructions from your wife? Then we'd better comply, though I'd be more than happy to sit here. I love kitchens like this, so full of character and warmth.'

'The view from the sitting room is better though, so perhaps we should adjourn there, once I've made coffee.'

Lippy rests a large multi-coloured bag on the edge of the Formica table. 'I really am pleased you agreed to talk to me.'

'Well, as yet it's more of an exploration as to whether I will talk to you rather than a definite agreement. I'm still a bit in the dark as to why you sought me out.'

'Simple. I want information. I'm an author and playwright and I want background detail for a play. Perhaps even a follow-up book.'

Ramsay pours boiling water into the cafetière, replaces the top and sets it on the tray. 'Afraid I'm not much of a theatre-goer, and besides I'm a bit out of the information loop, politically, culturally and every other way. Kat says I've grown into a hermit crab.'

'Don't waste a second thought on not knowing my name. It's only the culture nerds who've heard of me. Even TV addicts don't watch programme credits with sweaty palms, curious to see who wrote the rubbish they've paid some attention to.'

Ramsay jerks his head towards the door. 'This way to the sitting room.'

She follows him along a short passage into the square hall with tiled floor and etched glass in the top half of the door. The walls are painted pale blue, the trellis pattern of the previous wallcovering picked out in a darker shade by the light. The woodwork is painted white, giving a seaside feel that is heightened by a large wooden bowl filled with stones and shells. It sits on the floor beside a chunk of driftwood like a heron gorging a fish. A mirror framed with hawsers twined like tree roots, hangs above an old sea chest.

Ramsay balances the tray on one hand and opens the door to the sitting room. As she walks past him Lippy's glance takes in the brightness of the room, ocean light fed by the bay window with its brass telescope and green curtains the shade of mould, same as the walls. The room is sparsely furnished with little clutter and gives the impression it is rarely used but kept for the entertainment of occasional visitors. A three piece suite in floral covers dominates the room, a chair either side of the fireplace with its stripped oak surround and Aesthetic influenced tiles, with a large sofa directly in front. Above the fireplace stands a mirror, an overmantle the width of the surround, that stretches towards the ceiling in an oak frame carved with leaves and fruit. Lippy sees herself and Ramsay reflected in its glass, its silvering yellowed and mottled. The bubbles of her hair curls bounce about her face, bright with interest in the room's decor and in anticipation of her conversation with this man about whom she has excavated so much information, cherishing expectations of the essential details he can provide, the polish of authenticity he can impart to her manuscript.

Behind her face in the mirror, Ramsay's has an expression of horror. Eyes stare, mouth opens in shock as if about to let rip a gasp or scream. Her gaze drops below the mirror, below the fireplace with its sea green and red tiles to the hearth rug, mossy rather than mouldy green. A figure is sprawled across it, a man, face buried in the man-made fibre pile, arms outstretched, a length of blue rope wound round his neck.

14 - It's the ruthless that succeed

Brian strides along the road, past terrace houses, red sandstone, front gardens vanquished in favour of a gravel parking space for the car flanked by a narrow slab path, like a chalk-drawn line, that leads from pavement to front door. Late Victorian. Built for the new lower middle class, the managers of the city's industry, the small business people. Individualism paid lip service by variations in the woodwork — a round finial here, a decorative ogee bracket there. Otherwise the dwellings are structurally identical. The age of consumerism, though, has wrought havoc with the homogeneity of design and its integrity. Half glazed wooden front doors have been usurped by plastic and metal, fully glazed or partly glazed; the panels of storm doors now boast glass with or without wrought iron grilles to remind of the Costa Brava; sash windows with top and bottom panes bisected by astragals, now wear single panes that give the building a desolate stare, or a variety of pseudo modern, Tudor, or Arts and Crafts designs at variance with the style of the building. Victorian brown or green paint has been overlaid by white or brash purples, with one or two in black to reflect minimalist, neutral interiors.

Brian stoops to open the wrought iron people gate, squeezed between the stone wall that divides the garden from the neighbours' plot and the wrought iron car gates caging the green Micra. He strides to the front door of his parents' home to which, on the exterior, few concessions have been made to modernity. His father and mother prefer to retain as much as possible of the original façade and interior features. The asking price when they bought it twenty odd years previously reflected the fact the house required upgrading, not boasting double glazing or rooms knocked together to render them more suited to modern life. But Brian's parents wanted a Victorian house. Unmodernised. If they had lusted after a thirties bungalow or an end of century open-plan box then they would have bought whichever appealed. But they wanted Victorian. As built. More or less.

When growing up Brian never considered the style of his surroundings. They were comfortable, suited to his parents, not quite his taste…but fine. Now as he walks up the path he wonders if this house is more comfortable in its own skin than its more flamboyant modernised peers.

His mother opens the door before his outstretched finger has pressed the door bell, a white ceramic button, the word PRESS printed on it, within a polished brass collar.

'Hello, dear. Good to see you. How are you?'

His mother is exactly the sort of person who would be expected to open the door to the house. Although plumping out with middle age, she is still smartly dressed in tune with her generation, her barbed wire hair tamed by regular trips to the hairdresser, her make-up restrained, unremarkable. Every inch a primary school teacher of the kind he remembered. His mother's brown paper packaging of skin and bones hides a dragon of organisation. Every piece of paper, folder, letter, brochure, form, booklet, bill is allocated a home. In fact Brian often wonders how his mother would have survived without Ikea. She shares the Ikea philosophy so adds greatly to their profits by buying their files, boxes, baskets, drawers and shelving units in the quest for homes for her paper waifs and strays. What doesn't find a home is exterminated in the shredder, before it receives a decent burial in the compost bin by the vegetable patch in the back garden. His mother's computer sits four square on her tidy desk, mouse mat with a floral design to the side, facing a pin board with calendar and notes ranged in rows. Ordered, like the rest of her life.

Brought up with this regime, Brian has never thought to question why he and his parents have the two smaller bedrooms — his own not much more than a box room — whilst the main bedroom is a study for his parents. His mother's pulverised forests of paper commandeer two thirds of the space, leaving his father little more than a strip in which to heap his books and papers interspersed with political leaflets, CDs and bits of items the rest of which had either long since disappeared or no longer worked. The bits, said his father, just might come in useful for something. Someday. A widget to replace a high tech part which had died, a washer for his independence crusade.

There is a kinship between occupants and building. A no-nonsense solidity. A sense of authenticity with no pretence at being other than what their roles dictate. A home for solid lower middle class workers occupied by two solid upper working class people.

'Why do you still regard yourselves as working class?' Brian had asked his father at one time.

'Because I am,' replied his father.

'Yes, but you're a teacher, a head teacher. You have a good job, an important job, and you're reasonably well paid. And Mum, too. Surely that makes you middle class nowadays?'

'We work for a living, so in my book that makes us working class. The so-called middle class is only working class folk that have swelled too big for their boots, desperate to forget their roots, their beginnings.' His father flapped his hand dismissively. 'Nowadays it isn't 'cool' to acknowledge humble beginnings. Memories are appropriately curtailed to suit aspirational lifestyles in our consumerist society. But it's still working class blood that flows through their veins. Yours too, lest you forget.'

'So who would you regard as middle class?'

'You used the phrase, not me.'

'But you must acknowledge there's a middle class?'

'Why must I?'

'Because the vast majority of people nowadays regard themselves as such.'

'That may well be the case, but it doesn't necessarily make them middle class. To think of yourself as something, or hope to be something, doesn't make you that. You might think of yourself as upper class, a marbles-in-mouth toff, but no amount of thinking or hoping will make you a member of the aristocracy or the landed gentry. Not unless your circumstances have changed dramatically in the last few weeks. Have they?'

'Well, no. But that's different. I can't believe you think working class people, with the educational, employment and social opportunities now available to them, can't become middle class. Surely you as a good socialist should celebrate those opportunities. Celebrate success.'

'Leave socialism out of it. There's damn little about nowadays, and what lingers on has shrivelled like a dried pea. Become hard, tasteless, unpalatable. Dried peas don't constitute part of today's diet.'

'Now that's some admission coming from you.'

'Merely being realistic.'

'Well your precious Callyparty certainly isn't socialist, despite their protestations. Their policies come straight from the Tyke manifesto.'

'Och, don't stoop to that claptrap, Brian. Not with me. We brought you up to think for yourself, think things through. If you want a proper discussion on politics then that's fine by me. I'm ready for that any time, but don't demean me and yourself by pretending we're both stupid.'

'You're the one calling us stupid, Dad...'

'Stop baiting you father, Brian,' ordered his mother, entering the room in school teacher mode.

'Your tea's on the table,' says his mother as she leads the way. 'I could only manage an omelette as I didn't know you were coming until you phoned.'

'An omelette's great.'

'Douglas,' she says to his father who has appeared at the foot of the stairs, 'were you going to sow those spinach seeds before the light goes?'

Brian follows his mother through to the back room, the living/dining room. In the hall he passes, without a second glance, his father's portrait gallery — images of him accumulated over decades of his life, recording his presence at demonstrations. Anti nuclear, anti environmental hooliganism, anti status quo in the aftermath of the 1979 devolution referendum, anti Poll Tax, anti war when he was part of the mass not-in-our-name protests. Images badly composed, taken on cheap cameras often whilst on the move, so many were less than sharp in focus but eminently sharp in message. Several years ago his father had scanned his old photographs into his computer, enlarged their original size and printed them out on A3 photographic paper, framed in Ikea frames bought by his wife. Trophies. Events in his life of which he was proud as he believed he helped shape responses, beliefs; that his participation, and the participation of so many other ordinary people like him, had shaped the country he stayed in. He viewed his actions as essential to keeping democracy on track and relevant to his world. And while the demonstrations hadn't always had the effect hoped for, he considered his participation had at least earned him the right to criticise politicians and their actions.

Brian may now ignore the presence of the photographs but he still feels the strength of their message, and he allows himself an inward chuckle. To the parents of the primary school where he is headmaster, his father no doubt appears a stolid, sensible citizen. Tallish, still good-looking in a rather 1950s clean cut way, with short sandy coloured hair shot through with grey. Clean-shaven. Clean living. Brooking no nonsense from pupils or, Brian suspects, parents, but kind, considerate, always determined to help those with reading problems as he sees an ability to read as the key to life, the tool that opens all other doors. Without being able to read children cannot progress. Brian remembers his father spent his own money on books for some of his pupils, books with subjects he thought they would relate to, in an effort to unlock the magic of this ability to transform their young lives and shape their adult potential. And probably unknown to his pupils and parents was this other side to him, this campaigning side which at first seems wilder, more rebellious, but Brian knows it comes from a similar source to his reading belief. His father wants to shape the world the young pupils he is responsible for will live in, will inherit. He wants to tidy it for them, be able to explain it, ensure he can face them without shame about the changes his generation wrought. And if shame still finds a niche, then he wants to be able to tell them that he tried his best, but sometimes life is like that.

As he eats his omelette Brian's mother asks the usual maternal questions. 'How's the job, dear? Are you eating properly, dear? Are you getting enough sleep, dear?'

Brian waves his fork in the air, conducting his response. 'Yes, Mum. Yes, Mum. Yes, Mum. Of course I am. Remember, I'm a big boy now. I know how to look after myself.'

'Yes, I know, dear. It's just...' She raises her eyebrows by way of explanation. 'Have you a girlfriend yet?'

'Lots, but no-one in particular. And that's the way it's going to remain. Until I reach where I want to reach.'

'Yes, I know, Brian. We've had this conversation before. But time doesn't stand still, and if you put off settling down for too long you may find you've left it too late.'

'What I said before still stands, Mum. No encumbrances until I move up the ladder. I can't afford distractions. I need to focus, otherwise I won't succeed. And success looks as if it might be more difficult than I imagined.'

His mother throws him a sympathetic look. 'Do you want a slice of Victoria sponge with your coffee? Home made. I baked it last night?'

'Why not.'

His mother produces the cake then goes off upstairs to her study. She has work to do, preparation for the following day. Brian stuffs the sponge cake into his mouth and, coffee in hand, makes for the garden. The light ebbs and the air is cool. His father lightly rakes the area of the vegetable patch where he sprinkled the spinach seeds. The garden is small, though larger than its counterpart at the front. A path of slabs bisects it with the vegetable patch at one side, and on the other a paved area for the whirlie washing drier in front of which is a bed with low shrubs and flowers.

'So how's the world of politics, then?' asks his father, as he straightens his back and leans on the rake.

'Lurching on as usual.'

'Aye. I guess for your lot 'lurching' is an appropriate word.'

'Yeh, yeh. I didn't come home to go over old ground.'

'No? And here's me thinking you came because you enjoyed your parents' company.'

'Of course I do. You know that. But I want to talk to you about something specific.'

'Sounds ominous.'

'Rather depends…'

'Ah, there you are. Rosie said y'were out here. Communin' with nature. Gettin' your hands dirty, Dougie, that's what I like to see.'

'Hello, Steve. Just sown the spinach seeds. As it's dry I hoped I might get round to one or two others but the light's gone. You remember Brian, don't you?'

'Yes, yes, but it's a while since I last saw him. He's gone and shunted himself into the Parliament since then. How you enjoying it, Brian?'

'It keeps me busy.'

'Is that all y'can say about the place that cost us so much blood, sweat, tears, an', no' forgetting, money?'

Brian's father lays his rake against the fence. 'You must remember, Steve, Brian and I are on opposite sides, support different teams in the Chamber. He's red for danger and negativity, stay where you are and be grateful for crumbs that fall from our bounteous table. While we're yellow for getting ready, growing confidence for a sunny new start. Right? So he plays cagey in case he divulges any Party secrets that might rebound and bite him on the backside.'

'I didnae think the Party had any secrets these days. I thought they were all leaked, spun, divulged in memoirs and chewed over endlessly in the media. Like a herd o' trumpeting elephants at a water hole.'

'Don't listen to my father, Steve. We still enjoy the odd barney over Parties and policies.'

'And I still hope to persuade you of the wrongheadedness of your support for the People's Union Party.'

'Dad…'

'Okay, okay.' His father dusts off his hands on his trousers. 'You said you wanted to chat about something specific. What's on your mind?'

Brian looks at his father, his eyes swivel in the direction of Steve and back. 'Oh, nothing important. It can wait.'

'Come on, out with it, Brian. It must have importance for you, to have come all this way to talk to me about it.' Brian shrugs. 'Never mind Steve. Steve's been round the political block more than once. You can say what you want in front of Steve.'

Steve coughs. 'Maybe y'don't remember, Brian, but I used to be a member of the PUP. In days gone by. Even stood for Parliament for them. Westmunster, of course. That was in my unenlightened days.'

'I didn't know that. When was that?'

'Oh, more years ago than I care to remember. In the days when they weighed the votes. I was such a no-hoper I stood in one of the few seats where I didnae have a chance. Changed times, eh!'

'What made you leave the Party? Don't you regret your decision?'

'Regret it! Why in goad's name would I do that. Best thing I ever did, if you ask me.'

'What made you decide to leave?'

'I don't think there was ever one particular reason. It was more a build up o' things I disagreed with. Policies I didnae like. People I couldnae stand, peddling actions that appalled me. A few seriously hard bastards that made me question the meaning o' democracy. Those kind o' reasons.'

Brian's father nods. 'It's the ruthless that succeed in politics, that's for sure. How many good people have we seen shunted out because they couldn't take any more of the bad-mouthing and backbiting.'

'Well, you know the saying,' says Brian. 'If you can't stand the heat...'

'To survive in politics you need to have knuckles o' brass, a heart o' steel and a mind full o' shit. And as for the heat, aye y'need an asbestos suit to survive the heat o' the political hell.'

Brian's face shows surprise. 'You sound as if you were mightily disillusioned, Steve.'

'You could put it that way.'

'You didn't answer my question, Brian,' says his father. 'Quit the side-tracking.'

Brian sizes up the situation, decides to dip a toe in the water. 'In the course of a conversation with a colleague the other day, he happened to let slip a reference to The Galley. I wondered what you might know about it.'

Steve and Douglas look at one another, look at Brian, look around, look at one another again. 'We might be better to head inside,' Brian's Dad says. He covers the seeds he sowed with plastic cloches and leads the way inside.

They sit round the dining table at the back garden end of the room. Three bottles of beer appear along with three glasses. They sit and stare through the window at where they stood a couple of minutes previously. The creeping dark has now taken over, and lights have come on in houses round about. Brian wriggles in his chair. The situation makes him uncomfortable.

'It's akin to going back to the classroom. In front of the blackboard again. Explaining how things work,' muses Douglas.

'Yes, well maybe this shit should be taught as part o' history,' says Steve. 'Then folk might appreciate the need to scrutinise political parties and politicians. Then they might realise democracy's like a bar o' toffee. It can be pulled, stretched, twisted, reshaped, pressed into moulds, softened, hardened and swallowed.'

'And binned.'

'And binned,' agrees Steve.

'Do you want to tell him, or will I?' Douglas asks Steve.

Steve takes a long gulp of his beer, wipes his mouth with the back of his hand. 'I guess some things will never be laid to rest,' he says. He stares unseeingly in front of him, like a man who's just been told he will never see again.

'Look, I'm sorry. Forget it. I didn't want to cause...' Brian grasps his glass and moves it around on the table top.

'To cause what?'

'To resurrect unpleasant memories.'

Steve glares at him. 'First rule o' politics, son. Y'cannae no' ask questions because they might cause upset or unpleasantness. That's one o' the reasons people vote for others to represent them. So the bastards who get elected can ask the difficult questions. If y'cannae do that, then y'cannae survive in parliament. Neither o' them.'

Brian takes a deep breath. 'Okay. So, Steve, tell me about The Galley.'

'Any more beer, Dougie?' Steve asks. Douglas goes to the kitchen and returns with another bottle. 'Thanks. I always need a drink to wash away the taste in my mouth after I talk about this. Right. Where will we start?'

'With your departure from the Party. That intrigues me. And I have a feeling the subject of my question might have a bearing on that.'

'You're a perceptive bastard, aren't you. Just like your father. Yes, of course you're right. Though I'd made up my mind to leave anyway. You see, I worked in an engineering company, Brigg's Engineering. You might not mind it. Folded about twenty years back. I was a union member, active, I attended meetings, endless meetings. My goad the workers didnae half know how to chunter on in those days. But the union did bugger all to stop the company's closure, or to help its members. So there was I, without a job, of course, and without much prospect of another. Anyway, I found myself with all this time on my hands. I cannae stand no' having something to keep me busy, so I signed up for night classes and decided to learn some more about the background to the Party. I knew a fair bit about it, of course, but I spent my days in the library, delving into books and pamphlets, making notes. I'm no' quite sure why. It wasnae as if I could write a book or anything. It was just something to do that gave me an interest and stopped me feeling too sorry for myself.'

'This was before you stood as a candidate?'

'Oh aye. But after about six months I was asked to stand in a council by-election. Being unemployed I had the time to canvas, y'see. That way the local Party big wigs thought we might just win it.'

'And did you?'

'Naw, but I came fairly close. Anyway, shortly after that candidates were being reselected or selected. Shoehorned in. For Westmunster, that was. I'd managed to get on the list. All that reading in the library came to some use after all. But apart from myself I didnae have anything to offer. Just me an' my empty pockets an' a few mates from the union. I was up against folk, you understand, with more money than me, an' good contacts amongst the high heid yins in the Party, in the unions, even in business by this time. So I didnae get selected first time, but when a candidate had to withdraw in the Westonhill South seat, I was drafted in. They didnae have time to hold a proper selection, y'see. So there I was, unemployed an' fighting a Westmunster election. That was quite an eye-opener, I can tell you. I mean politics is politics an' the dirty tricks are part an' parcel o' the strategy, but my goad, I wasnae prepared for some o' the things that went on. An' I'd never realised to what extent the Party infiltrated all walks o' life. It had its fingers everywhere, poking actions, hooking in favours. To tell y'the truth, I was kinda glad I didnae win. For if I'd won I think some o' the methods used to get me there would have bothered me. I dinnae think I could have been an MP an' worked with folk who'd been pressured, whose livelihoods had been threatened, to get me elected. I guess I've been burdened with too many morals an' scruples to operate at that political level.' Steve cleared his throat and refilled his glass from the beer bottle. Lost in thought, he stared at the contents.

'So was that when you found out about The Galley?' prompts Brian.

'Aye. Of course I knew, everyone knew, there were some bastards, men of iron, who were known for 'arranging' things to achieve the desired results. They were looked up to like some sort of supermen. Wizards who could wave wands and make wishes come true. Great guys, with the interests o' the Party at heart. So it was said. Sons o' the working class who'd played the system, taken it on and come out at the top, cracking jokes with the great an' good, the toffee-nosed and blue-blooded. Y'know, its funny...No, funny's no' the right word... It's odd how we were taken in. No' just me, but everyone. Taken in. We honestly believed these people were worthy of being looked up to. Role models, I suppose you'd call them nowadays. Demi gods. No questions were ever raised, not that I know of anyroads, about the legality of what was done, about its morality. The black fist of enforcement. The end justifies the means, and dinnae ask any questions. That was the creed. And it wasnae challenged, because while you celebrated the results, and buried the methods used to get them, there was always this understanding that nothing was free. Some folks suffered, were shamed, found it necessary to compromise principles or to lower their own standards. But no problem. Nothing to concern yourself over 'cos it was all for the greater good. The good o' the Party — or at least some folks in it. I remember that I squirmed with discomfort, for I had this queer feeling that some day, for some reason that was deemed necessary for the good o' the Party, I might find myself one o' those the boot was put into.'

'Steve,' Brian nods in understanding, 'I understand that side of politics is unpleasant, but surely it's just eagerness, determination to win that cause the sometimes excessive — I agree with that — sometimes excessive energies that go into persuasion. The public are often goaded, mainly by the media, into thinking MPs and MCPs are self-serving, only interested in opportunities to live the high life. But the truth is, most are hard-working people, dedicated to the improvement of lives. And for our lot, focussed on bettering the lot of those least able to help themselves.'

Steve waves his hand, as if patting the air between himself and Brian. 'Ah, now, there I'm afraid we must disagree. I'm surprised, real surprised to hear you say that, Brian. Where've you been for the last fifteen years? Where were your eyes an' ears, your mind an' faculty o' reasoning during these years o' illegal wars when we licked the arse of the good old U S o' A? Where was your sense o' fairness hiding when we suffered cash for questions, cash for honours, cash for expenses to line the pockets o' our dedicated MPs? Where was your love o' democracy parked when the Party screwed those least able to help themselves, the ones you've just referred to, by ditching the lower rate o' tax to give higher earners a bit o' a bonus? And Brian, what were your thoughts when your Party let rip a culture o' bonuses to make the rich even richer and the poor even poorer? No, Brian, I heartily disagree with you. And the examples I've given are some o' the reasons I turned to another party.'

'Okay, Steve, so we disagree on areas of policy. But I wasn't asking about policy. I wanted information on The Galley, and you indicated you could provide me with some.'

'Well, it wasnae just policy I was pointing the finger at, Brian, it was people, too. People who thought they were superior to the common herd; who believed morals, the law even, didnae apply to them. They were above it. An' when that happens, then there's a serious sickness that siphons off the lifeblood o' your Party, a Party, dinnae forget, set up to give the ordinary folks o' this country representation. An' who represents them now? If you look at the analysis o' recent opinion polls, you'll see they support the party I'm now a member o'. That must surely shout a message in yer lug.'

Brian raises his hand, index finger extended to ram home his point. He opens his mouth. 'But Steve...' He hears footsteps thud down the stairs, muffled drumbeats on the carpet.

His mother's voice is raised, 'Douglas, Brian. I think you should read this.' She pushes through the door, laptop cradled in her arm. 'I thought I'd check the headlines on the Broadcasting Caledon website before I shut the computer down, and look...' She lays the laptop in the centre of the table where they can all see the screen. 'Look. The headline article. A Spin Doctor has been killed. Murdered. One of your lot Brian. Do you know him? You must, surely?'

Brian's eyes skip over the story, as yet short, skeletal. Brief facts and not many of them, lacking in trimmings until the hacks get to work. 'Doesn't give a name. Why the hell can't the bastards tell us who it is? Where did it happen?'

'It says he was found in a house on the coast.' His father has angled the screen towards himself and is reading carefully through the article.

'So, the house where he was found... you dinnae suppose it's the MCP's house? That's Bluebell McDaid's seat, isn't it?' Steve looks to Brian for confirmation.

Brian nods. 'Yes. I'm fairly sure her house is by the coast. I seem to remember her mention walks on the beach. But...em...let me think. Yes, I'm almost sure she's away for a few days on a Parliamentary visit.'

'So is the dead guy her assistant, a member of her staff, her lover, bidie-in?' asks his father.

'How the hell would I know! Besides, it doesn't say its her house.'

'True,' replies his father, though not many places along that stretch of coast.'

'I'd better contact Ming. Make sure he knows about it. Just in case.' He extracts his phone from his pocket and goes through to the hall, where he stares at a photo of a young version of his dad carrying a large CND placard as he listens to the ring of Ming's phone.

'Brian, can't this wait till tomorrow. You have this perversity about phoning me at the most inconvenient times. I'm with friends. In a restaurant. It really isn't a suitable time to speak.'

'Ming, listen…'

'I'll talk with you in the morning.'

'Miiiiinnnnnggggg. Don't hang up on me. Look at the Broadcasting Caledon website. Top story. A Party Spin Doctor has been murdered. Somewhere down the coast. Could be in Bluebell McDaid's patch.'

'What? What was that? Did you say murdered? Jeez! At Bluebell's, did you say?'

'No, doesn't say exactly where. Information is sketchy. Just says down the coast. But that stretch is Bluebell's fiefdom.'

'Who is it?'

'Doesn't give a name.'

'But it's definitely a Spin Doctor?'

'So the article says.'

'Jeez! I should phone Mutt. He needs to know about this. The media have probably been on to him already. Of course it's his problem. Nothing to do with us really. Right. Thanks, Brian.'

'Oh, Ming. Bluebell's away on that Parliamentary visit to Wales, isn't she?'

'Can't remember. Think she is. No, wait a minute. I think she called off. Can't remember why.'

'So she could have been at home?'

'Presumably, but I don't' see…Bugger! Must go, Brian.'

15 - That's what mudslingers count on

'There's a what on my hearth rug!' exclaims Kat, when Ramsay is eventually allowed to phone her. 'A man! A dead man?'

'Mmm. Afraid so.'

'Strangled, you say?'

'Yes.'

'So no mess. Right?'

'Well, I don't know. I didn't think to look.'

'Lord, give me patience. Just like a man. You ask a simple question and you don't know the answer.'

'I wouldn't agree it was a simple question. You forget, Kat, what a shock it was. I mean it's not every time we use the sitting room that we find a dead man sprawled on the rug.'

'Okay, I agree, it's a first, but that should have made you particularly observant, rather than blasé.'

'Kat, to please you I'd go and look. But the place is crawling with white suited bodies, a bit like a space travellers' convention, and there's no way they'll let us anywhere near the sitting room. It's taped off, out of bounds. We can't even walk along the back hall to the rest of the house. We're corralled in the kitchen while the space people use the front door.'

'We? What do you mean by we?'

'Lippy. The author. You knew she was coming. You told me to...'

'Yes, yes. But why is she still there?'

'Because she's not allowed to leave. We've both been questioned by a PC but someone higher up is to have another go at us.'

'Another go at you? Surely they can't possibly think you had anything...Oh, my lord. It's the expenses thing, isn't it? Being caught at that makes you a suspect.'

'This isn't connected with that — anyway I wasn't caught as you put it, I...'

'Save me another re-run, Ramsay.'

'Merely trying to point out that my previous life has no relevance whatsoever to this…this…incident. I don't even know the man. He's a complete stranger.' He could hear Kat suck in her breath, then mutter to someone. 'What?'

'Nothing. Updating Doris. Ramsay, are you quite sure you don't know this man. Someone from your past? Out for revenge?'

'Bloody hell, Kat. All that was years ago, and the only person who suffered and might want revenge was me.' He hears a noise behind him and turns. A man scrutinises him, like a security scanner. Interested in what he's just said.

'I need your version of events, Mr Dunn,' the detective says.

'Yes, of course. Kat, I need to go.'

'Is that your wife, Mr Dunn?' asks the detective. Ramsay nods. 'Tell her we need to speak to her. Ask when she can be here?' The request is an order.

'Did you hear that, Kat? The police want to question you.'

'Me? They can't think I had anything to do with it. I've been at work.'

'They're insistent, Kat.' He can hear a huff like a suction pump.

'Well, they'll need to wait until it's convenient.'

'That's not the way it works. You're wanted as soon as you can get here.'

'Mr Dunn, I'm waiting.' The toe of a cowboy boot taps the floor.

Ramsay's hand acknowledges the demand.

'But that means I'll need to take time off work. What can I tell them? They'll put two and two together.'

'Sorry, but your presence is requested.'

She growls in annoyance, like a cat in a fight. 'Oh, all right. But this is ridiculous. I'll leave in ten minutes and be there as soon as I can.'

'Fine. See you.'

'What was that?' The detective takes a step back into the hall and calls. Muffled response.

'Ramsay. Ramsay. Ask the detective about my hearth rug, will you?'

DI Raisin swivels back into the kitchen. 'Back in five, Mr Dunn. Don't leave.' Ramsay nods. 'And tell your lady wife I expect her toot sweet.' His feet click along the corridor.

'Ramsay. My hearth rug.'

'Ask him yourself when you get here.' Ramsay hears a strangled sigh as his wife cuts the connection.

Lippy places a mug of coffee beside him. 'Hope you don't mind. I'm faint with hunger.'

'Of course, we haven't eaten. Events took my appetite away, but now you mention hunger my stomach is telling me it's neglected.

'A sandwich? Would that be possible?'

'Oh, I think I can manage more than that. Kat doesn't have faith in my cooking skills so she leaves me prepared meals ready to pop in the microwave. Let's see what's available. Hmm. These might take a while.'

'Not to worry. A sandwich will be fine.'

'No, wait a minute.' He rummages in a cupboard. 'This is about as instant as you can get. Ham and spinach ravioli. That'll do. Stick the kettle on, would you Lippy. Now, a sauce. What have we? Tomato. Olive. Olive will do. And there's some salami I can throw in with it. Not quite à la carte, but given the circumstances...'

'Given the circumstances I'm surprised we're even contemplating eating. But, as they say, life goes on. And neither of us knew the man. You didn't, did you?'

'No. I've no idea who he is — or was. Or how he came to be lying in the sitting room.'

'It's just I thought your wife...'

'Oh my wife sees ghosts at every corner. Believes the world still rotates around what happened years ago. In another life.'

'You mean when you were in Parliament.'

'Yes, when I was an MP.'

'That's what I came to see you about, but it's been crowded out.'

'Perhaps that's best. There's not much to talk about.'

Lippy pours the boiling water from the kettle into the pot produced by Ramsay and adds the pasta. 'You must feel hard done by, surely?'

'At the time, yes. Perhaps still. But it's all in the past. As you've just said, life goes on.'

'But you were done over. You were made the fall guy. It was dumped on you whilst the main perpetrators got away with it. That must rankle?'

Ramsay opens a drawer, extracts cutlery and lays it on the table. From the fridge he takes out a bowl of salad. Jess his dog pads over, her claws clicking on the floor. 'What is it Jess? Want out, do you? No walk just now I'm afraid. You'll need to content yourself with the garden. OK, come on.' He walks down the passage and opens the back door. The dog pokes its head out. Sniffs the air. Looks up at Ramsay. 'We'll have a walk later, Jess.' The dog ambles out the door, picks up speed as it traverses the lawn and heads for the shrubbery. Ramsay leaves the door ajar and returns to the kitchen where Lippy has drained the pasta and stirred the sauce through it.

'Plates?' she asks.

'In that cupboard. To the right of the cooker.' Ramsay sits down. 'You ask if it rankles. I always respond that it doesn't. That I've moved on. The truth of course is that it still galls me. Always will. No matter what else changes, the resentment of my treatment will remain, fused into my bones. It's become a part of who I am. Some things you just have to learn to live with I suppose. There's no way to exorcise them. That's life.'

Lippy dishes up the pasta and puts the plates on the table. She sits down opposite Ramsay and leans her arms on the table. 'Tell me, if a play based on your experiences was written and put into production, do you think that might alleviate the frustration, the pain?'

Ramsay shrugs. 'I'm sure you're a highly regarded playwright, Lippy, but so much time has passed. It would merely resurrect the whole issue, the electorate's fury, and my disgrace. To be honest I don't think I could cope with that. Kat, my wife, certainly couldn't.'

'The issue is now at some distance, so makes a less hysterical evaluation of it possible. Besides, you paid the price. Merely one of the sheep that followed orders, but someone took the decision to dump the guilt on you. Aren't you curious to know who? Why? Besides, those who benefited most still clatter around, lording it over the rest of us. That's not right.'

Ramsay's curt laugh is like a machine slicing bacon. 'And since when, Lippy, was politics ever about what was right? About what's advantageous, yes. About what's prudent, yes. About the way you're directed to vote, yes. About lying, cheating, manipulating, backstabbing, yes, yes, yes. But never ever think politics has anything to do with what's right.' He rises from the table and walks to the back door, shaking, and pulls the door open. As he leans against the door frame he pants for breath, closes his eyes, lets the cool air dampen and beat down the flames of anger that threaten to erupt. Jess is suddenly beside him, her wet nose pushes at his hand, whining companionably as if she too is caught up in his pain and fury. He becomes aware of the tang of the sea. In the early evening stillness he can hear waves challenge the shingle of the beach to a tug of war, a duel, feels comfort flow from the nearness of the ocean though he doesn't know why. Perhaps the ghost of the old seadog who built the place is on the prowl, sailing in the wind around his old haunts. It may be that his love of the sea spills over to fold Ramsay in its octopus arms. His hand pats Jess. She wants to go in, and ambles into the hall. When he doesn't follow she circles him as if lassoing him, in an attempt to move him with her.

He hears the noise of a car as it jolts down the road. The engine noise changes down with the changing gears and the brightness of headlights torches through the branches of shrubs and trees. Is it Kat? She hasn't taken long, though she drives only at the speed limit when she passes speed cameras. Kat likes speed. Speed makes her feel powerful. Alive. So she says. Or does the arriving car herald more questions in the shape of another detective. As he can't make out the car it could be either. He sighs, like a puff of wind rustling the shrubs whose branches are as yet not fully clothed with leaves, and steps back into the hall. As he closes the door, he wonders on which side the comfort of the sea now is. Has it entered the house with him or has it remained on the outside, in its natural habitat.

'Your pasta will be cold. Will I reheat it for you?'

'No, It'll be fine. Sorry. I had to let Jess in.'

'You and she are great pals.'

'The greatest. She puts up with me as I am. More. She trusts me. Imagine that. Not many folk I can say that about. Trust. Fickle trust. I think I need a drink. There should be a bottle of wine around.' He finds a bottle of red and pours out two glasses.

Lippy holds up a hand. 'Wow, that's fine. I have to drive, remember. And the place is crawling with police. Never do if I was over the limit.'

'Do you honestly think a play would make any difference?' he asks after he finishes his pasta and pushes his plate to the side. 'You seem to set store by it. But can plays, or books, change the way people think? Or correct the record of events once impressed on minds?'

'Books, plays make people think, certainly. Encourage re-evaluation. Especially if the initial reaction has been knee-jerk, herd response, without overmuch thought devoted to it. Media goaded and galvanised.'

'Hmm! But it would dredge up the original garbage, the lies. Prodded wounds would burst open, to be exposed again to the pincers of public opinion, leaving them raw, vulnerable.'

'A play wouldn't necessarily be personal, though. The characters would be fictitious. Only the plot would be based on fact. Not even entirely fact. A bit of creative fiction is acceptable. Your name would never be mentioned. Nor any other actual names. No-one need know I have spoken to you, or that you had any input.'

'That's as maybe. But it wouldn't be long before some smartarse reviewer remembered, dug up the corpse — sorry, insensitive word — and brought the whole episode back into the spotlight, thinking it was overdue another rake over. The ideal piece for a slow news day. Good to promote the sale of additional copies or to drive more hits to the website.'

'That can't be discounted, of course it can't. But if a journalist were to do that they'd have to be careful about naming names and associating them with characters in my play, or they could find themselves accusing those never charged, and leave themselves open to accusations of defamation.'

Ramsay snorts. 'It's neither easy nor cheap to challenge accusations of defamation or wrongdoing, so whether true or not they get aired and they stick. That's what mudslingers count on. And they get away with it. Believe me, I know.'

'Yes, but my play is a work of fiction.'

'But only a stone's throw from fact . Besides, it could raise hackles.'

A car draws in beside the house, followed by sounds of a second vehicle. The back door opens and Kat strides down the hall into the kitchen, looking authoritative in her business suit, while the front door can be heard to open — hinges squeal like a dog with a hurt paw — then close. A voice directs the newcomer to the sitting room.

Ramsay rises from his chair and greets his wife. 'We've had some pasta. Can I make…'

Kat waves her hand. 'I ate before I left. Introduce us Ramsay. I presume this is the writer who wanted to talk to you.' Ramsay does the introductions. 'Your timing hasn't proved very wise.'

'Pardon?' says Lippy. She stares at Kat. The thought flashes through her mind that she reminds her of Eilidh. The hair, the way she holds herself, something about her attitude. Bloody Eilidh. Why after all these years has she suddenly become obsessed by her?

'You must curse yourself that you picked the same day as a body was found in the house. Rather upset your plans, I would think.'

'Not really. Writers are adaptable. There's always a gold nugget to be gained from a situation, even if it isn't the one anticipated.'

'I'll have a coffee, Ramsay. And is that wine? Pour me a glass while I go upstairs and change.' Kat throws her lightweight raincoat over her arm and disappears along the corridor towards the front part of the house. Voices are heard. A male voice, low, authoritative, decisive. A female voice, loud, haranguing, exasperated. Kat reappears and throws her coat over a chair. 'Would you believe it. These idiots won't let me upstairs in my own home. I'll have a word with their superiors. What a ridiculous situation.'

'Sit down, Kat. Have your coffee. I did tell you we were caged in here. Hopefully it won't be for much longer.'

'So who is the dead man on my hearth rug?'

'The police haven't said.'

'Are you quite sure you don't know him, Ramsay? I mean it seems impossible someone unknown should be murdered in the house.'

'It may seem impossible, but that's how it is, I can assure you. No signs of forced entry either, so I heard the police say. So why the murdered chap and the murderer were here I've no idea.'

'So if there are no signs of forced entry, how did they get in?' asks Lippy.

Kat shoots a look at her husband.

'This is the country, Lippy,' says Ramsay. 'People aren't as assiduous about locking windows and doors as they are in towns. I was only down on the beach, not far away. And not for long.'

His wife rolls her eyes. Men! But then she isn't prone to locking the doors either, unless the house is to be empty all day.

'Okay, understand that. So the doors weren't locked. But then, from what I saw, your visitor on the rug didn't look like a burglar, whatever burglars look like. He was wearing a suit. And black shoes. Do burglars wear business suits?'

Ramsay shakes his head. 'No idea.'

'So if there's a dead man in my sitting room, who killed him, and where is he now?' asks Kat. She gets to her feet and wanders to the window behind the sink, but all she sees is her own reflection interposed between herself and the waning light outside. 'So a maniac could still be wandering around the garden, lurking in the shrubbery, having a barbecue on the beach, for heaven's sake.'

'I rather think the police have thought of that and had a good look around,' responds her husband who remembers his feeling of the old seadog's ghost on the prowl outside. Fanciful, or prompted by an actual presence? No. Jess would have alerted him to an unknown person in the garden. He decides not to mention it. No point in further upsetting Kat.

'Ah, Mrs Dunn,' says a voice. Four pair of eyes swivel towards the speaker. A man stands in the doorway, brown leather jacket stretched over a pink shirt over a beer belly that bulges over the belt of his jeans. The bottom of the legs fray over boots with pointed toes and look suspiciously like cowboy boots. At the other end brown hair shot with grey flops over a face tanned and creased like an old shoe, a stalk of reed suctioned onto the inside of his mouth droops over his full lower lip.

Kat takes in every detail. She doesn't appreciate the gear. Thinks if this man has the nerve, the audacity to insist on questioning her, then the least he could have done was wear clothes appropriate to the occasion. She stands, and moves towards him. 'I am Kat Dunn. How do you do. And you are?'

'A long five minutes,' mutters Ramsay to Lippy.

'I need to ask you a few questions,' he says. The stalk of reed jigs up and down. 'Through here please. We're using your dining room. Ehm,

Detective Inspector Raisin, that's my name. I'll want to talk to you, Mr Dunn, and your friend there after I've spoken to Mrs Dunn.' He moves from the doorway to Jess's basket, bends down and pats her. 'Not much of a guard dog, are you lass? Big softie. There. There you are.' Jess's eyes are riveted on the stalk of reed, and follow its every gyration. She whines. The Detective Inspector turns to Kat. 'Well, what you waiting for? A limousine?' Ramsay sees Kat's mouth pucker like a shrivelled carrot as she bites back a response. She doesn't usually censor the words she utters to folk. Maybe it's a reaction to the Detective Inspector's outfit.

As the clicks of cowboy boots and killer heels retreat along the corridor to the front of the house, the noise of increased activity is heard. Voices jangle, phones burp, a voice commands, 'Get him to phone back immediately. Cut the claptrap. This is urgent.'

Lippy makes a face that conveys surprise, amusement. 'Things seem to be hotting up. Must remember the outfit for my next play, or book, though.'

'Did he say his name was Raisin?'

'Yes, so no references to dried prunes or pink champagne please.'

A hint of a smile hovers on Ramsay's lips. 'I'm sorry your time's being wasted.'

'Don't give it a second thought. In fact, it's a new experience and, now that the initial shock has subsided, I'm finding it quite intriguing.'

'You can include it in your play.'

'Now there's an idea. I could call it The Stuffed Pink Shirt.' She gives a giggle. 'I'm sorry. Not an appropriate occasion for that.'

Ramsay clears the plates and coffee mugs from the table and stacks them in the dishwasher. He washes the pan and leaves it upside down in the dish drying rack. Lippy watches him. 'If you don't get information from me, what will you do about your play? Forget it? Move on to another subject?'

Lippy takes a sip of her wine, puts the glass down, and twirls it on the table so the contents slurp around, swing backwards and forwards like a hula hoop. 'Forget it? No. I can't do that. Too good a subject. Besides, I've spent months on research — online, in the library reading newspaper reports. I've a contact who's an MP in another Party, and he showed me around the Commons, the scene of the crime as it were. I've talked to loads of people.' She studies him, half-turned away from her. 'The play's drafted, Ramsay. Your input is the detail, the confirmation of the assumptions I've made, the top stitching on the lapels. With or without you, this play is headed to the stage.' A look of confidence vies with one of sympathy on her face.

Ramsay is rooted to the floor in front of the sink, but his stance has been transformed. The friendliness is gone. He has become stiff, brittle. 'I see,' he says coldly. 'You owe me an apology.'

'Apology. Why?'

'You conned me into thinking you needed my input, my assent. I agreed to see you and invited you here in all good faith. And now I find you've merely strung me along. An accessory to titillate your work, totally uncaring about the effect this will have on me. On my wife. I want you to leave. Now.'

'I can't leave. The police...'

Ramsay rams a chair beneath the table and leaves the kitchen, heading for the back door. Jess trots after him. Lippy hesitates then follows too. She finds him leaning against a summerhouse, its blue planks streaked and faded beneath the remains of honeysuckle that swarms across the roof and dangles over doorway and window openings. She shivers. The evening has turned chilly and a dampness swirls in from the sea and rises up from the ground like a cold sauna. 'I'm sorry Ramsay. It was never my intention to trick you, I assure you. And I'm sure I never gave the impression you were my first port of call on this, or that your agreement was a determining factor on whether the play was written or not. That's not the way writing works. You get this idea, and...well...follow it, see where it takes you.'

'And it led you straight to me. Very neat.'

'But it was never based on you personally. It was based on an idea. I wanted to talk to you to give it authenticity. It was only today I realised how personally you're taking this, and yes, I then began to wonder about the effect on you.'

'Bit slow off the mark, aren't you. Slow at realising the misery you're intent on causing. Are your plays always so punch-laden, so thoughtless, so...so...uncaring about people? Now I understand why you're called Lippy. Lippy the egotist. You declare, poor sods cringe.'

'That's not fair, Ramsay. You hadn't heard of me, so you've no idea what my work's like. You accuse me of thoughtlessness, of being uncaring. But surely your actions are much the same in refusing your input for the subject to be explored, re-examined.'

'No, it's you that's not being fair, as you put it. You don't bloody well realise how traumatic that whole episode was. For me, and for others. You don't understand. Can't understand. Things happened. Bad things happened. Things I've spent years beavering to forget, to put behind me.' His fist thumps the blue wood of the summer house. 'My accusations, if indeed I've actually made any, will cause what? A bit of temporary annoyance? Slight bruising to your ego? Nothing more. Your career will trundle on and remarks I've made will be forgotten, buried beneath the exclamations of success. But have you stopped to think what repercussions your play might have on my life? The balm of years has been required for me to reach this stage where I still live my life on my own, but I can at least face each day with something approaching equanimity. If you dredge all that up again I'll be back where I started and my life will be back in shit.'

Lippy pulls her cardigan around her, and folds her arms to keep the cold at bay. 'Ramsay, I'm truly sorry you feel like this. What you did is in the past. It wasn't even anything particularly dreadful. You did what you'd been told to do, what most others were doing. Forget that. Let it go. What you should concentrate on is shifting the focus, pointing the stage finger at those who knowingly worked the system to its maximum. They're the wrongdoers. They're the ones left unfingered, untainted. Free. As I said before, the play's not about you per se, it's about an event in our political history. An interesting event with a story that needs told. If I don't do this, someone else will. It makes good theatre, too good to ignore.'

Ramsay's hands hold the sides of his shaking head as if to stop it bursting apart. 'Lippy, Lippy, you don't realise the quagmire you're stepping into. Things happen…are made to happen…to people. There's a system. Step out of line and… For your own good, drop it. Forget it.'

'Do I understand what you've just said? That there's more to your downfall—?'

'Leave me alone please. I want no part in what you're doing. I want to be left in peace.'

'But Ramsay…'

'Mr Dunn. Mr Dunn. Are you there? Time to share your story with me. Enlighten me. Convince me, if you can.' The pink shirt of the Detective Inspector glows faintly against the gloom of the house interior behind him.

'Huh! Five minutes, he said. More like—'

'Mr Dunn. I'm waiting. And I hate to be kept waiting.'

Ramsay pushes off from his leaning post and drags his feet across the damp grass, flattening it in the same jagged line pattern he left on the beach hours before. Jess, realising her master in on the move, cannons from the bushes and skitters over the grass after him. Lippy watches as the Detective Inspector, Ramsay and Jess disappear inside leaving the door ajar. She flexes her shoulders, pulls her cardigan firmly around her and heads off after them. As she feels the cold dampness of dew on her ankles, she wonders if, as she can't yet leave, a chat with Kat, the wife, might prove productive.

16 - Hungry lions await

Ming saunters into Brian's office, his mouth curled in a grin of satisfaction. 'Don't you just love it when things go well!'

'A pat's better than a skelp, for sure.'

'And a great article's superior to a snide paragraph.' He turns to throw a meaningful look at Brian. 'Or all that guff after my speech affair. You hung me out to dry there, Brian.'

'Absolutely not. I listed all the coverage—'

'Save your breath. Spare my ears.' Ming swings past Brian's desk towards the door to his own office.

'Interview went well, then.'

'Interview went swimmingly. That Jasmine gal is quite something.'

'Really! I heard she was…difficult.'

'Difficult! Where in heaven's name did you hear that? She's an absolute charmer. Had her eating out of my hand like a wee puppy. Frolicking too.'

'She liked the toiletries?'

'Went for the jobs angle — starving man to food stuff.'

Brian hides a sceptical frown by bending over a document on his desk. 'Great.'

'Gave her an idea for another piece. An in-depth review of rural employment. Told her the bloody Government should be doing much more. She listened. Nodded. Smiled. What a woman!'

'Sounds good.'

'She liked the product angle too. Thinks she might fly up to Barragh, do a piece on the company, interview the management, the staff. Human interest with a modern lifestyle angle. With a fistful of politics thrown in.'

'You certainly seem to have given her ideas to think about.'

'Said we should meet up again. That I should contact her with other suggestions for articles.'

Oh!'

'Always good to have a tame journalist in tow.'

'Can't say I know of many who fit that description. Maybe tame in terms of their willingness to tow the line of their media owners, but never tame when it comes to their victims.'

'You can't handle them properly, that's why. Remind me to send you on the next media handling course that's offered.'

Brian clenches his fists, his fingernails incising half moons across his palms. 'I left a pile of messages on your desk.'

'Ming sighs. 'No rest for the...no rest for us hard-working MCPs.' He bounces through the doorway to his office, then turns. 'Anything of interest in my absence?'

'Endless speculation about Wilkie Smart's death.'

'What's being said?'

'That he was having an affair with Bluebell.'

'Don't know what sane men see in the fat cow.'

'You mean—?'

'Anything else?'

'Vague, muttered-under-breath speculation.'

'Goes without saying. That's the norm.'

'Not so sure, this time.'

'What d'you mean? What's being said?' Ming's bounce is suddenly taut. His look of amiable bonhomie has disappeared with the flick of a conjurer's wand, replaced by a bland mask beneath which anxious concern squints.

'Mutterings. About dirty tricks.'

Ming's forced laugh sounds more like a growl. 'Dirty tricks! Huh! Wish the folks who uttered that would input the same amount of imagination into the formulation of Party policy. We'd make better headway if they did.'

'In my humble opinion the problem there is—'

'Your opinion doesn't matter, Brian.'

'Apologies. I thought this was a democratic Party.'

'Of course it is.' Ming senses a performance bomb, a minor one of little consequence, but the look on his assistant's face suggests, not an apology, but that a topic swerve is appropriate. 'Was referring to the... incident. That's the business of the police and we shouldn't speculate, but leave them to their work.'

Brian bites back his response, swallows hard and feels his rebuttal stick in his gullet like a large piece of gristle that he desperately wants to spit out, right into Ming's face. His ringing phone grabs his attention and after a deep breath he answers it. Ming hangs around to hear what is said, then, as the subject is of no interest, wanders back to his own office.

Some time later he reappears to sit on the edge of Brian's desk. 'Those mutterings about dirty tricks you mentioned. What's being said?'

Brian shrugs, stares intently at his computer screen. 'You wouldn't want me to repeat idle tittle-tattle, would you Ming?'

'A flare of anger lights Ming's face. 'You're the one who always tells me forewarned is forearmed. I merely thought it prudent to have a strong rebuttal should the mutterings be mentioned in my presence.'

'An interesting titbit for Jasmine?'

Ming's face hardens, his lips compress, his eyes reduce to slits that have Brian in their wintry beam. 'You've a foot over the precipice there, Brian.'

'Really? What precipice would that be, Ming? The same one the rumour-mongers are mentioning?'

Ming's gaze realigns itself. An item on one of the bookshelves draws his attention. He waggles his hand, rubs his nose as if a drip has formed there. 'Haven't a clue what you're wittering about. Haven't heard any rumours myself. Nothing beyond Bluebell's liking for fresh faces and firm behinds — a contrast to her own, I must say. But there you are. She hasn't by any chance dangled her hook in front of you, has she?'

'We sat beside one another for all of three minutes at the Parliamentary Christmas bash, but I wasn't aware of any hook.'

'You're probably not her type. She goes for the suave, intelligent types.'

'Same as Jasmine of the Callyman, no doubt.'

'Never advisable to let your jealousy show, Brian.'

'Not me. I've forsworn feminine distractions and their entanglements until...'

'Until?'

Brian seeks for a way to turn his indiscretion. 'Until I've saved enough for a deposit on a flat and can step off the rental ladder.'

Ming's shoulder's relax. 'Huh! Come the day of your retiral you could still be saving. In this city anyway.'

'True. But...you can but try.'

'You know, I had this creepy feeling you were about to say you'd forsworn women until you became an MCP. Wonder where the idea I should watch my back comes from?'

'Search me! The womb of your ideas is a thing of wonderment.'

Ming stares at him, unable to decide how to take the remark. He opts to accept it as a compliment, a pat on the back. 'The breadth and quality of my ideas is the reason Jasmine wants to keep in touch. She realises I can be of use in her journalistic career.'

Brian swallows hard. 'Did you know Wikie Smart? I mean you must have met him on a regular basis, but what was he like as a person?'

'Why d'you want to know?'

'Just interest in a guy — albeit a dead one — who's made the headlines. I've seen him on TV, heard him at conferences, meetings and suchlike. But beyond the occasional brief remark never really spoke to him. Got the impression he tried hard, perhaps found the job more difficult than he imagined, was ambitious…but beyond that I don't know much about him.'

'Interesting. Why d'you think he found the job difficult?'

'Can't put my finger on anything in particular. He was always one hundred per cent behind the Party, its policies, its direction.'

'Naturally. Aren't we all?'

'Yet I occasionally caught a whiff of frustration, indicative perhaps that the spin or direction wasn't quite what he advocated.'

'Thoughts of applying for the vacancy?' Ming's head jerks at the thought. His eyes widen, questioningly.

Brian shakes his head. 'Good grief, no! Not…' He is about to say not where my interests lie, but before uttered hurriedly changes his words to, 'Not my thing.'

'Hmm!' Mings flicks him a hard look. 'You mentioned frustration.'

'My overactive imagination no doubt.'

'I met him often enough, had a feeling he wasn't approved of in certain quarters, but didn't really know him that well.'

'Who didn't approve of him?'

Ming slides from the desk to stand over Brian who wonders why the question has caused a ripple of anxiety to cross the MCP's face, and why his hands agitate the air. 'Politics is a hard profession where there's no such luxury as approval. According to circumstances, there's right and wrong, good and bad for the Party. Politics is a tightrope. Slip and any number of hungry lions await. Best to remember that, Brian.' He turns on his heel and paces to his office. 'Hungry lions, Brian.' He closes the door behind him.

After Ming leaves for the day in a bustle of files, laptop and papers, Brian tries to contact Kevin again. His fellow Parliamentary assistant, who had gripped his interest with his mention of The Galley, had called off their meeting at The Wabbit Hen in a hurried phone call a couple of hours before they were due to meet. Brian has tried to contact him for a chat ever since, but Kevin always seems too busy, up against deadlines, or in company and can't talk. He promised to catch up with Brian but has not attempted to call or meet him. Brian suspects Kevin is avoiding him. Yesterday when he went to lunch he waved at Kevin who stood, tray of food in hands, at a nearby table one minute, then had disappeared the next. Apparition or fast exit?

Kevin's mention of The Galley was of interest, historic interest as Brian had believed it mainly a feature of the past, swept away by new brooms, a new political set-up and a new parliament. It is not something he has come across in his Parliamentary work, and his father's friend Steve's tales were of a previous era. Steve had left the Party years ago when it became apparent that the beliefs of Bleer, the new leader and PM, and his henchmen had veered off in a very different direction from his own long-cherished views. So, on balance, Brian tends to think the days of The Galley are over. Granted political manipulation and machinations surround him on a daily basis, but such stuff is an accepted part of politics — always has been, always will be. Like others, he is well aware of the undertones and the less than subtle attempts at persuasion, but these, after a bout of curses, are shrugged off, par for the course. Accept or get out. The ugly stuff that The Galley perpetrated was snuffed out long ago, the clique behind it shattered when its head honcho died. Wasn't it? Must have been.

Weird, though, that he now slaves away for an MCP who worked as Constituency assistant for that head honcho, the Galley Chef. Charlie Kintail. The realisation sends a shiver down his spine and causes his thoughts to stutter.

How much does Ming know about Charlie Kintail, about The Galley? Surely he can't have worked for him for years and been unaware of the iron grasp the MP and his clique had on the Party? Or was Ming calculatingly hired as a naïve, bumbling, unsuspecting front to their operations. A helpful but not too bright pawn who could be shoved around from square to square as required. On the other hand, Ming may not be too bright but he is far from daft, especially when it comes to looking after Number One. More recently, his background and hard work in his constituency, where, despite his recent grumbles, he usually trudges along to even the most dire of functions, means he is popular, and is going to prove trickier to shift than Brian had first anticipated. So Brian now finds it difficult to believe Ming knows nothing of what went on when he worked for Charlie Kintail. Was he even part of it, The Galley finding Ming's father's union contacts useful?

When he listened over the past few days to discussions on Wilkie Smart's murder — muttered comments about the man and his affair, and whispered asides about the likely perpetrator — what became clear was that, far from having been expunged from the Party, there is a belief (reluctantly acknowledged) that The Galley still sails amongst them, still controls, still pulls strings. The view expressed in cloaked terms is of it lying low, gliding through the shallows with sails furled, the dip of oars barely ruffling the surface of the political waters, ropes loosened, weapons disguised or hidden, but that it still wields significant power. Others vehemently ridicule the idea as fantasist twaddle.

Instances of The Galley's power and reach are cited in whispers, in behind-hand comments, to trusted colleagues. Most instances are hearsay, with little substance, about why a recalcitrant MCP backed down over a certain issue, why another was demoted by his removal from front bench to back, why a car was trashed, a boat burnt and sunk, why a particularly vicious media campaign was stirred up by apparent cyber bullies against a female MCP who voiced concerns over welfare policies, a former Minister has enjoyed a lengthy holiday in Florida, this Party stalwart or that grovelling Member has not been selected for constituency list or shortlisted for a safe seat. Then there are muttered comments about jobs refused or lost, promotion denied, eviction from houses long inhabited, and of people ostracised. One of the names Brian hears mentioned in a furtive remark is Pete whom he had tipped off about the by-election. Pete who attributed his failure to be selected to his Party Conference run-in with Carnoustie, the ex-Minister. Pete said he would either get out or grovel. Brian hasn't seen or heard of him since.

Carnoustie. Could he be part of it? With Charlie Kintail long gone who is Chef in The Galley now? Who are the other 'cooks'? And does Ming Dulse have an involvement with it? If he does, then Brian's remarks might have been risky. Ming's remark about hungry lions plays back to him. Brian's stomach knots in apprehension. If he doesn't want to end up on someone's hearth rug, a length of rope round his neck, then he'd better pay more attention to where he puts his feet and what words roll off his tongue. Get a grip, he orders himself, even The Galley wouldn't go that far. But as his thoughts revolve the naïve beliefs and simplistic aspirations of his university years seem long in the past. The present is more difficult to chart than he had ever thought possible.

Ming's phrase, the one he is so fond of repeating. 'Never let the buggers win.' Brian wonders where it came from. Had it been a favourite mantra of Charlie Kintail?

17 - It strikes me as odd

The city feels strange, like an old friend not seen or heard from for years. After his daily diet of sea and sand, seaweed and rocks, space, wide skies, the odd gull screech, voices of children at the other end of the beach, his own company during the week, few phone calls, and only Chrissie Derwent in the local shop keen for a chat to pass the time, or a trip with Kat to the supermarket at the weekend — after the muted tick of that the city is loud. Brash and noisy. Shop fronts scream for attention for their wares, music blares from the cavernous depths of others. The look-at-me culture is disconcerting after the quiet of the laid-back coast. But the fumes disturb him most. Petrol and diesel drive up his nostrils, ram down his throat, making him gasp for the briny air he has become accustomed to. The reek smothers. He covers his mouth and nose with his hand, but it makes little difference. He wishes he hadn't come, hadn't agreed to meet Lippy Nevis. Nothing good will come of it.

At the door of the café where he arranged to meet her, he stops and ponders calling the meeting off. If he turns away and retraces his steps to the car park, in an hour and a half, less, he can be back at home, can make a fuss of Jess, his dog, and take her off for a walk along the beach to meld into the peace of the landscape.

A couple elbow roughly past him. 'If you're not going in, move elsewhere, grandpa,' says the guy. 'You're blocking the bloody doorway.'

'Sorry,' mutters Ramsay as he shuffles aside.

He looks through the glass of the window, and decides this meeting is a mistake, a spur-of-the-moment weakness he should never have agreed to. Really he just wants to keep quiet, moulder in peace. But Lippy, seated at a table near the door, notices him. She waves, gets to her feet.

Ramsay takes a deep breath, but regrets it as he chokes on the unaccustomed fumes, and thinks, 'What the hell! I need to change the air I'm breathing.' He is grateful for the smoking ban as the air inside will be less obnoxious than in the street. Slowly he turns and pushes the glass door.

'Ramsay,' says Lippy, moving round the table to peck his cheek. 'I'm so glad you decided to talk to me. To come today. Have a seat. What can I get you? Coffee?'

Ramsay nods. 'Coffee would be good. Black. Nothing fancy. I'm just a plain, old fashioned, sandblasted, black coffee guy.'

She grins, and orders coffees and two chocolate muffins. 'I hope you'll eat yours. Otherwise I'll feel compelled to, and while one chocolate treat is bad, two is definitely sinful. Especially for my waistline.'

'I can probably manage my share.'

The coffee arrives. Lippy stirs in sugar and looks at Ramsay. 'Thank you for getting in touch – for coming.'

Ramsay shrugs. 'Fine.'

'What made you change your mind? I'm glad you did. But what brought about the change of attitude?'

Ramsay thinks as he sips his coffee. 'The guy on Kat's hearth rug.'

Lippy looks surprised. 'How so?'

'He was a Spad.'

'A......?'

'Spad. Special Advisor. Spin Doctor.'

'Ah, right. But why did that bring about a change of mind?'

'Because I had…what you might call a premonition…I don't know. Anyway, annoyance swept me along the beach yesterday, pretty damn mad with you and the world in general. Kat didn't appreciate her home being a murder scene, or the white suited ants, or the pink shirted Detective Inspector Raisin. She wasn't too keen on his attitude either.'

'Yes, he was quite…'

'Nutty?'

'Abrasive, I thought.'

'In the morning Kat was in a foul mood. I kept out her way until she left for work. At lunchtime she phoned from the pub where she eats to tell me, between mouthfuls of her sandwich, that there are all manner of rumours going the rounds. Word is the guy on the hearth rug was Wilkie Smart.'

'Yup, that's now confirmed.'

Ramsay plays with the spoon on his saucer, pushing it around with his fingers. 'Thing is, I think Bluebell McDaid was having an affair with him.'

'Really! But he looked quite young.' She shivers at the reminder of what she saw in Ramsay's lounge. The body of the young man sprawled out. Motionless. Lifeless. The blue rope around his neck. She shakes herself. 'She's…well, she's about my age, isn't she?'

'Takes all sorts.'

'Good for her. Perhaps that's what I need.'

'Hmm. Anyway, Bluebell McDaid's house is a short distance along the road from us.'

'Interesting.'

Ramsay takes a bite of his muffin. 'I was on my way out to the beach when the pink shirted one arrived. To let me know their investigations indicate the victim was not killed on Kat's hearth rug but elsewhere, and the body was then dumped in our lounge.'

'So perhaps at—?'

'Perhaps.'

Lippy plays with her spoon. 'Your wife didn't seem too upset by events.'

'Kat?' She had to grow a hard shell. But underneath she feels, believe me.'

'Okay.'

Ramsay takes a long, slow sip of his coffee. 'The guy was strangled. But not with the piece of blue rope. That was, as the pink shirted one put it, merely for show.'

'Even more interesting. The questions now are who was it meant to show, and what was it meant to show them?'

'I'll come to that in a minute. But back to the beach.'

A waitress, a young girl in a white blouse with black trousers covered by a long green apron butts in. 'Can I get you anything else? More coffee? A buttered scone?' Heads shake.

'We're fine thanks,' says Lippy. As the girl moves off she turns her face to Ramsay. 'So on the beach you'd an opportunity to think things through?'

'The beach is good for thinking. As my annoyance abated, I…began to wonder why he was killed.'

'Motive. Yup. Always high on the list for answers.'

'Why he was moved to Kat's hearthrug…well… our front room. Was he killed at Bluebell's? If so, why?'

'Wow, an MCP involved somehow in a murder.'

'Doesn't sound likely, does it? But you see that brought me back to my own situation.' Lippy's eyes widen to a stare, her mouth hangs open. 'Get a rein on your imagination, Lippy. Don't let it gallop off. There was no murder or anything like that involved with my kerfuffle.'

Lippy leans her arms on the table, and looks at him shrewdly, interest drawn in the lines on her face. 'But something has made you think there's a connection. You think there's a link between what happened to you and the body we found the other afternoon?'

'It's difficult to explain. That's why I mentioned a premonition. As I sat on the rocks yesterday thinking all this through, I was hit by a strong wave of belief that there's a connection. Why else would the body have been moved to our house? Surely it doesn't make sense to move a body? Danger of being caught for a start. Why not leave it and run?'

'Unless you want to send a definite message to some person.'

'That's the conclusion I came to.'

'And you think that message is connected to your own situation.'

'That was the only interpretation that seemed to make sense.'

'Unless of course someone, either the killer or another, wanted to rid themselves of a body, and of the implications of it being found in their house, by ditching it on one of their neighbours. Any of their neighbours. Perhaps they weren't particular as to which.' Ramsay dips his head in a nod. 'It's probably widely known your wife's away during the week and you spend an inordinate amount of time on the beach. Nor would it be difficult to discover you leave your doors unlocked — a welcome to anyone with sticky fingers or other nefarious intentions.'

'You're probably right, Lippy. I've got myself worked up into conspiracy mode. That's more or less what the pink shirted one said. That we were a convenient and easy dumping ground. Kat and I appear to have been erased from their list of suspects.'

'The police never erase, Ramsay. You should know that. They maybe rearrange, like the deck chairs on the Titanic, and insert you further down the investigative order, but you'll still be there. Make no mistake about that.'

'Perhaps, but the focus is elsewhere.'

Lippy pushes her empty sugar sachets around the table beside her cup. 'You know, it strikes me as odd.'

'What? What strikes you as odd?'

'Within a couple of minutes you tell me about a premonition of a connection between what happened to you and this murder, which presumably you never mentioned to Raisin because you're reassured he now thinks you've nothing to do with the body on the hearth rug. Has it dawned on you the pink shirted one might take a different view if you tell him of your feeling the two events are linked.'

A flustered look appears on Ramsay's face. 'I didn't say they were linked, Lippy. I merely admitted to…to…well to a vague notion there may be a connection.'

'Same thing.'

'Pah!'Ramsay throws his hands in the air, and pushes back his chair as if to get up.

Lippy grabs his wrist. 'Sit down, Ramsay.'

He sinks to his seat again. 'I shouldn't have come. Forget it. Just—'

'No, no. Your notion is interesting.'

Ramsay looks around, then leans over the table with head lowered. 'Lippy, I think I might be in danger.'

'In danger!' Lippy's voice rises. Coffee addicts at other tables look questioningly towards her.

'Look, I don't want to worry you. It was only an idea. Forget it.'

'You talked of messages to people.' Ramsay nods. 'That the message could be connected to your own situation.'

'Yup.'

'Why you think you've become a threat years after your downfall needs an explanation. Certainly to me.'

'It's complicated.'

'Okay, but try and explain why you feel there may be a connection. Let's discuss that and see where it leads.'

Ramsay glances around. Lunchtime approaches so the café is filling up with those from offices nearby. Their time is limited and they are intent on cramming it with food, drink, company and tales of office and private lives, set off by giggles and raucous laughs, all packed into fifty minutes. Already looks are directed towards them and their empty coffee cups. The atmosphere is growing stuffy and the noise makes talk of private matters increasingly difficult.

'Can we move? Go somewhere quieter where we can talk without being overheard?'

'Sure. Where do you suggest?'

Selina is walking home from work. She feels tired, drained, but thinks a walk will perk her up. The department store was busy today. Not so much customers who bought, as browsed. They asked questions, compared quality and price, debated with themselves, then said they'd think about it. At times she has to stifle screams of frustration, but she's learnt to maintain her face in a mask of helpfulness and understanding. And of course she does understand, money's tight with her too, but she doesn't like her time wasted, and she thinks some customers are merely out for amusement, to pass the time looking at goods with no intention of making a purchase. A trip around favourite shops, an entertainment

— like an outing to watch a film or a play, only one in which they are the central character, the one with star billing.

The streets are still busy and hum with life. 'This is a transition period,' Selina thinks. 'The first blink of better weather and a few brave souls ditch the winter woollies and go straight into sleeveless high summer gear, while other, more canny folk, retain heavy coats and boots but leave off scarf and gloves.'

It's much the same in the Home Furnishings department. The first glimpse of spring flowers makes the house-proud dream of a spring makeover. New curtains for here, accessories for there; major refurbishment or one or two focal point items. All designed to create a new ambiance to surroundings become boring by long months of short days, huddled within the same four walls. 'It's the same with life,' she reckons. 'We become bored by the daily grind and need a fillip occasionally, a treat, a change of surroundings to recharge our batteries, refocus our lives.'

Soon it will be a week since her husband left. She has not heard from him. She has told no-one about his disappearance. Should any mishap have befallen him, then her lack of action may cause comment by the police. Why didn't she notify them earlier, they will ask. She won't have an answer.

She stops to look in a shop window. Shoes. New styles like gladiator sandals, but with platform soles and heels like the wires on a suspension bridge. Not for her. But there are others in colourful leathers with fancy trims and nick knacks. One pair in particular draws her attention. She gazes, and thinks of the outfits she could wear them with. Each time she looks at them she would be cheered by their colour, their joie de vivre. She swithers. She can't afford them, but they're tempting. Perhaps she could try them on. If they don't fit or are uncomfortable then she doesn't have to regret what might have been. On the other hand, if she tries them on and feels as if walking on air, what will she do? The shop doors are wide open to the street as other shoppers drift out, shiny black shoe carriers clutched in their hands. She drifts inside.

The interior is calming, almost minimalist. More like an art gallery than a shop, with individual shoes displayed on transparent plastic stands. Pieces of sculpture for feet. Selina fears the prices might also be in line with works of art as no price tags are visible. As she browses, an assistant materialises at her side, offers her help when she decides what to try on. Selina knows the routine and isn't going to be rushed or bulldozed into a decision. After a browse around she hasn't been able to find the pair she likes in the window, so when the assistant next makes her circuit Selina asks about them.

As she walks back and forth, and stops in front of the mirror to turn front on, side on, a twirl to view them from behind, she decides to throw caution to the winds. Before she changes her mind she gabbles that she will take them. The assistant, who initially looked doubtful about her intentions, beams and goes off to bag them whilst she waits for the credit card to be handed over. Selina pushes the cost from her mind. She deserves a treat occasionally and the past week has been difficult.

As she walks through the doors, now shut in preparation for closing, into the darkening evening, she is conscious of the upmarket bag swinging from her hand. The thought drops her shoulders and lifts her chin. She turns to head towards her bus stop and finds herself face to face with her husband, Schaw.

18 - The face of democracy

'This birthday bash later...' Ming scratches his nose as he dumps a ream of signed letters onto Brian's desk.

'Birthday bash?'

'Okay, the invite for a drink to celebrate another birthday ramped up by one of our esteemed colleagues.'

'What about it?'

'Not many going apparently. Pressure of work, that sort of thing.'

'Serves the bastard right. Why should he expect others to celebrate with him? Fork out for their own drinks when he probably hasn't attended anyone else's bash. Bloody stupid.'

'My, aren't we in a twisted mood!'

'Stuff on my mind.'

'Not plotting, I hope?'

Brian throws down his pen with a grunt of frustration. 'Just stuff. Family stuff. Okay?'

'Fair enough.'

'Parents' twenty-fifth wedding anniversary. Need to buy them a present.' He runs his fingers through his hair. 'No idea what. I mean, what do parents need after years of home-building and acquisition?'

A look of amusement meanders across Ming's face. 'Never had you tagged as the dutiful and mindful son.'

'Not sure you have me tagged as anything.'

Ming raises his eyebrows and slowly shakes his head. 'It's a 'she', by the way.'

'It's a 'she'! She's a 'she', surely. You'll have the feminists and the equal opportunity fanatics after you.'

'Whatever.'

'Who's a 'she'?'

'Our esteemed colleague of the birthday bash...drink.'

'Who?'

'Whatshername.' Ming swivels his wrist to wave his hand dismissively. 'Anyway… Thing is, there's an attendance deficit. I can't go as another commitment calls, so I've volunteered you.'

'You've what! My time's my own after—'

'No, it's not. You look after my interests whatever the time…or place. Besides, it won't bite into your evening. A brisk foray into pub, grab a glass, deliver my congrats and condolences — no, not those — my regrets at missing the big event, then a smart dive for the exit. Duty done. Honour satisfied.'

'Eeeeek!' Brian thumps his desk. 'Okay, okay, sorry about the reaction. Had hoped for a look round John Lewis for a pressie for parents. But I understand your needs come first, dear master.'

'You know, Brian, sometimes I wonder if there's a ruddy wee devil in there instead of your own personality. Or perhaps it just gets blasted up from the furnace below every now and again when your mood dictates. Whatever it is, think you need to take care, old son. Reassess your position here. Where you see yourself headed. Otherwise where you're headed might not be the happy, sunny, parasol-drinky resort you envisage.'

'Yeah, yeah. It's the end of a long week, Ming. And there's at least one speech to be drafted for you over the weekend. So cut me some slack.'

Ming shrugs, 'Just saying.' He ambles back to his office, then reappears with his padded jacket, emblazoned with stripes and logos, slung over his arm. 'I'm off. Out to dinner this evening. Rather good eatery, too. Enjoy your weekend, Brian. Remember to be early on Monday morning, and in a more amenable mood, please. Toodle-pip.'

When Brian pushes open the battered brown door, with its Victorian etched glass, the Parliament folk who have turned up to the bash are already several drinks ahead of him. The MCP rides a wave of feminine bonhomie and hugs and kisses him as if a long-lost friend rather than a little-known colleague.

He thinks it better to deliver Ming's felicitations before he forgets. He is sure to be asked about that on Monday, and no point in handing Ming another omission ripe for criticism. 'Ming's devastated he can't make it. Would love to be part of your celebration but…necessary constituency business. You know how it is. So he sent me as delivery boy for his best wishes.'

The woman throws her weight onto one leg, elevates one hip and lowers the other, and stares at him as if wondering if she has discovered a new species. 'Ming? That'll be that Dulse idiot?'

A smile hovers on Brian's lips, unable to decide whether to bloom or wither. Eventually he settles for a twitch of his eyebrows. 'Yes, Ming Dulse.'

'Hmmph! The MCP swivels to her audience and raises her glass. 'Listen up, you bastards. The eminent Mingally Dulse sends his apologies for non-attendance. What do we say to that?'

'Three cheers,' shouts a voice. The company sniggers.

'Bloody bampot.'

Brian suspects his stay might be even shorter than Ming anticipated. But the MCP throws her free arm around his shoulders and snuggles into him. 'Boss man not here…lordy, I'm sorry but I don't know your name.'

'Brian. I'm Ming's assistant.'

She leans back like a tango dancer to survey him. 'My condolences.' She waves her glass in his face. Brian can smell the alcohol but can't put a name to the concoction. 'Anyway, as I was saying, boss man not here, so let your hair down, Brian, and show the bastard what you think of him.'

'I may already have done that.'

'Even better. We'll have a chinwag later. Ricky, hey Ricky, give this guy a drink for his sterling work.'

The barman appears, his stance a question mark.

'I'll have a pint.'

'That idiot of yours still as bombastic as ever?' asks a guy on the other side of the birthday girl.

'Don't know if I'd be so generous as to call him that,' replies an MCP with an office just along the corridor from Ming's. 'Bombastic indicates some knowledge of your subject.' A few guffaws rise above the chatter. 'Does that apply to Mingin?' Chortles of laughter.

'Mingin Ming! That's good. Must remember that.' Brian recognises the guy — another assistant like him. Unlike him, his boss is at his elbow, thumping the bar, enjoying the joke.

'Very funny, but just be careful,' someone mutters.

'Aye, remember his connection,' A few throats are cleared. Brian looks to see who made the remark, but the crowd has reformed, and circles as if slip stepping in the moves of a Dashing White Sergeant. Brian pays for his drink and takes a sip, wondering how long he needs to hang around. With a squeeze of his shoulder the birthday girl swans off to drape herself round another friend.

'Is he as bad as they make out,' asks a voice behind him.

Brian turns. The woman is young, about his own age. What strikes him most about her, almost hits him in the gut, is they way her grey eyes dance and the laughing curve of her mouth. In the drab and tired surroundings of the bar, vitality radiates from her, and makes him feel a tired, disillusioned sceptic. Disillusioned? Wonder what made him think that? 'I suspect most people underestimate him.'

'In what way? I heard his non-speech, by the way.'

'Ah, well — he was rather thrown in at the deep end with that.'

'No end should be too deep for a competent politician.'

'Fair point.'

'So what do his peers underestimate?'

Brian's mouth purses as he pushes his glass around a puddle on the bar, fascinated by its glide, reminded of a hovercraft he once saw though he can't remember where. 'Ming has his strengths.'

'Such as?'

'Believe it or not, he's a damn good Constituency worker, and he's respected for that.' He can't quite believe he's standing up for the bastard. What the hell's got into him!

'That could be down to your efficiency and that of his Constituency assistant.'

'We play our parts, I dare say. But it's Ming who presses the flesh, listens to the sob stories. He's the face of democracy to his constituents. And he plays the part well, whatever his shortcomings in the Chamber.'

'You give the impression you admire him.'

Brian is drawn by the dancing eyes, feels entranced by them. 'Heavens, am I! Must be the Friday flop. What about you?'

'I work for Bluebell McDaid.'

'Really! I thought her assistant was a stringy guy with long hair and buck teeth?'

The woman laughs, a musical sound like the clink of crystal glasses. 'He left. I've only been in post five weeks. Worked at Party HQ for a spell before this, so not totally in the dark about who's who and how the place operates.'

'Where is Bluebell? She doesn't seem to have been around since...'

'She's taking time off. The shock, you know. Upset her.'

'Not surprised. Can't think what state I'd be in if I found a body.'

'She didn't actually find him. That was someone else.'

'Of course. But rumours are that Wilkie Smart was murdered at her house?'

'Speculation.'

'Word on the grapevine is the police have been all over the place.'

The woman shakes her head. 'Like you, I only hear the gossip. I'm not privy to the police investigation.'

'No, of course not. I just assumed… I suppose as you work for her I assumed you knew what happened.'

'I'm not sure even the police know yet.'

'When did you last see her? Sorry, you don't need to answer. I didn't mean to interrogate you.'

She drains her glass of what Brian assumes is white wine. 'I saw her the Friday before it happened.'

'Poor woman.' Brian ceases the circling of his glass on the bar.

'We worked as usual. Nothing appeared out of the ordinary. She went off on constituency business in the afternoon — a meeting with a group of people up in arms about…a meeting with constituents. She attended that, then…disappeared. I know of no-one who has seen her since. Mutt sent word she was taking time off. That any work I couldn't handle should be referred to our deputy leader. So, there. You now know as much as I do.'

Brian's head bounces in acknowledgement of the information. 'I'm Brian.'

'Kirsty.' Her hand deposits her empty glass on the bar and glides out for him to shake. "Mutt suggested I should come along to this. He thought Bluebell would appreciate it. So, here I am.'

'Another drink?'

'No thanks.' She fans her outstretched fingers in front of her. 'Yes. A tonic water would be good. These places make me thirsty, but I'm driving.'

Brian waves to catch the barman's attention and orders more drinks. 'There's a free table over there if you fancy a seat.'

'Good thinking. Let's grab it.' They snake their way between drinkers to bag the table and two spaces on the red banquette.

As he strides up the fine line path to his parents' front door, Brian has a grin on his face. He noticed it in the mirror this morning when he shaved. He saw it again in his reflected image in the glass window of the bus he took into town to visit John Lewis. The chore of finding a present for his parents turned into a pleasant sortie. And as the six crystal champagne flutes were wrapped — when the sales assistant discovered they were a silver wedding anniversary present she offered to gift-wrap them in fancy paper with ribbon formed into loops and stretched into curls — he picks out a box of wine glasses for himself. Not as classy as the champagne flutes, and considerably cheaper, but better than the two or three assorted tumblers he uses. His purchase of the wine glasses emanates from an idea afloat in his mind that he should ask a certain person to dinner. Couldn't offer her wine from a cheap tumbler, could he!

His mother has set the table with her best china, the cutlery kept for good occasions, and rather utilitarian wine glasses. A small pot of pink begonias, container covered in kitchen tinfoil, stands centre stage between two Ikea glass candlesticks with red candles. Short lengths of silver tinsel from her Christmas tree decorations box are looped around the bases. Brian notices five places.

'If you had a girlfriend it would make the number even.'

Brian grins. 'You don't like irregularity, unevenness.'

'I like tidiness.'

'Didn't make much headway there with Dad, did you?'

His mother straightens a knife, nudges a placemat. 'I asked Steve and Phyllis. I thought another couple would make it…more of an occasion.'

'Dinner party rather than family meal.'

'Exactly. You know Steve and…? Of course you do.'

'Yup.'

'Ever since you talked to Steve last time you were here he asks about you. I suspect he's worried in case the information he gave you might… well, might have encouraged something silly.'

'Or something unwise?'

'Particularly something unwise.'

'The opposite might be more the case.'

His mother looks at him questioningly but is stopped asking what he means by his father breezing into the room.

'When you see the table laid for a dinner party, Brian, you'll think I've becoming the middle class guy you accused me of being.' Brian grins. 'A dinner party, no less!' He looks happy at the thought.

His mother elbows her husband. 'It's a celebration of a milestone. Others go out to expensive restaurants, some even get whisked away on cruises, we're having a quiet meal with friends.'

'Weather's too uncertain to go away. Besides, it's term time. You never know what the summer holidays might bring.'

'Heard that one before. And what it brought was two nights in a grotty B and B in midge-infested Argyll.'

Brian retrieves the box of gift-wrapped wine glasses from the chair where he left it and thrusts it into his mother's hands. 'Happy anniversary.'

His mother's smile is slightly flustered. Her son doesn't usually remember such occasions, never mind produce gifts, though this anniversary is rather special. Twenty-five years. How time flies! It seems little more than a handful of years since she met Douglas at an educational conference. Prior to that there had been one or two flings, nothing serious, she was concentrating on her career. And exploring the world. But fate sat her next to this untidy man with his penchant for taking things to pieces, and it had not been long before she decided she wanted to be there for him, help him put his projects back together again and sweep up the parts left over. Not the role she had envisaged, but she was happy with the result. They were late starters, she was nudging her thirtieth birthday, so hadn't delayed having a family. Brian was the only one to come along, a daughter to balance the act appealed…but she was content with her son.

'Hurry up. Open it,' orders his father, his hands ready to grab the package. His mother looks around for somewhere to lay the parcel, retreats to the chair Brian used, and carefully peels off ribbon and paper. 'Oh!' she gasps as the picture on the box lid is revealed. Her hands shake as she pulls off the lid and drops it on the arm of the chair. 'Oh, Brian! They're lovely.' Her fingers float like dandelion seeds over the glasses. She turns to face him. Kisses his cheek. 'We've never had champagne flutes.'

'Never had champagne to put in them.' His father looks pleased despite his remark.

'Of course we have.' His mother shoots her husband a look of reproach.

'I suppose Cava and Prosecco are good substitutes.'

Brian reaches behind the chair and pulls out a gift-wrapped bottle. He holds it out to his father.

'For me?' Brian nods. 'When did I last get a present that wasn't socks or ties!'

His wife shakes her head with a mock sigh. 'Incorrigible. Always has been, always will be.'

'Think you'd better wash these new glasses, Rosie. Looks like we've the means to hansel them.' The wire-topped bottle is waved in the air.

His wife beams. 'Thanks, Brian.' The glasses are removed to the kitchen sink.

The flutes have been hanseled, the fillet steaks devoured, the selection of puddings sampled with appreciation, and now mellow with wine and good company the chat flows.

Phyllis is slightly build but what she lacks in stature she makes up for in personality and an exuberance of energy which is directed into making things happen. A member of numerous organisations, she is the driving force behind car boot sales, amateur dramatic productions, exhibitions of artists' work, talks on local history, and whatever other schemes appeal to her seemingly tireless zest for a busy life. During dinner she relates stories, mimics those she likes to take down a peg, and keeps the party merry to the point of tears rolling down cheeks.

'How do you keep up with her?' Rosie asks Steve.

'Ach, I used to chain her down occasionally for some peace. But that didn't work. She was ten times worse when I released her. So I've just learned to live with it.' He looks at his wife. 'It could be worse.' His look becomes a grin within which his appreciation of her is obvious.

His wife chortles. 'You're as bad as me Stevie boy. At least I spread my interests. Yours all bang around in one political Party.'

Rosie nods her head. 'Politics grabs some people that way.'

Phyllis takes a sip of her wine. 'Too many men driven to wage too many vendettas.'

Brian looks up. 'Vendettas aren't the preserve of men. I could cite a number of women who relish that side of politics.'

'The bulk of our politicians forget what we send them to Parliament for,' says Brian's mother. 'In the run-up to elections they spout about all the changes they'll pursue, gush about the benefits their Party will bring to people's lives. But when it comes down to it, their only interest is their own self-aggrandisement.'

'Ach, Rosie, you shouldnae believe the media.' Steve has moved from banter to solemnity.

Brian leans forward, waving his glass. 'Much of the vendetta stuff — the cheap jibes and insults — they're mostly window-dressing.'

'Not with your Party, Brian. Cheap jibes and insults are all they have these days. No policies, no direction, no leadership. Just jibes and insults.' Steve warms to his subject.'

'Have to agree the Party's not been on top form recently.' Brian purses his lips. 'There's a sense that the future has closed down as if it didn't exist, shut up shop. Britain appears to have turned its back on tomorrow, and instead revels in a reimagined version of its glorious past. You only have to turn on the TV to see the number of costume dramas, period dramas, films set in the past or else in an unimaginable future. Any other eras, to escape the reality of the present.'

'I like to watch costume dramas,' admits his mother. 'They're usually well done, though not always historically accurate.'

Phyllis bounces in to say, 'Most of them are too artificial sweetener for me. Gooey, with all the nasty reality airbrushed to shadows.'

Rosie agrees. 'That can be the case. But it's entertainment not history.'

Brian's mind remains on politics. 'Voting reform for Westmunster needs to be tackled — but not much chance of that. Too divisive. So we lurch on.'

Phyllis's face clouds. 'Why discuss this dire stuff? It only makes us gloomy.'

Her husband shakes his head. 'This dire stuff, as you call it, impacts on out lives.'

'Here we go again.'

'It does, too. Take austerity. Look how that affects the poorest in society, the out-of-work, pensioners. While bankers and other high heid yins continue to rake in obscene bonuses. And Brian's Party sits on the sidelines.'

'Knitting,' quips Rosie.

'Ha, ha. I was going to say twiddling its thumbs.'

'No, definitely knitting. Scarves for the necks of the aristocracy, like crones at the foot of the guillotine, as they watch heads roll, lives ruined, and revel in the spectacle.'

Laughter whips round the table. Glasses are recharged.

Douglas' hand slaps the table. 'You're on form tonight, Rosie. Crones at the foot of the guillotine. Like that! That image will haunt my mind every time I see the Westmunster opposition leader get up to speak.'

Steve enjoys the image. 'Wonder whose heads are for the chop?'

Douglas wags his finger. 'Could well be the head of that very same person.'

'Decapitated leader and decapitated Party.' Steve hoots with laughter.

'Steve, this is Rosie and Dougie's twenty-fifth anniversary, don't forget. You're not at a Party meeting.'

'It's fine, Phyllis. It keeps the wee chaps happy.'

Douglas raises his glass to his wife. 'Look forward to another twenty-five years with you, Rosie. And more.' He goes to fetch another bottle of wine from the sideboard and does the rounds with it.

'Just as well we can walk home,' laughs Phyllis.

'Another glass and you'll no' be walking. It's me that'll have to carry you.' Phyllis makes a face at her husband.

'It's a special occasion,' says Rosie, lifting her glass to Steve.

'How's Holygood?' Steve asks Brian, with a wink at Douglas.

'Same as always.' Brian gives a curt laugh. 'You surely don't expect any change?'

'The building's to be changed — an extension for security or something. But no, politics isn't about to change. That would be like expecting Caledon's climate to turn tropical.'

'We had hopes at one time of change, of a more consensual approach,' reminded Dougie.

'Och, that was just a daydream. You're a headmaster, Dougie, you should know consensus is never going to break out. No' in the playground, no' in the Parliament.'

Douglas leans back in his chair and drapes his arms over the back. 'Perhaps with devolution we hoped for more reality.'

'Reality!' Steve settles himself for a good discussion. 'Which reality? Politicians have two— the one they spout and the one they're forced to live in.'

'You mean politicians have different realities according to circumstances? Interesting.' Brian helps himself to another of the chocolates his mother has put on the table in one of her good crystal dishes.

'Certainly looks like it when it comes to a debate on devo max, independence, whatever.' Steve's hand also shoots out for a chocolate.

Brian waves his chocolate in the air. 'The People's Union Party is perfectly clear where it stands on those issues?'

'Oh, yes!' His father looks sceptical. 'Where's your Party's vision, its ambition?'

Steve titters. 'Lost in a third reality — an alternative reality — never to be rediscovered.' He licks chocolate from his fingers.

Brian waves his hand. 'We're the ones who're realistic, who ask the hard question that need asked. You can't jump into the pit of the unknown, blindfolded. Heaven knows what you might end up with, apart from a hard landing.

Steve and Douglas shake their heads, and groan comically.

His mother looks up. 'Well, you know what George Bernard Shaw said in "Back to Methuselah". *You see things; and you say 'Why?' But I dream things that never were; and I say, "Why not?'*

19 - Informing on an informer

Schaw looks thinner. His face is gaunt and the steady, often truculent gaze of both truth and lies has been replaced by one of worn scepticism, while eyes that are watchful have taken over from unwavering scrutiny. The clothes he wore on the Friday morning he left, now have the appearance of having lived roughly and uncomfortably with him for several days.

He wants to drag Selina off to sit in Princess Gardens, on a bench overhung by the branches of still-bare trees in a secluded part of the area used mainly by those with a reason for privacy. But it is now dark and a chill wind funnels up the valley where the Nor Loch once flowed but where the railway now grinds and shrills.

Selena shivers, pulls her coat around her, and with one hand rearranges her scarf at her throat. To save money she eats a substantial breakfast before she leaves for work, and foregoes lunch, which even in the subsidised canteen, is expensive —especially if she opts for the healthy alternative to burger and chips. So she now feels hungry as well as cold, and is voluble in her annoyance at being dragged to this out-of-the-way corner of the gardens.

Reluctantly Schaw propels her by the arm back to Princess Street, along to the end and down Leitham Walk, in search of a quiet pub where they can have a drink and talk in privacy. Selina doesn't understand why all the secrecy, and why they can't head home.

She knows better than push him for an explanation for his absence — that is fruitless; she knows that from his previous disappearances. But she wonders why he is acting in this furtive manner. It's out of character.

Schaw pushes the battered door of one establishment. His head jerks back and forward like a pigeon's as he surveys the place. A dislike of something about the interior or the drinkers makes him grab her arm and hurry her further along the road.

'Schaw, this is ridiculous. I'm cold and I'm hungry. Tired, too. I've been on the go since seven this morning.'

He throws her a glance weighed with disdain. 'I've been on the go since Friday.'

They sit at a table in Schaw's chosen pub – a working men's howf from the look of the grim surroundings. Selina is no sooner settled, with her handbag and shiny black shoe carrier on the stool beside her, than Schaw decides to change tables. His second choice has a clearer view of door and clientele.

'I'll have a rum and coke,' says Selina. 'And get some crisps and nuts. Otherwise I'll collapse under the table from hunger. And I don't like the thought of any part of me meeting that manky floor.'

Her husband squirms from his seat and sidles to the bar to order. He returns and places her drink in front of her. A packet of cheese and onion crisps and one of cashew nuts are scliffed across the plastic table top, hatched with a random pattern of scratches and gouges. Selina throws out her hands to stop the packets continuing their journey over the edge. She selects the crisps and rips open the top of the packet.

'They suspect I'm a police informer.'

Her husband's head is bent over his drink and Selina wonders if she has heard correctly. 'What?'

'Either a police informer or a spook.' His hands cage the pint of beer.

'Eh? Who thinks—?' Selina's fingers with their cargo of crisps halt their journey to her mouth.

'A police informer or a spook! Classic. After all these bloody years of service.'

'Schaw, I haven't a clue—'

'No imagination.'

'Who?'

'Rich, too, when you think who's watching me! But maybe that's where the idea comes from. Informers informing on an informer.'

Selina's fingers drop the crisps back into the bag and push crisp and nut packets away from her. 'I don't understand what you're gibbering about. Where've you been the last week?' She never intended to ask the question but it's out now, so nothing to be done. She can hardly claw it back.

'Did you realise I was watched?'

A frown cuts the landscape of her brow. Selina slowly shakes her head. Is Schaw ill? Unknown to her, does he suffer from hallucinations? Is he on a drug that causes paranoia? 'No. I'm not aware of you being watched.'

'Must be a bloody good operation. Wasn't aware of it either. Maybe one or two peculiar instances, now I think of it — but nothing to raise my suspicions. And I'm careful. Always have been. Had that drummed into me. Jeez!' He takes a gulp of his beer as if it might be his last.

'You mean someone's following you? Why?'

'Why? Usual reasons.'

'Which are?'

'They suspect me.'

'Suspect you of what, for heaven's sake?'

'Dealing drugs, I understand.'

'But that's ridiculous!' Selina grips her glass more firmly. She looks at Schaw for confirmation of her assertion. 'Isn't it?' The words are half whispered, half gulped.

'Course it is. But the polis need to be given an excuse. And that's the most likely to interest them.'

Selina's body tenses. 'Let me get this straight. Someone told the police you're a drug dealer because they suspect you're a police informer—'

'Or a spook.'

'Or a spook, and want you to come under suspicion and be...taken out of circulation?'

'Looks like it...

'To save them — whoever them are — doing it?'

'Smells like it.'

'Oh, dear heaven! Who...who would do that?'

Schaw shrugs, hikes his eyebrows up his head. 'Pretty damn obvious.'

Selina sighs. Hits the table with her fists. 'Not to me, it isn't.'

Schaw grabs her hands to silence them. 'Don't draw attention to us, for goad's sake.'

'There isn't anyone whose attention I can draw. Just a guy over there, blootered like a soused herring, who looks as if he's trapped in seaweed. And a wee barmaid who wasn't sure whether she was giving you change of a kroner or a kopek.'

'But you never know. It's often the most unlikely...'

Selina's fingers rub at a stain on the table. 'Right. So tell me, who's spinning creative stories to the boys in blue.'

'Surely Charlie Kintail's daughter doesn't need to ask that!'

Selina raises her head to look at Schaw. Confusion is drawn on her face. 'What's my father got to do with anything?'

'Jeez, Selina!'

'Oh!' His wife's eyes open wide. Her mouth flaps in an attempt to force the words stuck in her throat out into the open. 'Jut.' The name is catapulted from her moth and explodes into the air.

'Shh!'

'Jut appeared last Saturday. Asked for you. Forced his way in.'

'Bloody hell. You all right?'

'Shaken.'

'He didn't…do anything?'

Selina shakes her head. 'No, but he's a scary guy. He…he left something.'

Schaw stares at her, his mouth twitching. 'Left what?'

His wife tells him of the piece of paper left in her bed, a piece of paper with a logo printed on it.

'That settles it. Drink up.'

'I don't feel like it.'

Schaw throws his head back and pours three quarters of his beer down his throat, places the glass on the table and dashes a hand across his mouth. His hand then shoots out to grasp his wife's arm and pull her from her seat. 'Let's go.'

'We can have a drink at home. Well, you can. I'm fine with tea.'

Schaw checks his watch, waggles his head as he calculates. 'No time. Got to shift ourselves.'

'No time for what?'

'Distractions. Like eating. Least not till we're on our way.' Schaw half pulls, half pushes his wife out into the street and searches for a taxi, arms waving like a tree in a gale.

When seated in the back of a cab en route for home, he gives his wife her instructions in a low, insistent voice. 'I'll wait in the cab, right. Engine running. Meter running. So two minutes. Grab a few clothes for us both. Something warm. Just a small case, though. And maybe a bag. Never mind toiletries and stuff. We can buy these on board, or when we arrive. Okay?'

His wife nods, flustered, but understands he is serious so she needs to follow his instructions.

'Passports,' she croaks. 'What about—?'

'Never mind passports. Other arrangements.'

'What d'you— ?'

'Hurry. Or we'll miss the train.'

20 - She enjoys anything

Lippy replaces the phone on its charger. Grins. Hugs herself. A theatre company is interested in her play. Perhaps even for performances during the festival if she can finalise it. The director wants to read the draft. Had a brainwave about who could play the leading roles. If they are available. It is down to Lippy to deliver. She curses Ramsay, genteelly. In the cafe when she thought they had progressed, when she thought they were off somewhere quiet to talk about his experiences, he took cold feet and bolted back to his seaside hideout.

She sighs. It's not as if he committed a major crime like murder or arson. All the man did was fiddle his Parliamentary expenses in the manner approved by his Party and a large part of the political establishment. Expenses were seen as a perk of the job, a necessity for poorly paid MPs to live in the manner Westmunster believed appropriate to rulers of the realm, and to keepers of the flame of Empire. Everyone was at it. Or most. Expenses, directorships and any other freebies on offer. Wrong, of course, yet accepted. And Ramsay was a fairly minor offender. A minnow compared to the political bully boy whales. The bigger miscreants could ensure colleagues watched their backs, ready with alibis, defences, justifications if necessary, in return for similar favours should their names be paraded in the media.

Ramsay was short on back-watchers, had even, on more than one occasion, been told he was too honest for his own good. So was seen as the ideal fall-guy, a tasty piece of meat to throw to the lions. Ramsay was the expendable idiot whose demeaning and demotion would satisfy the media's and the public's demand for payment, for retribution. The fall-guy, so others, faces straight and pleading honesty, could intone how reprehensible his actions had been, whilst they ensured their own backs were well covered as their own perks piled in.

Lippy is aware of an alternative hierarchy in most political parties, an unofficial clique at a distance from the leader, whose hands can be seen to remain clean. The clique usually does the necessary —mucks out stables to ensure the spotless credibility of the party, whips the beast to gallop to win or succeed. At times, when leadership change is deemed necessary or unavoidable for the good of Party and country, the men in grey rise to the challenge, do what is necessary and advise the leader to go as he, or she, no longer rides on the trust of Members or followers.

Lippy has no idea whether these 'men in grey' are the same people who muck out stables and deal with problems and people like Ramsay. Or whether certain of the more menial duties are delegated to keep the hands of the grey men clean. Or whether another unofficial clique, perhaps devolved, perhaps stand-alone, exists to deal with the minions.

Ramsay was certainly done over by a clique in the People's Union Party. He knows it and she knows it. But she is no wiser as to structure and identities.

She taps her pen on her desk in frustration. Tomorrow she'll phone Ramsay again. If he doesn't answer she'll drive down to his lair and squat beside Jess until she receives answers. Meantime, to the kitchen, to throw together a sandwich to munch with a quick cup of coffee before she changes. She thinks she'll wear the dress she wore the evening Derek and Gail came to dinner, though she hopes the evening will turn out more satisfactory. Tonight she is off to Parliament — to a reception in the Garden Lobby.

The process is similar to the preliminaries prior to a flight. No customs, but security is much the same. Coat and handbag in plastic tray. Shoes off. Watch and jewellery stowed in handbag that has disappeared into the maw of the scanner. She knows if she wears them a bleep will earn her a frisk by a woman with the build and look of a jailer. Why does she always feel guilty as she goes through security? No sgian dubh snuggles in her cleavage, no plastic explosive in her beads. Yet she invariably expects to feel the vice-like hand of a security officer on her shoulder, the other in the small of her back, to guide her towards the interrogation chamber. She can almost see the rack, the thumb-screws, the tray of hypodermics with truth-inducing drugs. Oversight of the third-degree operation is by a scar-faced, leopard-stroking ringmaster wearing the braid-adorned hat of a senior security officer.

The press of bodies behind her forces her through the scanner. Once through, she stops. No bleep sounded. Relief. But why does she feel the impulse to stride across to the officious-looking guy over there to insist there was a malfunction. That in the hem of her dress lurks…whatever.

She shakes herself. The crush behind propels her forward to reclaim her coat and other belongings and to make for the cloakroom.

A queue trails from one of the desks in the reception area where invitations are checked. Lippy flaps hers like a fan. She feels warm. Those already processed hang about like bees hovering around a patch of flowers. A few examine a wall of display stands with an exhibition. The letter or letters of a previous grandee are on display. Lippy's curiosity is aroused. She wants to look but doesn't want to lose her place in the queue.

This is not the first time she has been in the Caledon Parliament. Occasionally she comes to watch debates. The better ones are pure theatre, but more often they resemble dire rehearsals. Whichever she sees is immaterial as they provide her with valuable insights into human behaviour, and ideas for her characters and plots. In the past she has attended events here, too, having received invitations to various receptions. The reception this evening is for a writers' organisation of which she is a member and occasional office bearer.

A friendly MCP who supports writers and writing and other cultural matters agreed to host the event. No doubt, for there are benefits in being seen to engage with the riff-raff, a few other MCPs will put in a brief appearance as they wend their way between office and the exit that leads to home, or to local pad. Expenses again. Though Caledon has kept these under a tight rein.

At last she is approved, a badge clipped to her lapel in evidence, and can take in the exhibition, though she barely has time to glance at the panels before an official appears to drive them, like a sheep dog marshalling errant sheep, through convoluted corridors to the Garden Lobby.

Glass of wine in hand, Lippy samples the nibbles being waitered around by a pack of girls in white shirts, black trousers and waistcoats. Like magpies. Lippy doesn't like the look. To her mind, there is no valid reason for people who serve nibbles to be men, so why dress women as if they were. Surely the Caledon Parliament is meant to be different, yet here it is slipping back into stereotypes. She decides to raise the matter with whichever MCP she can collar.

Other groups are ushered into the Lobby to join the melee. The volume of chat rises as clusters form, greetings are loud, stories animated. Lippy wanders around and exchanges a few words with acquaintances. She bumps into Marsha, her publisher, who is desperately trying to avoid writers in search of publishers, then joins a group of fellow authors and listens to their moans about publishers and the quality of e-books. A flutter of comments swirls around as the MCP hosting the event makes an appearance with his entourage.

The chairwoman of the organisation bustles up to him, the smile on her face ingratiating, pushing out towards him. She gushes, the MCP is enthusiastic but formal, and wants his part in the event over speedily so he can repair to a nearby restaurant. An imposing staircase waterfalls into the Lobby, its bottom steps widen and curve to make an impromptu platform. The chairwoman and MCP climb the first half dozen steps and stand like actors on a set, ready to woo the audience with their lines. Chairwoman speaks of her gratitude, her delight, her hopes. MCP effortlessly kicks a joke to his audience, flatters, lobs selected bon mots of encouragement before he rejoins his entourage who form around him like a shell, to protect him from those who want to field questions or make innocuous remarks.

The chairwoman, the main part of her starring role over, leaves the elevation of the stairs to mix with her subjects. She has played the role for nearly a decade, guider of their efforts and vetoer of their perceived excesses. She may be one of their women in grey.

'That's it then,' says Lippy. 'How many minutes of his time did the MCP deign to devote to us? Three?'

'He's very busy,' says one of her companions, an author of romantic novels. 'It was good of him to come.'

Lippy looks at her in surprise. 'That's what we pay him for. You and me. And everyone else here.' The woman looks affronted by her response.

Lippy is about to turn away when a thought flashes across her mind and stops her. The woman who believes MCPs attend such events out of the goodness of their hearts reminds her of herself, a younger, more naïve version of herself — herself as she was that summer with Eilidh. Thankfully she has changed since then, become less of a wimp. She has learned to question, stand up for herself and her beliefs, challenge others when she thinks them wrong. Perhaps she has Eilidh to thank for that. Perhaps —though a hard way to learn a lesson.

Years ago, she met a guy who insisted people never changed, but developed. Is that true? Is your character set in your genes, unable to be altered in any way, except through your development as a person? If she thinks of an apple seed, she supposes it might be true. The seed develops into a seedling, to a plant, and over years into a tree that bears fruits that contain more seeds. So she can appreciate the development argument, a case of natural evolution, she supposes. But she isn't so sure the same applies to human beings who have brains to think and feelings that develop, yes — but surely these thoughts and feelings can also bring about real change. If, between childhood and now, she has developed, then she is certain that development has made her a different person, changed her into a more outgoing woman, more comfortable in her own skin. So are development and change the same? Different? Development, change. Whatever the process, she is no longer the same person she was that summer. Eilidh's treachery ensured that.

With a roll of her eyes, a tall, reedy woman who writes historical who-done-its (Agatha Christie meets frilly eighteenth century) moves the conversation back to well-worn channels and Lippy moves off from the knot of people, her thoughts stifled before uttered.

From a passing tray she liberates another glass of wine, though she thinks vinegar a more appropriate name, when a voice behind her exclaims, 'Lippy! Is that you, dearest? Jingle jangles, it is!'

'Jasmine! Long time no see.'

'Thought I recognised the voice berating that misguided woman. How are you?'

'Same as always. You?'

'Oh, telling myself I'm enjoying my new job.'

'Wondered why you'd put in an appearance at the Callyman.'

'Needs must, dearest. Needs must. Journalism is not what it used to be. The Internet is playing havoc with standards. You have no idea how difficult it is to find an angle on a story that has not been covered ad infinitum on the bloody Internet.'

'Yet in a few weeks you've made your name known on the Callyman.'

'Not hard. Though I fear for the harm it might cause my reputation.'

'I didn't expect to see you here.'

'Our dedicated chairwoman sent me an invitation. I suspect she wanted to swell the hordes to impress that smarmy MCP who dipped in, wrinkled his nose, and flew out.'

'Why should she want to impress him?'

"She belongs to his Party. I rather think her sights are chasing an OBE, perhaps even an MBE. For services rendered to writing, of course.'

'I see. More fool her.'

'Good luck to her, I say. It's grab what you can time.'

'Another flurry of activity. Have we more illustrious visitors? Looks like it.' They waggle heads to see who has descended to the Garden Lobby from on high.

'I should really shoot off,' says Jasmine as she checks her watch. 'Only popped in to see what was on the boil, and so I could assure our chairwoman I was here.'

'Who's that?'

'The MCP? Haven't a...no wait. Oh, Lippy, my dear. You must meet this character. A laugh a minute, I guarantee.' Jasmine steers Lippy by the arm to the side of the MCP who has been abandoned by the chairwoman after a brief welcome and farewell. 'Ming, dearest, how good to see you again. The piece on your morning routine hasn't been forgotten. Just awaits an appropriate slot in the paper. So keep your eyes peeled.'

'Err, right…though—'

'So wonderful of you to provide such good material for a story! The toiletries were inspired. I still intend to follow up on them — once the weather is warmer.' Her hand touches Ming's arm. 'And the photos of your family… So heartrending.'

'I hope the article… Not too long before it appears, I hope?'

'Keep reading, Ming, keep reading.' She taps his arm reassuringly. Ming's face glows. 'So sorry, I should have introduced my friend. This is the writer, Lippy Nevis.'

Ming's face registers that a bell has rung somewhere in his head. 'Pleased to meet you. Writer, did you say?'

Lippy sticks out her hand to be slid over by his. It feels like being stroked by a wet fish. 'Yes. I write novels. At present I'm finishing a play about —'

'Lippy Nevis! How good to meet you,' Ming gushes. Lippy looks taken aback. 'I've a copy of your book. You signed it. Has my name on it. My wife bought it for me.'

Lippy remembers the woman with the chunks of rock and yellow plastic around her neck at her last book signing. So this is husband-with-all-the-mobiles Ming. 'I hope you enjoy the book.'

'Mmm. Perhaps…not quite my taste in reading matter. Us MCPs have so little time for fiction.'

'Maybe your wife will enjoy it.'

'Oh, she's bound to. She enjoys anything. Comics, magazines, any old rubbish.'

The face of the young guy beside Ming cringes in embarrassment. 'Other people for you to meet, Ming,' he mutters.

'Of course, Brian, of course.' An oily smile flows over Ming's face. 'What it is to be popular, eh! Excuse me ladies. Good to meet you.'

Brian throws a look of apology towards Jasmine and Lippy as he steers his charge through the knots of people chatting in the Lobby.

'Wow!'

Jasmine starts to giggle. 'I had to write a piece on that idiot. Can you believe it!'

'Poor you.'

'I thought I did brilliantly. But the editor isn't so sure.'

'Can't be your writing, so why…'

'On combat duty.'

Lippy looks puzzled. 'Combat duty?'

'Yup. Old bastard's a member of the same Party — People's Union — so challenges or vetoes any piece that, in his flaky opinion, could damage them.'

'Old Boys Network writ large.'

'Absolutely. He has this thing about women, too. Sexist bastard. No, I didn't say that. Got to stay focussed and positive.'

'What was Ming what's-his-name like to interview?'

'An absolute hoot. He turned up with these toiletries. Fair enough it was a lifestyle piece on how MCPs start their days. Then he brought up this stuff on his ancestry.'

'Different. Pity your editor has vetoed it.'

'Oh, he'll probably capitulate…if I make the changes he wants.'

'You need to toe the line.'

'Mmm. Always been the case, but either it's become worse or I've reached the age when it irks more. I'm sick of promoting shallow, second-rate idiots like Ming thingummyjig at the expense of half-decent politicians.'

'Poor Jasmine. In the doldrums this evening.'

Jasmine throws her head back. 'Nothing a good story wouldn't cure. But I probably should make the changes to the Ming piece. Keep my employers happy.'

'As you say, think positive.'

'I suppose a follow up piece on Ming is always possible — if at any time I'm totally and absolutely stuck.'

'As bad as that?'

'It was the old photo. Jingle jangle! If I had a family photo of great grannie in rags, last thing I'd do is flout it — especially to a journalist. I wanted to know if he jogged, how long he spent on the rowing machine — that kind of thing. And there he was, flapping this photo in my face. I couldn't get away from the wee creep fast enough. Oh, the low points of a journalist's job.'

'Commiserations.' Lippy chortles. 'She enjoys anything. Comics, magazines, any old rubbish.' She mimics the MCP. "How do idiots like that get into Parliament?"

'Easy?'

'Easy! How?'

'They wheedle, strong-arm, blackmail or otherwise persuade the necessary people.'

'The play I'm presently tweaking and polishing has a plot not a million miles from that.'

'Sounds interesting.'

'Hopefully. But I need to tie down Ramsay Dunn to dot and cross the necessary details.'

'Ramsay... The guy who was done for fiddling his expenses?'

'The same.'

'Do tell more.'

'I'm sure he was made the fall-guy.'

'Wouldn't be surprised.'

'You know something about it?'

'I might?'

'Willing to share it?'

'Perhaps.'

'So?'

'Not here.' Jasmine glances around.

'Where then?'

Jasmine checks her watch again, a Gucci with a black face and large link gold bracelet. 'Need to rush, dearest. Lunch on Tuesday?'

'Fine by me.'

'Here's my card.' She thrusts a business card from her pocket at Lippy. 'Give me a time and place and I'll be there. Good to catch up.'

21 - A slug of acid

It hits him as soon as he enters the building — an atmosphere like steel shavings. Jaggy, ready to scrape egos, squeeze thought and enmesh the uncertain in a tangle of endless strands. Steel spaghetti. Like a seaweed cage. Brian feels as if he is walking through a Brillo pad, with little certainty he will reach the other side. The steel shavings have gouged their way in, infiltrated every cranny, caused rust, promoted decay, a chemical reaction has formed sizzling acid that corrodes and eats through the very girders of the Party.

Though still early, the corridors on his Party's floor of the Parliament thrum, twang as if a harp of steel hawsers is being plucked by giant fingers. Other staff have arrived early like him as the Sunday papers left them in no doubt of the serious work ahead. Faces are haggard, the result of weekend revelries, and unpalatable media coverage. Both have taken their toll. Voices boom loudly. They query, question, insist the stories are a ploy by a governing Party that does little more than play at politics, up to its dirty tricks again. Ocean deep anger storms from wall to wall, smashes words and warps expressions. The anger swells and swirls, is caught up in the steel shavings where it gets twisted and corkscrewed and becomes destructive.

'Not true.'

'Can't be true.'

'No way.'

'We've back-pedalled of late. Can't deny that.'

'Opinion polls not good for us either.'

'A blip, that's all. Nothing to worry about.'

'But the stuff in the media…'

'Garbage.'

'Mutt has been subdued of late.'

'Busy. Pre-election preparations.'

'Aye, it's just over a year away.'

'No time at all.'

'We're still ahead. Have a substantial lead.'

'But reducing. Steadily.'

'So time to stand and fight, not cower.'

'Who says we're cowering?'

'That bilge in the Sunday papers isn't good.'

'A concerted attack.'

'Dirty bastards.'

Brian drags himself away and with reluctant steps enters the office where he knows a pile of newspapers will greet him, and gleefully retell the stories that already fill his mind after his trawl through the Sunday editions and this morning's online coverage. He wonders whether he should tip the pile into the wastepaper basket, but there are too many, and they'll overflow, spill around it and across the floor. He can't sit and look at them as their front pages leer at him, and spew out a load of rubbish about the Party, and about Mutt, their leader. The sight of them is too disconcerting. He doesn't need to pick up the top paper to read the headlines as he already knows them by heart. Someone has done a thorough job.

A well-planned attack has been let loose against them, headlining in every news outlet. Nor do the lurid accusations stop with the front pages but run into full page spreads in other sections of the papers. Journalists have been fed a travesty of half-truths, massaged facts, quotes taken out of context, unsupported allegations and Photoshopped images. Mutt's private life is savaged with comments from call girls, copies of supposed emails of a highly suggestive nature, and more doctored photographs. In one rag, Stella Silveri, whose photograph looks suspiciously like a page three blonde, provides graphic descriptions of sex romps, threesomes and other mind-boggling combinations, complete with dates, and details of what they had for dinner. A broadsheet omits much of the bedroom allegations carried by the red tops but features donations to both leader and Party and tracks their course. The media is in full hunting pursuit, its gasps of indignation and howls of frothing rage pound through fields of stories. With rousing cries and horns blasting, they chase a chimeric fox across rutted fields and the sucking goo of swamps.

The former secretary to the CEO of a large company gushes details of what the knighthood to her boss cost in terms of cash, shares, holidays and other inducements. And then there are the reams of space devoted to the jollies and the lolly targeted to guarantee the burial of potential legislation — by votes for or against — or the emasculation of it to the point where it became an irrelevance. More columns of figures and a sprinkle of dates fill another section of page. Quotes from vociferous trade unionists and party members insist on investigations, radical change, the necessity for heads to roll. And the head everyone apparently wants to roll is Mutt's. Overnight, he has become a liability. Mutt must go.

In the course of one weekend Party and leader are comprehensively trashed on the flimsiest of evidence and manufactured fairy-tales. Brian feels saddened. Is this really what now passes for journalism? For democracy? He sighs, for he knows it is.

The governing Party are responsible, of course — so those around him believe, if he goes by comments he still hears rattling backwards and forwards along the corridor. The Callyparty has sunk to black propaganda. The nasty twits, steeped in bile and shit. Strident voices hope Mutt has organised suitable retribution, an appropriate response that kicks the bastards where it will hurt and seriously damage future hopes. The Party needs to rally, and teach those sewer rats a lesson they won't forget.

Brian stares at the pile of papers, his mind strangely blank. Retribution? Yes he'll support that. But retribution is never easy in politics, especially when an election hurtles down the line like a steam train out to beat a record. Election strategy can't be derailed by an all-out attack on their opponents, no matter how hated they are. The election has to come first, to win that convincingly will be the ultimate retribution. That is the sensible tack. But he knows the demands, especially by backbenchers, for immediate action will be hard to ignore.

And one or two of the comment pieces amongst the heaps of garbage are spot on. They hit home with Brian. Mutt does have his drawbacks as leader. He can mirror Ming in the way he deals with members of the public — that writer woman for instance. For heaven's sake couldn't the guy just have confirmed his wife would greatly enjoy the book and leave it at that. But no! Ming has to add a slug of acid to the brew.

And if he is really honest, which he thinks it necessary to be with himself at this juncture, then Mutt has a smidgen of Ming's gaucheness. After nearly thirty years in politics he shouldn't have. But there it is. He does. A touch of the foot in mouth. Though much superior to Ming in most other ways, he lacks the elusive ingredient that transforms a competent, or at least reasonably good, councillor in local government into a bloody good Party leader.

Wired into the DNA of a few lucky people is that magic ingredient — whether it is a sense of presence, well-honed communication skills, a thorough grasp of policy (your own Party's and those of other parties for comparison) and an inherent understanding of how people and politics work. Mutt is reasonably intelligent, has achieved good things within the Party, redrawing and revamping policies for instance, when they bothered with these. He wasn't a bad speaker and could enthuse Party members, but he falls far short of being an orator who can swell hearts and move minds.

Brian sighs. If forces both without and within the Party are pushing for Mutt to be replaced, what are the alternatives? Too dire to contemplate, is his first reaction. The deputy leader, Brankton, is known to have ambitions. But he is the right side of fifty, so has time to realise these when Mutt eventually stands down. Presumably at some unspecified time in the future after his stint in government as First Minister. Yet if Mutt is pushed into resignation now, to provide a successor with a clear but truncated run to the election, then Brankton is the obvious successor. No, that would be madness. With their cumbersome leadership process, they'd be half-way to the election before he was in place. Though he supposes Brankton can argue that as deputy he'll become transitional leader as soon as Mutt steps down, so the campaign can continue unhindered with him sharpening its blades, until the new leader is in place. And if the new leader is him…

Brian shakes himself. Is he questioning whether the Sunday onslaught is anything other than a dirty tricks campaign by their opponents? He decides he doesn't want to answer the question. The answer might be uncomfortable. He chivvies himself into action, sweeps the bundle of newspapers into his arms, staggers through the door, and dumps them in the corridor outside the office. They slide across the carpet like a broken fan, and somehow lose some of their importance. Brian wipes one hand against the other as he turns his back. At least he won't now have to eyeball them on his desk.

He hears Ming's approach down the corridor as he zigzags from one side to the other, exchanging views on what needs to be done as he pops his head into other offices and shouts comments about the need to get their own back on the maggoty lot in government.

'That corridor's like a recycling tip,' he complains as he barges through the door. 'Get onto the appropriate gaffer to remove the garbage.'

'A recycling tip?' Brian goes to look. Outside each office door splays a pile of newspapers. They form a paper pathway along both sides of the corridor. He grins. Guess he started a trend.

Ming stomps through to his office, then returns to perch on Brian's desk.'

'So, your thoughts?'

'Brian knows to play careful. 'Much the same as everyone's, I would think.'

'Bloody bastards. There should be rules against this sort of thing. A law should be passed. Defamation of Party and person.'

'You're one of the law passers, Ming.'

'It's not right. It's…it's…' His fist thuds the desk.

'I seem to remember, when such a bill was under discussion, your tack, was the need to retain free speech, the right to freedom of expression. A free press.'

'That was different.' He picks up a letter from Brian's desk and glances at it.

Brian decides it is best to be conciliatory. 'I suppose it was.' He takes the letter from Ming's hand and returns it to his correspondence pile.

'Any word of a meeting? A talk from Mutt?'

'Not as yet.'

'What, nothing?'

'Nothing.'

'Hmm. Perhaps I should have a word.'

'With Mutt?'

'Yes.'

'Is that wise? I mean—'

'You suggesting Mutt won't listen to my advice?'

'No…not exactly. I'm sure he'll take all advice into account when he's ready. It's just…'

'Just…?'

Brian swallows. 'Busy. He must be extremely busy — in consultation with the Shadow Cabinet, Headquarters. Working out a campaign plan. I'm sure he'll appreciate your input when he's had time to gather his thoughts and ideas.'

'Mutt has had three bloody years to gather his thoughts and ideas. And where has that brought us? Eh? To this sorry state. With a bloody election staring us in the face.' He glowers at Brian.'

'The opinion polls still show us in the lead.'

'Pah! Tell me, if you can, what d'you think of Brankton?'

Brian gasps a breath. 'Brankton? He's…personable. Keen. A tad… arrogant perhaps, though that may just be my impression. I don't know the guy that well. Good on policy — though as many of our policies are under review and have been for… Look, Ming, I'm not sure I'd be in favour of a change of leader at present, of ditching Mutt for someone else — Brankton or whoever.'

'Suddenly found an opinion, have you?'

'A leadership change would give credence to the stories.'

'Not if Mutt suffered...say a heart attack, and resigned for health reasons.'

'The election is approaching—'

'Exactly why we need strong leadership. And an end to this namby-pamby stance. We need a man who can go for the jugular. Strong. Decisive. A man who can lead us over the winning line with a margin to spare.'

'Yes, but—'

'A man who can crush the bloody Callyparty.'

'But a leadership campaign takes time, Ming. Time we don't have.'

'Who said anything about a campaign?'

22 - Good fish, chips not bad

Schaw sits hunched in the taxi. He refuses to talk, refuses to say where he has been or where they are headed. Selina watches the lights of houses, shops and offices slither past, a small case at her feet, an overnight bag clutched on her lap. They are driving back towards the city centre, retracing the route taken in the other direction not long before. The cab stops at traffic lights.

Schaw sits forward, his feet anxiously tap the floor. In the artificial light from the outside world his face has a peculiar colour — yellowish with green and purple tinges. It appears thinner with the bags beneath his eyes more pronounced. He looks at his watch but has to swivel towards the window and raise his wrist to the outside lights to read it. His mouth pulls to a straight line, lips compressed. 'Come on, come on, come on,' he breathes rather than says. The driver ignores him, probably can't hear him. Schaw's hands are restless. They tap and squeeze his knees, scratch his neck, then dive for cover into his jacket, to reappear with his wallet. Peeled open, he fans through the notes before he extracts a couple. The wallet is returned to his pocket while the notes remain clutched in his hand.

As she watches the outside world pass, Selina again wonders where Schaw is taking her and why they need to leave. What about her job? Non-appearance is not looked on kindly unless your excuse is cast iron, so she's in danger of losing it, and then what will they do? What will she do for money? Jobs are difficult to come by these days, even jobs in department stores. Her husband's job probably went several days ago when his firm didn't hear from him. Unless he took holidays. So much she doesn't know, she feels as if they are caught up in a game of blind man's buff in the pitch dark.

Money! What about money? They'll need money and she can't remember how much remains in her purse. But they can always find an ATM. In silence, she frets about how little time she had to pack and of the clothes, toiletries and makeup she will need to do without. Why the rush? She doesn't understand. When she glances at her husband she is horrified by the weariness and apprehension in every line of his face and a pallor that has a very unhealthy tinge. That frightens her, yet it also melts much of her annoyance with him, and the idea ripples through her mind that she would like to reach out her hand and stroke his, or, if possible, put her arms around him in a cuddle of reassurance. The feeling underlines her worry, as embracing her husband is an act long out of fashion. Emotions and feelings are kept to themselves, confined in their own hearts and minds, caged.

They roll in to Waverlie Station. The taxi halts with a squeal of brakes. Schaw jumps out, shoves notes into the driver's hand and without waiting for change, pulls Selina from the cab and rushes her across the concourse to the ticket office. He looks at his watch again, looks at the station clock. 'Come on, come on,' he fumes.

Selina notices a newsagent, still open, and is about to make for it to buy crisps or chocolate, when Schaw thuds his hand into her back and propels her through the station towards a platform. 'Move. It's about to leave. With a wave of their tickets they sprint onto the platform as the train clanks into motion. Schaw wrests open a carriage door, throws in the case and bag and thrusts Selina on after them. As she gathers herself and the bags her husband lands at her side.

'Whew! That was close.' He drags himself to his feet, dusts the knees of his trousers. 'Through here.' He leads her further along the train until he stops at empty seats and stows the luggage on the rack above. He struggles out of his padded jacket and slouches into a seat.

It dawns on Selina she still doesn't know where they're headed. Earlier, Schaw mentioned buying stuff on board, that sounded like a ship as trains didn't boast shops, and the offering on planes was limited. But at present they're on a train hurtling through the darkness to an unknown destination. 'Schaw, where are we going?'

'Not now Selina.'

'But—'

'Later. I'll tell you later.'

So she has to content herself. She sits back in the seat and closes her eyes. Her Kindle is in the bag — she threw it in with a few grabbed clothes — but doesn't want to disturb Schaw by asking him to get the bag down, and besides, her mind and thoughts are in too much turmoil to read. Perhaps later, if the journey drags. Meanwhile she uses the time to untangle and rewind the little her husband told her, figure out who he referred to, why certain people want the police to believe he's involved with drugs, where scary Jut fits. In her mind she sees again the piece of paper with the logo, the same logo she occasionally saw when her father was an MP. Unconnected pieces of information rattle around her mind like parts of a jigsaw, but she can't make them fit together, though a sinking feeling in her stomach tells her they do, and she might not like the completed image.

The movement of the train jolts her. She can't remember when she was last on a train. Years ago. Probably the time she, Schaw and her mother travelled down to Westmunster for her father's retirement party. The size and lavishness of the celebration, held in a large central hotel, surprised them, blew them away. Still, they supposed, his years there meant he knew hundreds of people — those who worked in and around parliament, people he came into contact with through the committees he sat on, the visits he undertook, the speeches he gave, his campaigning, the many fundraising projects he was involved with, a few businesses he had an involvement with. Charlie was always busy. If he wasn't wearing himself out for his constituents, then it was for the Party. His dedication deserved a medal, perhaps even a gong. Charlie would like a gong, her mother sometimes said.

All that evening, colleagues, friends and acquaintances trailed in and out, slapped backs, threw their arms around his shoulders, laughed very loudly at nothing, squeezed hands, exchanged knowing looks and innocent words loaded with meaning.

Her father was the centre of attention, but Schaw seemed to know people too and he spent the evening in banter and earnest tête-à-têtes, while she and her mother sat at a table and admired the décor. Her mother constantly exclaimed over the chandeliers — how big, how glittery, how expensive they must have been.

'It's a hotel Ma. The function suite.'

'Look at the size of the mirrors, the gilded frames.'

'What about them.'

'Not bought in the Co-op, I wouldn't think.'

'Unlikely, Ma.'

Occasionally her father had sallied over, and with a benevolent, well-oiled smile burnishing his face, asked if their drinks needed replenished. Once or twice he towed a woman across the sea of floor to introduce them. But neither she nor her mother had much in common with these elegant figurines with their chromium lives and eggshell chatter, so they departed fairly swiftly to be swallowed by the swirling mass of promenaders. Both Selina and her mother had bought new outfits for the occasion. Charlie had been generous in his donation of money to foot the bill, but Selina realised as she studied the other women in the room that their outfits were high street while many of the others were haute couture, or if not quite that then pretty damn close.

The evening was a watershed. After years of her mother's marriage, and of her own formative years, it brought home to both how little they knew about the man. He rode two personas at home, family man and constituency worker; and a further two, MP and bon viveur, down here. Four different people, two distinct lives, Selina thought. Two lives at odds with one another. Were both real or was one a sham, a façade for the other?

Four people, two lives, and that was without taking into account his other activities of which she knew almost nothing — manipulator and fixer, so her mother had let drop not long before her wedding to Schaw. Manipulator and fixer of what? She was kept in the dark about that, with her mother knowing little more. That added another persona. Five different people inhabiting the same skeleton, the same polished and perfumed skin, the same cunning mind. She wondered if she or her mother knew the man at all. They were compartmentalised into a small segment of his life that barely impacted on the remainder of it.

And the man who sits, blank-eyed, staring through the carriage window, unaware of the dark landscape features outside, is a man in a similar mould. Schaw isn't the same, he lacks her father's engaging charm, his streak of utter ruthlessness. That trait had only come to the surface after his death, gleaned from the odd phrase in a letter, a few files of photographs whose significance she refused to acknowledge by placing a name on them, the occasional remark dropped by Schaw. Her mother shut her mind, said she would hear nothing derogatory about the man who had been a good husband and father, but Selina knew that however much they wanted to deny it, Charlie had brokered...incidents... occurrences that were highly questionable. Beside the colossus that was her father, Schaw is a mere maquette.

The taxi takes them to a small hotel near the station that is accustomed to late arrivals. The receptionist is a chirpy guy in his fifties whose trim figure fights a losing battle with flab, though gives the impression of previous athleticism. His squashed nose, and an eyebrow that veers jaggedly in the middle, suggests a boxer. Perhaps night receptionist in a city centre hotel is an obvious career move for an ex-boxer, thinks Selina. A key secured to a large brass tag is handed over by a hand, square in shape with prominent knuckles, which also points them in the direction of a nearby fish and chip shop that remains open till midnight.

'Good fish, chips not bad. But by this time, folks, both are probably crispy outside, soggy inside.' He shrugs. 'But if you want to eat…'

A young woman is stacking chairs on top of tables when they arrive. She looks up and growls to someone in the back shop. She continues to pile up the chairs, sending a message that if they want to make a purchase the great outdoors will be their restaurant. The woman disappears through to the back, then returns with a pail and mop. Selina reckons they have about thirty seconds to complete their purchase before the mop hassles their feet.

Outside the wind blows rubbish along the street. A knot of youngsters, voices loud, sing and swear as they zigzag towards them. Selina tucks her arm through Schaw's, and folds herself in his lee while they rollick past. Schaw follows them with his eyes until they recede into the distance, then hands her the box with her meal and they walk back to the hotel. Outside, a plastic table with a large ashtray full of cigarette ends, and some chairs provide an area for smokers, and for those in search of a place to eat late night fish suppers. The wind blows rain and rubbish along the street, and a nearby banner for a ten kilometre race flaps angrily between its lamp posts. Selina huddles into a chair and leans over the cardboard container on her lap in the hope of keeping her meal dry. The chips are lukewarm, their greasiness cloys her tongue, and the fish batter has long since lost its crispness and become slimy and tough. Part of her wants to throw it away, but she is hungry and perseveres.

Schaw crumples his box, and throws it on the table. 'Could've done with a drink.'

'There's a kettle in the room. We can have coffee or tea.'

He doesn't reply.

The roar and clatter of traffic wakens her. Selina didn't expect to sleep. Despite her exhaustion she was wound up about Schaw, about his reappearance, about his behaviour and his dragging her off to she doesn't know where. The fish and chips wallowed in her stomach like a dead whale and despite brushing her teeth their greasiness remained in her mouth. Used to the relative quiet of their flat, the noise of traffic grinding past on the road outside the hotel room rarely lessened as late evening became early morning. Her husband began to snore almost as soon as his head hit the pillow. Before he collapsed into bed he had checked the window, ensured the door was locked and wedged the chair by the dressing table beneath the handle. He swept up the small case and was about to add it to the door defences when it dawned on him it would be tantamount to adding a brick to the top of a dam, so he threw it into a corner. At some point, after she restlessly tossed and turned, she fell asleep.

The clock shows it is just before eight. The bed beside her is cold. Selina listens. No sound from the cupboard that is the bathroom. She props herself up on her elbow. No sign of her husband. His padded jacket hangs over the back of the chair that was on door duty so he has obviously gone out, but probably not far. She glances around. The décor looks even sadder in daylight than it did the evening before — eighties fantastic, still hanging around thirty years later. The dark green and red with cream stripes held apart, never to meet or clash, by a deep border of rococo swirls that are repeated in the dark carpet. The curtains, though, are light and bloom with cabbage roses. The walls feel as if they crowd in on her, with intent to smother or otherwise extinguish feeling and all aesthetic thoughts. Selina wriggles into a sitting position, and rubs her arms. The small case contained no nightgown so she slept in her pants, and with no dressing gown to throw round her she feels cold.

As she braves a tepid shower, the thought crosses her mind that Schaw might have dumped her, decamped on his own and left her to manage as best she can. But why do that now? He could have ditched her any time since he caught up with her yesterday. So she expects him to return, in which case she should stir herself, dress to be ready for breakfast when he reappears.

She's ready now, and sits on the bed waiting for him. Her mind wanders to work. She feels guilty, for she will be regarded as having let her department down by her non-appearance, and staff who let the store down have a habit of losing their positions. Perhaps if she explains... But what can she say? She shakes herself and goes over to the chair with Schaw's jacket, feels in the pockets. She pulls out his mobile. Switched off. She wonders why, remembers he hasn't used it since reappearing. If she switches it on she can phone the store, make an excuse for being away for a few days, perhaps save her job. The phone jangles to life, downloads messages, notices of missed calls that confuse her. Her phone had been a basic one, not a piece of electronic wizardry, but she had dropped it into a puddle last winter and after a few weeks of ambivalence it had decided to die. As she rarely used it she hadn't bothered to replace it.

She hears the phone ring, an efficient voice answers. 'Kathy, that you? It's Selina. Hi. Afraid I won't be in for a day or two. It's Schaw. He's taken ill. He's in hospital and— Where? Neucastle...he's in hospital in Neucastle. I came last night as soon as I found out. What's wrong? Well, that's the thing. They don't know. They're doing tests. May take several days. Don't feel I can leave him. Thanks, Kathy. I'd appreciate you passing it on. Yes, I'll pass your good wishes to Schaw. Thanks. Bye.'

She hears a noise, a key in the lock and spins round to see her husband elbow his way through the door with a heap of newspaper cradled in his arms.

'Out of action for a week and the Party goes bananas.'

'What?'

He thrusts the pile of papers towards her. 'See these. See this pile of garbage. Swallowed a load of bullshit hook line and bloody sinker, they have. It's mayhem. Bloody 'our-side's-losing mayhem.' He dumps the papers on the bed. 'All-out war. Not what's needed.' As he raises his head he notices the mobile clutched in Selina's hand. 'What the blazes you doing with that?'

'I needed to phone the store. Tell them—'

'You've used the sodding phone!'

'I didn't think you'd mind. I—'

'Jeez, I don't believe this! What the hell do we do now?'

'It was only a call to the store.'

'It doesn't bloody well matter who you phoned.'

'Sorry. If you'd let me in on things, I might have known not to use it.'

'Jeez! I suppose you told them where you were?'

'Emmm…I did mention—'

Schaw runs his hands through his hair, grabs fistfuls of it. 'Bloody hell.'

'Sorry.' Selina rakes in her pocket for a hankie and blows her nose. 'I didn't know…you didn't say…'

'You bloody well didn't think, woman.'

The phone rings, startling both. Schaw lunges, grabs it and switches it off. He throws it on the bed. 'Shit.'

'Can we go for breakfast?' Selina asks, her voice barely louder than a whisper.

Her husband throws her a cold look. 'Get your stuff. We need to get out of here.'

'Now?'

'Now.'

'But what about breakfast?'

'You haven't a bloody clue, woman. Grab that bag.'

'Haven't a clue about what?'

'We're slap bang ding dang in the middle of Black Square territory.'

Selina shakes her head. 'Never heard—'

Schaw hauls her out the door, checks the corridor. 'Like your father's lot, but more ruthless, with more modern technology.'

'You mean another…? She grabs the banister in case she loses her footing on the gloomy stairs.

'Yes, another… With that bampot Jut.'

They check out. The guy behind the desk looks them up and down, as if searching for visible signs of treasure nicked from their room. 'Ye no' havin' breakfast?'

Schaw throws notes on the counter. 'Sorry, mate, no time.'

As they scuttle through the lobby Selina asks, her breath coming fast, 'This is their territory?'

Schaw holds the door for her. 'Yup. Here in the North East and up the coast into Caledon. The east's response to your father's lot that originated in the west, in the shipyards.'

Outside, they head towards the taxi rank at the station. A fine drizzle wets the pavement. Selina shivers and pulls up the collar of her light raincoat, wishes she was wearing her winter coat or at least had an umbrella. She hadn't thought to change last night, hadn't had time to think

'You mean that guy Jut belongs to this Black Square lot?'

' Uhuh. Brought up here, but now stays near Edin. More's the pity!' Schaw marches across the road, dodging traffic.

'Wait for me.'

'South Sherds,' he mutters. 'Maybe a bus would be better.'

The city jerks past in stops and starts. Schaw spends the journey deleting names and information from his phone. Before they walk into the ferry terminal he runs across to a line of lorries about to head off across the country and, in a feat of bowling worthy of Lords cricket ground, lobs his phone onto the top of one. 'That should keep them guessing for a while,' he says.

23 - A whiff of seaweed

Lippy is enjoying the drive. The day is breezy and tree branches dance a gavotte across the sky, while shrubs and flowers bow and curtsey as if formally robed and attired participants in the eighteenth century dance. The sun shines, and washes fields and villages in bright colour, though the air contains a chill, a reminder of the reluctance of northern winter to loosen its grip through spring. But from the inside of the car Lippy can imagine the climate as Mediterranean.

She has telephoned Ramsay several times in the last forty-eight hours, left messages, asked him to return her call, but no response. Ramsay doesn't want to talk to her. Fair enough, but she has too much at stake to let him sulk. The director interested in her play liked what he read, has a theatre slot, and sufficient arts funding left in the kitty to move forward with it. She gets the impression she is a stand-in for a writer whose play has not materialised or which has been delivered but failed to meet expectations. That seems the direction of her life at present, being a stand-in. First Marsha with the bookshop event, and now with her play. But she isn't complaining, far from it. Instead she bows and curtseys in thanks to her lucky stars that she stands near the head of the hopefuls queue.

So pressure is now on her to extract information from Ramsay. Lippy laughs, thinking it sounds like pulling teeth, but acknowledges there seems a similarity. She's the mad dentist, the torturer with thumbscrews at the ready. She'll toss him onto her rack, installed in a basement kitchen somewhere, roll up her sleeves, torture manual propped on her cast iron cookbook rest, and get to work. What is it with her and thumbscrews and racks these days? She remembers thinking along similar lines whilst going through security at the Parliamentary reception. Maybe on the lifelong road of development from apple seed to tree to apple seed she is developing further, or — heavens — mutating even! Mutating into a crabbit apple out to skew the normal lifecycle.

Her glance is drawn to a view of the sea and she snorts dismissively. She really needs to get out more. Enjoy the normal company of normal people. Her head nods in agreement though she queries the definition of normal company. What she would refer to as normal company is usually bland, one dimensional, and provides no meaty material for her writing. She needs the unusual, the quirky, the flawed characters like Ramsay. She can then dig around his mind and winkle out the material that's the lifeblood of her books. That's why she is bowling down the coastal road in search of him.

A book she read some time ago about Robert Louis Stevenson comes to mind. No, it wasn't about Stevenson. It was about his wife, Fanny. Fanny van de Grift Osbourne. Wonderful name.

She took a liking to Fanny. Was enthralled at her sense of adventure, her willingness to tackle with cheerfulness the challenges life threw at her, the challenges marriage to a husband in dubious health led her to overcome. Fanny had guts. She was a gutsy woman who rolled up her sleeves and got stuck in; hands calloused with clearing swamp and jungle; roughened by the construction of furniture for the shacks and apartments where she stayed. She created gardens from wildernesses and grew food to feed her family; sailed unknown oceans, made a home amongst people very different to those she left behind in San Francisco. Fanny was a woman who loved colour, Polynesian garments and old Mexican jewellery, and who cooked, painted and wrote with verve. A woman with talent for whom life was always a challenge.

Her husband's friends and colleagues had little time for her — a siren, a gold digger, she would be the death of his writing. Heavens, what did Stevenson see in her! He could have the pick of women in reception rooms and salons in Edinburgh and London. Anywhere. Women of good pedigree, accomplished, genteel and well-dressed. But Stevenson had abandoned law to write. And Stevenson, so it seemed to Lippy as she read the book, needed a wife who would be unafraid to accompany him on his adventures, and share the highs and lows of living precariously far away from family, friends and home. Stevenson, believed Lippy, found the qualities he sought in Fanny, his 'steel-true and blade-straight' wife. A woman who would be by his side in the adventures he needed to experience in order to write his books. Of course, she was sure Stevenson scholars would disagree with her conclusion. But that's what she believes. And she has reached the stage in life when she believes her opinion is as valid as anyone else's.

Not that she's comparing herself to Stevenson or her writing to his — good grief, no! Nor does she compare herself to Fanny, whose determination shines as a reminder of what can be achieved if you put your mind and hard work into a project. What she does subscribe to is the necessity to experience, for her writing. It is essential. And if she can't experience a situation personally, then the only other option is to pump someone who has. Why it's so important to persuade Ramsay to open up to her.

Nearly there. The road has been unusually quiet and she has made good time. She fervently hopes this won't prove a wasted journey, and that Ramsay will be at home. Given his frame of mind there is always the possibility he has taken himself off to mope on some remote peninsula or island — Ardnamurchane or Orknie for instance. She is beginning to understand Kat's attitude, her relocation to Edin to stay with her sister. More than convenience for her work lies behind that, Lippy is sure.

She likes Ramsay, likes him very much, and has been surprised at the easy manner that has developed between them, yet he will not open up about his past, and adroitly sidesteps her efforts. Ramsay has suffered humiliation, has hinted at other suffering too. Pressure has undoubtedly been put on him, unrelenting pressure. And no doubt a handful of misdemeanours were unearthed from his past life and worked on, blown up, to add to the intimidation. Rather than his expenses fiddle, her instincts tell her it could be the possibility of future duress and threats that keep Ramsay incarcerated in his seaweed cage.

In a gap in the scrubby seaside vegetation on the left side of the road she notices a large white house, not by the roadside but way across the rough field near the cliff edge. It has a Victorian solidity that gives it stature within the landscape. Idly she wonders about the access but the question is almost immediately answered when she sees the bonnet of a white car edge out from a narrow rutted road. As she passes she sees the bonnet belongs to a police car. She throws her foot on the brake and curses as she checks her speed. She hasn't noticed thirty-mile speed limit signs. A speeding ticket is the last thing she wants. When she checks her rear view mirror she sees the police car drive out behind her. She slows more, expecting to be pulled over, but as she reduces speed and hugs the grass verge the police car overtakes and bullets off along the road.

Lippy brings the car to a halt. She realises she is trembling. Deep breaths, she instructs herself. Deep breaths and a blast of sea air. Slowly she climbs from the car, walks to the verge and calms herself as she looks out over fields to the vast expanse of pewter sea that, here and there as the sun catches it, sparkles like silver.

Lippy breathes in air and view until her heartbeat returns to its normal pace and her thoughts turn back to their usual channels. The police car has unnerved her. Usually marked police cars are only found in rural areas when a speed trap is in operation. The reason she kicked herself for missing a speed limit sign. She turns from the view and looks along the road, the direction she came from and the one she will take. No speed signs. No signs of any kind. Another house in the distance, a farm possibly, but apart from that — isolation. She wonders what the owner of the Victorian house has done to merit a visit from the cops. Must be serious. She swivels to look at the house again but from this angle it is hidden by a shelterbelt of trees, conifers that block the view as effectively as a high concrete wall.

Her hand is on the car door handle when the thought hits her. Could that be Bluebell McDaid's house? Is that the explanation for the police car? Ramsay said she lived just along the coast from him. She isn't far from Ramsay's house, so perhaps…' Bluebell appears to have dropped off the face of the planet. Apart from speculation in the media that Wilkie was killed there, Bluebell has barely been mentioned. No comments, no laments for her dead lover. Strange, surely? The police have been tight-lipped about her too, with no indication they are looking for her or that she is sought for questioning. Surely in such a case the lover is the first person spoken to, the one centre frame, as most victims are killed by people close to them.

The Internet is awash with rumours. Some believe it was a burglary gone wrong, that Wilkie disturbed the intruder before he could start his trawl, the reason why there are no reports of missing items. Others advocate a lover's tiff taken to extremes. Bluebell is known to have a temper which she lets loose with devastating force. Yet others think these explanations simplistic, that there might be more to it. Veiled and not so veiled comments about death threats from sick idiots — Callyparty people mostly. That's where, some say, the police should look for the perpetrator, in the ranks of the putrid Party in government. The occasional voice calls for calm, points out that as yet no arrest has been made. But anger lunges from numerous postings, anger and a demand for retribution against those considered, but by no means proved, guilty or even implicated in any way.

If the big house is Bluebell's, Lippy wonders if she's in residence? If she rings the doorbell will she answer? If she does, what will she say? That her writer's imagination is curious? That having seen the body sprawled on Ramsay's hearth rug she wants to see if the original crime scene differs? As a follow up she can say she has a journalist friend who can't pay like the gutter press, but would write a sympathetic article. Perhaps sympathy, rather than money, is what Bluebell needs right now.

No, she can't be there. If she were, the press circus would be loitering at the gates, desperate for a growl from the lion. There could be an intern slouched by the house, but the police would no doubt have sent the poor soul scarpering.

Bluebell could be there but not answering doorbell or telephone, though she'd have to slip out for food and bits and pieces. But she may have organised a friend to deliver the essentials.

Lippy pulls open the car door and plumps herself on the driver's seat. With a glance around she executes a nifty three-point turn and swings the steering wheel to point the car up the track to the Victorian house. Jasmine indicated at the Garden Lobby reception that she had information relevant to the subject of her play. Lippy reasons she might open up more if she can provide a juicy titbit in return. The lowdown on Bluebell would throw Jasmine a meaty tip-off to follow up, help boost her towards the politics slot she covets.

From the track an open gate leads to a drive. Lippy swings her car through the gate and arrives at a wide area in front of the house. A former stable building to the side is presumably now used as a garage. Its doors are shut and there is no sign of a car. Lippy climbs out and surveys the property as if a potential buyer. It's in good repair; the windows have a fresh coat of paint as does the deep red front door. She climbs the wide steps and rings the modern doorbell beneath the brass nameplate with McDaid etched into it. Despite pleasure at her hunch being correct, no feet dash to answer, nor is there any sign or sound of life. She rings again, returns to the open space and studies the windows for twitched curtains or peering eyes. Nothing.

Frustrated, Lippy is reluctant to leave without an enticement for Jasmine. She takes the path that leads round to the rear of the house. This looks more like the main façade as a balcony pushes out from a room, presumably an upstairs lounge, over the round bay of the room below which boasts French windows onto a flagged patio. From here the vista is wide and open, sea stretches from the end of the grounds to infinity. A breeze gusts round the garden and rebukes plants trying to grow and flower. She can smell the salt, a whiff of seaweed. And blown in on the waves she can almost hear the cries of mariners whose ships were wrecked on rocks after they headed for deceiving lights. From the rocks it would be simple, with a few strong men, to manhandle casks and crates from a foundering ship onto the shore and up to the house. She wonders whether, beneath the Victorian pile, cellars from an earlier era lurk.

The French windows are too tempting not to be checked, so Lippy, with another glance around, pads across the flagstones and peers through. Presumably originally a dining room, it now appears to be an office cum snug. Lippy shivers as she wonder if this is where Wilkie was murdered. The room has a look of normality, no crime scene tape is draped across the part open door, or across the French window, so perhaps the deed was done elsewhere. The bedroom seems a possibility. She moves along the back. A room with curtains drawn raises her interest but gives away no secrets. On to the kitchen quarters. Through two long windows she can see a large room with original-looking cream painted cupboards and wall shelves. A range cooker of some kind stands in the alcove where the original range probably stood. And in the centre is a long table with brightly coloured wooden chairs at one end. The kitchen is reasonably tidy — tidier than her own — so no reason to think Bluebell left in a hurry, apart from an opened bottle of wine and two glasses on the table.

Not much more to see, Lippy thinks. She strolls across the wiry clumps of grass, noticing the weed-smothered flower beds at the side of the garden. Doesn't look as if Bluebell enjoys pottering in her garden. She probably doesn't have the time. At the end is a low stone wall with a gate. Lippy opens it and ventures through. From there a path leads to the cliff edge — not so high here as in most places — and the path develops into a steepish ramp that runs down to the rocky shore. By the top of the ramp squats an old dinghy. Paint peels in long tongues from its weather-greyed wooden planks and the interior is filled with sand in which sea pinks and grasses grow. Bluebell doesn't sail either, surmises Lippy.

The ramp is pitted and the edges have crumbled from the assault of high tides, but it isn't difficult to walk down. She picks up a stick thrown up by the tide and thrashes the air. On the beech she looks around then walks from the rocks out to a sandier area where she can look back at the house and along the coast. In the sand she trails the stick, and bends to draw shapes. The stick digs a channel in the sand. She likes the way the edges of the channel curl and heap, magnifying the original mark.

At the water's edge two gulls squawk and squabble, bad tempered, each determined to secure the prize, whatever it is — a piece of fish, a mussel. Lippy watches them soar and dive. One drops the prize, both swoop. One nabs it from under the beak of the other, flutters a few yards before being attacked by the loser with harsh screeches and beak wielded like a rapier. Both jig around, twirl and twist before they take off to repeat the circus. Mock indignation, evasion and bluster, thinks Lippy. Just like politics. Two parties at war over what's in it for them. There she goes again. Cynicism. She's definitely turning into her Dad.

Her feet march through massed ranks of seaweed, dried by wind and sun to brittle wire, barbed with wizened pods, laced with shells and feathers, to the water. The sand sucks and slurps beneath her shoes. They leave blurry indentations that fill with water. She is leaving a trail of mini pools behind her. Is that what making her mark on the world amounts to — blurry puddles that will be washed away by the relentless onslaught of years? The sea is calm today, calm and cold looking. The water shushes up the sand in long lazy waves, picot edged with white, reaching and retreating right along the beach to a rocky headland. She sees no sign of Ramsay, the sand gives no indication of a dog having romped and prodded and sniffed, so perhaps their beach lies beyond the outcrop. A waves roams close to her feet so she steps back and with a final look at the view walks slowly back up the beach to the ramp.

Through the seaweed she scrunches, swinging the stick. Did something catch the sun and glint? Or was it her imagination? She pokes around with the stick, bends closer and peers. There. What's that? She flicks the stick and something jumps like a tiddlywink onto the sand. Lippy picks it up. The stick is parked under her arm and she wipes sand, gritty on the pads of her fingers, from the tiny object. It's a badge — one of those small lapel badges that many men wear. She looks closer. The surface is scuffed, the colour faded, but it looks like a black square.

24 - Want to join the big boys?

Brian's father, Douglas, drummed into him years ago that factions are inevitable in any political party where a wide range of views and opinions coalesce under one leadership and group of policies — broad church is the oft used phrase. That is why Douglas advocates discussion to resolve problems. He ushers fighting pupils into his study, sits them down, surly face to sulky face across a narrow table and with the palms of their hands flat on the table top, tells them to talk, first the one, then the other, telling each other what drove them to fisticuffs. His belief is that organisations and political Parties should use a similar means of settling disputes, a face-to-face soul-bearing without the involvement of others. Apart from him.

Brian doesn't believe you can treat a political Party in the same way you treat aggressive primary school kids, though he occasionally is driven to believe there are similarities between the two, but his father is adamant that life is about communication, and a lack of it can be found at the root of most problems. His mother grins behind her husband's back and tells him to grow up. So Brian is realistic enough to expect disagreements, the cracks usually hidden behind compromises, fudges, metaphorical paper posters or large pot plants. Every so often an eruption by one faction or another causes uncomfortable headlines that make it necessary for the hierarchy to trail round media studios, and turn on charm offensives, or spew out dismissive rants that malign the opposition. All part of power politics.

As Brian trails into the Parliament building this overcast morning he is aware the atmosphere has changed. The recent annoyance, frustration, open discussion of retribution, has been replaced by an air of fragility. Eggshells are not beneath feet to be trodden on, but instead form a dome in place of a ceiling, their frailty doomed to be shattered by loud or inappropriate words. Or words spoken to the wrong people.

As he exits the lift and walks along the corridor to his office, the atmosphere pushes down on him. He feels his skin freeze and crack like ice, with the iciness ready to seep into his insides to spread and numb, until he is unable to function normally. He has worked through periods of Party infighting before when Parliamentary colleagues spat bile like warring children, and plotted downfalls as if an X box game. This, sadly, is the usual stuff of politics. But the intensity of the current fracture signals its difference.

Previously it was possible for him to sit on the sidelines, attempt to show even-handedness whilst favouring one side and despising the other. No — despising is too strong a word. Usually he thinks the other side crass, foolish, misguided, childish, bitter, wrong-headed, unthinking, gullible, demanders of instant action, immediate righting of past wrongs, and with no capacity to think strategically of longer term objectives. And these are people in his own Party! Perhaps it is his father's influence, but there are times when he thinks the governing Party has more going for it than his own. Heresy. The Callyparty suffers its own problems. Since fighting a mock election at school he has been convinced of the stance of the Party of which he is a member, certain it offers the best road ahead, despite its sporadic loss of way. He still views it as the only Party worthy of his support. But recently he has questioned if its stance has become too negative to woo voters and secure a return to government.

This current furore, merely the most recent in an endless chain, contains the ingredients for a more serious fracture of the Party, though few would probably admit that. Of course the Party consists of more than the soundproofed glass cube of the Parliamentary cabal. The ordinary punters — members and supporters - are the Party, too, though their numbers are diminishing. But it is the Parliamentary cabal, along with a small management team, that calls the shots, guides policy, controls publicity, shapes its image into what is regarded as the most likely model to keep its numbers at a healthy level in Parliament, if not in power.

The Party image over recent years has changed. The Party has changed. Followers for years have been praised for their loyalty, but how far does the elasticity of that loyalty stretch, for according to Headquarters a worrying number of membership subscriptions have not been renewed. Furthermore, ambivalent, sometimes critical, comments by a number of union leaders have been snatched by the media and puffed and blown out of shape. Any rift between spender and purse is serious. Brian is of the opinion more should be done to scotch such stories instead of allowing them to run and gain traction. However, it appears others know better.

These relatively minor spats pale into insignificance against the stories that now rain down like outsize hail stones around Brian and his colleagues, stories that claim the Callyparty is not the instigator of the campaign against Mutt. According to a sympathetic though unnamed journalist, said to be a reliable source, the campaign emanates from a faction within their own party. Twisted faces and howls of disbelief hide a few glances of relief that the truth will emerge. To this few, the Callyparty was too hastily painted culprit in a typical knee-jerk reaction, it was too easy a target. A political journalist in the broadcast media has even hinted to an unnamed Member that the shenanigans are not merely a campaign aimed at Mutt's removal, but are a means to ramp up a vendetta between two factions within the Party. On the face of it Brian is sceptical of this line. Why would one faction destroy leader and Party, and the Party's chances of power, merely to get their own back for some long-forgotten slight or dirty trick? To risk everything worked for, so a rush of misplaced satisfaction can be enjoyed. Too silly to be true, surely? Such extreme machinations could never happen. Yet Brian, when he takes the time to think about it, is aware such plots wreaked havoc previously in the history of his Party. And the likelihood is that the Party may again be in the throes of such a vendetta.

The Parliamentary Party seems to be fracturing before his eyes. The consensus of previous days, when it was widely believed the governing Party was behind the campaign, has shattered. The jagged shards of co-worker friendship, amicable rivalries, getting-on-together-for-the-cause strategies, lie around them, ready to slash the unwary. Mistrust strides the corridors. Internationally nation does not speak peace unto nation, so — in the warrens of Parliament — faction does not speak peace unto faction.

His feet slow as he nears his office, as if to enter signs him up to an involvement in the fray, and he is reluctant to become embroiled in it. To stand on the sidelines this time will be more difficult. This has all the hallmarks of a tournament to the death — unwise phrase! — a tournament to cleanse opposition within the Party, and to hell with the consequences.

In contrast to the hubbub in his corridor a few days ago, today it slumbers in silence, empty. A door clicks closed, muffled footsteps fade to nothing, a nearby phone coughs apologetically for attention then stops, the hiss of lift doors is muted. The corridor is devoid of chatter, of speculation by querulous voices as to who was the perpetrator of the Mutt attack. In five or ten minutes a flurry of activity will kick it to life, as committees will start their sittings. But Brian doesn't expect the mini exodus for that will generate much conversation.

The door flies open. Ming dives through to his office, grabs a bundle of papers and crashes past Brian, stopping to ask, 'You sure I have everything I need?'

Brian thinks it politic to check, so he shuffles through the folders splayed in Ming's arms. 'All present and correct.'

Ming is halfway back through the door into the corridor as he responds, 'You're for the high jump if anything's missing.'

Brian sighs. It's shaping up to be another difficult day. To navigate his way through it without foundering, he needs a treat to look forward to. His hand reaches for the phone.

'Kirsty? Brian here. I enjoyed our chat the other evening.'

'Same here.'

'I was wondering…I wondered if you'd like to meet up for a drink when you finish?'

'You mean this evening?'

'Yes…or if that's not convenient, whenever is.' There is a long pause. 'Look if you'd rather not…fine…no hard feelings.'

'No, no it's not that. I'd like to. It's just…'

'Just?'

'The strains within the Party at present.'

'Nothing to do with me, or with you surely?'

'There's no certainty as to which faction anyone belongs to. The Party's paranoid at present with suspicion and mistrust.'

'I assure you, Kirsty, I've no involvement with any underhand dealings, and I'm not a member of any faction.'

'Hmm. I want to believe you, Brian, but there's the small matter of…' Her voice trails off with the realisation she is entering dangerous territory, being explicit and uttering names on the phone.

'I'd like to see you. What if I undertake not to recruit you to any faction, or involve you in a dastardly plot? Would you agree then?'

'You shouldn't make light of the situation, Brian. Nerves are raw and bleeding. At such a time caution is advised.'

'Merely trying to persuade you I want your company, not the company of your politics.'

'Not sure the two can be separated.'

'Urrrgh! I'm sinking in a quagmire of my own making!'

'Perhaps we should leave it until a more settled atmosphere returns.'

'Suppose that might be sensible. But I'm not sure I want to be sensible and let silly events dictate who I can see and when. Not in this instance anyway. Heavens, Kirsty, you have a similar position to me, with another MCP. Surely we can't be regarded as a danger by meeting for a drink?'

'Normally there wouldn't be a problem, but…'

'But these aren't normal times.'

'Exactly.'

Brian sighs. 'Okay, point me to the nearest monastery. D'you think I'll suit grey robes?'

'Thank you for calling, Mrs Killin. Do call again if the problem isn't resolved. Goodbye.'

'What the…?' The line is dead. 'Okaaaay, you've made your feelings clear. Better if you'd said no thank you and left it at that. Bloody women!' His foot lashes out and kicks the wastepaper basket beneath his desk.

For ten minutes he stares into space, then he gathers his thoughts and turns his attention to the revision of a speech for Ming to deliver at a constituency event — the opening of an environmental centre. Environmental topics are not rated amongst Ming's strong points, so Brian aims to keep the speech simple with several mentions of the number of jobs, including in the constituency, dependent on the environment. Ming delights in mentioning jobs — an area he knows little about, but on which he can spout convincingly.

As he prints out a draft to leave on Ming's desk, his phone rings.

'Sorry to cut you off, Brian. A visitor. MCP for Bluebell's next door constituency. Wanted to look at files. Meet me at the Wabbit Hen. Nine thirty this evening.'

Snide remarks, and objections caused by his being miffed, well up in his throat, but all he says is, 'Okay.' The phone goes dead. 'Careful lady. Perhaps even twitchy lady.'

Ming's mood appears to have improved as a result of his committee stint. 'Ladybank was his usual idiot self. Raised one or two chuckles. And that bloody awful Callyparty woman — what's her name? The one like an elephant on wheels.'

'Batty Braidburn?'

'That's her. No wonder she's nicknamed Batty. The woman's a few hundred chromosomes short of a human being. Where do they find these people?'

'Obstructive, was she?'

Ming perches himself on the edge of Brian's desk, prepared to chat. He rubs his nose. 'No, not obstructive — at least I don't think she meant to be. But she kept mentioning these reports. Bangs on about them. Insists they're relevant, for heaven's sake!'

'And they're not?'

'Well, I haven't read them, and I can't think any other committee members have. Except that lawyer guy. He's a nut for reading.'

'I see....'

'Reports, huh! They tie us up in irrelevances. Waste the committee's time.' He purses his mouth into a squashed tomato shape. 'Maybe a word in the ear of the Chair.'

'Halliday?'

'Invite him for drinkies. See if I can get Batty shunted off and replaced by a more normal idiot. What d'you think?'

'Can't say I know the woman, Ming. But your judgement is usually sound on such matters.'

'Usually?'

'None of us can be right all the time.'

'Speak for yourself.'

Brian swallows hard. Taps a pencil on his mouse mat. 'Your speech for the environmental centre opening is on your desk.'

'What opening?'

'The environmental centre at—'

'You mean I'm giving the opening address, cutting the red ribbon and stuff.'

'Uhuh.'

'Why didn't you mention it before?'

'Been on your schedule for the last six months, Ming.'

'Hell, you can't expect me to read... What do we say about the environment?'

'Jobs.'

'Jobs. Good. Can't go wrong with a mention of jobs. Any particular types of jobs?'

'If you read it through and let me know of changes, I'll let you have the final copy and send out a media release.'

'Good photo opportunity, I hope?'

'Excellent I would think.'

'That's what I like. Keep on top of the pile. Never let the buggers win, eh Brian?'

'Absolutely. Em... Ming...while you're here... I thought I should mention. I've put my name forward for the regional top up list for the next election.'

The smile drains from Ming's face. His eyes narrow and his mouth becomes a hard line drawn across a face that gravitates towards flabby. He slides from the desk and stands, towering over Brian. 'Not standing for a constituency?'

Brian shakes his head. 'No, not sufficient experience. Besides—'

'Sure you're not plotting to stand against me?'

'Definitely not.' Brian's reappraisal of whether to go for constituency or list resulted in him plumping for list. Too late now for a constituency and more chance on the list, he reckons. Though the fight for a constituency appealed. Still…maybe next time round.

'You wouldn't stand a chance anyway.'

'I realise that.'

'You against me at a selection meeting! The constituency wouldn't even bother with an interview. Minnow versus shark. No contest.'

Brian forces a smile to his face. Yes, even if he were an iron strong candidate, Ming would swing it his way. He'd make sure of that, no matter what it took. Ming has a fighting structure behind him. Brian has only himself. Under the circumstances he's unsure he can even count on his few supporters. 'No contest. Exactly. That's why I've decided to try for the list. Who knows, if I'm lucky you might find me working alongside you in Parliament.'

A cloud passes across Ming's face and turns into a scowl. If Brian hadn't been watching so intently for his reaction, he might have missed it, but he doesn't, and it causes him concern. Eyes bore into him.

'Want to join the big boys, do you?'

'I want to give it a shot.'

Ming stomps towards his own office. He turns at the door. 'You're not ready for it,' he spits. His slammed door shakes the office like a minor earthquake.

'Brian jumps up, lunges to the door, throws it open. 'Sorry that's how you feel, Ming. I happen to disagree with you. My application's been submitted.'

'You're wasting your time.'

'I have a reasonable chance.'

'You think so! More fool you.'

'My qualifications are better—'

'Qualifications aren't everything.'

'My application's in, so let's wait and see.'

'On your head be it,' spits Ming without raising his head.

Brian's impression from the phone call of Kirsty's reluctance to be seen with him is reinforced when he arrives at the Wabbit Hen. She strolls up and down outside, waiting for him, and instead of them entering the Victorian encased warmth, she suggests they walk.

'Bit chilly,' says Brian.

'But safer.'

Brian feels confused. She appears to have dressed up to see him, and as he brushes her arm a whiff of perfume drifts up to him. 'We could go to another pub.'

'Let's walk a while. I like Edin at night — something to do with the atmosphere.'

'Me too — thought I prefer to enjoy it from the inside.'

'Couch potato?'

'No. Only kidding.'

'You not a fresh air man?'

'Depends on the fresh air.'

Kirsty raises her head and sniffs the air like a dog. 'I like it high up. I used to be into Munro bagging. Climbed fourteen while I was at uni.'

'Those are hills over…well, high ones?'

'Yes, hills over 3000 feet.

'You're obviously fit. I'd better watch my step.' His look of surprise shows he's impressed, yet a wriggle in his gut warns him he may have to pech up number fifteen, sixteen and onwards if their meeting this evening leads to a more permanent arrangement.

'I'm not so fit now, so I'd probably struggle. My legs would buckle and my breath pant.'

Brian stops, and his eyes wander over her. 'You look plenty fit to me.'

Kirsty laughs. 'Thanks. But I spend too much time on my behind these days. And when on my feet it's usually for a slow waltz through a shopping centre to hand out leaflets, or a twirl to perch on someone's desk at two in the morning with a mug of coffee and a pie to discuss strategy.'

'Discuss strategy? Who with?'

'Oh…when I worked at Headquarters. Since moving to the Parliament life has been pretty desk-bound.'

'Can't have been easy for you — what with Wilkie's murder and Bluebell's disappearance.'

'Far from boring, granted but…' She shrugs.

'But?'

'Let's just say I prefer to be on the inside rather than the outside.'

'You don't want to be inside a murder investigation.'

'No. But I like to be at the centre of what's happening. Not the centre of attention — the centre of action. I like to be part of the action, make things happen, achieve. I suppose you could say I'm ambitious.'

'You like to be at the heart of what's happening? I hope that doesn't mean you've an involvement with…' He waves his hand in the air.

'With the campaign against Mutt?'

'Sorry, I didn't mean to ask. That was crass.'

'Logical question, given my spiel.' She continues to stroll, swinging her handbag.

Brian stops, and leans over a railing. 'Great view, even in the dark.'

Kirsty's steps slow. She swivels round and walks back towards him, leaning her arms on the railings. 'No way am I associated with that. The opposite.'

'Amazing to see lights in all these different colours. Like a kaleidoscope.'

'Mmm.'

'Good to know you're not involved in the machinations against Mutt. I didn't think you were.'

'Really? Why not?'

Brian watches lights move in the distance, a never-ending rearrangement of a pattern of luminous dots. 'To say my instinct whispered you weren't, would be wrong. It's the vibes you give out. They're the vibes of someone concerned by what's playing out.'

'Vibes! I'll need to watch those, keep them under better control, camouflage their transparency. But how do you know they weren't vibes of concern lest I was found out?'

'Not what I was picking up.'

'So, do you have concerns about my non-involvement with the Mutt campaign?'

Brian straightens, looks at her, eyebrows raised questioningly. 'Why on earth would I have concerns about that?'

She straightens, too, so they stand face to face. Her voice is low. 'I'd have thought that was obvious.'

'Obvious?' Brian's voice has risen in tone and volume. 'Sorry, you've lost me. Why should your lack of anti-Mutt involvement concern me?'

Kirsty raises her eyes to heaven but not to look for stars. 'Brian, Brian, Brian! The guy you work for. Your MCP.'

'Ming?'

'Who else.'

'I work for him. Wasn't my first choice by a long shot, but I was desperate to get a foot in the Parliamentary door. I write his speeches, answer his correspondence and wipe his nose. Beyond that I don't step. No. Wrong. I have to admit to a suggestion that he buy toiletries for his interview with Jasmine Stane.'

'Callyman Jasmine?'

Brian nods. 'Uhuh.'

'That must've made her day.'

He shrugs. 'Long story, and irrelevant to what you seem to be suggesting I'm involved with. Though I'm not sure what that is.'

'You know Ming's history? Right?'

'Some of it.'

'Who he worked for?'

'Charlie Kintail, so I've been told.'

'What do you know about Charlie?'

They start to walk again. 'My knowledge of him is sketchy, gleaned from a couple of sources. Recently, too. Believe it or not I knew nothing about him until…until someone supplied a few nuggets of information. Thing is, I haven't been able to contact that person since.'

'No surprise. It's how the system works.'

'So I'm discovering.'

'Who else filled you in?'

'A former Party member.'

'I see.'

'I thought it was all in the past, had died out with the death of Charlie. However, the odd remark recently by various people made me question that. And then Wilkie is murdered and Mutt gets trashed, and I wonder…'

'You wonder?'

'Talk in office corridors is of two factions at war.'

'That about sums it up.'

'You seem much better informed that me.'

'I told you, I worked at Headquarters. It's our job to be informed.'

'You said… When I asked you about the campaign against Mutt…'

'Yes?'

'You said no way were you involved. The opposite. What did you mean by the opposite?

'Faux pas.'

'Come on, explain. You can't leave me wondering.'

Kirsty stares at him, searches his eyes, probes his mind. She nods slowly and takes a deep breath. 'I hope to heaven I've read your vibes correctly.'

'If you're about to tell me something sensitive then I assure you now that I won't pass it on. I don't like the viciousness of what's happening. It can only harm the Party big time.'

Too right. That's why… Okay, you promise to keep it under your hat?'

'Absolutely.'

'Bluebell came into Headquarters a couple of months ago. Said she thought something was brewing. I wasn't at the meeting but I saw her when she arrived and when she left, and she certainly looked worried — as if about to fight a by-election with no funds, no workers and a cupboard full of skeletons.'

Brian chuckles. 'Given those odds, she's the kind of person who'd win.'

'Probably. Anyway turns out she thinks a plot is being hatched. Why, I don't know, but presumably she convinced the high heid yins and named a few names. There was sufficient concern for the Party Manager to decide on a course of action. Bluebell's assistant, the guy you described as stringy with long hair and buck teeth, wanted to leave — personal reasons — but with hours reduced he'd undertaken to postpone his departure until as near the summer recess as possible. So, as he was more than happy to leave right then, it was decided I'd take his place, keep my eyes and ears open, and pass on whatever information seemed of importance. Unfortunately I didn't pick up on moves against Wilkie — with tragic results.'

'Not you fault.'

'Hmm! Can't stop thinking about it, though.'

'No word about Bluebell?'

'No. I half wonder if the Party has her stashed somewhere to keep her safe until the murderer is apprehended and the other nonsense stops.'

'Could be. They wouldn't want her put at risk. Could explain why the police aren't looking for her. They know where she is.'

'Makes sense, doesn't it?'

'Yup, but better if we keep such thoughts to ourselves.'

'Agreed.' She turns towards him and smiles hesitantly. 'So there, that's my dark secret. I trust you not to repeat it. I'm a bloody fool to trust you, but I feel I need an ally in the lion's den.'

'I thought you relished being at the centre of events, so why the need for an ally?'

'I didn't bargain on a murder. Besides, four eyes and four ears are better than two when it comes to covering the Parliamentary Party.'

'You're roping me in?'

'What better place to have an ally than in Ming's office?'

'Ming burbles on about jobs and the opposition. He gives no indication he knows about this sort of stuff. Though, come to think of it, a couple of days ago he suggested Brankton would make a more effective leader than Mutt.'

'He did, did he!'

'Mentioned that there wouldn't be a campaign if Mutt resigned because of a heart attack.'

'A heart attack! Bloody hell! You sure about that?'

'Yes. I remember saying a leadership campaign would take time we didn't have, and his response was, Who said anything about a campaign?'

'Thanks. That's going straight back to Headquarters.'

'We're a team then?'

'We're a team. Now what about a drink?' She tucks her arm through his.

25 - It's not funny

She sits on the edge of the bunk. Through the window all she sees is sea — grey sea that somewhere in the grey distance merges with grey sky. It's as if land, buildings, everything that makes up the world, has been sucked from its surface to leave only air and water. The sight sends a wash of hopelessness and fear through her. Brought up in a city, she likes the buzz of people around her, the noise of traffic, streets and spaces that are easily accessed, a landscape that is lit naturally or artificially twenty four hours a day. And here she is, staring at nothingness, and that unnerves her. Though still daylight, brightness has left the sky and soon the dark will creep in with charcoal cloak and silent footsteps. And then there will be black sky and black water.

Never before has she travelled on a ship like this. She vaguely remembers boats to destinations on the Firth of Cliede when they went on holiday. Her father booked the crossing months in advance to ensure the car could be accommodated on board. Crossings to wherever they went took between half an hour and a couple of hours. They were fun mostly. Her mother would go off to find a seat inside to stop her hair being blown around, or the pattern on her coat being trashed by a pesky seagull. She would stand at the rail with her father, and they would watch their holiday destination become larger as the expanse of sea between land and boat grew smaller. She was probably closer to her father on these holidays than at any other time. Part of each day was set aside for her, and then all three of them would bundle into the car to explore, or go to a cafe for a Knickerbocker Glory, or to somewhere posh for afternoon tea.

But this vessel that throbs beneath her feet is a far cry from the wee boats of her long gone holidays. This is a floating tenement, ungainly and ugly. And on this vessel all she can see is sea, and she is at its mercy for many more hours. She has heard stories of rough crossings, of travellers suffering sea sickness, and hopes she won't be affected, though the small cabin is stuffy and the faint throb of the engines travels from the deck through the soles of her feet into her body to unsettle her further.

Schaw stowed her in the cabin then left to book dinner. He said if you didn't book early you could miss out and the fish and chips munched in the rain was the last meal both had eaten. He said he wouldn't be long and she should stay in the cabin till he came back. That was some time ago, and since then she has sat here, on the edge of the bunk.

She had wondered what would happen about passports, for they appeared to be bound for Amsterdam. Schaw told her to keep quiet, say nothing, but if asked mention they were off to spend a few days in the city to see the sights, the canals and the Van Goghs. When nearly at the security control, two passports were slid from his inside pocket. One was thrust into her hand and she was told in a whispered instruction to open it and see who she was. As she swallowed she flicked the document open. Mrs Elsie Ravenscrofte. Her eyes widened as they took in the photograph. Mrs Ravenscrofte looked surprisingly like her — same nondescript hairstyle, small eyes, thin lips. She looked like a startled rabbit — the startled rabbit effect of photo booths. Selina looked closer. Mrs Elsie Ravenscrofte was her, Selina. The photo was one of a strip taken at a photo booth a year or so ago for…something. Some document for which she required a photograph. Schaw must have taken the others. But the passport? Was it her own — doctored? Or was it a passport that belonged to another person? No time to question Schaw, not the place anyway. Selina handed it to the security official and tried to stop the twitch of her face muscles and prevent guilt flooding her eyes.

The officer was middle-aged with a face that looked as if he had seen every scam in the book, lined with determination and resignation, eyes blank as concrete slabs. Even his mouth was rigid. Throughout the process it didn't once open or relax its steely pout, and looked more like a waxwork than a living, breathing human. Selina drove her mind to think of what she could visit in Amsterdam as she'd never been to Holland. She focussed on canals and windmills and wondered if the guy studying her and the false passport could hear the drum of her heart. After what seemed hours it was flipped back to her and with a hand she was sure shook, she grabbed it and walked as fast as she dared from the hall, without sparing a glance to see where Schaw was and how he fared.

He made it through without mishap too, and sidled up behind her, grabbing her arm. She shrieked and turned her head in expectation of seeing a customs or security official, but instead it was her husband. Through the hall he propelled her and out onto the walkway to the boat. Selina wondered if their shortage of luggage might be noticed but whilst a number of passengers trundled large cases, many carried small bags. Mini cruises were popular, it appeared, so a scarcity of luggage went unnoticed.

Further along on the dockside a long line of cars boarded, driven from dock to ship with hardly a lessening of speed. Dozens and dozens of them. Hundreds probably. Selina wished they were driving on in the car. She thought she would feel safer, though why she didn't know.

'The car?' she asked Schaw. 'Where's the car?'

Schaw had looked surprised. His mouth flapped. 'Eh…It…eh… broke down.'

'How will you get it repaired if—'

'Quit the questions, Selina. Let's get on board.'

A steward glanced at the tickets held out by Schaw and a string of directions were rattled at them before his smile and attention was turned on the next in the queue.

So now she sits here, waiting for her husband, waiting for an explanation for this whole rigmarole.

'Okay,' says Selina when her husband eventually returns to the cabin. 'Sit down,' she bestows one pat on the bunk beside her. 'Tell me what's going on.'

Schaw slides past her to the window and peers through it at the rapidly darkening sea and sky. 'I've booked dinner.'

'Fine, but I'm not going to be batted off subject. I want to know what's happening'

He turns to face her. 'You must have some idea.'

'Not much.'

'That's probably best.'

Selina springs to her feet. 'Look, let's get something straight. You've dragged me away from home, away from work, with not so much as a whiff of an explanation. I've had to brazen out a dodgy passport and gone without meals. I'm sitting here with at best a change of clothes, no make up or toiletries, and without a bloody clue where we're going or what happens once we arrive. I've gone along with it so far. Not asked questions. But this far and no further. I need an explanation.'

Schaw swivels round to look at her, opens his mouth as if to fob her off, then thinks better of it, gulps a deep breath and blows it out through his nose like a sigh. He takes her elbow, pushes her back to a sitting position and plumps down beside her on the lower bunk. 'Bloody beds. Can't sit up straight. Should maybe have lashed out on a more upmarket cabin, further up the ship, instead of down here in the—'

'It'll do.'

'Jeez! If I sit here I'll be a hunchback before I've finished.'

'We can go—'

He slides to the floor. 'No, I'm fine here.'

'You don't look comfortable.'

'Stop fussing.'

Selina shrugs. 'Please yourself.'

'You're the one insisting on a tête-à-tête.'

'Just get on with it.'

Schaw stares at his shoes. They are scuffed and in need of a polish. 'What d'you want to know?'

'Everything.'

'Everything? Bloody hell.'

'Start at the beginning.'

'Which beginning?'

'Schaw, don't be so bloody difficult.'

He bangs the toes of his shoes together, apart, together. 'Well, you know about your father? What he did? Right?'

Selina shakes her head. 'Not really. I was thinking about this earlier. Mother and I knew only a small part of the man. I've had a feeling for a long time that mother believed she lost him when he became an MP. Before that he was just an ordinary guy, worked in the shipyard — I was never sure what he did.'

'He was a riveter — until he got involved with the union and moved to work for it.'

'Is that how he was able to become an MP, through the union?"

'Yup. Usual route.'

'Mother said he changed after that.'

'I gather working for the union was a steep learning curve. Your father harboured ambition. That ambition had the door to its cage opened by his time with the union. As an MP, the cage door was thrown open wide. In fact the cage was squashed underfoot and dumped.'

Selina leans forward, elbows on knees, hands cupping chin. 'You've lost me with this talk of cages.'

Her husband throws her a glance. 'His time with the union showed him what could be done, what could be achieved with ambition and... and the will. Determination, too.'

'You mean determination to break out of the constraints of convention?'

'If that's how you want to phrase it.'

'You've an alternative?'

'He became...proficient in methods that could be used to achieve what he wanted.'

'Underhand stuff?'

'Persuasion by different means.'

'So my father resorted to underhand methods to get on?'

Schaw half turns and props his elbow on the bunk beside his wife. "Don't sound so shocked, Selina. You don't get anywhere in this life by being nice and considerate.'

Surprise and confusion fight with one another on her face. Her mouth twitches. 'When did you become so hard, Schaw, so cynical?'

Schaw almost imperceptibly shakes his head. 'Get real, Selina.'

'I always suspected you were like him. Now I know.'

'Look, you're the one who started this. You're the one who insisted on knowing it all. That means everything. Warts, verrucas, ingrown toenails, corns, the lot. Otherwise I'll shut up.'

She thumps her hands on the bed and sniffs, blinks rapidly. 'Okay. Okay. Carry on.'

'Sure?'

She nods. 'Yup.'

'Well, with all he learned at the union he managed to wangle his way onto the candidate's list. Not as difficult in those days as now. Unions always wanted men they could rely on in Parliament. Your father had proved himself reliable. He was a union man, and the union played their part and looked after him, sponsored him, contributed finance and manpower to his campaigns. In return he fought their corner in Parliament, introduced union people to others who could be useful.'

'It's the other side that are lambasted for acting like that now. Donations, cash for questions, old boy networks, old school networks.'

'It's a way of life in Westmunster, whichever Party. That's how the power game is played.'

Selina mulls over what has been said, her lips purse, a frown line deepens between her eyebrows. 'Where did The Galley come in?' Her voice has fallen to a whisper, as if she dares not say the name of the organisation any louder in case she is overheard.

Schaw shifts his position, pulls up his knees and embraces them with his arms. 'I suppose you could say The Galley came out of that. Unions wanted MPs they could trust to keep those they couldn't trust, or those they feared, in line. When a government has its back to the wall over a vote or a policy, the whips are active, ping-ponging around in a frenzy. Why d'you think they're called whips? Your father was a whip for a time, and got a feel for persuasion and arm-twisting. Learned about weaknesses and pressure points, secrets, too. His set-up was an extension of that. I suppose you could say it was an almost logical extension of all his previous experience.'

'But The Galley did more than persuade fellow MPs to vote in a certain way?'

Her husband wriggles on the floor. 'Times were changing, Selina. Politics were changing. An MP needed to be more than one of the lads to be effective. And governments are only as effective as their MPs. It was necessary to ensure the election of the right people, to have the right people in place, so there was a constant supply of bright young things waiting to take the Party forward.'

'You've just swung from explanation mode to excuse mode.'

'It's the way all parties work, Selina. Like it or not, it's the way the world works too. Survival of the fittest.'

'The nastiest and most manipulative, you mean.'

Schaw gives a laugh of contempt. 'Pah! What a sheltered life you've led. Unbelievable you're Charlie's daughter. My wife.'

'Well I am. Though I daresay my life was sheltered. My mother did her damnedest to distance me from whatever my father did. Not that she knew much about it either. But I'm sure she knew enough to know she wanted to protect me from it.'

Schaw shakes his head. 'Like what he did or loathe it, he was bloody good at it. You saw the turnout when he retired.'

'Based on what you've said, most of those folk probably didn't dare not turn up.'

A smile creeps onto her husband's face. 'You're probably right. Most of them probably hated his guts, but they would kowtow to him without a whimper. In the main — though there could be the occasional unwise outburst.'

'Why? I don't understand why.'

'Power dictates the route to achieving it.'

'That's someone's throw-a-way soundbite. You don't actually believe that, do you?'

'A sniff of power can do odd things to people. It can make lions of pussy cats.'

'So it's power that matters, not people.'

'No politician can achieve much for people without power. You need power to get things done.'

'What a lousy lot politicians are.'

'They do what's necessary.'

'They do what people like my father make them do.'

'That, too.'

'I can't believe I didn't know about this.'

'Didn't know, or didn't acknowledge?'

Selina shrugs. 'I suppose maybe I'd a vague idea, but… She stares at him, and wonders vaguely whether history habitually repeats itself. Her mother must have had similar discussions with her father. Now here she is doing what her mother must have done, wondering how she married one man and ended up with another. 'Where do you come into the saga?'

Schaw's shoulders move in a slow flex. 'Your father was looking for another member of his team. Someone outwith Parliament. A freelancer who could undertake the occasional commission.'

Selina's eyes widen. 'You worked for The Galley?'

'Occasionally to begin with, then more regularly.'

'But your job…?'

'A bit of juggling was required, but I managed.'

'The evening meetings? The weekends away?'

'Yup. Amazing how much you can shoehorn into a weekend when your mind's focussed. And Charlie couldn't abide people whose minds weren't focussed. Besides the cover it provided, it gave me links to unions and contacts.'

Selina shifts on the bunk, and grasps the edge of the duvet in her hands. 'I can't believe I'm hearing this. You involved with… Urrrgh!'

'Of course, things changed after Charlie died. There was a helluva bunfight. Kept well out of that, I can assure you. Thought I'd be dropped like a hot potato. But no. The skills I'd acquired were too valuable to lose apparently. According to the new Galley chief. Different story this time round, though.'

'Whoa, whoa. You're getting ahead of yourself.'

'Didn't think you'd be interested in the story after your old man departed the scene.'

'Why on earth not? You had, and obviously still have, an involvement.'

'Had.' Schaw runs his hands through his hair. 'My involvement's in the past. There's been a change. A power struggle we shouldn't have lost…but we did.' He turns his face towards Selina. 'You'll have seen the stuff in the papers about Mutt?'

She nods. 'Were you involved with that?'

Schaw rouses himself, checks his watch. 'Lordy, lordy! Ten minutes till dinner. Must go for a pee, then we can trot along and enjoy a decent dinner. You never know, it might be our last.'

'For heaven's sake! Don't say things like that. It's not funny.'

'No, it's not.'

26 - More or less will not do

The windscreen wipers smear dust and rain across her vision and she pulls the steering column stick for water to clear her view. The smell of the washer solution wafts through the car — sharp with an artificial lemon tang, not too objectionable. Lippy squints at the sky where a black cloud hangs threateningly, nudged by billowing white ones and pushed by the breeze. Probably just a shower, she thinks, not wanting to trudge along the beach in a downpour in search of Ramsay. Personally, she feels he would be better employed finding himself an occupation of some sort, rather than mope on the beach every day. His wife Kat no doubt tried persuasion, she might even have resorted to threats to jolt him from his self-imposed isolation. His lack of response is probably why she takes herself off during the week to the bright lights of Edin.

But responses to events are personal, and different people have different reactions. Ramsay obviously has been wounded by the whole expenses debacle, cut by the lack of support from friends, and left deeply sceptical about the democratic process. In the mix of his emotions lurks fear, and Lippy isn't yet sure whether that's justified or not. If Ramsay still feels the need to watch his back, does that apply to her, in view of her probes and questions? Her play?

Her intention is to park the car and head for the beach but as she drives through the gates she notices another car parked near the door. It's small, red and sporty — not the mode of transport she envisages Ramsay's friends drive around in. Her interest is aroused, though if another visitor is ensconced her journey might prove wasted. All her wiles have been brought to bear on him to provide her with details of how he was entrapped in the Parliamentary expenses debacle, but his reluctance is proving hard to crack.

She manoeuvres the old Volvo alongside the red interloper whose owner still has acres of space to back round and head out the gate, leaving her to pump Ramsay for the information she needs. As she climbs out the car she hears a laugh, a bright, crystal ting of a laugh that undoubtedly belongs to a woman. She stiffens, feels her hackles rise. The bastard. He wouldn't open up to her because he had someone else after his information — someone with a better offer, no doubt. There it is again. It sounds as if it's coming from the front of the house. As her feet scrunch the gravel of the path round the old sea salt's house, Jess decides to become guard dog and barks excitedly. Ramsay, alerted by Jess, comes to investigate and they bump into one another at the corner.

'Lippy! I wondered who was arriving.'

'You're a difficult man to contact, Ramsay. So thought I'd attempt a face-to-face meeting.' Lippy pushes past him and the bed of dead daffodils and round to the front of the house, her curiosity goading her on. 'Jasmine! Well, well, well.'

'Lippy, dearest, so good to see you again.' She steps towards her, cheeks are air kissed. 'You didn't phone about lunch.'

'Here to pinch my story, are you?'

'My understanding was you were writing a play, a drama only vaguely based on Ramsay's adventures.'

Lippy notes the use of the word adventures. As if Ramsay is some latter-day swashbuckling hero. 'Yes, but—'

'Plenty space for us both, dearest. A good article by me will help promote your play.'

Anger rises through Lippy. All her research and writing, her patient pumping of Ramsay — all for nothing if Jasmine spills the beans on him. Does she realise Ramsay does not want to be identified? Even the idea of a play based on a fabricated version of what happened, no names mentioned, had sent him winging off on paranoia. So what will Jasmine's article do! And yet when she arrived there had been laughter, not shouts of annoyance.

'Ramsay and his wife don't care for publicity.' Lippy is aware her voice sounds peeved, and she feels guilty speaking for the man beside her, who is perfectly capable of defending himself, and his own interests. But she is annoyed, both with herself and the reporter. At the Parliamentary reception she had mentioned her play to Jasmine, was given the impression Jasmine could divulge information she was in need of, and to entice the information from her she had sought to dangle the murder in which Ramsay is implicated. Now Jasmine has driven a tank through her strategy by seeking Ramsay out and turning up on his doorstep.

Jasmine has always been pushy. No shrinking violet, she rides full tilt at the object of her interest. And, judging by the red car parked behind the house, she still drives with foot full down. What a fool she was to mention the play and its subject matter. She might have known this would happen, but then Jasmine has been away working on a paper in Downsouth, and in recent years thoughts and ideas have been safe from her plundering. Lippy wonders why she has returned. Last time they met before she went off, her complaints of Caledon's small size and inward focus were numerous and scathing. Downsouth was where opportunities waited to be plucked like apples from laden orchard trees. The mud of Caledon streets was scraped off her killer heels so Jasmine could tread the polished pavements of fortune.

Yet here she is back, after six years and no contact, and expects to pick up what she had so decisively thrown down. But Jasmine is a journalist, and stories often require to be hacked from rocky ground. And with cutbacks due to the shrinkage of print readership, Jasmine is driven to earn a living like everyone else.

Besides, annoyance like this aside, Lippy rather likes her. Jasmine is fun, fun to be with and around. She knows so many people, can always conjure up theatre tickets at short notice, likes to arrive at parties with a host of friends in tow and is invariably in the loop when it comes to scandal and wicked titbits of information. Jasmine enjoys a good time and isn't averse to sharing it with friends.

Lippy is surprised Ramsay hasn't commented, but when he does it's merely to say, 'I'll get you a coffee.'

The black cloud has blown over with merely a christening sprinkle of rain, and now the sun plays tag with the clouds. Though the house is situated by the sea and must receive the spray-laden force of winds for most of the year, today it is surprisingly calm with spring warmth in the air. Only a couple of miles separate the house here from Bluebell's, yet the climate seems different, or perhaps the position of one is more sheltered than the other.

Lippy glances towards the lounge window, hoping for no surprises today. She wonders if Ramsay and Kat have used the room since the body was discovered, and imagines the awkwardness of a relaxing evening snuggled on the settee whilst remembering the body of Wilkie Smart sprawled on the hearth rug. It might not bother Kat as she didn't see the man, the piece of blue rope, but she's sure Ramsay would be upset. To put a log on the fire he would need to step across the space where Wilkie Smart had lain. It would be like walking across his body. Lippy shivers. She remembers the room has the shop-window-display feel of a place little used, and she guesses an excuse now exists to use it even less.

'Must have been a shock,' says Jasmine, her voice smoothed by sympathy, her head nodding towards the lounge window.

'Not what I expected to unearth on my visit, no.'

'Poor you.'

'It's not me that has to live with it.'

'Ramsay said Bluebell McDaid lives near here.'

The badge from the beach, so small and insignificant, feels a dead weight in Lippy's pocket. She wonders about pulling it out, displaying it on the palm of her hand, her beach find, while she watches for reactions, for signs of recognition. The badge is a trophy to show off, but her better judgement advises caution. Jasmine has already elbowed her way into the Ramsay story, she'll have no qualms about running with this, building it into a major development in the case, to secure headlines and column inches. Jasmine seeks a route out of Lifestyle into whatever position gives her prominence — preferably Political Editor. So Lippy keeps her hand away from her pocket and opts for an empty reply. 'Does she?'

Ramsay appears from the open front door and hands her a mug of coffee. 'The garden seat is reasonably comfortable.' He indicates a bench the other side of the shallow steps to the door, beneath the lounge window. 'Or perhaps that's too near...' He folds himself onto the steps and stretches his legs out in front of him. Lippy joins him while Jasmine, after several glances at the steps and her coat, opts to stand. Lippy hopes that is a sign she will soon leave.

'Can't remember when I last had the company of two intelligent ladies.'

'My last visit when...'

'Apart from that. That day will forever stand on its own, unattached to anything else.'

Jasmine's shoes, with lower, more sensible heels than those she normally wears, scrunch the gravel, whose mix of pebbles and broken shells suggests it has been carted from the beach. Lippy cups her hands round her mug and watches Jasmine while Ramsay stares out to sea. Jess snuffles loudly and collapses at the edge of the grass, opposite Ramsay, head resting on front legs, eyes closed but ears alert.

A fishing boat rat-a-tats across the water, bouncing on the waves like a bright red duck. Gulls formed into a ragged, growing circle swoop, squawk, soar, zoom in and harry it. Their cries of indignation carry on the wind, across sea to shore where Jess's ears twitch and swivel in their direction.

Ramsay's eyes focus on the boat, and track its jaunty progress towards the harbour. Another catch safely home. 'You'll have seen the papers — the garbage about Mutt.'

'Comprehensive hatchet job.' Jasmine prods the stone path with the toe of a shoe. 'Media have gone overboard on it. Whoever's behind it must have influential support. Money, too.'

Ramsay's eyes follow the boat as it slows and swings towards the coast to make for the nearby harbour. 'Made my blood boil.'

'Word in the media is of an almighty internal struggle. And Mutt's backers lost.'

'Certainly looks like it.'

'Old Charlie wouldn't have tolerated such mutiny in the ranks.' Jasmine throws Ramsay a glance.

He gives a curt laugh. 'Aye, old Charlie kept a tight rein. The bastard.'

'No internal upheavals under his regime.' Jasmine's gaze is now fixed on Ramsay, as is Lippy's.

'He was a nasty, manipulative, lying, underhand bastard, and I can't think of one good word to describe him, but...he knew people. Knew what motivated them, how they would react. That let him shuffle the deck chairs, promote special members of the crew whilst others were ditched on a desert island inhabited by cannibals.'

'Must remember that description,' says Lippy with a smile. 'Was it Charlie that went after you?'

Ramsay's eyes are prised from the fishing boat as it disappears round the headland. 'Oh, no, no, no. Not Charlie. Never Charlie. His spotless hands with their manicured nails were on public display. No, not Charlie. A number of his henchmen, yes. Charlie boasted an army of squaddies eager to carry out his orders, desperate to foment political fun and games. Bloody bastard.' A foot kicks the gravel. 'But, you have to hand it to him, he knew how to keep his favourites at the top.'

'So how did his henchmen go about— ' Now that Ramsay has broached the subject, Lippy is keen to find out more.

Jasmine takes a couple of strides along the path and back. 'Who replaced Charlie?'

'Who replaced him?'

'Yes, I went away about then, kind of lost touch with political machinations here. The eyes and minds of the media in Downsouth are enslaved by Westmunster. Compared to bankers, and phone hackers, the Charlies of this world are mere fleas.'

'Yes.' Ramsay's face hardens. 'Yet Charlie exerted considerable influence, there as well as here. I don't think most people realise quite how much.'

Lippy jumps in. 'So tell us what he influenced.'

'You haven't answered my question, Ramsay.' Jasmine's friendly persona reverts to her professional investigative journalistic one. 'Who took over The Galley after Charlie's death?'

Ramsay's mouth twitches. His long silence on the subject makes it difficult to talk of it, but the words bubble in his veins and in his muscles, determined to erupt onto the surface and make themselves heard. The attack on Mutt is the last straw. He would have held his peace for he no longer matters, but Mutt is different. Mutt is the Party's big hope for the next election. And some sodding idiots are out to put that at risk. His foot edges over the red line. He sighs, and in the explosion of breath comes a tumble of pent up emotion shaped into words and incoherent phrases.

'That bastard Charlie organised it, no doubt about it. Spoke to me about it. Took me aside and sympathised, arm round shoulders, buddies together bullshit. Wanted to winkle out the details, used his lead plumb line to gauge how I'd react when he threw me to the cannibals. I should've known, should've twigged what was going on. But they were all at it. We'd been told to do it to top up our salaries, advised it was perfectly legal. So stupid me thought everything was hunky-dory, never envisaged it turning against anyone, never mind me. I hadn't been greedy, not like others who'd dredged up receipts from years before and set up bogus businesses to submit bills for work never done, or stuff done at grossly inflated prices. I just put in for every-day expenses. Okay they were more than I'd have spent had I not been told to claim. But hey, we were working bloody hard. My amounts claimed were tiny compared to the big hitters who were into musical chairs with their houses. If you don't bag a chair it's your turn to pay the taxes. Dear heaven, when I think of what went on — and what I got done for!'

'Ramsay,' Jasmine's foot taps the gravel with impatience.

But the dam has been breached and Ramsay's words gush on. 'Mutt even came to see me. Now I like Mutt, have a lot of time for the man. I was one of the people that angled for him to become Leader in the Caledon Parliament. Mutt and Charlie got on well, so when Charlie said jump for Mutt I joined in. The day he came to see me, his back was ramrod straight but his face drooped like soggy spaghetti. I could tell he didn't like what had happened, what was still happening, but his room for manoeuvre was tight, though I've a feeling he called off that sidekick of Charlie's — his son-in-law. What's his name now? Funny name. Schaw, that's it. Schaw with the paw, some folk called him. He kept a low profile. Knew how to spread the dirt in the pub, though. No story too fantastic. And all those sods reeled home, nudging one another with their elbows, his words sucked into their beings. Damage done.'

Lippy wishes she had paper to takes notes. 'Charlie seems to be something of a legend.'

Ramsay smiles wanly at her. 'You had to hand it to the guy, Charlie was good at what he did. Born to it. Charlie could take an insignificant fact, and before you knew what was happening he had feathers fluffed, wings flapping and people rabid and straining to be let loose on some poor innocent wee fall-guy. It was like a cock fight with a vicious conniving cock and a fluffy wee duckling. No contest. And all over some insignificant occurrence no-one in their right minds would raise an imaginary eyebrow over.' He shakes his head, partly in admiration of a force gone, partly in sorrow at the damage that force wreaked.

'His successor, Ramsay.' A hint of impatience roughens Jasmine's voice though her face still smiles.

Ramsay shifts on his step. 'I was stupid enough to think the whole Galley thing was Charlie's fiefdom, and when he died that it would be laid to rest with him, like grave goods at a chieftain's burial. Long past time it was. I was sure The Galley had finally hit the rocks. How wrong I was! Democracy, huh! Don't make me laugh. Bloody stupid me. I should've known that much power would never return to dust. Such a wealth of power attracts the power-hungry, the power-crazed. Charlie knew that, and he and his cohorts had carefully secured the succession.'

'Name, Ramsay?'

'Carnoustie.'

'Carnoustie?' Lippy gasps with surprise. 'The ex-Minister guy who's restyled himself as Party grandee?'

'The same. How d'you think he managed the new image?'

'Carnoustie. Hmm.' Jasmine's face shows excitement. 'Need to have a wee rummage in the Callyman's files. See what I can dig up.'

'Let me tell you this about Carnoustie—' Jess jumps to her feet, tail wagging as she barks and feigns attempts to dive to the corner of the house to see whose feet scrunch the gravel.

Ramsay rises to his feet and bounds along the front of the house.

'Ah, glad to find you in residence, Mr Dunn,' says a voice.

Lippy shifts in surprise. She recognises the voice and wonders if the pink shirt will again be on display.

'Detective Inspector Raisin,' responds Ramsay. 'I hope your visit means good news?'

The two men walk together to where Lippy and Jasmine now stand. Lippy stretches out her hand. 'We met before. The day of the...'

'The playwright lady.' Lippy nods. 'Never forget a face. Names can evade me, but every face I've met is catalogued.'

Ramsay's hand indicates Jasmine. 'Jasmine is a journalist with— '

'Ah, cavorting with the press, are you Mr Dunn? Tut, tut. Not to be advised.'

Jasmine steps forward and switches on her man-eating smile. 'Sorry, didn't catch your name.'

'Raisin. Detective Inspector. And you are?'

'Stane, Jasmine. Lifestyle journalist.' Her eyes start with the unruly brown grey hair and travel downwards to the leather jacket, the pink shirt, the jeans and the cowboy boots. 'I can't say I remember every face I see — too many for that — but I can say I catalogue each and every name in their appropriate place.'

Lippy senses Jasmine is sending out a challenge to the DI, but doesn't know why. Perhaps it's as simple as her finding him intriguing. Jasmine is a journalist — an extremely good journalist, if a tad opinionated — and contacts are the lifeblood of journalists. So Jasmine probably wants to add his name to her address books. A bit like Gail, her son's girlfriend. When Jasmine wears that cheeky, challenging look on her face she reminds her of the Eilidh of long ago. The stance is the same too — a sort of come and get me I'm waiting for you but will fight you all the way attitude, conveyed both by look and posture. There she goes, dredging up Eilidh again. Why the hell can't she stay buried! If Eilidh turned the corner of the house now she wouldn't know her. The years will have dulled the chestnut hair and her figure has probably ballooned with gobbling chocolate and the birth of six kids. She'll live in a caravan, take in washing to make ends meet, and have a husband who repairs television sets. So she doesn't have a clue why Jasmine should remind her of Eilidh.

The Detective Inspector accepts Ramsay's offer of a coffee and Lippy agrees to a refill. Jasmine's remains largely undrunk, so she refuses.

'Am I interrupting a powwow?' asks the DI. 'Was a war council in progress?'

Lippy raises her eyebrows in surprise. 'Heavens, no! What gives you that impression? This is merely a follow up visit to my previous one. One or two details to check.'

'For the play?'

'For the play.'

'How's that coming along?'

'It's at the checking, revising and tweaking stage. I have a director and a theatre company interested.'

'You have? Hmm. Must look out for it. Who knows what I might learn.'

Lippy glances at Jasmine who looks amused. 'How are the investigations going? Found the perpetrator yet?'

The DI checks his hands, studies his fingers. 'Our enquiries are progressing.'

Jasmine snorts with laughter. 'That's doublespeak for they haven't a bloody clue.'

'Not so, Miss — am I right in addressing you as Miss?'

'Why don't you settle for Ms?'

Detective Inspector Raisin looks pained. 'I so dislike the Mizz form of address. It's neither single, nor married, neither one thing nor the other — like a not proven verdict in court.'

'What not proven verdict?' asks Ramsay as he steps carefully from the tiled floor of the hallway onto the stone steps, a tray held in his hands.

'Do I see a plate of biscuits, Ramsay?'

'Specially for you Lippy.'

'With all your visitors Kat'll think you've broken out your shell.'

'What progress have you made with the case?' prods Jasmine. She has been standing for some time and her feet and legs are complaining. The sea air is fresh and she would much rather have this conversation in a quiet upmarket pub. But a DI makes a good contact and since her return she's had to restructure her contacts book, so she sips her cold coffee — too strong for her and definitely not caffè latte — and leashes her impatience.

'Police investigations are about being meticulous. We are meticulously sifting our evidence and statements taken.'

'So you haven't any leads.'

'Mizz Stane—'

Jasmine's mood changes and she grins at him. 'Oh, do call me Jasmine. You dislike the Mizz stuff anyway, so you might as well.'

'Mizz Stane, we are actively following a number of leads.'

With his place on the steps taken by the DI, Ramsay wanders across to stand beside Jasmine. 'Glad to hear you have leads. I won't feel comfortable in my own home until the perpetrator is caught, and we know why the body was dumped here.'

'Hardly dumped,' says Raisin. 'Quite artistically arranged I would have said.'

'You know what I mean,' mutters Ramsay.

The DI pours half the mug of coffee down his throat. 'And why are you here today Mizz Stane?'

Lippy straightens up, keen to hear the answer. Why is Jasmine here today?

Jasmine stands very still. Her eyes seek Ramsay's. Ramsay's head dips almost imperceptibly. 'I came to…' She shuffles her feet. 'I came to give Ramsay information.' Her voice is low, flat.

'Did I hear correctly? Did I hear you say you came to give Mr Dunn information?'

'You know that's what I said.'

'My, my!' DI Raisin places his mug on the step, and both hands migrate to his knees where they tap out a rhythm. 'Uhuh! So, Mizz Stane. What's this information you wish to share with Mr Dunn?'

'A letter.'

'A letter? Interesting. A letter to whom? From whom?'

'A letter to Ramsay. It was sent to me at the paper.'

'Hmm! A letter for Mr Dunn that was sent to you at the Callyman? Even more interesting. Now, Mizz Stane, I wonder if you can tell me this.' His eyes take in the other three and land on Jess who has decided to play no part in the shenanigans taking place in her garden. She shows her disgust at the intrusion by snoring and letting rip the occasional snort. 'Can you tell me why a letter to Mr Dunn should be sent to you at the newspaper you work for?'

'Haven't a clue. That's how it was.'

'Hmm! Let me get this straight — I need all my pieces of information lined up like ducks in a row. This letter for Mr Dunn was in an envelope addressed to you at the paper? Yes?'

Jasmine nods. 'Ten out of ten.'

'So, let's sketch a picture of this. You arrive in your office, pile of mail on desk. You work your way through it and come upon this envelope that you open. And, lo and behold, inside you find another envelope addressed to Mr Dunn? Yes?'

'More or less.'

'Oh, Mizz Stane. More or less will not do. I need facts. Definite facts, not more or less facts. So, tell me the facts.'

Jasmine rolls her eyes heavenwards. 'It was the only letter. Letters are rarely used as a method of communication these days. Most connected people use email, phone, Twitter.'

The DI sighs. 'Yes, I'm aware some of us still live in the stone age. But humour me, Mizz Stane, humour me with the facts.'

'I opened it, saw it was for Ramsay whom I hadn't met but whom I'd heard of from Lippy. So as soon as I could leave I hotfooted it down here to deliver the letter.'

'O…kay.' His fingers play the piano on his knees. 'Okay, but that still leaves one question which you have omitted to answer.'

'Urrrgh! What question?' Jasmine's face looks peeved, as she makes an effort to control her temper. She is not a person who enjoys being toyed with, and she suspects this bloody DI is doing just that.

Detective Inspector Raisin studies her, pleased to have riled her, but doesn't let it show. 'You have failed to inform me, Mizz Stane, why you were the recipient of the letter?'

'Why don't you ask the bloody sender when you find him?' Jasmine spins round to face the sea. Ramsay places his hand on her arm then removes it when he sees the gesture has been noticed.

'I can assure you I'll do precisely that. But until I run the sender to ground I would ask for your version of the reason.'

Jasmine takes a deep breath. She hands her coffee mug to Ramsay and slowly turns to face Raisin.

'This is police harassment. I don't know why you're treating me in this manner.'

'This is a murder investigation, Mizz Stane, so I'm allowed to question in whatever manner I think fit — with one or two exceptions of course — in order to establish the facts of the case. Now, if you climb down from your dashing white high horse, we might be able to do that without further waste of time. Yours and mine.'

Jasmine's fists are clenched. 'I've absolutely no idea why the letter was sent to me. I was working elsewhere and only returned a couple of months ago to take up the Callyman position. So I've few contacts here. It's a total mystery to me why I received it.'

DI Raisin stares at her as if sifting through her for any indication of a malformed truth or a diseased fact. 'O...kay, I'll go with that for now.' He scratches the side of his nose. 'So where's the letter and the envelope addressed to you?'

'Ramsay has them both.'

The Detective Inspector's eyes travel to Ramsay. 'Mr Dunn, you must know what I need from you.'

Ramsay nods. 'It's in the house. I'll get it.' Hand clutching Jasmine's mug, he slips between the DI and Lippy who listens as his footsteps pad along the hallway to the kitchen.

'Do you suppose whoever sent the letter didn't know where Ramsay stayed but thought a journalist might know, or be able to find out?' ventures Lippy.

'A possibility. But why send it to a journalist who's only been here for two months so isn't widely known? Why not send it to one who's been around since the ark?' Lippy and Jasmine both shrug. 'And the most intriguing question of all — which I have every expectation will soon be answered — is why send a letter to Mr Dunn at all? Unless perhaps it has to do with a certain body and the investigation into that person's murder.'

27 - Urrrgh, politics!

Ming blows into the office like a squall of autumn wind, disturbing the air and atmosphere around him.

'What the hell does that bastard think he's playing at?' he throws at Brian as he gusts through his office.

'Who you talking about, Ming?'

'What right does the bampot have to utter such garbage?'

'Brian grins widely. His boss can't see him, so no problem. He suspects he knows the subject of Ming's ire, but thinks it wise to play along. 'Who's this?'

The noise of files as they cascade to the floor comes from Ming's office. 'Shit! Shit! And double shit!'

'Something wrong, Ming?'

'Get your double-crossing arse in here, toot sweet.'

The double-crossing reference sobers Brian. Does it refer to him and Kirsty? If so, how does Ming know? Hmm. But rather than stride, he saunters in to face Ming. 'Problem?' he asks as he bites back a chortle and surveys an artistic installation of folders and papers spread across the floor. 'New filing system?'

'You're too glib for your own good. Know that?'

'If you say so.'

'If you hadn't left these bloody folders on the edge of my desk this wouldn't have happened.'

'Sorry. I'm certain I placed them—'

'So you can bloody well pick them up and put the papers back in order. I haven't time for such things.'

Brian hunkers down to retrieve the papers he put — safely — on Ming's desk earlier. Ming will need them shortly for the debate in the chamber, so a bit of speedy shuffling is required if he's not to incur further wrath. 'Who were you talking about?'

'Talking about? When?'

'When you came in. You seemed less than pleased with someone.'

'Oh, that. I assumed you'd know.'

'Perhaps I've missed—'

'Don't play silly buggers, Brian. You know damn well I was referring to that idiot Mutt — his performance on television last night. The brazen-faced cheek of the man. To go off in the huff, hide himself for... for ages, then pop up on our TV screens like a slice of toast, dripping honey as if nothing had happened.'

'Did something happen — apart from someone taking a pot-shot at him in the media?'

'Bit more than a pot-shot.'

'Par for the course I would have thought for a leader.'

'How would you know!'

'Mutt batted it off well. Came across as being in charge of events. That appeared the popular verdict.'

'Huh! Who says? He was like a monkey at the zoo. Swinging this way and that, performing tricks, preening himself — all to please the audience.'

Brian squares up papers and folders and rises to his feet. 'Can't see Mutt as a monkey. He's his own man. Doesn't perform to any organ grinder's tune. Perhaps that's why a few disgruntled people in the Party want to damage him.'

The glare that stretches Ming's features gives him a comical look, like a child pulling idiotic faces. 'A few! You're out of touch, Brian. Mutt's trod on too many toes, sidelined people with valuable contributions. He's become a liability.'

'Really! I thought his poll ratings were fairly good. Of course, not as good as—'

'Joined the enemy, have you?' Ming's icicled voice cuts through his assistant's support of their leader.

'I'm only voicing solidarity with our leader in the run up to an election. That's what's expected, isn't it?'

'Think again. You're taking a dangerous swerve off the main road.'

'I understood I was on the main road.'

Ming holds another folder at arms length and, with a theatrical flourish, drops it to the floor. He compresses his mouth into a scar. 'I was mistaken about you Brian.'

'Mistaken? In what way?'

'I judged you as an assistant that would support me.'

'I do. I support your Parliamentary work.'

'But you don't support me?'

'I don't regard now as the correct time to challenge the leadership. That's a different matter.'

'If a leader or a policy fails to come up to scratch, then it requires to be challenged, changed.'

'Agree. But the time for change should be chosen with care.'

Ming looks for another file to throw on the floor but none are to hand. Instead he beats his hand in the air. 'Rubbish. Prevarication breeds weasels. We need to show the electorate we've the strength, the single-mindedness to take the actions required.'

Brian keeps his head down. The same words were uttered in his hearing recently by another MCP — by Brankton. Ming the Unoriginal is parroting them. Brian decides to jump in the deep end. 'I'm not convinced the Party has a suitable replacement for Mutt.'

Ming's hand slaps his desk. 'What a bloody disappointment you've proved to be, Brian. I don't usually make mistakes, but you're a big, gangly, stringy, one. A big mistake and a big disappointment.'

'You've been pleased with my performance to date.'

'I made it clear on your appointment what was expected of you, and you've failed in your duties. Failed big time. Instead of supporting me and my decisions, you decide to challenge me. In challenging me you challenge the person the Party wants as leader.'

'That's bullshit. I've challenged no-one.' Brian jumps to his feet. 'I support today what I supported when I started to work for you. I'm not the one that's changed.'

Ming splutters, his face contorted. 'Get those papers sorted. I need them.' His hand cuts the air in dismissal of his assistant.

When several minutes later Ming tornadoes out the door and down the corridor to the lift, Brian is left to wonder if he has burned his boats. His confrontation with Ming has been brewing for some time, but he'd rather matters hadn't come to a head quite so soon. Support of his application for the list would have been useful, but now looks unlikely. A significant number of Parliamentary assistants put their names forward to stand as candidates. It is one of the reasons people take on the post — to learn the ropes and make contacts prior to standing themselves. So why Ming is so annoyed by his application Brian doesn't know. Now, to further complicate matters, Ming is openly supportive of Brankton as leader, and is suspicious of Brian's opposition.

Brian thuds his elbows onto his desk and ruffles his hair with his hands. His life is falling apart. Sure there have been rough patches, but all was trundling along fairly well until... Until when? Until Wilkie Smart's murder — an event that had nothing whatsoever to do with him, yet seems to have changed the course of his career.

He looks up as the door opens and a figure sidles in. 'Kirsty, good to see you.'

'Quick visit. Best if I'm not seen here.'

'Just had a barney with Ming.'

'Over what?' She looks concerned.

'Mutt. And my application for the list. Looks like he's—'

'Blast. You should've been more careful.'

'Not easy with him.'

'Yeah, well, keep your lucky rabbit's foot with you.'

'These are frowned upon in our environmentally conscious times.'

'That merely means you don't broadcast your ownership of one.'

'The thought makes my skin crawl.'

'Cross Ming openly and you'll need all the luck you can conjure up.' Kirsty stands by the not fully closed door. Her hand still grasps the handle, half taking in Brian's response, half alert for sounds in the corridor.

'You're full of the joys of spring.'

'Full of the woes of the Party more like.'

'Mutt's reappeared, thank goodness. He was in full flight on TV last night. Did well I thought.'

'He's no fool.'

'So why the long face and jerky stance.'

Kirsty carefully sticks her head round the door and surveys the corridor. 'This thing against Mutt…it isn't over.'

'I didn't say it was. But he came out strong last night. That must've given his opponents pause for thought.'

'Don't you believe it. Attack becomes a way of life. Decapitation and filleting to some are as enjoyable as a win on the Lottery.'

'I was mulling over events when you appeared. I wondered when the problems between Ming and me surfaced and reckoned it was about the time of Wilkie's murder. So perhaps we're all on edge, and once the perpetrator's arrested tensions will ease.'

Kirsty glares at him, her eyebrows slanted. 'You don't believe that guff surely? Tell me you don't.'

Brian leans back in his chair and swivels it towards her. 'I'm an optimist.'

'You could've fooled me.'

'The all-out attack on Mutt must've taken considerable organisation. The Party black sheep can't come out with that every day.'

'Who says they will? Plenty other ways to cause discontent.'

'You think there's another attack in the pipeline?'

'I don't think — I know.'

'What?'

Kirsty checks the corridor again. 'It's bloody quiet here today.'

'Yup. Weird. But what about—?'

'Can't talk here. Can we meet later?'

'Sure. Where?'

A door opens further along the corridor, voices murmur, recede towards the lift.

'Must go.'

'Where?'

'Where we met before…and we can move on from there.' She slips through the door.

'Time? What time?'

'I can leave anytime. What about you?' Another door opens. Kirsty jumps back into the office until the corridor is clear again.

'Six. I'll leave then. Ming can like it or lump it.'

'See you.' She slips into the corridor and is gone.

When Ming returns from his committee meeting he stands outside the door and chats with a couple of other MCPs. As Brian's fingers rattle over his keyboard he can hear the rise and fall of voices, one of them a woman's, laughter, a whine of attack against a colleague, perhaps Mutt —he can't hear the conversation clearly. The sound of the voices is like an organ playing softly in church, almost more a vibration of sounds than actual music. Brian hopes Ming will leave soon. He has left nothing on his desk for his attention, so there is no reason for him to linger, and this evening Ming's wife hopes to catch up with friends on an evening out, so she wants him home sharp. Brian knows this as she phoned and asked him to remind Ming of it.

Brian tidies up and is about to shut down his computer when Ming throws open the door and with a wave at colleagues stomps into the office. His face beams with the look of a child who has been given a present but instructed not to tell others about it.

'Not shutting down your computer I hope.'

'Yes. I've finished for the day and have plans.'

'My, you have plans, have you!'

'Yes, so—'

'Too bloody bad.'

Brian looks at his boss and wonders what has brought about the recent change in his attitude. His eyes look mean, and instead of his usual relaxed but blustering stance he has become aggressive and petulant. His skin has developed a grey tinge and his laid-back nature has drawn in on itself until he has the appearance of a hedgehog rolling into a ball to present a wall of spines to the world, and especially to Brian. Until this sudden change Brian has been surprised that his time with a bruiser like Charlie Kintail has apparently left Ming with a naiveté untouched by the nastier and more questionable aspects of Charlie's machinations within the Party. With Charlie long gone, something or someone else has impacted on Ming, and the change is not for the better. Brankton must be pulling his strings, though he questions whether Brankton has the nous to mastermind the campaign mounted against Mutt. If it's a case of the blind leading the blind, then some clear sighted and determined person must be switching the levers. But Brian has no idea who that might be.

As thoughts flash through his mind, Brian decides to play it safe. 'Your wife phoned.'

'Karen? What did she want?'

'Asked me to remind you to be early home. She's a get-together with friends this evening.'

'Bugger. Right, well you'll just need to do the report on your own.'

'What report?'

'All in my notes, Brian, all in my copious notes.' Ming dumps his folders on the desk. A snide look twists his face. 'Needs a bit of research, of course. Just to make it all hang together. I've written the conclusion down for you, so the facts and findings need to be consistent with that.'

Brian sifts through the notes. 'This will need a bit of work. Hope you don't want it anytime soon.'

'I promised the final report would be distributed to the rest of the committee by lunch time tomorrow.'

'What! Not possible.'

'I've given an undertaking. I'll take a dim view if I have to go back on that.'

'Be reasonable, Ming, there's days of work in this.'

'Lunch time tomorrow.'

Brian bites back words of annoyance and stills his hands by squaring up the files into a neat pile. 'I'll need coffee and sandwiches to keep me going.'

Ming shrugs. 'Nothing to do with me.' He turns on his heel and stomps into his own office.

Brian slips out. The coffee and sandwiches were an excuse to let him phone Kirsty, but it dawns on him the food will be needed too.

'Kirsty. Brian here. Hi. Look, really sorry but my dipstick of a boss insists I work on a sham of a report he has magicked from the ether. Says he needs it by lunch time tomorrow. Yes, afraid I'll have to call off. It's a ploy to piss me off, I'm certain, but—. Sorry, what was that? Okay. Will do.'

Back in the office he sips his coffee and goes through Ming's notes. Undecipherable twaddle as far as he can see. Ming appears to have it in for him, but he reckons at present it's better to humour him than further challenge his authority. That could see him booted out the door before he has time to draw breath.

With a triumphant look burnishing his face Ming strolls from his office, raincoat thrown over his shoulder. 'A good dinner and feet up by the fire to watch footie, I think. Just me and a nice single malt.' He bends to retie a shoelace. His raincoat slides to the floor and he heaves it back on to his shoulder as he straightens. 'Enjoy yourself, Brian. Remember, lunch time tomorrow.' He swings out the door.

Brian grits his teeth and mutters under his breath. Urrrgh, politics! He picks up a pack of sandwiches and rips it open. Cheese and pickle. Not his favourite, but this late in the day there is little choice. One down and he tackles the other, tossing the packaging into his wastepaper basket. It hits the edge and slides to the floor. As he bends to retrieve it and stash it in the bin, light glints on something, like a piece of tinfoil or metal, and catches his eye. He gets up to investigate. Bending down, he picks up the item. It must have fallen from Ming's pocket or coat as he can't think where else it might have come from. He lays it in the palm of his hand and looks at the small square item, enamelled black on one side and with a pin on the other. Brian recognises it as a lapel badge, but he has never before seen one in the design of a black square. He wonders what organisation Ming belongs to, thinks it odd he, as his parliamentary assistant, is unaware of it. He moves towards Ming's office to leave it on his desk, then thinks better of it. With the factionalism and fracturing of the Party, he might be better to show it to Kirsty and see what she thinks. If Ming misses it, then he could have lost it anywhere.

28 - Salting slugs

Out in the open sea the ship rocks gently, like a cradle set in motion by a guiding hand, the movement measured, sufficient to lull without causing concern. Then, as if the guiding hand is distracted, an occasional heave causes the vessel to thud and send shockwaves juddering through the length of the ship and the bodies of passengers.

Selina concentrates on walking up stairs and along passageways, one hand clutched tightly onto the rails. 'It's rough.'

Schaw seems to enjoy the rocking experience. His gait rolls easily with the motion as if accustomed to it. 'Nah, this is calm. Rough means —'

'Don't tell me. I don't want to know what rough means. I hope it stays like this — no worse.'

'Forecast is good, so it'll probably be fine.'

The passageway with its rail gives way to a circulation area with no rail, so she grabs her husband's arm. They pass wide doors out to the deck across which the light from inside spills. They open to admit a young couple into the warmth. A blast of cold clean air accompanies them. It dances around and partners with the inside atmosphere that smells of warm people, perfume, hairs pray and alcohol. The doors close, cocooning them, and through the glass, apart from the lit rectangle, Selina sees nothing but dense black. Not velvet black, for this black has no texture, no softness, but a hard wall of black nothingness. For someone used to a town and its lights — welcoming in colour and brightness when near at hand, in the distance still bright with pinpoints of red, blue, green and yellow — the endless black unnerves her. To step into it would be to step off the end of the world, the end of everything.

'I might have enjoyed this in summer — in June when nights are light and I can see what the blackness covers.'

'Not much to see out there. Water, that's about it.'

'You sound as if you've made this journey before.'

'Woops! Another biggie.' They halt to steady themselves as the ship lurches.

'Ugh!' Selina holds tight to Schaw's arm.

'Nearly at the restaurant.' Her husband puts his arm round her.

'Thank goodness.'

'You'll be fine once you're seated.'

Passengers, mainly young, mill around. They shriek and giggle at the lurches, feign falls against members of the opposite sex, hands thrown against their bodies to steady and explore. Youngsters heavy with make-up but light on clothes swirl around, their male counterparts slouched in drooping jeans and sleeveless T-shirts emblazoned with wild images. They twirl, shout, gesticulate to one another as if on a dance floor. Selina and Schaw push their way through the throng intoxicated on high spirits and find the restaurant which is surprisingly full considering the main holiday season is still months away.

A waiter with a face like a monkey, and hips that sway like a pendulum between tables and diners, shows them to their table.

'He sounds Spanish,' remarks Selina.

'Probably is. Spaniards work on cruise lines. Good on the hospitality front, not so good when the weather turns rough.'

'Quit talking about rough weather. You'll put me off dinner.'

Wine lists fly down from the hands of a waiter with a hint of superciliousness gilding his face.

Selina leaves the one placed in front of her unopened. 'Can I have a glass of water?' she asks.

The waited bows his head. 'Still or sparkling?'

'Still.'

The waiter scribbles on his notepad with studied gravity, as if she had ordered an expensive cocktail.

Schaw takes his time to leaf through the pages, hums and haws, asks about this wine, then another and eventually settles for a different one. The waiter bows — an incongruous gesture, thinks Selina — and hurries off to weave his way through tables and fellow waiters in a fair rendition of a paso doble.

The buzz of conversation in the restaurant is loud, occasionally strident, like the percussion section of an orchestra — the boom of drums, clash of cymbals, ting of chimes, rattle of maracas, supplemented by a blast of trombone and a squeal of flute. As she glances around Selina can match instruments to people. The guy opposite, given stature and voice, is a drum. The woman with him she reckons is a wind chime with that slightly breathy sound they give as the breeze plays around and through them. The man further along the table has just shown by his laugh that he is a pair of clashing cymbals. She wonders what she and Schaw are as they sit here, looking out of place — grey phantoms of the orchestra.

Many passengers are seated at tables in large groups. Selina watches with fascination as they lean forward to converse, dance in their seats, throw heads back in laughter, all bent on extracting as much enjoyment as possible from the evening. Dress is casual but fancy. Women wear trousers or leggings and tops in jewel colours. Earrings, necklaces, bangles catch and keep light from overhead or the softer glow from miniature table lamps. Selina feels drab in the black skirt she wears for work. She changed her white blouse for a plain black cotton top but wishes she'd packed a chiffon scarf to soften the neckline and add interest. She toys with her cutlery as she listens to the various languages that ping around her like plucked guitars. With a darted smile at her husband she picks up the menu and flicks through it.

She can't remember the last time she and Schaw ate in a restaurant. When first married, they often ate at a local Chinese restaurant, that or the Indian further along the road. Occasionally, if a special occasion such as her mother's birthday, her father would book a table at a city centre place that was glitzy, and shiny and as pretentious as paste jewellery, and where her mother rarely enjoyed the food. *What's this?* she would sniff, as she poked the mound on her plate with the prongs of her fork. *I'm not going to like this, I know I'm not.*

Other young married friends would invite them for dinner. Those were good evenings when food like spaghetti bolognaise or fish and chips and bottles of plonk would have them surfing the waves of hilarity and enjoyment. After many such evenings they would walk the deserted streets home, through the chill of the breaking dawn, and watch the city wind itself up for the ticking past of another day, as they wound down for a few hours sleep. Such a great period in their lives, so why did it suddenly peter out? Yes, they had Janice, their daughter, but other couples had families too, and they just carted them along to wherever the dinner was, and left them in a bedroom to sleep in carrycots, prams, or snuggled in sleeping bags on inflatable lilos on the floor.

Have kids will manage, was the motto. Maybe the kids reached the ages of being too disruptive for such an arrangement to be practicable. Yet other couples were able to continue with their social lives, so perhaps something else had impinged. Her mind turns to Schaw, and what he told her of his work for her father. Had she been the only one out of the loop? Had their friends been aware of her father's activities and of

Schaw's association with her father? If so, was that the reason for a log-splitter being driven through the trunks of their friendships? She looks at her husband whose eyes rove through the menu, mulling over which of the exotic dishes to choose, and wonders if the working relationship between husband and father — two men she now realises she knows little about — has limited her menu of life, has constrained the life she has led. A wave of regret foams through her, but she drives it back, as she decides lamenting the past is pointless, better by far to pin her thoughts on the good times they shared as a family.

'This place is expensive,' she whispers to Schaw, leaning across the table.

'Not unduly.'

Selina wonders where the money came from for this, and remembers the name on the ticket and on the passport she showed customs. Mrs Elsie Ravenscrofte. Did someone by that name book and pay for tickets, tickets Schaw somehow managed to lay his hands on? Or did Schaw buy the tickets under that name? She'll ask him, though perhaps later, not now, for she wants to enjoy this meal. Rarely has she been taken to a restaurant like this, except by her father — and again his leaving party flashes through her mind — so she would like to revel in the experience and enjoy the meal but— In her life there's always a but. How can she enjoy herself when she still has no idea why they're here and where they're going?

The waiter takes their order, and the wine waiter, with a flourish of bottle and napkin like a conjurer, pours a small measure into Schaw's glass. He swirls, sniffs, tastes, rolling the wine round his mouth before he slowly swallows. He hesitates to get the full after-effect then nods. 'Nice wine.'

The waiter pours the ruby liquid into both glasses, deposits a bottle of water beside Selina and zooms off as if on a skateboard.

Selina takes a sip. 'Schaw, who's Mrs Elsie Ravenscrofte?'

'You are.'

'You know I'm not.'

'That's your present identity.'

'What about my real one? The real me?'

'It's still there, waiting for you.'

'But why the shenanigans? Why can't we use our own passports?'

'Jeez, Selina, not here, for heaven's sake.' The boat lurches. 'Oops! Watch your wine. Too costly to waste.' He puts his fingers around the bases of the wine glasses to steady them and stop their slide towards the edge of the table.

'But Schaw— '

'Sit back and enjoy. Things will work out.'

'Where are we going?'

'Amsterdam.'

'Yes I know, but are we staying there? And for how long?'

'To be accurate we dock at the IJmuiden ferry terminal, about half an hour from the centre of Amsterdam.'

'So do we get a train, bus, what, to the centre?'

'We'll sort that out tomorrow. No problem.' He puts his hand over hers.

'But—'

'I know a guy in Amsterdam.'

'You mean someone who'll help us?'

'Uhuh.'

'So we need help. You're in trouble.'

'Things'll cool down.'

'When?'

'Soon.'

A frown creases Selina's forehead. She unscrews the top from her bottle of water and pours some into a glass. 'Soon?'

'Soon. When the police get their arses in gear and apprehend Wilkie Smart's murderer.'

'What! But that's nothing to do—?'

'Course not.'

'So why…?'

Schaw glances around. People at nearby tables are too engrossed in their own frolics to pay them attention, and the talk is in Dutch or German, nevertheless he lowers his voice as he leans towards Selina. 'I know who did it.'

'You know who killed…?'

'Shh!' Schaw glances around again. 'Yes. So better we remove ourselves until he's arrested.'

'Dear heavens! You mean your life's in danger?'

'No, no. Don't be so dramatic. Just best if we're not around.'

'We?'

'Eh?'

'You said best if we're not around?'

'Slip of the tongue.'

'You sure?'

'Of course.'

The waiter delivers their starter, sliding a plate in front of each with an, 'Enjoy your meal.'

Selina watches his departure, swings her gaze back to her husband. 'Have I…met this person who…did it?' She remembers the visit paid to her a few days ago when she waited for Schaw's return. 'I have, haven't I?'

Schaw slowly picks up his cutlery. 'Drop it, Selina.'

'Have I? Tell me.'

Her husband sighs. 'Yes.'

'I knew there was something weird about him. I could see it in his eyes. No feelings, just icy coldness.'

'Look, everything's fine. He and his mother have been left behind. And we'll stay away until the police have done their stuff. So nothing to worry about.'

'Easy to say.'

'I wouldn't put you at risk, Selina.' He drops his knife and grasps her hand. 'I know we've hit lows, but we enjoyed highs, too.'

'They seem so long ago.' She shakes his hand away and picks up her cutlery to eat her prawns.

'Selina, I did what I did to pay for holidays, ballet lessons for Janice, her bike, school trips, to pay bills.'

A wan smile curls his wife's mouth. 'Life rarely turns out the way we dream.'

'True. But dreams are just that. Not reality.'

'You haven't been an easy person to love…not recently…not when you shut me out. But I still do, you know. Not in a sloppy, romantic way, but I can't imagine life without you, Schaw.' Her fingers find their way to his cheek, and stroke it. They move a strand of his hair from his eyes and Selina notices a mark on Schaw's forehead — a large yellowish area like an old bruise. She doesn't remember seeing that before.'

Schaw tracks her hand and grasps it, lowers it to his mouth and brushes his lips across its back. 'It was safer to keep you in the dark.'

Like a leaf fluttering from a branch, she lets her hand fall to the table. 'But by doing that you changed.'

He plays with his glass. 'Your father…his views of women were… traditional.'

Selina gives a curt laugh. 'So my mother informed me not so long ago. She said he didn't think women had brains. Regarded them as ornaments for the mantelpiece.'

'About right. He'd never have stood for me telling you. And by the time he died…well… there didn't seem much point.'

'One man with so much influence.'

'You don't know the half of it. Not even a fraction.'

'Probably better that way now.'

'Probably.' They munch their food. Schaw finishes his mushrooms and carefully places his knife and fork on his plate. 'They nicknamed me the Galley Cat, you know.'

Selina looks up. 'Weird. Why?'

'Because my job was to rid the Party of those considered rodents and pests.'

'Rid? Not literally, I hope?'

'Heavens, no.'

'I see.'

'I thought of it as salting slugs.'

'Assaulting slugs! Ugh!'

'Salting slugs. Though I'm not sure there's a difference.'

Selina stares at him, one eyebrow at an angle to the other. 'You're kidding me.'

'I used to watch my father salting them. He'd go into the garden with the tin of Saxa salt and pour it onto slugs he winkled out from beneath leaves.'

'Why on earth did he do that?'

'Revenge.'

'Now I know you're kidding me.'

'No, they ate the veg he grew. My mother was a vegetarian. Didn't like veg that had been chewed before it got to her plate. Hence the salting.'

'What a weird upbringing!'

'It seemed very normal. They shrivelled up.'

'Ugh!'

'Probably quite a painless way to go. Though he moved on to beer traps.'

'That must've caused the slugs some merriment.'

'I couldn't stand around and watch that. The trap was left overnight and checked in the morning.'

Selina flaps her napkin at him. 'So because your father salted slugs, you thought it okay to…to…shrivel…rodents for my father.'

'I think it made it easier. Childhood teachings stay with you.'

'Perhaps.'

The next course follows seamlessly. Waiters whirl through the spaces between tables, whisk used plates to the kitchen, and carry tempting dishes from it. By sleight of hand their starter plates disappear and are replaced by others. Cutlery is changed, their wine glasses refilled.

Schaw grins at her. 'Posh, eh!'

'Maybe after this…when it's over… maybe we could go away —

abroad, somewhere warm. Portugal or Greece or somewhere, and spend time together. Go sightseeing, enjoy meals in tavernas. That sort of thing.'

Schaw grasps her hands in his. 'That's a promise. We'll make up for lost time.'

Selina blinks rapidly, but it's not enough to stop a tear journey across her cheek to her chin, and leave a trail like a slug. She frees a hand, grasps her wine glass and raises it in a toast. 'To making up for lost time.'

Her husband raises his glass and they clink them together, tings on a xylophone of the orchestra of sounds around them, before taking sips.

'Now let's enjoy our meal.'

A passing waiter stops, asks if their meal is to their satisfaction, if he can bring them more wine.

Selina takes a roll from the basket on the table and tears it. 'When did you start to work for my father? Before we were married? After?'

'This isn't the place—'

'Tell me. For anyone listening my father could be a painter and decorator or an IT consultant. So tell me. I need to know.'

'I did one job before — a simple bit of business that I sorted. He was stuck. I helped him out. That's all.'

'And after?'

'One of his regular guys left. I wasn't keen to be involved…not exactly my usual line of work. But he paid well. Give him his due, he was never stingy. So the money was a big incentive.'

'My mother never saw much of his money.'

'No.' He takes a mouthful of his steak. 'Still, what he left ensured she could be well looked after.'

'No thanks to him.' Selina leans her arms on the table and glances around. 'Nice décor.'

'Functional and modern. But fine.'

'Och, you! You never show any interest in your surroundings.' She thinks of the soft furnishings and nick knacks she brought home from the department store, bought with her own hard-earned money. Unless she pointed them out to Schaw he never noticed. 'You'd be happy living in a cardboard box.'

'Shit!' Schaw's cutlery clatters to the plate.

'What? What's wrong?' Selina's blood runs cold at the distraught look on her husband's face. His body has stiffened, tensed like a bow with its arrow poised to shoot

He stares over her shoulder in the direction of the restaurant's door. She turns to look. 'No, don't. Keep still.'

'Tell me, what?'

She sees him relax, his manner snaps from alert to watchful calm with a whoosh of breath. 'It's all right. Nothing.' He gulps a breath of the restaurant's boozy air.'

'You saw something...someone?'

'False alarm. Thought I did. But it wasn't him.'

'You sure?'

'A sprinkling of paranoia to enhance the sauce.'

Selina stares intently at him. 'You wouldn't...?'

Schaw pats her hand. Her wavering fork nearly stabs him. 'It wasn't him. I caught a glimpse, and thought...thought I recognised the features, the hair. But I was mistaken.'

'You frightened me.'

'I frightened myself. They can't possibly know we're on the ship. So relax. Let's enjoy our meal.'

'Okay.' Selina takes another mouthful of her sirloin, but now it tastes like stewed rubber.

29 - Others will have turned the screws

Detective Inspector Raisin pulls on a pair of gloves dredged from a pocket before he takes the envelopes from Ramsay and examines the larger envelope, the one addressed to Jasmine, twisting and turning it between his fingers. He grasps all, lightly but firmly, in the fingers of one hand while he extracts a polythene bag from a pocket. This he places on his lap and drops the inspected envelope onto it. The process is repeated with the second, until he is left with the sheet of paper.

Lippy squints across to see if she can read what it says and is surprised to see it does not comprise letters cut from newspaper headlines and pasted onto the paper like a child's collage, but is computer generated in a bog-standard typeface and printed out.

'Hmmph!' DI Raisin folds the sheet and inserts it into the appropriate envelope then places all in the polythene bag which he seals.

'Any clues?' Lippy's face looks hopeful of information.

The DI unfolds himself from the step until on his feet, and towering above Lippy. He turns to Ramsay who loiters outside the front door. 'You have nothing to add to your earlier comments, Mr Dunn?'

Ramsay's eyes meet his. 'Nothing.'

'Hmm!'

He twirls, in a surprisingly graceful manner for a man. 'Mizz Stone.'

Jasmine cocks her head like a bird, eyes beady. 'Detective Inspector.'

'A word please.' DI Raisin turns and strides into the house, passes Ramsay without giving him a look.

Ramsay shrugs at Lippy. 'My home's become Waverlie Station.'

During Jasmine's interview Ramsay and Lippy sit companionably together on the front steps. Their eyes scan the sea, trace the line of the horizon, zigzag between there and shore below where they sit, and occasionally track back into the garden, to a flower bed where a particular flower is either in bloom or struggles to make its entry into the world. Conversation loups easily along as they discuss plants, weather, seaside living and Ramsay's belief in mulching his roses with seaweed. The letter is not mentioned. Lippy gets the impression the seaweed is of more interest to him than the roses, though they are probably Kat's favourite flowers. Of more interest even than the letter under discussion by the DI and Jasmine.

For the first time Lippy notices a long tangle of seaweed hanging beside the front door, bladder wrack by the look of it though there may be other varieties caught in its fronds of bulbous sacks from which droop opened mussel shells and bits of crab.

'Is it accurate?' Lippy's head nods towards the garland.

'Probably as accurate as most weather forecasts.'

'You like seaweed, don't you?'

'Very under-rated plant. Though it isn't a plant. It's a form of marine algae.'

'Under-rated?'

'Yes. Apart from the habitats seaweeds provide for millions of marine creatures — there are over nine thousand varieties of seaweed, you know — they provide an amazing amount of oxygen, through photosynthesis. We usually attribute oxygen to trees, and forget our hard-working seaweeds.'

'I didn't know that.'

'Mmm. It's also a food, and its iodine content makes it useful in wound dressings. Research is on-going into further uses. I'm sure they'll find plenty.'

'And as we gobble up resources on land...'

'Exactly.'

'Not sure I fancy eating it.'

'The Japanese appreciate it. Think of sushi.'

'Not a big fan of raw fish.'

'I must make you some sushi. Quite a dab hand at it, though I say it myself. One taste and you'll be hooked. I guarantee.'

'Fish isn't my favourite food.'

'Just you wait. My sushi is...was...renowned.'

Lippy smiles at Ramsay. He looks more relaxed now than he has since she first met him. Despite the murdered body on his hearth rug, the letter and another visit from the Detective Inspector, Ramsay's face has lost the haunted look of their previous meeting, his eyes have more lustre, though that could be down to the sun, his hair is springier, even his body has more life. It has lost its stiff, stay-away-from-me stance, and is interacting with those around him.

'I hated seaweed when I was young. Always got caught in it when I went swimming. Whenever I felt its fingers touch my skin I thrashed around in the water, terrified.'

Ramsay gives a soft chuckle. 'Frightened its tentacles would drag you down to its lair in the dense kelp forest?'

'Something like that'

'The sea is another world. You need to accustom yourself to its inhabitants.'

'Think I'd rather it was more like a swimming pool. Filtered, aseptic. But without the chlorine.'

'You're a writer. You like people, engage with them, tell them about the world. Why shut yourself off from another aspect of the world you could relate to your readers?'

'Seaweed's slippery.'

'As were many of the characters I've known.'

'Thank you, Mizz Stane. Thank you.' The DI bounces through the door and Ramsay jumps to his feet to let him past. He comes to a halt on the gravel looking at Ramsay, Lippy and Jasmine who has followed him out and stands behind Lippy, arms folded, weight on one leg. The stance and the look on her face say defiance, yet a challenge is evident too. Lippy's glance travels from Jasmine to the DI to find that his eyes are staring intently at her. She shifts uncomfortably on the step.

'Miss, Mrs or Mizz?'

Lippy places her hands on her knees as if to provide additional support. She is concerned by the tone of his voice. 'Mrs is fine, though a relic of the past. Or you can call me Lippy.' Did his mouth twitch at that she wonders.

'Mrs Nevis, you get around.'

'I'd hardly call down the coast around. I mean around makes me imagine places like Barcelona, Istanbul—'

'Down the coast is sufficiently around for me. My patch doesn't stretch beyond the border.'

Lippy flicks her head. 'I get around then. Makes me sound like a fast woman.' She stiffens her fingers, clawing them into her knees. What an idiot she sounds. Though it weighs only a few grams, she imagines she can feel the drag of the lapel badge in her pocket. What was cold has now become hot, sufficiently hot to burn a hole through her jacket and fall with a clink onto the stone step. She gives a nervous cough.

'As I say, you get around.' He stares at her. Lippy shifts uncomfortably. 'Before your visit here, you investigated another house up the coast.' Lippy swallows hard. 'You were at Miss McDaid's.'

Jasmine starts with interest. 'You were at Bluebell's, dearest? What did you find?'

'Mizz Stane, thank you. I'm asking the questions here.'

Jasmine beams at him. 'Sorry, DI, dearest. Professional interest and all that.'

'Professional interest! Huh!'

'Ooh! You don't think journalism is a profession? Or perhaps you don't think women can be—?'

The DI ignores Jasmine's retort. 'Why were you at Miss McDaid's, Mrs Nevis? You were seen.'

Lippy glances around three faces, each taut with anticipation. She doesn't like the way the DI is treating Jasmine, and feels a compulsion to support her friend who is as much a professional in her own work as the DI is in his. 'Professional interest,' she says, with a toss of her head and an arch look directed at him. Jasmine sniggers. The DI huffs. 'I didn't have any intention of visiting Bluebell McDaid. It just...happened. Fate.'

'Indulge my thick detective mind, Mrs Nevis, and explain what fate had to do with your visit.' His feet scrunch the gravel as he takes a step towards her. Lippy, sitting on the step is forced to push back her head to look at his face.

'I was on my way here, to visit Ramsay...about my play...I wanted his input.'

'And?'

'I saw a police car edge out a drive. I stopped to...to look at the map, see how far I was from Ramsay's... Bloody hell, I just wanted to see where the body Ramsay and I found in his lounge came from.' Jasmine sniggers again. The DI looks stern though little else can be read from his features. 'Ramsay said Bluebell's house wasn't far along the coast. I wondered if that was where the police car came from.' The DI continues to stare. 'I rang the doorbell, but no answer.'

DI Raisin gives a slow shake of his head without moving his eyes from her face. 'Oh, curiosity! Curiosity did more than kill the cat, you know.'

'A perfectly natural action, given the circumstances, Detective Inspector. Lippy and I had a traumatic experience. Perhaps you don't realise how traumatic. We deal with such experiences in different ways. In Lippy's case she—'

'Yes, yes, Mr Dunn. I understand that.'

'So why hound her as if she's committed a crime?' Jasmine has donned her investigative journalist pose. Lippy can almost imagine a tape recorder or a microphone thrust into the DI's face.

'Hound? I merely asked a question. I'm allowed to do that, you know…in order to find a murderer.'

Lippy squares her shoulders against the expected accusation. Accusations rake up the past, a specific day in her childhood that still has the power to overwhelm and crush her. She struggles to keep her mind on topic. Bluebell's house. It wasn't as if she stole anything. She hasn't committed a crime, though she did pocket the badge from the beach. But the beach wasn't the crime scene, so it's not as if she removed evidence from the scene of the crime. Though perhaps the DI won't view it that way. Evidence is evidence. Though she knows apparent evidence is not necessarily real evidence. Ramsay discovered that to his cost. As did she. As the past closes in, and tightens its arms around her like a boa constrictor, her eyes flicker closed.

The morning had been wet with horizontal rain that blasted into every nook and cranny. In the old caravan it infiltrated its cladding, saturated its frame, oozed from the pores of the ceiling and ran down the skin of its walls. Lippy could almost see mould form before her eyes — runnels darkened to streaks, thickened and coloured into the green of a furry fungal growth. Windows steamed up, and water coursed down them like a pelmet of squeezed sponges. The air was clammy. Windows and door begged to be thrown open to air the interior and chase out the damp, but the rain poured and any opening meant more water blown in.

Lippy's mother kept herself busy and her spirits from flagging by grabbing the opportunity to do some chores. Her vigorous brushing of the carpet added dust to damp. Then she wiped out the narrow wall cupboards that contained dishes, tins and packets.

'We could do with a top up of food,' she said as she shuffled a few cans around. 'Might be an opportunity for a trip to the supermarket. I'm fed up with the shop here — it's so limited.'

Her father had extracted as much information as he could from his newspaper and had now moved on to a paperback purchased in the caravan park shop. 'Mmm. A more lively book wouldn't go amiss either.'

By the time lunch had been eaten and cleared the weather had improved. Deluge had changed to heavy showers in between which the sun deigned to squint from behind scudding clouds. Lippy's mother and father, desperate for an excuse to leave the caravan, opted for an afternoon of window shopping in a nearby town where plumps of rain could be dodged by a wander into the nearest shop, the afternoon topped off by a trip round the supermarket. Lippy declined the pleasure. Her mother swithered about leaving her on her own, made her promise to stay put, not to touch the gas for cooker and lights, to behave herself, and if there were any problems to hotfoot it to the shop.

After they had trundled off, Lippy lay back on the seat her father usually occupied where she squirmed to get comfortable on the cratered foam cushion, and read. She could hear voices of holidaymakers coming and going, shouts, car doors slam and engines fade as vehicles drove off. The site became unusually quiet. She wondered what Eilidh was doing, and that sent her out the door and running to the hedge to see if the cocoa tin contained a note. The stubby branches of the privet, with its tightly crowded leaves, shed plump droplets onto the sleeve of her cardigan and her fingers which slithered across the surface of the tin and made it difficult to grip. Eventually, she prised off the lid, but the tin was empty.

Back in the caravan she rummaged in the bag that contained her night things, amongst the as yet uneaten treasure of sweets given to her by Eilidh, and took out a bar of white chocolate to mouth-melt while she read.

She needed the loo. The box in the corner or a dash to the toilet block? She opts for the latter. As she pushed open the door the rain began to sheet down. She hesitated, looked at the box in the corner, then grabbed her red rain jacket from a peg and, throwing it over her head and shoulders, made a dash for the toilet block. Black clouds darkened the afternoon light and gave it an oppressive feel as if warning of a dire event. The rain bounced off the ground; its force created mini fountains as it hit puddles and bounced back into the air. As she ran she hopscotched between puddles, but landed in one, and splashed muddy water up her legs. The mud sucked off her shoe and as she bent to retrieve it and reacquaint it with her foot, her rain jacket trailed through the sticky ground beside her.

Inside the utilitarian concrete building where the only colour was the battered royal blue of the cubicle doors gouged with graffiti, she swung her jacket from her shoulders and assessed the mud damage. She turned on the hot tap and ran the cuffs and bottom edge of it beneath the flow of water, rubbing the material together with her fingers. The slimy brown stain swirled off in the arms of the water in the direction of the plug hole. With the mud gone, her jacket was clean but the colour was darkened by moisture from bright red to dark rust. Lippy squeezed it out, dabbed it with a paper towel and left it draped over the surface by the basin while she dashed into a cubicle.

When she came out two women were propped by the sinks, engaged in a fiery argument. As they flopped around, staccato words and disjointed phrases battered the walls. One waved a bottle threateningly at the other. 'Leave him. Unnerstand? Leave him or…or I'll batter yer face in.' She brandished the bottle like a club. It missed the woman's eye by a hairsbreadth and dribbled alcohol down her coat.

The opened cubicle door swung back and the handle hit the wall. One woman turned towards the basin to wipe her coat, the other spun round. 'Gettin' an eyeful?' she spat at Lippy, swinging the bottle menacingly in her direction.

Lippy dismissed any idea of washing her hands and fled from the building back to the caravan. The rain had almost stopped but her feet gathered more mud as she squelched through the puddles on the path, so she took her shoes off, cleaned them with kitchen roll, and left them by her bed to dry.

She heard a car draw in beside the caravan opposite. Passengers spilled out. The man opened the boot and clawed out walking boots and poles, and an assortment of jackets. Lippy remembered her own jacket. Her eyes travelled to the peg allocated to it. It was empty. Her red jacket had been left in the toilet block. She felt annoyance, fear lest it might have been stolen. Her parents would be angry, might not buy her such a good replacement as it had been expensive and was only bought after much pleading and promising.

So she plucked up courage and decided another trip across the mud was necessary. Her shoes, feeling cold and damp, were slipped on, and with no jacket she wrapped her cardigan around her and made a dash for it. At the door to the toilets she stopped, listened. All seemed quiet. On tiptoe she crept inside, ready to turn and bolt back to the caravan if the women were still there. The place was empty, creepy like a haunted house, and the slightest noise rolled around the walls and came back to her. Hurriedly, before other visitors appeared, she grabbed her jacket and ran.

When her parents returned, they dumped plastic bags bulging with tins and packets on the table, and asked about her afternoon. She assured them she'd spent a quiet afternoon reading. Her eyes flicked to her jacket on the peg. Over its surface a large damp area and various smaller ones oozed out in various shades of red. She was sure it would catch her mother's attention. But her parents busied themselves with unpacking and restocking the cupboards, too keen to put away purchases to notice.

Two loud bangs on the door shook the caravan. Lippy's mother and father looked at one another, surprise scribbled across their faces. Her father went to open it while her mother stood by the sink, a packet of macaroni clutched in her hands.

'Where is she? Where's that daughter of yours?'

Lippy could see her father stiffen as he moved to block the doorway.

'Why d'you want my daughter?'

'A sneekit wee thief, that's what she is. I want my stuff back, or payment for it. That's why.'

Her father threw her a questioning glance. 'Are you saying my daughter stole something from the caravan park shop?'

'Yup. The missus saw her in the security mirror.'

'That's not — '

'Didn't like to go after her. You bein' here for the season an' all. Too soft by far, my missus.'

'Your wife's mistaken. My daughter—'

'Mistaken? Nah! See, look… He pushed past Lippy's dad to point to the wet red jacket hanging on the peg. 'That's the jacket. That's the red jacket she saw.'

'Lippy's dad licked his lips. 'When…when was this?'

'This afternoon. About an hour ago, give or take.'

'You said your wife…'

'I was at the cash and carry. The wife looks after the shop when I'm away.'

'And she saw a red jacket?'

'Sure did.'

'There must be others with red jackets.'

'Stuff's been going missing for weeks. You've got to expect a bit, but not this much.'

'My daughter's rarely in the shop.'

'She was there this afternoon, for sure. Ask her.' He pointed a nicotine stained finger at Lippy who was trying her hardest to escape through the cratered cushions and caravan's thin walls.'

Her father turned to look at her, his eyes perplexed. 'Lippy?'

"We told you to say in,' said her mother.

'I did. I only went out to the toilet. I didn't go near the ghastly shop.'

'Enough, Lippy,' said her father. 'Did you take…? What's she supposed to have taken?'

'Sweets.'

'Did you steal sweets from the shop?'

Lippy squirmed. This was too embarrassing. 'No, of course not. I wouldn't do that.'

The caravan park owner drew himself up, and threw out his arm to indicate her jacket. 'How d'you account for the red jacket, then? It's wet, too.' He grabbed it and waved it in the air.

Lippy's frantic look pleads with her parents. 'I told you. I went to the toilet. It was raining. My shoe stuck in the mud and my jacket fell on the ground when I tried to put it back on.'

'Hmmph! Likely story. Though you might have gone there before or after you pinched sweets from the shop.'

'I didn't take sweets. I didn't go to the shop. I haven't been there for ages,'

'You're in most days.'

'No I'm not. I don't have money to buy sweets.'

'So you nick them.'

'No.' Lippy's voice has risen to a squeal.

Her mother laid the macaroni on the table and sat beside her. 'Lippy, you must tell us what you did when we were out.'

'Pah! Another crime. You two left a daughter of…what's her age? Too young to be left on her own, that's for sure.'

Lippy's father stamped his foot in annoyance and struggled to control his temper. He turned to his daughter. 'Lippy, dear, just tell us what happened.'

'I told you. I went to the toilet. I never went near the shop.'

'I believe you, but how d'you explain the woman in the shop seeing a red jacket.'

'It wasn't mine. I wore mine to run over to the toilet but…'

'But?' asked her mother.

Lippy twisted her fingers together and gulped. The words splashed out. 'I washed the mud from it and left it by the sink.'

'That's why it's wet?' Her mother stroked her shoulder.

Lippy gave a jerky nod of her head. 'When I came out the cubicle, two drunk women were arguing. One threatened me with a bottle. I was frightened. So I ran. I forgot my jacket. That's all. I promise.'

Her father bristled with indignation. 'Drunk women! What sort of place has drunk women brawling in the afternoon? In a place where there's kids! Jeez!'

'She's made it up. You didn't expect the wee beggar to own up, surely.'

Her mother jumped to her feet. 'No she hasn't. I've seen them there. More than once.'

'You didn't say.' Her husband turned to her, a shocked look on his face.

'So how's your jacket here now?' asked her mother.

Lippy gulped back tears and dragged the back of her hand under her nose. 'I went to get it…just before you came back.'

'See!' Her father glared at the caravan owner.

'See what?'

'Lippy's jacket could've been worn by someone else to visit the shop.'

'Not bloody likely.' The caravan owner's exasperation and anger were mounting.

'Why not?'

'Ask her where the sweets are. Ask her where she's put them.'

Her mother turned to her. 'Tell him you don't have sweets, Lippy.'

Lippy twisted her hands. Head lowered to hide her shame, she scrunched her body into a ball in the corner of the caravan.'

'Lippy.'

She raised eyes full of guilt to her mother. 'In the…' She unfolded one arm to indicate the bag where her night things were kept. 'I…there's sweets in there.'

'Oh Lippy!' groaned her mother.

'How?' demanded her father.

'See, told you I was right. The wee thief.'

'I didn't steal them,' insisted Lippy, raising her head. 'I didn't. I swear I didn't. Eilidh gave them to me.'

'Eilidh?' Her father sounded astonished.'

'I knew that wee madam couldn't be trusted,' spat her mother. 'There's something about her I don't trust. Never did. Not from the first day—'

'How convenient,' drawled the caravan owner, as he lurched across the caravan and made a grab for the bag. Onto the table he poured its contents as if emptying Santa's sack. Lippy's floral cotton nightdress, her hairbrush, toiletries, two clasps, a hairband, a few coins, and a cache of sweets.

In a silence that she will always remember with scorching humiliation, Lippy curled up. Tears fell and sobs shuddered her body. Around her a gaping chasm developed, deep, burning, sulphurous, with a complete lack of sound that drove a rift through the crust of her life. It was a silence that stretched, extended to the horizon and beyond, and encompassed fury, embarrassment, grief, the injustices of life, the treachery of friends, the difficulties and realities faced by parents.

'Eilidh gave you these?' asked her father very quietly and calmly, picking up the tubes and bars of sweets and letting them run through his hands to land back on the table.

With a heaved gulp, Lippy muttered, 'Uhuh.'

'When?'

'Every time I see her she has some. If I don't see her she leaves them in the cocoa tin.'

'The cocoa tin?' queried her mother. Lippy explained between gulps and sobs. 'I see.'

'Huh! Some story!' insisted the caravan owner. 'Nice couple, that wee lassie's parents.' He pursed his lips. 'Don't see their wee lass pinching stuff.'

'But you can see our daughter stealing?' retorts her father.

'I didn't take them, Mum, Dad. Honest. I wouldn't do that. You know I wouldn't. I kept the sweets there because Eilidh gives me more than I want to eat. That's why they're there.'

Her mother turned to the caravan owner. 'Okay, you've heard our daughters side of the story, now go and accuse Eilidh.'

'No way. Why would I do that? Your wee lass has the stolen sweets. There. In front of you.'

'I didn't steal them,' shouted Lippy.

Her father flapped his hand. 'Shh!'

'Honest, I didn't. I'd never have taken them if I'd known they were stolen. Eilidh always has stuff — money, sweets, jewellery. I didn't steal anything.'

Lippy's mother straightened up, glared at her husband. 'Okay, if he's not going to tackle Eilidh, then you'll need to go and sort it out.'

'Me?'

'Yes. It's your daughter that's being accused.'

'But… I can't. I can't possibly do that.'

Her mother folds her arms, and sighs in frustration. 'Why on earth not! Are you going to sit there and let your daughter be accused of being a thief?'

'No, of course not. But—'

'Well?'

'I can't do that. For heaven's sake, the man's my boss. My job—'

'Oh, you never take a stance on anything but politics.'

'That's not fair.'

'Never mind. I'll go.'

The caravan owner blocked her exit. 'Hang on there. I can't have you annoying my visitors.'

'What the bloody hell d'you think you're doing? Let me past.' She tried to elbow him aside but he stood firm.

'This is a good site. Taken me years of hard work to build it up, so it has. Me and the wife.'

'Let me past, please.'

'So I'm not going to have a thieving family spoil my site for me and my visitors.'

'Get out of my caravan,' yells Lippy's father, finally losing his temper. 'You've no right to make such accusations.'

'I've every right, mate. The proof's right there in front of you.'

'Get out.'

'I'll expect you to be packed and gone in an hour.'

'This is outrageous,' shouted Lippy's mother. 'Outrageous. We've paid till the end of the season.'

'Yeah, well what's left of the site rental fee will recompense me for your wee devil's pilfering.' He turned on his heel and stepped through the door, thrusting his face back through the opening. 'An hour. Or I call the police.'

As he marched away from the van, the occupants noticed a crowd of onlookers had gathered outside. Heads craned towards the caravan, their curiosity on display in eyes, mouths, muttered remarks to one another, and behind hand comments. On the edge of the crowd was Eilidh. A large smile gashed her face. 'Vinegar sticks,' she shouted. 'To think I played with a wee thief!'

30 - Naughty, naughty

'Lippy, Lippy. Are you all right?' Ramsay's voice is raw with concern.

'Get her a glass of water,' barks DI Raisin.

She hears the clack of heels as Jasmine's shoes disappear into the house, and along the corridor to the kitchen.

When Jasmine returns she sits on the step beside her, an arm round her shoulders, and offers her the glass. The water is cold. She can feel it swirl and prickle its way inside her. 'I'm fine. I'm fine.'

'You sure, dearest?' Concern softens Jasmine's voice.

Lippy flaps her hand. 'Yes, fine. Just got waylaid by the past.' She sweeps a hand through her hair and takes another gulp of water. 'Sorry, Detective Inspector.' She rests the glass on a knee and supports it with a hand. 'You wanted to know about my visit.'

'If you don't mind.' Concern softens the edge of sarcasm in his voice.

Lippy takes a deep breath. 'Well, I rang the bell, and no answer, so my...artistic curiosity overcame my common sense, and I went round the back.' She hears the DI draw in his breath as if about to comment, so she rushes on. 'There was always a possibility the bell hadn't been heard and someone might be in the garden...or on the beach. But there was no sign of anyone.'

'No sign of anyone?' DI Raisin shuffles his feet, shifting the gravel until he stands on a bare patch of ground. 'Not quite true, is it?'

'Don't badger—'

The DI holds up his hand at Ramsay. 'Don't interrupt, please, Mr Dunn.'

Lippy moves her other hand to cradle the glass and pushes her free hand into her pocket to extract the badge. She feels it red hot in the palm of her hand, can smell the searing flesh and can't wait to rid herself of the thing that is about to bring censure on her head, and which has dredged up an ugly and shameful incident from her past to collide with her present. With a toss of her hand she throws it to the ground. Heads jerk to see what it is. The DI bends to pick it up from the bottom step where it fell.

'My, my, my! Anyone tell me what this is?' He holds out his hand, palm upwards. The badge is a small black square, lying between stubby fingers and strong wrist.

Jasmine's eyes narrow but she shakes her head. 'Sorry.'

Ramsay stiffens. His tongue flicks round his lips.

'Mr Dunn?'

'I'm…not sure.'

'But you think you know?'

'It's one of those lapel badges that have become fashionable.'

'Ten out of ten. Now tell me what organisation.'

'They weren't around in my time, but…'

The DI's hand waves in a circular motion, indicating he wants more, now — a stream of information not a few words dropped like a plum in winter. 'But?'

'There was…is an unofficial organisation inside the People's Union Party.'

'You mean The Galley?' asks Jasmine. Ramsay nods. 'But that's not their logo. They never used a black square.'

'You know about this organisation?' On the DI's face surprise battles with amusement.

Jasmine flicks her hair back from her face. 'I'm a journalist, Detective Inspector Raisin. And just as you have your sources, we journalists have ours.'

'You don't say, Mizz Stane!'

'It's not a Galley pin, though they did have a square badge not unlike that.'

'Mr Dunn. Do continue your tale of enlightenment.'

Ramsay looks at Lippy as if for encouragement. 'The Galley logo, as far as one was used, was — surprise, surprise — a galley. One of those many oared boats.'

'I can see my history education was sadly lacking. What has a galley to do with the People's Union Party?'

'The Galley…takes care of problems…of troublemakers.'

The DI is aware of Ramsay's background and senses his reluctance to be explicit about the nature of The Galley so decides research in the office will be more productive. Perhaps even another chat with Mizz Stane. She obviously knows more, so can fill gaps in his knowledge. To accomplish it over a drink might be fruitful. Pleasant, too.

'Okay, so it's not The Galley, but the feeling is that — and correct me if

I'm wrong — this badge has to do with a…let's say a similar organisation. Am I correct?'

Relief crosses Ramsay's face, as if an unseen hand has fast-peeled the layer of discomfort away. 'I'm only hazarding a guess, but I'd say you could be correct.'

'Thank you, Mr Dunn. Can you add any further observations to that?'

'I've heard…vague mutters of it — of another organisation. Black Square. I don't keep up-to-date with the political world — I'm pretty isolated here — but from odd remarks by infrequent visitors and the stories that headlined in the media last Sunday—'

'You refer to the stories about the leader of the main opposition party?'

'Yes.'

'Carry on.'

'It looks to me like…like a turf war.'

Jasmine has become enlivened. She scents a story and all her senses quiver with anticipation. 'Jingle jangle! You mean between The Galley and this …Black Square organisation?'

'Possibly.'

The DI has also had his interest ratcheted up. To date, information on the murder has been slim. But infighting between two factions might provide meat for his teeth to chew on. 'Any idea who runs these…err … organisations?'

'It started with Charlie Kintail.'

'Charlie Kintail? Name rings a bell. Yes, MP for a time. Dead now, though?'

'Several years ago. When he died the operation and some of Charlie's henchmen, including his son-in-law Schaw somebody-or-other, was taken over by…' Ramsay's glance travels again to Lippy. She smiles as if in understanding that the information she sought is now being handed to a wider audience — to the police.

'By?'

'Ramsay drops his voice to a murmur. 'Taylor Carnoustie.'

'Taylor Carnoustie! You mean the guy who used to be Minister for Education?'

'The very same.'

'But he's still in Parliament.'

'Yes.'

'Are you certain? Have you proof?'

'Certain, yes. Proof would be hard to come by. Anyway he's the head man, the action is carried out by others.'

'Names?'

'Apart from Schaw whatever-his-name-is, no idea. Out of my current sphere.'

'There's Ming Dulse,' suggests Jasmine.

'The MCP?'

'Yup. He was Charlie Kintail's Parliamentary assistant. Must have learnt a few tricks or two in that office.'

'O…kay. So this other lot…the Black Square folk…any names there?'

'Mere speculation,' says Jasmine, 'but the campaign against Mutt was aimed to benefit Brankton.'

'You've been doing your homework,' jokes Lippy.

'Once a political journalist… Old habits die hard. Besides I need a scoop to get me out of Lifestyle and back into Politics.'

DI Raisin looks serious. 'You can't finger the deputy leader of a political Party because a campaign is run against the leader.'

'Why not?' asks Lippy.

'I'd have thought that was obvious.'

Ramsay waves his hand from side to side. 'No, no. You can't discount him on the basis of being obvious. Because he's obvious means neither you nor anyone else will find a shred of evidence against him. For his fingers will have been kept well away, and others will have turned the screws.'

'So Brankton could be head of the Black Square outfit?' asks Lippy.

Ramsay makes a dismissive sound. 'No, hasn't got the chutzpah. All bluster no action.'

'Then who?'

'Ramsay's right about Brankton,' says Jasmine. 'Though…'

'Do share your thoughts with us, Mizz Stane.'

'He has a son.'

Ramsay's eyebrows shoot into his hairline. 'Brankton's married! First I heard of it.'

'Second time around. You're behind the times,' says Jasmine. 'I rather think the marriage is…kept in the background. Rumours suggest he puts up with her because of her business acumen. Though what the business might be is open to speculation.' Jasmine looks to Ramsay for reaction but he merely gives a slight shrug and shake of his head.

The DI paces along the path and back. 'What makes you mention the son, Mizz Stone?'

'Umm, I'm having to dredge my memory for this. But I think he was in trouble — years ago, before I left. Bit of a psycho, I seem to remember.'

DI Raisin looks impressed. 'Any more titbits?'

'There was a court case which journalists were discouraged from reporting. Not exactly unusual, but…'

The DI purses his lips and takes another turn along the path in front of the house.

'You wouldn't have a name?'

Jasmine shakes her head. 'Long time ago. Crime wasn't my bag.'

'Okay. Let's see where that little lot takes us.' His phone buzzes. 'Raisin. Yup. Yup.' He checks his watch. 'Forty minutes.' He pockets his phone and turns to Lippy, holding the lapel pin in front of her with one hand and wagging the index finger of the other. 'Naughty, naughty. Never remove evidence from a crime scene.'

Lippy is stung by the rebuke. 'It wasn't a crime scene.'

'Oh no?'

'There was no indication, no tape, no notices. It was the bloody beach. And let's face it, that badge could've lain there for months, dropped by someone perfectly innocent with absolutely no connection with this mess.'

Ramsay puts his hand on her arm. 'Lippy anyone wearing that badge wouldn't be innocent. Maybe of Wilkie's murder…but not innocent.'

'Always possible. But in that case it would most likely have become buried, not remain where it could be noticed.' The DI scratches his cheek as he stares at Lippy. 'Look where our little discussion over this pin has taken us. Reflect on that.'

Lippy's response is, 'Urrrgh!'

He swivels towards Jasmine. 'Mizz Stane, I may need to speak to you again. For background information, you understand.' Jasmine inclines hear head, before she bestows on him a smile full of encouragement.

His eyes meet hers. A curt nod to all and a wave of his hand then Detective Inspector Raisin scrunches along the gravel and disappears round the corner of the house.

Ramsay puffs out his breath. 'I think we need another coffee.'

Jasmine jumps down the steps to the path. 'Not for me, Ramsay. Thanks. Need to get back to the office.' She slings her bag over her shoulder. 'Interesting afternoon.'

'Coffee for me please.' Lippy sighs and clambers to her feet. 'Large and strong. My nerves need a pick-me-up.'

'Would you rather have wine? Something stronger?'

'Heaven's no. I might meet another police car.'

'Another police car?' queries Jasmine.

'I'll walk you to your car and enlighten you.'

Jasmine laughs at Lippy's tale, consoles her about her removal of evidence and the DI's scathing remarks. 'He's quite dishy, don't you think?'

'Raisin of the pink shirt?'

'Yes.'

'You have to be kidding!'

'No. I rather like him. Slightly abrasive on the outside but I suspect quite squishy on the inside.'

'He had me fooled.'

'And a quirky sense of humour.'

'You think he has a sense of humour?' Lippy's rounded eyes and open mouth show her disbelief.

'Mmm. Wouldn't mind a wee romp with him at a suitable time.'

'You're married.'

'Only technically.'

'He's probably married, though can't think who'd have him.'

'So, no problem! Sex and money, dearest, they push this old world around.

'Still the same Jasmine.'

'Still the same Lippy. Though if you play your cards right…' Jasmine bends double to slide into the red car.

'I'm not with you.'

'Oh, come on! You must see the way Ramsay looks at you. Quite smitten, I'd say.'

'Jasmine, you live in a fantasy world.'

'We'll see.' She closes the door, revs the engine, and lowers the window. 'Let's have that dinner soon.' With a spurt of gravel she swings the car round towards the gate and is off.

Lippy wanders back to the front of the house, pulling her jacket around her.

'It's become cooler,' says Ramsay from his seat on the step where he has been joined by Jess. 'Maybe we should have our coffee inside.'

'Ramsay, what was in the letter?'

31 - Woven to deceive

Brian waves his arm, fingers curled into the palm of a hand that beats the air, to emphasise his point. His head bounces in time with his hand, his eyes shoot anger and disbelief. He has been in a state of perpetual fury since he saw his face splashed over the online media when he logged on to his laptop this morning.

'I've no idea who fed it to the media.'

'Where were you the day of Wilkie Smart's murder?'

'Where was I? Surely you don't—'

'Routine question, Mr Coldstream,' Detective Inspector Raisin assures him as he walks, hands stuffed in pockets, beside Brian through Holygood Park.

'The DI had appeared not long after Brian arrived at his Parliamentary office and was subjected to the full blast of his annoyance, disbelief and feelings of betrayal. A walk was suggested as a way of dispersing steam and to allow them privacy. Ming hadn't put in an appearance when they left so Brian has that tussle to look forward to.

Brian kicks a stone into another dimension. 'Where was I? How the hell... No, wait. I was at home.'

'Home? As in...?'

'Home — at my parents' house. In the opposite direction from Bluebell's place.'

'And your parents...?'

'They can vouch for me. As can a friend who dropped in.'

'You were there from?'

Brian kicks another stone. 'Around seven I think. My mother will know the exact time...she notices such things.'

'And before that?'

'Before that... I was at work. In the Parliament. Stayed on after Ming left to work on my application — for the approved candidate list.'

'Oh, we could see you in Parliament!'

'I've opted for the top up list. Interview next week.'

'Hmm! You were seen by others in the Parliament?'

'Yes, you can check.'

'And you left when?'

'Takes about an hour, hour and a quarter to reach my parents' house. Depending on traffic. So around five forty five.'

'As I said…just routine.'

'I needed the fresh air.'

Detective Inspector Raisin paces in silence before he comes to an abrupt halt. 'The media story—?'

'Not one bloody word of truth.'

'But you knew Wilkie Smart?'

'Not really.'

'Expand.'

'Saw him around, heard him speak, knew of him but didn't have a personal connection.'

'Your impression?'

Brian ponders the question. His mouth twitches, eyebrows wiggle. 'Hard worker, ambitious.' His feet slow their motion. He stops, turns to take in the view of the Crags on one side of the road, the Parliament building and a large swathe of Edin flowing out on the other. He pulls up the collar of his jacket. The sky is overcast, mist hovers in patches, warm breath on cold air. He feels the dampness seep into him, into his hopes and ambitions. 'Merely my impression but…' He takes a deep breath.

'Carry on. Impressions are useful.'

'Not sure whether he was stressed by the job, found it more difficult than expected. Yet he seemed capable of handling problems. I don't know.'

'You think he was under pressure?'

'We're all under pressure. Brian's forehead furrows in the pattern of a tractor tyre. 'But frustration bubbled beneath his actions.'

The DI studies the view without taking it in. 'Tell me, I've heard mention of… factions.'

'Every party, every organisation has its factions.'

'Of course. They're even rife in the police. But — and let's just throw caution to the winds and indulge in some speculation here — is there a likelihood that friction between factions may have…let's say may have made Wilkie Smart's job additionally difficult?'

'Factions? You mean…?' Brian swirls the air with his hand.

The DI expels a breath of exasperation. 'I'm talking about The Galley which appears to be supportive of your Party leader, and Black Square which, according to my information, backs Brankton, the deputy.'

Brian stares at the DI, eyes wide, mouth flapping. 'Ehm…ehm…'

'Ehm is not a particularly informative answer. I hoped for more.'

Brian stabs the tarmac with his toe, making loose gravel spurt. 'This may seem odd to you, but until recently I knew little about The Galley. As for…what's it called?'

'Black Square.'

'Never heard—' A gasp propels itself from Brian's mouth, as if he's been punched in the solar plexus. His head tilts to the side, his eyes narrow to slivers of grey.

'Yes?'

'I've never heard of them. But…'

'Mr Coldstream, I don't want to spend the night out here. So if you could just spit it out.'

'It may be nothing…'

'But it could be the breakthrough needed. So spit it out.'

'Black Square — does it have a lapel badge?'

Interest like a spark of electricity flares from the DI, his body starts, his hair stands on end, his eyes bore into Brian, while words explode from his mouth. 'You've seen a lapel badge with a black square?'

Brian nods, transfixed by the DI's reaction. 'Mmm.'

'Where?'

'On the floor.' DI Raisin's expression indicates the thought of shaking Brian has sped through his mind. 'On my office floor. It fell from Ming's coat.'

The DI purses his lips as he kicks at the ragged raised edge of a pothole. 'Ming is the MCP you work for?'

'Ming Dulse, yes.'

'Interesting. Most interesting.'

'I don't understand Ming.'

'Few of us do understand politicians.'

'No…you see… Ming is the protégé of Charlie Kintail. Heard of him?'

'Heard the name.'

'He started the whole Galley thing. To tighten discipline in the Party. The top brass were afraid of dissent, you see. Voters don't like it. They like to think everyone works together like happy bunnies. So, Charlie… volunteered…to keep the ship…well, shipshape.'

The hand of the DI travels to his hair, his fingers plough it into furrows, rake, plough. The toe of a scuffed brown cowboy boot again harries the edge of the pothole. 'Uhuh! So — correct me if I'm wrong here though I suspect I'm not — you wonder why Mr Kintail's protégé would jump ship, as it were, for another vessel.'

'Yes.'

'Perhaps you've too many scruples for politics.'

'Pardon?'

'You heard me. Most politicians I've come across would sell their grannies if they thought it would buy them advancement. Most police, too.'

'I thought he was well placed for a post of some kind under Mutt. Recognition for loyal service, that kind of thing.'

'But he considers his chances better under another leader.'

'Appears so. Brankton's avid supporter.'

'Ever meet Brankton's family? Know anything about his wife? Son?'

'No. Might've seen his wife, I suppose. Out on the stomp at a by-election or at conference. But no idea.' Brian shivers.'

'Yes, bone-numbingly chilly. Let's head back.'

As they head back towards the Parliament Brian watches energetic figures, bent forward, braving the steep path up the Crags, while on the grass below women with prams and toddlers stroll around, and allow their offspring to run, chase balls and imagine they're aeroplanes or vampires or dragons. A young woman in black Lycra gear jogs past, taking a swig from a water bottle clutched in her hand. Behind her a couple stroll, arms wound around one another, sharing remarks and secrets.

'One way to keep warm,' says the DI, as he turns to watch their progress. He makes a mental note to phone Jasmine Stane, Mizz Jasmine Stane, when he's finished with Brian.

Brian wonders what Kirsty will make of the media headlines implicating him in the murder of Wilkie Smart. 'Who the hell could've given them the fabricated story?' he wonders out loud.

'Who indeed?'

'Why didn't a reporter even check it? Bloody idiots. It's Mutt mark two.'

'Looks like it.'

'I can see the point of targeting Mutt — if you're a political buffoon. But why me?'

'You've grazed someone's shin.'

'The only swords I've crossed recently were with Ming.'

'Over the Party leadership I presume.'

'Yes. That and my application for the candidate list.'

'You've made him twitchy.'

'You think he's behind the media crap?'

'Steady on, there. I didn't say that.'

As they leave the park the traffic surges past and they have to wait to cross the road. Behind them sits Holygood House and the Royal Picture Gallery, a gilded, and stolid reminder of historic Caledon. In front sits the contemporary Parliament building, since its outset mired in controversy over its design and escalating cost. It is still sufficiently new for controversy to hang around its windows and poles, swirl around the upturned boats structure. The DI wonders how many decades or centuries will pass before the structure is regarded with similar tacit approval to the one behind him. In the meantime he postpones judgement on its suitability for purpose.

Outside the Parliament a scatter of tourists take photographs or sit on the security barriers, fashioned to resemble seats but designed to stop vehicles being driven at the building. Brian is quietly proud his country opted for a modern structure for its new parliament, and proud so many visitors hang out here. The poetry wall, he is sure, is unique, and each time he passes he stops to read another quote and ponder its meaning for him. The integration of culture into politics and Parliament appeals greatly to him. Culture, like political democracy is an essential strand of living, he believes. Culture from his mother, politics from his father. Perhaps that amalgam is what gives him his affinity with the wall and the poets commemorated there.

As they walk round the concrete barriers and along by the shallow ponds that reflect building and Crag, the DI slows his pace. 'Have you indulged in any literary efforts recently?'

'Don't have much time for reading, apart from reports, but I've—'

'Not what I mean. Try writing.'

Brian looks confused. 'I write all the time. That's my job. To research and write speeches, letters—'

'Letters. Go with that.'

'I can't divulge the people I've written too. That's confidential.'

'O…kay. Let's focus on one letter in particular.'

'What letter?'

'One that was brief to the point of curtness.'

'I'm often brief, but I deny my letters, or rather Ming's letters — as he signs them — are curt.'

'This one was. So curt it didn't even bear a signature.'

'So if it wasn't signed how do you—?'

'The desk sergeant took a phone call this morning. Early.'

'You've lost me.'

'It was a woman's voice, so he said.'

'So?'

'The woman said you'd written a certain letter to Ramsay Dunn.'

'The expenses fiddler?' The DI nods. 'Don't know, never met, haven't a clue where he stays to send a letter.'

'It was sent care of a journalist.'

'Odd.'

'Jasmine Stane. Mizz Jasmine Stane.'

'Callyman Lifestyle journalist.'

'You know her?'

'Haven't met her. She's the one who interviewed Ming on his morning routine. His wife bought him a load of toiletries to impress her with. Ming said the interview went well, though the piece hasn't yet appeared.'

'So you've had no contact with her.'

'No…wait…yes. I remember. I was with Ming when we bumped into her at a recent Parliamentary reception.'

'Expand.'

'Not much to add. She was with someone…a writer. Ming seemed to know her for some reason.'

'Lippy Nevis by any chance?'

'That's right. Knew it was a silly name.'

'You say Mr Dulse knew her?'

'Mmm. Emm…yes…his wife. She'd been at an author event at a bookshop. She was the author, and his wife bought a copy of the book and asked her to dedicate it to him. Ming remembered the name.'

'As you've met Mizz Stane, that provides you with a reason for sending the letter care of her.'

'This is becoming bloody ridiculous.'

'Do you know where Ramsay Dunn stays?'

'Haven't a clue. Nor do I have reason to contact him. He's a stranger.'

'I see.'

'If I wanted to write to him, which is extremely unlikely, but if I did, I'd try Party Headquarters for an address, not send through another person, especially one who's a journalist.'

'Quite the tangled web, woven to deceive.'

'I'm not deceiving you.'

The DI looks Brian straight in the face, eye challenges eye. 'Did you write a threatening letter to Ramsay Dunn?'

'No, Detective Inspector, I did not.'

'Uhuh. Any idea who might have phoned to say you did?'

'Jasmine Stane has to be a possibility if the letter—'

The DI raises his head to take in the building above him. 'No, no. It wasn't her.'

Brian hunches his shoulders and scliffs his feet on the pavement. 'Then I haven't a clue.'

'O...kay.' DI Raisin lowers his eyes from the upper part of the building, gives a nod of his head and steams off then turns and loups back. 'The lapel badge. The one you say you found. Where is it?'

A flicker of annoyance crosses Brian's face. 'The lapel badge I found on the floor of my office is in my desk drawer. I did think of handing it to Ming, but decided against.'

'Go get it.'

'Could be difficult. If Ming's there...'

'Hmm. Quandary. I've the solution.'

'Fine.

'I go in this entrance, right?' The DI points to a wood and glass door.

'Yes, I use the entrance round the corner.'

'Off you go. By the time you reach your office, Mr Dulse will be on his way to see me at this entrance. Get the badge and bring it back out here for me. Mission accomplished.'

Kirsty puts her hand on his. It feels soft, with the warmth of an invitation. She waited for him near the exit, loitered, pretended to be waiting to cross the road when someone came out. 'At last,' she breathes, as she circles him like an out-of-sorts puppy. 'Need to talk. Follow me.' She wings it up the pavement, diving between sightseers and people making their way home from work. Brian twice thinks he has lost her but pushes on, wondering where she is headed. He catches up with her at traffic lights and together they push through the door into a pizza chain restaurant, and select a table near the back. Brian orders coffees.

The place is busy and the hubbub of conversation, the demands of children and the hiss of the coffee machine ensure their conversation will be difficult to overhear.

Brian leans across the table, concern stiffening his features. 'Kirsty, I had nothing to do with...I swear. I couldn't believe it when I saw the photo and read the guff in the media this morning.' Kirsty looks sympathetic. 'Heaven knows where they got the stuff, who fed that garbage to them, but I had nothing to do with it. You must believe me. I didn't even know the guy.'

Kirsty looks around, takes in the walls plastered with posters for specials and extra big or extra great offers, before her gaze drops back to Brian. 'I believe you, Brian.' She pats his hand again.

'I have a rock solid alibi for the— You believe me? Relief smooths his face and voice. He throws himself back in his chair and expels breath like an old locomotive letting off steam. 'What...great, but...? How?'

Her fingers doodle patterns in a damp patch on the table. 'I was out for a drink last night — after a meeting. Wasn't going to go but...well, it was an opportunity to pick up info. At first, there was all the usual banter. Next thing, two guys started to act funny — like kids with toys to show off, brag about. They began to mouth off about people who were in for a surprise, an unpleasant surprise that would cause grief and damage reputations.'

'Peculiar company you keep. Where was this?'

Kirsty waves the hand that isn't drawing masterpieces. 'Thing is, they were obviously Brankton supporters, and I'm certain one of the people referred to was you, amongst others.'

'Me! But what have I done—?'

'The talk made it clear there's a campaign afoot to discredit supporters of Mutt as well as Mutt himself.'

'Jeez!' A shadow of unease settles on Brian's face. He cradles the coffee cup in his hands as if he needs to hold tight to something. 'The police... they spoke to me today.' His voice is low, gravelly.

'Why?'

He clears his throat. 'A woman phoned. Said I'd written a threatening letter to a former MP.'

'I hope you don't think it was me.' Kirsty looks taken-aback. Annoyance lurks around her eyes and mouth.

'No, of course not.'

'Good.'

'There's no way I—'

'Who was the MP?'

'Ramsay Dunn.'

'He stays near Bluebell.'

'Does he! Perhaps he's under suspicion?

'Maybe.'

'Anyway, what with the letter and the accusations in the media...'

'What did the police say?'

'It was a Detective Inspector Raisin.'

'Raisin?'

'Uhuh.'

'No kidding?'

'Hardly a kidding matter.'

'No, of course not. It's just...well, Raisin!'

'We went for a walk in the Park. To let me cool. I was pretty pissed off when I saw the stories—'

'I'm not surprised.'

'I have an alibi, you know — for the time of Wilkie's murder. Just as well it's solid or Brankton's bastards could have me in the frame for it.'

'Where were you?'

'In my office…and yes lots of people can confirm that. Then I left to travel through to see my parents. They stay in the opposite direction.'

'So, an alibi.'

'A friend of theirs called in, so further proof. Wasn't back till late.'

'As you say, just as well it's solid, given the accusations. You didn't say what the Raisin guy said.'

'Just asked where I was. He accepted my alibi, though no doubt he'll have it checked. Asked whether…?'

'Whether?'

'The media stuff could indicate a war of factions?'

'Hope you didn't agree. The last thing we want is for the media to prod its ballpoints into that scenario.'

'Of course not. Said I'd no idea. Pointed him towards the other lot — the idiots in power.' Brian had intended mentioning the conversation around The Galley and Black Square, including his find of a lapel badge that appeared to fit the name. But the media coverage of his supposed involvement with Wilkie's murder, and the letter which a woman said was sent by him, has made him clam up, wary, even of Kirsty. The DI required the information as part of a murder enquiry, he's reluctant to divulge it to others lest it lead to a witch hunt.

'Right call. Better only to share info with me.'

Brian glances around. The smell of hamburger and chips is making him feel hungry, but he doesn't want to eat here. 'You say my name was mentioned by guys in the pub?'

'Uhuh.'

'But why? Why am I being targeted? I'm not a threat to anyone.'

'Someone thinks you are.'

Brian's fingers chase spilt sugar crystals around the plastic table top. His hands have become warm, clammy, and the crystals melt against his skin and make it sticky. He takes out a handkerchief and wipes them. 'Whatever way I look at this there's only one person who might worry about me posing a threat. I'm not, but…'

'Ming?'

'Ming. He's worried about a challenge, though I assured him I'd applied for the List not for a constituency. But he feels threatened.'

Kirsty nods. 'Recently, he's developed ambitions far beyond his capabilities. People at HQ have noticed. I suspect Brankton's at the root of that. He wants to train up a crew to take over from Mutt and his allies.'

'Yeah, well I was stupid enough to disagree with his support of Brankton. So doomed on both counts.'

'Only if his lot emerges on top.'

'What should I do?'

'You might want to have a quiet word with Mutt.'

'But will he want to talk to me?'

'Don't see why not. I'm surprised he hasn't spoken to you already.'

'The hierarchy weren't to be found today.'

'Interesting.'

'I thought I'd be mobbed by irate colleagues. But the place was like an off-season fairground.'

'Mmm, I noticed that.'

'I bumped into a guy dashing into a committee room. He looked like Special Branch.'

'Wonder what's afoot. Perhaps movement on the Wilkie case.'

Brian stares at the table. 'Suppose it's about Bluebell? A body—'

'No, I was going to tell you. HQ phoned this afternoon. Bluebell's been in hospital for tests and exploratory procedures. She didn't want word to get around. Didn't want speculation. However results are more positive than she feared, so she's expected back in a couple of weeks.'

'Whew, that's a relief! Last thing we need is a body and a by-election.'

'Quite.'

'That raises questions.'

'What do you mean?'

If Bluebell was in hospital and not at home, how come Wilkie was killed there?'

'No idea. But keep Bluebell's whereabouts under your hat meantime.'

32 - Why do you think he's a politician!

She stretches, arms thrust upwards towards the ceiling, then flops, arms hanging, swinging like a pendulum in dire need of oil and a dust. Another afternoon spent on the computer, tweaking, re-reading, becoming mind-bleached and bored. For a break she logs onto Facebook and replies to friends, readers, and comments on a few of Derek's posts. She has a feeling her son views her intrusion in his online life with less than relish, but it amuses her to discover what he's up to, and staple together descriptions and characteristics for his friends who post inane, raunchy, but occasionally intelligent observations and quirky links. It provides material to feed her imagination with its voracious appetite. Words and ideas require to be fed.

Facebook she quite likes. It is similar to email — she can log on, post, leave comments, follow links, share what amuses her, whenever she feels in the mood with no pressure on others to respond. Not like her mobile. Which reminds her, where is the blasted thing, and is it switched on or off? She unearths it at the bottom of her bag — dead as a dried fig, uncharged for too long. Hurriedly she rummages for the charger on her kitchen work surface, and eventually runs it to ground on a chair beneath a pile of clothes that patiently await ironing. The two reacquainted, she stands tapping her foot on the kitchen linoleum until there is sufficient charge to turn it on and see if Marsha, her publisher, has tried to contact her. She has a message. 'Blast.' She presses to access it. Relief, not from Marsha. But surprise, surprise, from Jasmine who has information. Lippy leans her forearms on the work surface, backside in the air, legs apart so she can rock from one foot to the other whilst she waits to be connected.

'Jasmine Stane here,' comes a voice, authoritative yet candy coated. Only Jasmine could pull that voice off, reckons Lippy.

'You left a message. It's Lippy. Hi.' Her voice by comparison seems an uncertain gabble.

'Been doing a bit of nifty digging, dearest. In the archives. Thought you might be interested in what I've found.'

'Tell me more.'

'Are you at home?'

'Yes.'

'Good. Be there in two shakes of a lamb's tail.' She cuts the connection before Lippy has time to ask if she knows the address. She obviously does. Jasmine is a journalist who likes to have her fingers on pulses and in pies. The image of where else she may also have her fingers brings a spot of red to Lippy's cheek.

Before she manages to whisk unwanted clutter from her sitting room chairs, the doorbell tings. Jasmine stands on the step with a broad smile and a bottle of wine.

'Your car supersonic?' Jasmine's eyebrow lifts. 'You've made it here from Edin in four and a half minutes flat.'

Jasmine gurgles. 'Fast, but hardly supersonic. Unfortunately. At a restless loose end, so decided to zip down on the off chance. When you phoned back I was passing through Lawder. Quaint place.'

'Just as well I'm at home.'

'Are you going to invite me in? Or have you a naked toyboy lounging on the sofa?'

Lippy shakes her head. 'One track mind,' she mutters as she leads Jasmine through to her sitting room.

'Would you have a sandwich, dearest?' Jasmine asks as she flops elegantly down on a chair and waves the bottle. 'It would go well with the vino.'

'I take it you haven't eaten?'

'Been too busy.'

'I was about to throw a stir fry together. Want to join me?'

'Sounds good. Then we can have a proper chat.'

Jasmine follows Lippy along the corridor into the kitchen and plonks herself at the table while Lippy pulls out a wok, noodles, and food from cupboards and fridge.

'I took my info to Detective Inspector Raisin.' She looks up at Lippy to watch her reaction.'

'And?'

'I don't know why you don't like him.'

'I never said I disliked him.'

'You're not enthusiastic.'

'He's just a policeman.'

'You don't think he has a certain…charisma?'

'Charisma!' Lippy drizzles olive oil into the wok. 'About as much charisma as…as a stick of rock. No, right colour but you couldn't call Raisin sweet. He's a trifle acidic. Tart.' She adds a chopped onion to the oil, screws up her eyes and wipes them with the back of her wrist. 'Oh, the onion's strong.' She stirs the onion around. 'He defies comparison. A one off.'

'Maybe that's what's so attractive about him — a style all his own.'

'Pink shirts and cowboy boots.'

'Better than a pinstripe suit and black business shoes.'

Lippy slices two carrots into thin orange batons. 'If you say so.'

'We get on rather well.'

'I thought I detected tension between you at Ramsay's?'

'That was business tension. On a personal level we…harmonise.'

Lippy turns, wooden spoon clutched in fingers. 'What is it with you and men, Jasmine?'

'I like them. They like me. Bingo.'

'Don't tell me you've—?'

'Give me a chance. The guy's in the middle of a murder investigation. His time's limited.'

'So your harmonisation is all in your imagination.'

'Of course not. When I saw him this afternoon there was a definite frisson between us.'

'Perhaps he merely shuddered at the way your lime green blouse clashed with his pink shirt.'

'Lippy, Lippy, Lippy. Where's your sense of romance?'

'More grounded than yours.'

'How do you write novels and plays without experiencing the finer things in life, like sex, good wine and great food — your onions smell as if they're burning, by the way — paintings that blow the mind, and…?'

Lippy grabs the handle of the wok and moves it off the heat. 'I said it was more grounded, not buried six feet deep.'

'As soon as this business is over I'm going to ask him out.'

'Perhaps he's happily married.'

'No, divorced. I asked him.'

Lippy shakes her head. 'I might have guessed.'

'What's so wrong with wanting to enjoy the company of a man who intrigues me?'

'What is there to intrigue? The cowboy boots?'

'No. His character. His dry sense of humour, his quick mind. A quirky side that hooks me and tantalises me.'

'Jasmine, if you were a fish you'd never be in water. And you know what happens to fish out of—?'

'They morph into dishes that captivate taste buds and entrance gourmet diners.'

Lippy drains the noodles and slurps them into a dish. 'You're impossible.'

'Not as impossible as that Ramsay of yours.'

'He's not mine.'

'Mind you, a half decent woman would soon snap him out of that cage he's built round himself.'

'He has a woman. His wife.'

'Huh! Has he not got his hands on you yet?'

'Jasmine!' Lippy shoves a plate and cutlery on the table in front of her.

'Don't do yourself down. You're still a good-looking woman.'

'Gee, thanks.' She puts the noodles and stir-fry on the table. 'Help yourself.'

Jasmine waves the wine bottle. 'Glasses? Clothes could do with an update, though.'

Lippy thuds two wine glasses onto the table. 'I live in the country. I write, so often see no-one for days. I don't need high fashion.'

'No, Ramsay thinks along the same lines. So you're still dancing around one another, are you?'

Lippy's mouth softens into a grin. 'He kissed my cheek when I left the other day.'

'Daring! Probably is for the guy. Still, a first step.'

'Eat before it gets cold.'

Over coffee Jasmine asks, 'Did you find what was in the letter to Ramsay?'

Lippy nods. 'Mmm.'

'Come on, spill.'

'Not sure I should…you being a journalist and…'

Oh, for goodness sake. It'll all come out anyway.'

Lippy pauses. 'Okay. It said *Stay schtum or you're next.*'

'Good grief! Upsetting. Frightening.'

'The last thing he needed. Kat will be livid.'

'Kat?'

'His wife.'

Jasmine twitches her mouth. 'Ah, I thought for a minute you meant… The invisible woman.'

'She found the expenses furore difficult.'

'I guess Ramsay must find the present situation even more difficult. An invisible wife and threats from someone unknown. I presume our dapper Detective has ruled him out of the murder.'

'Yes, he was seen on the beach by a reliable witness, as they say, and then I was at the house.'

'Of course. If I was him, I'd hotfoot it somewhere I couldn't be found.'

'I gather there's a police presence.'

'Even so...'

'Lets' move to more comfortable chairs.' Lippy gets up and leads the way to the sitting room where she closes the curtains and turns up the electric fire. 'What's the information you unearthed?' she asks when they are settled, Lippy in an armchair by the side of the fire, Jasmine on the settee, lolling back on the cushions with her feet tucked under her.

'It's about Brankton's son.'

'The one you mentioned—?'

'Uhuh. The DI was pleased. I wasn't able to give him a name the other day. But today I arrived with name, background and other details all in a neat parcel tied with a bow. Figuratively.'

'Sucking up to him.'

'I'm determined to make Political Editor on the paper.'

'Watch you're not shunted into covering Crime.'

'Heaven forbid.'

'So does this character look like he might be in the frame?'

'Well, considering the speed with which Raisin dearest barked to his sidekicks, I'd say very much so.'

'Sounds as if you're definitely in with a shout for Senior Crime Reporter.'

Jasmine straightens her legs and swings her feet to the floor. 'This guy's a nasty character by the look of it.'

'Like father like son.'

'According to the coverage at the time of his trail, he's not Brankton's son — he's his step-son.'

'Oh!'

'Brankton and his first wife divorced and he married this other woman. Reading between the lines, the reporter who covered the trial considered her rather odd, disturbed even. The DI had his people looking for a guy called Brankton, whereas his name is Colcannon. Jut Colcannon.'

'You said he'd been in jail?'

'I thought he had, but he got off on a legal technicality. There was quite a stushie about it. Our crime reporter certainly thought it weird. I came across letters in a few editions that alluded to funny handshakes and rolled-up trouser legs. Of course that never went anywhere.'

'What was he charged with?'

'Beating up a man who didn't agree with him basically. In a pub. A few hints he wasn't the only one but was a member of a gang.'

'He must've been quite young.'

'Yup. Late teens. But there's more.'

'You have been busy.'

Jasmine drains her wine glass. 'Investigations create a thirst.'

'I'll open another bottle.' Lippy springs to her feet and makes for the kitchen.

'Hang on, dearest. I've already drunk half a bottle. I've to drive back to Edin. Unless you have a spare bed I could crash on.'

'It's covered in sheets of manuscript, but I'll remove them.'

'I'd hate to be responsible for mixing up your scenes or chapters.'

'Might improve the book. It juddered to a halt several months ago. No problem.'

'In that case bring another bottle.'

Lippy returns, unscrewing the cap of another bottle of wine. She glances briefly at the label. 'Should be reasonable.' Glasses are refilled. 'You said there was more.'

'The benefits of computerisation. Instead of working your way through enormous tomes of back issues, you can bring articles up on screen and search for similar ones. Or for other articles on the people involved.'

'So?'

'Our friend Jut was imprisoned for two years for assault. The guy he attacked nearly died. He got out eighteen months ago.'

'Nasty piece of work.'

'That was DI Raisin's response.'

'So is he now chief suspect for the murder? Is there a link?'

'Someone is organising media campaigns against Mutt and a number of others — Mutt supporters, presumably. Brankton's the one who stands to gain by becoming leader if Mutt is forced to step down. Colcannon is Brankton's step-son and a known trouble-maker. Looks like links in a chain to me.'

'But for Brankton to revert to murder — somewhat drastic.'

'He may not have known about that. Colcannon may have taken matters into his own hands. From what I could glean from the reports in the papers, he and his mother are very close, and she exerts considerable influence over him. Negative influence seems the belief'

'Does she have a criminal record?'

'Not that I could find, but I don't know her maiden name. I expect the police will root around and see what can be dug up.'

'This …Jut character. Does Raisin think he's head of the Black Square outfit — given that Brankton's been dismissed as not having the guts?'

'He may be the muscle, but I don't get the impression he's the brains.'

'Back to square one. Black Square one.'

'Hmm.'

'Jasmine, humour me. Do you think it possible Black Square has a woman at its head?'

'Possible. There's undoubtedly a certain type of woman that's sufficiently cold and calculating. You're thinking of Jut's mother?'

'Uhuh. Whoever she is.'

'Mother decides on actions, son carries them out, husband provides the cover and benefits by getting top job. Quite a set-up — if that's the case.

Lippy squirms in her chair. 'The thought gives me a sickening feeling. Makes me want to rush around and check doors and windows are locked.'

Jasmine glances around. 'And check your mobile is always to hand.'

'Never thought of that. Where does Bluebell McDaid come into this?'

'I don't know. Raisin, dearest, is keeping quiet about her. No attempt has been made to find her, which suggests the police know where she is. Perhaps she's stashed somewhere for safety.'

'Ramsay didn't seem to know, but…'

'You're keeping information from me.'

'I shouldn't—'

'Of course you can. I'm a friend, for heaven's sake.'

'You're also a journalist.'

'Oh, pah!'

'He told me before I left. He…he…'

'He what, Lippy?'

'When he came back from the beach that day, he saw a car. Just a brief glimpse.'

'Has he told Raisin this?'

'Not initially, though he did the other day. In view of the letter he could hardly….' Her voice tails off. A look of worry creases her face.'

'Jingle jangle! The car — did he recognise it?'

Lippy nods. 'Not exactly recognise, but…'

'He either did or he didn't.'

'He's seen it around.'

'Hmm! Just as well there's a police presence at his house then.'

'You think he might be in danger?'

'No idea. But…'

'But?'

'Brankton stays not far from Bluebell and Ramsay.'

'Dear heavens! A viper's nest down the road from Ramsay. Psycho son, ambitious step-father and disturbed wife.'

'Looks that way.'

'Cosy — like a fakir's bed!'

'At the first trial, the address given for Colcannon was a Neucastle address. For the second, he was said to live with his mother and step-father. As an MCP, Brankton's address isn't difficult to find. Took me about ten seconds.'

'Wow, no wonder you feel you and DI Raisin harmonise. Your information must have pushed the enquiry forward by a mile.'

Jasmine grins. 'Always useful to have good contacts.'

'Speaking of contacts. The media barrage against Mutt and company. The Callyman was awash with it. You must know who it came from, or at least have some ideas.'

'Not me, dearest. The editor says *Jump*. I ask if I've jumped high enough. Same for the editor. The owners say *Print*. And our arse-licking editor bows and says *Of course masters. How often?*' She twirls her glass in her fingers.

'And editor, owner, or both, could support the People's Union Party and be anxious to... safeguard its reputation. Understand that. But why Brankton? Why turn on Mutt?'

Jasmine's hand flies to her mouth to cover a yawn. 'Lordy, I'm suddenly dog tired. Mutt got where he is by hard work — more or less. Brankton, despite his weedy, reedy, seedy appearance, is rather well connected. So can pull strings.'

'Don't tell me. Bankers.'

Jasmine shakes her head. 'No, he has a couple of interesting directorships — one with a large construction company, and one with an outfit that provides medical services and appliances. His father owns a large estate up north. He won't inherit as he's not the eldest son, but they stand to make a not insignificant sum from a proposed wind farm. So, as I say, he has connections.'

'And is willing to use them?'

'Of course, dearest. Why do you think he's a politician!' Jasmine yawns again.

'I'll go and sort your bed.' Lippy pushes herself to her feet. 'Do you need anything? Nightdress? Toothbrush?'

'Thanks, no.' Jasmine raises her large brown leather handbag onto her lap. 'Always carry everything I need for an overnight stay in my handbag.' She pats the bag affectionately.

Lippy looks at her in surprise. 'You always carry…?' She nods at the bag.

'Of course, dearest. Us journalists…us women never know when an overnight stay might be necessary. Or enjoyable, for that matter.' She arches her eyebrows and curves her mouth into a wicked grin.

33 - Slippery as a strand of seaweed

Schaw pours brandy from the miniatures he bought in the duty free shop into plastic tooth mugs and hands one to his wife. He perches on the edge of the bed and raises his glass to her. 'Sorry to have caused this upheaval in your life.'

Selina shrugs her shoulders. 'My father started it. So no use blaming you. You've only played out the hand he dealt you.'

'I should've said no, refused to become involved.'

'My father was a hard man to refuse.'

'True. He'd so many compelling ways of being persuasive.'

She plays with her glass. 'Difficult to believe I never knew what was going on.'

Schaw gets to his feet. 'You must have. Or at least suspected.'

Selina studies the carpet as she considers. 'Perhaps. But I was shielded from it — by him and my mother. You followed suit.'

'That's the way he wanted it.'

'His retiral event — that was a shock. That's when it was hammered home to me that he wielded power — power I knew nothing of. It frightened me.'

'He wielded power all right.'

'Illegitimate power?'

Schaw raises his hands and lets them fall. 'When it comes to power, what's illegitimate?'

Selina shrugs.

He paces back and forth in the confined space of the cabin. 'Selina, there are papers...'

'His papers?'

'Yes.'

'Mother mentioned men had visited her wanting papers. I thought she was havering.'

'They were in the house. I took them...after Charlie's death...before the house was sold.'

'You knew about them?'

'I knew something of them, but had no idea where they were. I came across them during the clear out.'

'You should've burned them. Sent the deals and dodgy doings up in smoke.'

'Believe me I thought of it, but they were — still are — my insurance policy. Though only against certain people, unfortunately.'

She looks at him; concern floods her eyes. Her voice is low with a slight tremble. 'What sort of papers?'

'Documents — that sort of stuff. Photos, quite a few photos — explicit, compromising, damning to certain reputations and careers. Recordings, too — indiscrete, shocking in some cases.'

Selina shifts on the bed. 'Dear heavens!'

'Jut and his mother want them, want the power they contain.'

'Where…where are they?'

'Before I tell you, there's something you must promise me.'

She clutches her glass, squashing its shape from circular to oval. 'I suppose,' she clears her throat, 'I suppose I've no option but to say okay.'

'You must promise if anything happens to me—'

'Schaw, stop it. Quit frightening me. Nothing's going to happen to you. This is Caledon, not some tribal dictatorship.'

'It's the Northerly Sea actually but—'

'Stop it. Stop. Stop. Stop.' She pounds her knee with her clenched fist.

Schaw drops down on the bed beside her and puts his arm round his wife's shoulders. He touches his head to hers and feels her hair tickle his nose. 'This is important, Selina,' he says, straightening. 'The papers… they're are at Bluebell McDaid's house.'

'Where? Bluebell… Why there?'

'We've known one another for years.'

'I didn't know.'

'Thing is, Selina the papers are in an old steamer trunk. In the attic. Not such a great hiding place at present…but…'

'Is that what Wilkie Smart's murderer…?

'No. I don't know. Might have been, though I don't think so. But…'

'But what?'

'You must promise if anything happens…I'm just being careful here and thinking ahead — just in case…but if anything happens you need to get hold of them. The papers must be destroyed… immediately.'

Selina swallows and nods. 'I promise.' Her voice is an uneven whisper.

'Good. Because if Jut or his mother believes you have them, or know their whereabouts, then you could be in trouble. They need to be convinced you know nothing about any of this. Okay?'

'Okay.'

'They'll be others after them too, if I meet a sticky—'

'Don't even think such a thing.'

'The papers must be destroyed. That's all.'

'Okay. But it's not going to come to that.'

'Let's hope not.' He squeezes her shoulder.

Selina dashes a hand over her eyes. 'I thought...I thought Bluebell had disappeared?'

'She'll be back.'

'Right.'

'Chin up. We've got away. Put a sea between them and us. Things will settle.'

'Heavens, I hope so.'

'Yup. Time and a jail cell will work wonders.' He squeezes her shoulders again. 'Drink up.'

The boat heaves upwards then bellyflops, and sends their drinks churning like merry-go-rounds in the plastic glasses. For several minutes it lurches and pitches before it settles into its previous rolling motion.

Selina glances round at her husband. 'So where were you last week?' she asks, turning her head to stare at the toes of her shoes. 'You went off to work on Friday and stayed away nearly a week.'

Schaw gets to his feet, wanders to the window and raises the blind. He bends, and peers out, stares into the unending black, then pulls down the blind again with a clatter. 'I didn't mean to. I got...waylaid.'

'Couldn't you have let me know?'

He turns to face his wife. 'Not really. Not possible.'

'Okaaaay.' Selina draws out the word, to infer she isn't happy with the answer but will accept it for now. 'But where were you?'

'Where was I? Ummm...well...' He fiddles with two more miniatures of brandy on the table beneath the window.

'Were you... with another woman?' Selina's voice is breathy, her screwed-up courage shows through in its tone.

'Jeez, no! ' Schaw shuffles the miniatures. 'Well...'

'A man then?' Her voice is more insistent.

'Well...'

'For heaven's sake! You were away, but you're not telling me where, or who you were with.'

'It's difficult.'

'Urrrgh! So, it's difficult.' Selina sighs in frustration. 'I deserve an explanation.'

'You do, of course you do.'

'So?'

Schaw walks to the toilet door and plays with the handle. He takes a deep breath that makes the frame of his body shudder. He moistens his lips with his tongue. His arms flap like a bird trying to take off into a gale, before one hand is directed upwards to scratch his head. 'Despite everything…well, your father wasn't bad to work for. I would've left after he died but Carnoustie…well he wanted me to stay on…for continuity.'

Selina gives a curt laugh. 'Continuity! That's a good one, given what you were up to — wreaking havoc with the democratic process.'

'Nevertheless, that's the way it was put to me.'

'Huh!'

'Your father's regime ran smoothly. Carnoustie was your father's anointed successor and they both wanted an uncomplicated transition.'

'Hmmph!'

'Look, if you don't want to hear this…'

'I never said that. I just have problems with the continuity argument.'

'It was run like a business so—'

'Okay. Fine. Carry on.'

Schaw resumes his pacing. 'After an initial dirty scuffle, everything went fine for a time, then Brankton began to throw his weight around, muzzle in on decisions and actions. Carnoustie's rod of iron wasn't anywhere near as strong as your father's. Charlie could stamp out an insurrection with a few well-chosen words and a twitch of his pinkie. But Carnoustie — nah! – he's too easily overcome, quite a weak character in fact. A good French brandy with too much lemonade. So all fizz and no body.'

'And Brankton took over.'

'Yup. At least he's the front man. Impression is he represents a new, somewhat questionable, faction in the Party. Has his sights set on the Party leadership.'

'The exposés in the media?'

'Yup. The Mutt attack. Not convinced he engineered that, though.'

'What's he like?'

'Not a bad sort really — apart from his misplaced sense of ability. But he married the wrong woman. I suspect she inflated his ambition and pushed him into it, aided by her nutcase son.'

'You still haven't told me where you were.'

'I'm coming to that. I told Brankton I was finished. I'd persuaded and strong-armed for long enough and wanted out. Wanted my life back.

He seemed quite relaxed about it, but asked me to reconsider. Said they were having a weekend house party and I should join them.'

'A house party. Quelle posh!'

'More like an eon of forced bonding. Endless discussions about the Party, its future under his leadership, the possibilities, stances to be taken on issues, people-shuffling — that sort of thing. In between pontifications there'd be clay pigeon shooting, archery and fishing. It sounded... well, it sounded a bit cranky but nothing much to be concerned about.'

'A weekend of bribery. That's perturbing surely?'

'Par for the political course. Brankton thinks he's a piston when in fact he's only a humble washer.'

'Sounds to me as if you were about to change allegiance.'

'Nah! In my game, Selina, you need to stay nimble-footed. Besides, *Better inside the tent...*as the saying goes. Anyway, I was getting out.'

'Bye-bye Charlie.'

'Bollocks. Brankton assured me senior Party people would be there, so cranky but above board. He insisted he sought consensus on how like-minded people could take the Party forward — so he said.'

'You believed him!'

'No reason not to. Though chances of him being Party leader are...I was about to say nil, but in this game... He's very plausible. Always been an MCP amenable to discussion. So I reckoned over the weekend I could persuade him to let me go.'

'Not purely a jaunt then.'

'I even had a couple of names lined up as possible successors. When I left that Friday morning my hopes were soaring like a hot air balloon.'

'I knew something was up.'

'I was set to get my life back, so I thought. No repercussions. But I reckoned without the scheming wife and crackpot son.'

'Jut? You'd met him before, though, so you knew what he was like.'

'He was around. I kept out his way as much as possible, but he gave me little reason to distrust him. Not any more than most political hangers-on.'

Selina shifts her position on the bed and stretches out her legs. 'I never liked the bastard. Knew he was a rum one first time I clapped eyes on him.'

'Maybe you're senses are more acute when it comes to character evaluation.'

'For heaven's sake, you only have to look at the guy! Shifty, devious, as slippery as a forest of seaweed.'

'That's him. And more.'

'That Sunday he came looking for you…I knew in my bones he was up to no good.'

'Sorry about that. He wanted to find out what I'd told you. Didn't believe me when I said you knew nothing.'

'He had a knife. I saw the shape under his jacket.'

Schaw thuds down on the bed beside his wife and takes one of her hands in his. 'I put you in danger. I'm sorry. It should never have come to this.'

'Well it has. While you were enjoying yourself.'

'No, no, Not enjoying myself. No way!' Schaw's voice has risen.

'Shh. You'll be heard.'

'You don't understand. It was work. A job I was trying to extricate myself from.'

'Looks as if you've made a right mess of that. Far from extricating yourself you're now hunted.'

'That's because…because of what I was…made…forced to do.' He slides his glass onto the table and lets his head fall into his hands. His shoulders heave and his wife wonders if her husband is crying — something she has never seen him do.

She puts a hand on his shoulder and moves it around as if kneading his muscles, massaging his back. Schaw winces and she lets her hand fall to the bed. 'This weekend party…who was there?'

Schaw lifts his head and gulps air. 'About ten of us. Mainly MCPs, with me and Wilkie Smart.'

'Wilkie Smart?'

'Yup. He and I…we appeared to be invited along for much the same reason — to be persuaded to stay on and shift allegiances.'

'I thought you said—'

'We went to see what was hatching. Out of curiosity, not to change sides. And to get our freedom. Wilkie wanted out too. Had a big job lined up. A position he was desperate to accept because it offered more challenges. Huh!'

'So how come he…?'

Schaw shakes his head. 'It…got out of hand. On Sunday morning Jut and Wilkie had been with the clay pigeon shooting group. I opted for fishing but took a book to read instead. It was bloody cold. Felt as if I had frostbite after an hour or so. At lunch Jut gibbered nonstop, kept prodding me, wanted to know who knew about my work, did I boast about it, blab about it in bed? I said we'd better things on our mind, that I wasn't a blabbermouth and neither Charlie nor Carnoustie had any complaints.'

'Nasty piece of work, for sure.'

'I was fed up with fishing so in the afternoon I joined the archery lot. Jut barged in but became bored and left. That must've been when he took a run back to Edin to visit you.'

Selina shivers. 'I'll never forget his slimy intrusion.'

Schaw takes a sip of his drink. 'The archery lot was a pretty staid bunch, and the target kept being moved nearer. Some of them found difficulty seeing it never mind hitting it with an arrow. In fact it crossed my mind at least one of them thought the long thing with the sharp end was a backscratcher rather than a weapon.'

'You're talking of senior Party people.'

'Exactly. Anyway, Jut was fired up by banging at the clays in the morning, and no doubt by his intimidation of you in the afternoon. By dinner he was even more off his trolley. He was loud and raucous, told risqué jokes and hooted uproariously at them. He downed wine by the bottleful, and became pretty objectionable. Brankton suggested he go easy. Jut swore at him — a right mouthful. I could see Brankton swivel his eyebrows at his wife and flick his head towards Jut. He wanted her to shut him up, but she thought it hilarious and encouraged the bampot.'

'You should've left.'

'Too much vino drunk to drive. I fully intended to leave after breakfast on the Monday.'

'Why didn't you? You'd have saved me days of anguish.'

'Coming to that. Most of us went off to bed—'

'Quite a mansion to accommodate everyone.'

'A small country estate. Chunks of land have been sold off over the years for executive houses, but still a significant number of acres.'

'By the coast?'

'Slightly inland, with a small river running through the property.'

'Didn't know an MCP's salary ran to estates in the country.'

'He comes from money. Might well be what attracted the wife.' He leans across to the table and sweeps up the miniature bottles of brandy. 'Another?' Selina nods and holds out her plastic tumbler. Schaw unscrews the caps of both bottles and pours the contents into his wife's and his own glass.

'Don't stop. I want to know what happened.'

Her husband takes a slow sip of his drink. 'Wilkie didn't come up with the rest of us. He and Jut, and his mother, were discussing unemployment figures or workfare or something, and they didn't agree. Words got pretty hot. Jut cursed and swore, poked fun at every sentence Wilkie uttered, made him look a right fool. I was glad to see the back of him. I don't know why Wilkie didn't just leave. If he had…things might've turned out different.'

'How? What happened?'

I'm coming to that. Let me tell this in my own way. It's difficult enough without you hassling me.'

'Sorry.'

'I couldn't sleep. I wasn't in one of the main bedrooms but in a wee shoebox tucked under the eaves — originally a servant's room probably — and at the back of the house, so didn't hear comings and goings. The roof sighed and creaked in tune with the bed and I'm sure rats scrabbled in the attic. Eventually I dozed off. I woke later than intended. Breakfast was a help yourself affair and I was finishing when Jut crashed in. No sign of Brankton, or his mother, or anyone else. I felt a shiver of alarm climb up my spine. He was wild, and still ranting like the previous evening. I asked if he'd eaten breakfast but no response.' Schaw takes a slug of his drink. 'Reliving this is bloody difficult.' His breath grates in his throat. 'He waved his arms around like a windmill, and I gathered he wanted me to go somewhere with him. I said I needed to get back. I had work. But he insisted. Started to curse and swear at me, so eventually I gave in but said I couldn't be long. We took his car, not a good idea as he was still pissed. It was one of these four wheel drive efforts, a Land Rover, in a muddy brown colour. At the time I remember thinking it wasn't a car for a young guy, but…' Schaw swallows hard.

Selina grips his arm. 'Take your time.'

'We didn't drive far. Jut turned the car up this track and into the drive of a house. I was sick with fear as I knew whose house it was. Anyway, no-one was around. We went round the back — more like the front as it faces seawards — and went in through the kitchen door. Jut had a key.' He takes another gulp of his drink. 'Then I saw him.'

'Saw who?' asks Selina, her voice as quiet as swirling mist.

'Wilkie.'

'You saw Wilkie Smart? Was it his house?'

'No, you don't understand.' Schaw's voice is flat, devoid of expression. 'It's Bluebell's house.'

'Bluebell's! So how—?'

"Wilkie…he…he was lying on the floor. Dead.'

'Oh, dear heavens!'

'Jut…well, he wanted help to move him. I told him no way. I dashed out and he stormed after me. Grabbed my arm, pulled me, swore, threatened. I thumped him one and pulled free, ran. Ran blindly, unaware of direction. I found myself tripping and stumbling down a path to the beach. Jut's footsteps crunched on the gravel behind me, so I kept going.'

Selina sits very still as if a mannequin in a shop window. The revelation has drained her face of any expression, but in the cabin light she appears to have aged. The lines on her face are etched deeper, the shadows under her eyes are more pronounced purple grey, while the skin of her face has an artificial green hue. As her husband shudders, she blinks rapidly. 'Oh, Schaw!'

'He tore down behind me. I could hear his feet slither on the path. He lunged at me on the beach and sent me sprawling in the shingle. My face landed in a heap of seaweed and I could feel it prick my eyes. It smothered me with its rotting smell, and worked its way into my mouth to choke me. It clawed my skin with its prickly bits, and slithered around my face like some horrid animal. I coughed and spat, crawled to my feet, still coughing and spluttering, and before I knew it Jut was on me again. Round and round in the wet sand and stones we rolled. Round and round, up and down, we pounded the daylights out of one another. Then we lay. My body screamed with pain. I wondered if I'd a broken rib. My nose was bleeding over my shirt and jacket.' He stole a look at his wife. 'Haven't been fit for that kind of exercise for a long time.'

Selina points to Schaw's forehead. 'The bruise…?'

Her husband nods. 'Plenty of those. All over me.'

'But who…killed him, killed Wilkie?'

'Jut. He was still arguing with Wilkie at breakfast apparently. When he left Jut followed him. Wanted to know where he was going. Wilkie had gone to pick up bits and pieces for Bluebell who's in hospital. All very hush-hush. Barged in at Bluebell's, and took Wilkie by surprise — thought that was funny, laughed himself stupid over the look on Wilkie's face, so he spouted later. Even opened a bottle of wine to keep himself topped up. Then I assume it all went downhill, and Jut…well, he…he strangled him.'

'Oh, it doesn't bear thinking about.'

Schaw sniffs. 'Bad, yup.'

'Why did he want to move…it?'

Schaw shakes his head. 'I suppose if he was left there it was too easy to tie him to Jut and Brankton.'

'So you…'

'Mmm. Jeez he was heavy. And I was in no state. Neither was Jut. That's why Jut had brought the Land Rover. We needed somewhere close by to dump him, somewhere with easy access, before traffic increased and there was a greater chance of us being noticed. And missed. Besides we didn't fancy driving around with a body for long.'

'Bloody stupid to pick Ramsay Dunn's place.'

'Jut knew he would be mooning around on the beach and that Kat would be in Edinburgh. He knew the place would be open too. Think he might have been watching him. Anyway, we drove up, not a soul to be seen, unloaded our cargo and left him in the sitting room. Jut pulled this piece of blue rope from his pocket — must've picked it up on the beach — and thought it would be a hoot to loop it round Wilkie's neck. Some laugh! I felt sick but Jut bundled me back into the car. Had to stop further along the road, though.'

'So you're an accessory to a crime.'

''Fraid so.'

'Dear heavens.'

They sit in silence as the ship hums, rises, dips, bellyflops. 'Jut's mother took my clothes to wash. They wanted to keep me there in case I...'

'In case you told the police.'

'Uhuh.'

'Don't know how long they'd have kept me. Who knows what my fate might have been. Same as Wilkie's, I suppose.'

'Oh, Schaw!'

'I'm a liability, Selina. A threat to them, and their schemes.'

'Dear heavens!'

'They locked me in the attic room, let me out for dinner in the evenings. That's when they told me I'd been watched, and Brankton's dragon of a wife accused me of being a police informer. That or a spy. Take your pick. Any excuse to—'

'They kept you prisoner! These people think they're above the law.'

'They certainly think they can manipulate the law.'

'How?'

'Easy. Networks, that's how. Tentacles that reach everywhere.'

'Unbelievable.'

'Maybe, but it happens. Especially when you're regarded as scrap for recycling.'

'Thank heavens you got away.'

'This day they were running around like chickens harried by a fox — something had upset them big time — and I managed to give them the slip when I was let out for a pee. Sneaked out the door — it was usually locked. Walked a bit, well...half staggered, half lurched, and hitched a lift from a lorry driver. Not supposed to lift hitchers, but the poor sod was being made redundant so didn't give a fig about rules. The rest you know.' He leans his head on his wife's shoulder and she locks her arms around him.

'Oh, Schaw! What're we going to do?'

34 - Why the special treatment?

His day has been difficult. He has been the butt of snide remarks and ridicule, unpleasantness and jostling, hostility and pranks more attuned to wee school kids than mature Members of the Caledon Parliament. When he walks into the dining room for lunch a hiss travels round the tables of a significant number of those in his own party. Brian feels he is being stalked by a snake, something large and poisonous, that is gearing up to strike and fell him with one attack of its fangs. He eats marooned at a table near the centre of the room. Around him, Members of other parties pick up the vibes and titter. He looks surreptitiously around for Kirsty but doesn't see her and he wonders if she has stayed away on purpose.

This morning Ming was icily formal like a frosted flagpole. The flag of his bombast drooped and hung lifeless, frozen stiff like a board. This afternoon he is off on a committee visit so Brian will have the office to himself. That will give him time to mope, so he almost wishes Ming was going to be around. At least his frigid presence and chilly remarks would keep him from wallowing in a trough of self pity spiked with fury.

The hostility around him depresses his appetite and he pushes his plate away and gulps his coffee, which burns his mouth. A loudmouth member from his own Party scrapes his chair out from the table where he sits and struts towards Brian. In anticipation of action, heads turn, eyes follow him, and voices fall silent. As he approaches he fakes a trip and careers into Brian's table sending his plate of barely touched food spinning to the floor where the plate smashes and the lettuce, tomatoes and other salad stuff waltz in different directions. His coffee leaps to the edge of the table, tumbles into his lap and sends the hot liquid to pierce clothes and skin. Brian jumps to his feet, aware all eyes are riveted on him. He wills himself to keep quiet, not to swear or call the idiot names. With one hand he wafts material from skin while with the other he searches in a pocket for a handkerchief. Sniggers can be heard along with the odd mumbled remark.

Into the scene rolls a motherly, middle aged woman from the servery. With one hand she offers a cloth to Brian to mop the moisture from his clothes while with the other she wipes the table, her cloth meticulously folded and turned, paying no heed to those who watch her. She straightens and surveys her work, then turns her attention to Brian. 'Are you all right, hen?' she asks. Concern coats her voice.

Brian thanks her and scrubs at the coffee that has seeped into his trousers.

She gives the table top a final polish. 'Some folk are awfy careless,' she announces. Her voice carries to nearby tables, where faces turn away in the pretence of not having ogled the spectacle. A few grins are hidden behind hands. She leans towards him, and in a more muted voice says. 'Jist let me sweep that lot up an' I'll bring you another plate o' salad an' a fresh cuppa.'

'No, please. Thank you. I appreciate your offer, but I'm not hungry.'

She leans closer. 'Dinnae let the bastards win, son. I'll bring it — up to you what you do with it.' She nudges his arm with her elbow and catches his eye conspiratorially. Suddenly Brian sees the funny side of the situation and his face creases into a grin, then a chuckle rumbles up from his throat. 'That's great. Thanks.'

The woman straightens her back and takes her time to amble back to the serving area, swishing her cloth over a few other tables en route. With exaggerated actions, for she knows every eye in the room is on her, she selects a salad and pours a cup of coffee. A tray is wiped and the plate and cup are placed on it along with a serviette. Then, with the tray supported on one hand and balanced by the other, she makes her way back to Brian's table where she lays the dishes before him with all the pomp of a maître d'hôtel. Once that is accomplished to her satisfaction she fetches a brush and shovel to clear the mess on the floor. As she sweeps, the edge of the metal shovel accidentally rasps the ankle of the perpetrator of the incident. He yelps and bends to grasp his ankle. His leg collides with the leg of the table he sits at, while his elbow connects with the top, and over it goes. Crockery and food are launched into orbit, whilst others round about jump up and brush pieces of gooey hamburgers and sticky sauce from their clothes. Brian lowers his face to make his twitching grin less noticeable.

'Is there somethin' wrong with you?' The woman asks indignantly, waving her brush at the guy. 'That's the second time in ten minutes you've messed up my floor. The big floor brush and mop are in the kitchen.' She indicates the direction, leaving the guy in no doubt what is expected of him. Brian decides a box of chocolates needs to wend it way to this matron in shining armour.

As Brian walks rapidly back to his office, head down, eyes riveted on the corridor ahead, he tells himself he has to ride it out. That's the only option. Another couple of days and the media will move on to another story, another target, and the nonsense about him will be history, relegated to fire-lighting or chip paper. But that does little to assuage the bitterness and deep sense of injustice that grips his heart, and the outrage that is in danger of paralysing his mind. Accusations, serious accusations, have been made against him, splashed in all the media, about his implied involvement in the murder of Wilkie Smart, and he is powerless to contradict the calumnies. The media have their story, and have plucked headlines from a pit of vitriol. After their success at character assassination the article will be relegated to the archive, unless more can be milked from it. To secure readership for another edition the process will be repeated with a hatchet job on another poor soul.

But for him the damage will have been done. The public will shake heads, tut over their cornflakes, not necessarily believe it in total but, with sucked intake of breath and what they consider a wise-owl look, will intone remarks of no smoke without fire. The media can say and do whatever it wants. Its victims have no redress, unless they are backed by six figure and more bank balances. So he needs to state his innocence and ride it out.

As Brian treads the corridor he fears his career is over before even begun, dazed at how the wheel of fortune has spun so dizzily from a Parliamentary assistant with potential to a figure of ridicule. And not for the first time he wonders what part Ming has played in this. Ming the bumbling, Ming the ruthless, Ming who learned his craft from the founder of The Galley, Charlie Kintail.

Gullibility is not confined to voters, so a few of his colleagues will believe the story — at least in part — while others will happily go along with it for the sport, and for the opportunity to do down a potential rival in the employment or selection stakes.

As he enters his office he feels despondent. The world is against him, has ganged up on him ready to squash him underfoot like a bug. He thought himself so smart. Huh! Even cherished high hopes of outmanoeuvring his idiot boss, only to find he is the one who has been ruthlessly played. He, Brian — not Ming — is the sucker. The lesson is as bitter as the pill to swallow.

For an hour or more he answers letters and emails, telephone calls, jots down notes for a speech he needs to write for Ming, but his heart is not in his work and his thoughts roam elsewhere. His actions are automatic; the responses he does not need to think about; his fingers pound the keyboard of their own accord while his brain is numb with misery. The time on the computer clock moves onwards at a snail's pace. Brian toys with the idea of leaving early. If challenged he can make the excuse of arrangements for an event or liaising with constituency staff. He is on the point of shutting down his computer as the door is pushed open. When he raises his head the sees the leader of his Party scrutinising him.

Brian jumps to his feet whilst offering the information that Ming is not around.

'It's you I wanted a chat with…err…emm…Brian.'

'Oh…I'll find another chair.'

'No need, I'm merely passing.'

Brian hovers, unsure whether to remain on his feet or sit down. He stays on his feet.

Mutt paces back and forwards between the outer door and the door to Ming's office. He pauses to read the names of books and reports ranged along the shelves. 'Uhuh. Managing to keep your head above water, do you think?'

Brian's brain thaws sufficiently to send a warning signal. In normal times he would feel confident of an interview with Mutt, but he's certain this isn't a normal time, and the interview is shaping more like an interrogation. 'The work's interesting, but not unduly difficult.' He sneaks a look at Mutt, and wonders if that's an appropriate response.'

Mutt perches on the edge on his desk and waves a hand to indicate Brian should sit down. 'Bad business this.' He gives a theatrical sigh.' Nasty business.'

No need to ask the business referred to. Brian squares his shoulders and draws a breath to launch into his rebuttal of the allegations in the media. 'I had nothing to do with it. The media have either been misinformed or they made up the entire story.'

Mutt stares at him, but Brian gets the impression the eyes don't see what they are looking at. His lips purse like a dried prune. 'The police have interviewed you?'

'A Detective Inspector Raisin spoke to me, yes.'

'Hmm.'

'He accepts I have an alibi for the time of Wilkie's murder and that I couldn't possibly have had any hand in it.' He doesn't intend to mention the letter he supposedly sent to the ex-MP. The less Mutt and others know the better. His reputation has been sufficiently damaged.

'I see.' Mutt inspects his fingernails. 'Pleased to hear that. Still…'

Brian understands he needs to show some fight. 'I had nothing to do with it. I've been set up — just as you were. There are people—'

Mutt holds up his hand. 'No regurgitation of faction stories, please.' His hand moves to pat the knot in his tie then slides down his front, fingering his tie as it drops.

'Look, the police accept I had nothing to do with what happened. If you don't believe me phone them.'

'No need for that. No, no need at all.'

'Good, because I'm totally innocent of the allegations in the media.'

Mutt glances around, and checks his fingernails again. Brian wonders if this is how a Party leader should act. The man seems ill at ease. His face is haggard, the bags beneath his eyes are more pronounced than usual and have the look of bruises, his mouth is under a tension which pulls it down at the corners and a mist of sweat beads have settled on his upper lip. Brian is surprised how ill the man looks.'

'Like I said, a nasty business.' He coughs. 'Thing is…the Party is on election footing and we can't…we can't afford scandals that deflect attention from our positive stance.'

'It's a scandal I have nothing to do with.'

'This story about you — it got more coverage than my visit to the factory of our largest pie maker.' Brian looks at Mutt in disbelief. 'Their workforce has increased by ten. We need to push the positives.'

'Agreed, but—'

Mutt waves his hand again and slips from the desk to pull a book from the bookshelves. He flips idly through it then puts it back. 'You need to withdraw your application for the candidate's list.'

'Pardon?' Brian feels anger rise within him, gush up his windpipe to his throat and splatter into his mouth. He swallows hard to keep it under control.

'Bad timing. We can't allow you on the list — not with all this hoo-ha. Some jumped-up journalist would resurrect the story, and before we knew what was happening another media frenzy would erupt with even more legs. And who knows what good news story about me that might scupper.'

'That's ridiculous. I'm innocent. The story's a fabrication.'

'No, not ridiculous. It's politics. And as Party leader I'm a better judge of that than you.'

'You're condemning me when I've done nothing wrong.'

'Oh, I don't know about that. A smidgeon strong perhaps.'

'But I had—'

'Ming is less than happy with your work. Missing papers for speeches and suchlike.'

Brian fumes. Mutt has chosen the one aspect of his conduct he can defend least well. 'Ming's not the best organised person.'

Mutt tuts. 'Loyalty, loyalty…err…Brian. Loyalty. You should show loyalty to your MCP.'

'I am loyal.'

'Not what I've heard.'

'My only disloyalty in Ming's eyes was to support you when he favoured Brankton.'

Mutt shakes his head in slow motion. 'You need to be more circumspect, Brian. I rather think Ming was correct when he suggested you allow your feelings to over-ride your brain.'

'What!'

'Calm reflection is what's required. Calm reflection. And a great deal more experience. That's why you'll withdraw your application for the list.'

'I don't believe this.'

'Now that's sorted I must push on.' Mutt heads for the door. As he disappears into the hall he turns. 'You might want to consider whether politics is the most appropriate career for you, Brian.' The door swings closed.

The office is strangely quiet until Brian kicks the wastepaper bin and thuds his fist onto his desk. He can't believe what just happened, he can't bloody well believe it. 'Shit. Shit. Shit.' He sinks onto his chair and lowers his head to his hands. The room spins. His eyes won't focus and all he sees is a blur, a whirl of red blur. The furniture and contents of his office gyrate around him. Into their stream is pulled his hopes for the future; his ambitions; his hard work to get this measly position with Ming; the tickets (in lieu of bribery) for the football match that left him penniless for months but which he reckoned worth the sacrifice as they levered him into the Parliament; all the tripe he's put up with, the condescension, the late evenings and early mornings and the weekends of campaigning. All are now up in the air, whirling dervishes that sweep up everything in their road and hurtle it away from his grasp.

Has he been a fool? He underestimated Ming, for sure. Misjudged the depth of his vindictiveness against someone perceived as a threat, and his determination to safeguard his own career. Bumbling Ming. He viewed him as a pushover, then realised he had his strengths and would have a fight on his hands to oust him. But never in his worst nightmares did he anticipate that Ming would turn the tables and oust him. Worst of all, he has manipulated and engineered matters, and used the leader he supported to kick him out. In his naiveté he considered any threat most likely to come via Brankton, but Ming has outwitted him, outmanoeuvred him. That rankles, hurts in every fibre of his being. Rage and humiliation burn and grate through him as if an alien hand force-feeds him barbed wire.

The phone rings and is left unanswered. His tensed fingers form claws and he grasps for items to destroy. Ming has destroyed him. So he in turn has an overwhelming urge to crush and decimate. His fingers find a pen and curl round its blue length. They grip hard. His fist rises and falls and the pen stabs and stabs and stabs at a sheaf of papers, the point sinking in, leaving blue-ringed holes. His breath heaves in short bursts as if doled out in air packets, a sachet every twenty seconds. The casing of the pen cracks then splinters over the top sheet of paper. With one hand he sweeps the jagged pieces into the palm of the other and hurls them at the wastepaper bin.

He gulps a breath of air that feels rough on his tongue and throat, and drapes his arms down the back of his chair. A glance tells him the time is approaching home time, not that he usually manages to finish so early, but today nothing will stop him. Why ensure Ming's briefings and papers, his correspondence and media releases are up to date? Ming has played executioner, so Brian feels under no compunction to smooth his Parliamentary path.

Kirsty. He should phone Kirsty. Ask if she could meet him. Kirsty will be furious at the treatment meted out to him, and by Mutt of all people — Mutt whom she has been so anxious to protect. Kirsty, with her HQ knowledge and contacts, will have ideas for ways to change Mutt's mind. And Kirsty will know the words to let flow to sooth his fury and wounded pride. His hand moves towards the desk. No, don't use the office phone. Use his mobile. He pulls it from his pocket.

He thinks at first she isn't going to answer. Then he hears her voice. 'Can you meet me? It's important.'

'Sorry, no can do. Important meeting.'

'I've been shafted.'

'What d'you mean?'

'Mutt visited me. Told me to withdraw my application for the list.'

'Ah!'

'The media coverage of my alleged crime, and totally false accusations, is not appreciated. I got a higher billing than his visit to a pie factory. Can you bloody believe it!'

Kirsty does not answer immediately. 'You're upset.'

'Too right I am. Fuming, searing red hot upset.'

'Poor Brian.'

'This was Mutt who did this. Our Party leader. Mutt. The guy whose back we've worked to cover. Not Brankton. But bloody Mutt.'

'I can understand you being upset, but—'

'But? You'll be telling me next you agree with him that I'm not up to the job.'

'Brian, you have to realise—'

'Jeez! I don't believe this. Today is obviously gang-up-on-Brian day.'

'No, Brian, but you need to understand Mutt's in a difficult position.'

'You mean I'm not! Being accused of a crime I'd absolutely nothing to do with. Even the police agree I'm innocent. The article was pure, bloody fabrication.'

'Calm down, Brian.'

'Calm down! Did you take in what I said. This is my life I'm talking about. My future. Mutt can't bloody well do this to me.'

'Get a grip, Brian. These things happen. I'm sorry but—'

'You're taking this very calmly — almost as if you knew about it.' He hears Kirsty sigh. There's a hint of exasperation in the sound.

'Look, Mutt did what he had to do. He came to an arrangement — an accommodation with Brankton.'

'Jeez! You mean he sold out.'

'No, he was pragmatic.'

'Same thing.'

'It's not personal — well, not really. It's politics.'

'Bloody politics.'

'You got in the way, that's all. Wrong place at wrong time, working for the wrong guy. Ming's got form. You must've known that. Form and experience.'

'I see, so I just shake hands and accept it.'

'Got any better ideas?'

'Kirsty, I thought you of all people might have shown me some consideration. I mean we've got to know one another. Things were going well between us.'

'So? What d'you expect me to do?'

'The phone's rotten for discussions. Can we meet? Please? Just for half an hour. Ten minutes even.'

'Sorry. Another engagement. In fact I need to shift.'

'What's so important?' Brian hears drawers closing, stuff moved around, a computer being shut down. He can hear Kirsty's breathing. He can almost hear her squirm out of giving him an answer. Suddenly he's not sure he wants to hear her reply.

'If you must know, I'm off to a selection meeting.'

'A selection meeting! Where for?'

She pauses. Brian can almost see her weigh up what titbits to feed him. 'There might be a by-election in the offing. Can't say where. A candidate is being selected…just in case.'

'But you're not on the approved list yet.'

'Mmm. I was…fast-tracked.'

'Fast-tracked! Why the special treatment?'

'Not special treatment. An all women short list is wanted so I was fast-tracked. Look I must go.'

Brian stands very still, phone jammed to his ear. His world is disintegrating around him. 'The fast-tracking, the inclusion on the short list…are they in return for…for information…services rendered?'

'Don't be silly.'

'That's the last thing I'm being.'

'Ugh! You know how these things work as well as I do. Let's just leave it at that.'

'I see.'

'I don't think you do, Brian. But I haven't time to argue.'

Brian's hand moves the phone from his ear, then slides it back. 'You'll make a good politician, Kirsty.'

As he slinks out the Parliament building and, shoulders hunched, strides up the Royaume Mile, Brian regiments his thoughts into deciding which of his nonpolitical friends he can invite to the pub to assist him in slagging off people — women in particular — and in drowning his sorrows and anger.

35 - The fathomless grey of the sea

In the no-man's-land between sleep and wakefulness, an alien noise makes itself heard. Indistinct, quiet, yet sufficient to prise her from the depths of slumber. Her mind gathers her thoughts and shoves them in the direction of listening. Another wisp of movement, a whisper of breathing. Eyes are prised open with a butterfly wing flutter. Dark. It must still be early — so why the noise? Selina listens intently and discerns a movement out of her line of vision that extends to a rectangle of the opposite wall and the corner of the stool beside the window table. Her clothes are draped over the stool, and as the dark lightens to shades of grey she makes out the folds of her top and jacket.

The noise interrupts again. If she were a dog her ears would prick and swivel in its direction. This time she can identify the noise. She understands what it is. The door is being inched open, carefully, but gives a faint whine as if in protest. With an effort she raises her head and swivels her shoulders, letting a gust of cool air chill them, and peers towards the end of the cabin. Her mind understands that the bulk of the dark door has moved and reformed into a long narrow sliver that allows a wedge of insipid light to intrude into the cabin, giving colour back to carpet and handle of the toilet door. So the cabin door must be open. But why? Is someone about to enter the cabin? A thief? Dear heavens, could it be Jut? She blinks rapidly and sees her husband's jacket-clad back slip between door and frame out into the passageway. The door is pulled shut behind him and returns to its usual shape. The lock clicks — the click has a sound of finality about it.

'Schaw.' Her voice is heavy with sleep. 'Schaw,' she calls, this time louder though she realises he will now be too far off to hear. She props herself up on her elbow, and scratches her head as she wonders why her husband has left the cabin so early in the morning. He was restless after their talk, but said he was dog-tired and the brandy would help him sleep. She hadn't been aware of him lying awake, but, despite her fears and worries, she had dropped off. Schaw was upset, unsettled, only natural after what he's been through and given their present situation, so his disappearance worries her. Still wanting to sleep, she drags herself from the bunk and pulls on her clothes, shivering in the cooler air outside the bed's warmth. From her bag she yanks a woollen scarf and throws it round her neck and shoulders. As she hasn't bothered with tights she thrusts her bare feet into her shoes, and grabbing the cabin key from the table, she lurches towards the door.

The ship rolls less than the previous evening. The corridor is empty and silent. Unaware which way Schaw has gone she turns in the direction they took to the restaurant. At the bottom of a flight of stairs she stops, listens. The hum and creak of the ship is all she can hear. She feels as if she's entombed in an insulated box. Then a door closes, that full-throated bass thud of a door fabricated to withstand the elements. Footsteps clatter across a hard floor. Does she hear the burble of muted voices? Though it could be the twang of wind through an opening. Another door closes, or perhaps it's the same one. She runs up the stairs, slipping her hand along the handrail, and at the top lingers to listen again. Restaurants and bars are long closed so where is Schaw headed and why? Would he venture out on deck for a breath of fresh air to clear his mind, help him sleep? Surely not. That would be foolish.

Selina peers through the glass of the doors, reluctant to take herself from the warmth and security of the interior to the hostile environment outside. She pulls her jacket and scarf tightly around her and ventures through the door, pushing at it with hands and body. The cold and damp hit her with such force she almost staggers but she steadies herself against the door frame and looks around while she catches her breath. Light seeps through the mist, its pre-dawn bloom muted like a candle that glimmers through a charcoal grey chiffon scarf. Yet even that feint flush of dawn catches the foam and froth of waves to emphasise the blackness of the sea around the ship. She can hear its swishing sound as the hull arrogantly cuts and pushes its way through, throwing water to one side or the other of its bow, like a knife cutting a cream sponge, the displaced filling oozing out both sides of the blade.

The sea is alive, a giant mammal — what she can't see she can feel. It ripples with breath, coughs and sneezes, wheezes, teases, squirms in impatience, swishes and swirls around the ship, lashes out in anger, pounds home the message that it is stronger, deeper and more chilling than can ever be imagined. Selina is frightened to move in this hostile environment. Like a limpet, she clings to a rail that runs along the outside wall of the mingling area at the top of the stairs. Inside glows, bright and comforting, smiling colours and soft furnishings. Out here a nippy breeze chills — already her hand is so numb with cold she can hardly keep hold of the rail — and all the colours of the spectrum have given up the ghost and muddied together into grey: the fathomless grey of the sea; the dense grey of the sky; the throbbing grey, splashed with dirty yellow from lights, of the deck beneath her feet; the yellow streaked white grey of the icy wall against which she leans for comfort; the thudding grey of the beats of her terrified heart; the menacing grey she feels gathering around her trembling body, set to pounce.

As her eyes accustom themselves to the gloom she starts in surprise and alarm. Way in the distance…up near the bow…she makes out a blurred shape. It moves. She strains to see. Is it a figure…two figures, leaning on the ship's rail, silhouettes that shimmer dully in the mist? A metal grey sliver of fear darts through her. She steadies herself, fights to control her breathing and pushes off from the rail, the only thought in her mind that she must reach the figures. Without doubt she knows in her shaking bones one of the figures is Schaw. But who is the other? If pushed, she can understand her husband coming on deck for air, to clear his head, to think, after a horrific ten days, but surely he wouldn't arrange to meet someone — not on deck, not at this early hour. So why another figure? She concentrates on her trek along the shifting deck and pushes from her mind the surging belief of the identity of the other person.

Along the deck she lurches, clutching the rail when she can. As the ship rolls, strings of la-la-la-la-lahhhhh, de de de deeee steps cant her towards the deck rail and sea, towards never-ending greyness. The next roll returns her to more safety. Thoughts of her own wellbeing are pushed away from her mind, and she perseveres in her journey. Now she can hear voices, as yet indistinct. No words leap out, merely grey sounds in the grey seascape. One of the figures raises its arms, a gesture which indicates menace to Selina. She opens her mouth to shout, wants to tell whoever it is to stop, but words stick in her throat. Her tongue flaps around her mouth in an effort to ease their passage but all that comes out is a high-pitched squeal.

Both figures turn with a jerk. She hears the one with the raised arms growl. The other looks towards her. 'Jeez, Selina!' she hears him gasp. His attention is now focussed on her. The other person takes advantage of this. Arms are raised again. Selina's ears are filled with the gush and grumble of the sea as the hands bring a heavy object down on her husband's head. He crumples on the deck, making no sound that she can make out. Schaw could be an empty jacket that's slid to the floor, bundled in a heap. Motionless.

The object that felled him is tossed overboard. Somewhere in Selina's mind this fact registers and she is aware of a splash far below. Another squeal. The person standing by the rail glances up, and sees she is rooted to the deck, unable to move, unable to speak. He hauls Schaw to a standing position and drapes him over the rail. He works fast now. His legs are spread to steady himself, he bends, grasps Schaw's ankles and with an almighty heave and expulsion of breath, like a Highlander tossing a caber, he decants Schaw over the rail into the grey sea.

Horror and fury galvanise Selina. She uproots herself and charges like a catapulted stone towards the assailant. Arms flay the air while guttural sounds from her throat split the mist. The man flexes his shoulders, adjusts his jacket and strides past her, flinging her pounding fists away as if swatting off flies. Through the moisture from her eyes — salt water and salt tears — Selina forces herself to the rail over which her husband's body disappeared and stares into the dense grey of the water. 'Schaw. Schaw.' Her cries sound like wails, an eerie keening for her lost husband, for her inability to save him. 'Schaw.'

Screams break free of her throat and fire into the air as she holds the rail with both hands and throws her head back. She screams and gasps. A door opens and footsteps pound the deck but she hears nothing. Hands grasp her arms, prise her hands from the rail and drag her to the shelter of the superstructure. A face swims into view, to be joined by other faces. Voices demand to know what's going on, what's happening. Selina gulps and screeches an explanation. Feet pound away from her. More faces arrive, more voices — like tuning-up instruments in an orchestra — demand lifebelts, lights, for the ship to stop, to turn back. Every thread of Selina's body shivers and her knees buckle beneath her.

'Take her inside,' orders a voice.

It has been a nightmare. From the moment she thought she was wakened by a noise she has been dreaming. Schaw will be asleep in the cabin, and is now probably wondering where she is. She must have been sleep-walking. Dangerous on a ship at night. Something she's never done before. A combination of the recent stress, the heavy meal followed by the brandy and Schaw's deeply disturbing confession, has been too much for her, shunting her mind into hyper-reaction mode and causing her to sleep-walk as part of a nightmare.

She holds a cup in her hand. It feels hot. A voice tells her to drink, but she doesn't want more brandy. Her hand is nudged towards her mouth and she is forced to sip. Peculiar brandy, besides being hot it's sweet, more than sweet, it has a sweetness overload. She sips again.

The faces around her dissolve, another takes their place. His white shirt dazzles her eyes, and he has epaulettes with braid that catch the light and blind her. The person in the shirt and epaulettes pulls a chair close to her and sits on it.

'Tell me what happened,' he orders, his voice low, authoritative, urgent, yet not unfeeling.

Selina blurts out words, phrases, disjointed and awash with salt. The man probes, gently but firmly. Her husband — how had he been? Had he been depressed recently? Under strain? He nods to a woman and bounces orders against another gold-braided man who marches off. Hands guide her along corridors to a bed somewhere, not in the cabin she and Schaw occupy, but to somewhere with the aura of her GP's surgery. Hands help her peel off the clothes she donned in such haste at the start of her nightmare and another man appears at her side. She is going back to sleep now. And in the morning when she wakes she probably won't even remember this disturbing dream. She can tell Schaw about it and he can comfort her.

The mist and greyness of early morning continue to enclose Selina. Wracked by sobs and wet with tears, her face puffy, and her mind in a daze of disbelief and horror, the following hours swirl like the sea around her. A void now occupies the centre of her being — a large spherical void like a distant planet, full of raw nothing. It pulsates and demands her attention, engulfs her, blots out thoughts and all other feelings except this sense of emptiness and despair. The sides of the void are pliable as if made from rubber, yet are enormously strong and she can see no door, find no window that might provide a way out. Just wet, salty nothingness.

Other uniformed people appear and take charge. The sentences they speak are tinged with another language and at times she becomes more confused as she doesn't understand what they say. Further questions, probing and not so gentle as before. Faces harden. Voices become flatter, devoid of inflection and warmth. Their sympathy is now spiked with suspicion as investigations reveal Mrs Elsie Ravenscrofte is not Selina and Selina is not Mrs Elsie Ravenscrofte. More questions to which she has no answers. More nightmares. And no sign of Schaw. Schaw is salting slugs.

Schaw has been salted by slugs.

36 - The opposite effect

He rises and kisses her cheek. Jess bounds up, tail wagging so hard it wags her whole body, and kisses the parts of her she can reach with her slobbering tongue.

Lippy bends to pat her, scratch behind her silk ear. Jess whines and hwaaows, vocalising her pleasure.

'Thanks for coming, Lippy. I needed to talk to someone.'

'No problem.'

'I didn't know who else to call.'

'Glad you feel I fit the bill.'

Ramsay puts a hand in the small of her back and guides her over to the wicker table and chairs that have appeared at the front of the house since her last visit. 'Have a seat.' He pulls one out, scrapes it over the gravel where the legs gouge channels, for her to sit down. 'You've turned my life around, you know. Brought me back to the present from a past that sucked me ever deeper into gloom.'

'Pleased you feel that way, Ramsay.'

'You've dragged me back to an even keel.'

Lippy's eyes are drawn to the view; to the sea glowering under black clouds that drive relentlessly across the sky, a charcoal landscape on the move; to a tiny yacht etched in brilliant white against the wide pewter sea that ripples and wrinkles in the breeze; to the headland of purplish rock, dressed in golden and green mosses, lichens and grasses, where gulls (she calls all seabirds gulls) form large kites that soar and swoop and dive, before they hitch a ride on the breeze and again fly off to circle the stack of white-splattered rocks. Even at this distance their squawks and screeches, skimmed across the water, are plainly heard, the sound angry and plaintive — just as Ramsay had sounded on the phone earlier.

'Sorry to hear about Kat.'

'Hmm. Thanks.'

'Must have knocked you for six.'

Lips fold together, eyebrows travel up his creased forehead. 'For two, perhaps.' He glances at Lippy then looks away, his eyes tracking to watch a bright blue inshore fishing boat as it putters across the waves, loaded with multi-coloured pots for catching lobsters and crabs, and marker boys from which small red flags flutter. 'It's been coming. Even I could see that.'

'Still.'

'It's been on the cards since the expenses fracas. It's merely taken Kat time to make an alternative life. Now she's achieved that.' His eyes wander back to survey his hands lying on the table onto which a scatter of petals and leaves has blown. He picks up a curled leaf in his fingers, smooths it and flicks it between them before he rubs it against the table surface and shreds it.

'I'm sorry.'

'Don't be. People have felt sorry for me for too long. It's isolated me. I need to break free of that.'

'But Kat…you have an excuse.'

'No. We should have parted years ago. Made a clean break to let us both start again. Instead we dragged it out in the belief things would come right. That helped neither of us.'

'But you must feel—'

'Must feel what?' He looks into her eyes. 'Lippy,' he clasps his hands together on the table, rubbing his thumbs against one another, 'what I feel is…relief.'

'Surely not, Ramsay?'

' Yes. I knew it had to come. The wait stopped me moving on. Now it's happened. Now I can draw a line under the whole sorry expenses episode.'

'But on the phone—'

'Yes, sorry. That was the reaction of my bruised ego. I've reprimanded it, and we had a frank discussion, and now my ego and I see eye to eye.'

Lippy's eyes catch a flash of deep pink. A bush in the border by the side wall is smothered in a mass of pink flowers. She wonders what it is. Further along is another with white flowers that cascade over it like water frothing over stones. The garden looks tidy. The grass has been cut and the skeletons and ghosts of dead plants removed. There is evidence of pruning and staking, weeding and mulching. Ramsay's work she presumes, as she has difficulty envisaging Kat at work on her knees with fork and trowel.

'You're making a new start?'

'I'm trying.'

'Good for you. If there's anything I can do…'

He grabs her hand. 'I'm counting on your help, Lippy. To chivvy me when I falter, encourage me when I collapse in despair.'

'Happy to help.'

'I hoped you'd say that.' Their eyes meet and they smile hesitantly. Lippy feels self-conscious and glances away lest she misinterprets the look that hovers around Ramsay's blue-grey irises. She lowers her gaze to study their hands, admiring the way they fit together, his strong square shaped ones curled around her long fingered ones; his with reddish patches where the skin is rough, perhaps from his recent gardening; hers paler and soft from the hand cream she works into them every night before bed.

'I can't possibly understand the nightmare you went through. But there was an incident…long time ago now… A girl I thought a friend… I couldn't believe her treachery. It was a rude awakening.'

'Invisible scars — though sometimes not so invisible.'

'True.'

'If we could see them they could be labelled — badges of honour almost — *For survivors of skirmishes and wars.*' Ramsay gives a wistful grin.

'*Awarded for bravery in the face of manufactured hostility.*'

'Yes. That's good. How about *For retaining silence and dignity in the face of trumped up enemy fire.*'

'*For outstanding courage under verbal bombardment.*'

'*For bowing to the inevitable.*'

Lippy playfully slaps Ramsay's hand. 'No, we all do that at some time. Not worth a scar, just a pat on the head.'

'Okay. *For the realisation you've been an idiot but learning to live with it.*' Ramsay feels Lippy's hand tighten on his in a gesture of understanding and encouragement.

A gust of wind swirls along the front of the house and blows fallen petals and blossoms around their feet, patterning the shingle with yellows, pinks, whites, purples and blues.

'Will you stay here?'

'Haven't thought about it. I expect so. It's home. The sea and I chime with one another, empathise with each other's moods.' Lippy nods. 'And Jess likes it here. She'd be bereft without her walks on the beach, all the exciting smells that can be found in the shingle—'

'And the seaweed.'

'That, too. Couldn't possible forget the seaweed. In fact—'

'Urrrgh! Rain.' Lippy disengages her hands and holds them up, palm skywards. Wet splodges the size of fifty pence pieces pepper the table top and darken and emphasise the colours of the shell-strewn shingle. The petals become limp and sag, moulding themselves to the contours of the chuckies.

Jess gets to her feet, shakes herself and sniffs the air, then turns and pokes at Ramsay's legs with her nose, whining. 'You think we should go in girl, do you?' He studies the sky, the banks of clouds, sullen grey and ballooning with rain. 'Yup, you're probably right.' He ruffles the dog's coat with his hand. 'It was meant to hold off till we had lunch but... better make a move.'

In the kitchen Lippy sits at the table while Ramsay howks dishes and cutlery from cupboards and drawers. He switches on the light above the table and in the rain gloom it casts a warm glow. Jess laps a drink from her bowl, her pink tongue curling and uncurling like a spring to move water from bowl to mouth. She leaves a trail of dribbles on the floor as her claws clack across the floor from bowl to basket where she heaves a sigh and flops down, head resting on paws. Her eyes look closed but she holds the lids fractionally open to watch events at the table.

'I passed a police car.' Lippy twirls the knife at her place, and sends it whirling on its axis like a rotor blade.

'Uhuh. Twenty-four hour security. I feel like a celebrity.'

'It's serious.'

'Yes, though hopefully not for much longer.'

'You've heard from the police?'

Ramsay goes to the tall fridge and retrieves a plate that he places with care on the table. He stands back to survey it, a look of pleasure on his face. 'Sushi. Told you I was a dab hand at it.'

Lippy peers intently at the shapes, and wonders which of the black wrapped rolls she'll manage to eat. Even the look of raw fish makes her queasy. 'Oh, right.'

'Don't look so apprehensive, for heaven's sake. I'm not out to poison you, just to...' He waves his hand as if mixing elements in the air.

'To what?'

'Expand your culinary horizons.'

'Okay. Anything to go with it? Salad?'

Ramsay delves back into the fridge and produces a bowl of salad and a jar of mayonnaise. 'You'll probably appreciate this more than wasabi,' he says, indicating the mayonnaise.

'Wasabi?'

'Eaten as an accompaniment to raw fish.'

'That doesn't tell me much.'

'It's a paste made from a plant root. Tastes like extra, extra strong horseradish.'

Lippy's shoulders hunch in a slight shiver and she wrinkles her nose. 'Don't like horseradish.'

'I surmised correctly then. Help yourself.'

'You made these?'

'Yes. I told you I'd let you sample my sushi.'

Lippy moves one piece onto her plate. "Hmm.'

'Next time I'll break out the chopsticks.'

Lippy pokes the black wrapping with her fork. It looks like black polythene that's failed the quality test as it surface is not completely smooth but lined and grainy.

'Seaweed,' says Ramsay.

'Should've known. I'll need to refer to you as the seaweed man.'

'Rather appropriate.'

'Ramsay...,' she pushes the sushi around her plate, 'my play... rehearsals start next week.' She sees him stiffen slightly then relax.

'You must be over the moon.'

'I never thought it would happen. So...yes.' Ramsay dips his head. 'You're...you're okay about it, aren't you?' A cloud of apprehension moves across Lippy's face.

Ramsay takes a deep breath. 'I'm okay about it. Thanks to your sterling work. In fact, I'll come and see it.'

'Promise?'

'Promise. If I can sit beside the author.'

'Wouldn't have you sitting anywhere else.'

'Hope it busts the box office.'

A grin spreads over Lippy's face, and elbows the cloud away. 'Thanks.' She takes a tentative bite of the ingredients rolled within the seaweed, liberally spread with mayonnaise, and munches slowly, experiencing taste and texture. Her head bounces and flicks to one side. 'You know, it's quite good.' Ramsay gives a weak smile. 'I might develop a liking for these.'

'Any time. Made on demand.'

'You didn't answer my question about the police.'

'Detective Inspector Raisin — by the way, your friend Jasmine appears to have developed a penchant for the pink shirted one.'

'His sense of humour and cowboy boots appeal to her.'

'Perhaps I should try a pink shirt—'

'Not your style, Ramsay.'

'No. I'm more a hair shirt man.'

'Some people fall for stray dogs...' Jess's ears prick to alert mode and swivel. '...Jasmine falls for odd people. She likes the idiosyncratic. Men who are unconventional. They hypnotise her.'

'That's me ruled out.'

'She's always been like that.'

'There's a Mr Jasmine?'

'In the past. I'm not sure whether the position is separation or divorce. They keep in touch.'

'I might have guessed.'

'When he's back in civilisation.' Ramsay's eyebrow hoists into a question mark. 'He's some kind of anthropologist — studies remote tribes in various parts of the world, their weird and wonderful customs.'

'I could say appropriate, but best not to.'

Lippy chortles. 'Parts of the world Jasmine wouldn't travel to within thousands of miles of.'

'Think of the despatches she could have written from such places.'

'Too dreadful to contemplate. Jasmine relishes the comforts of civilisation.'

'Granted, they're hard to give up.'

Lippy waves her fork. 'But you adroitly changed the subject. What did Raisin say? Any leads in the case?'

'Definite developments, it would appear. Which reminds me...' He glances at his watch. 'You don't mind if I switch on TV for the news, do you?'

'Carry on.'

Ramsay switches on a small television that sits on the work surface and surfs channels. 'There should be a news programme about now. Gotcha!'

'What are we interested in?'

'You haven't heard?'

'Something's happened?'

'A man fell overboard from the Neucastle to Amsterdam ferry. During the night. Though the word fell is disputed.'

'Who fell or—?'

'Shh! Here it is.' Ramsay listens, sitting forward in his chair, tenseness in his posture and in the lines gouged on his face. The brief facts as they are known are given in an impassive voice over shots of a similar ferry and the port at IJmuiden near Amsterdam. Then with a flick of expression from serious to ridiculous, the news reader is off on another tack.'

Lippy shrugs. 'Name doesn't ring a bell.'

'No, but I gather the name too is disputed.'

'Did Raisin tell you about this?'

'He mentioned it, yes.'

'So what's the connection with the murder.'

'Raisin suspects the person who fell might be associated with either The Galley or Black Square factions'

'I see. Fleeing to Amsterdam.'

'Fleeing the consequences of his actions. That's what Raisin thinks at any rate.'

In the afternoon the rain clouds drift off and blinks of sun appear in chinks in the cotton wool cloud cover. Jess pads to and from the door, whines pathetically, and looks in expectation at Ramsay.

'She wants her walk.'

'Does she miss Kat?'

'She's my dog. I got her for company. To Jess, Kat has only ever been a rare visitor — one who demanded the attention she usually enjoys.'

Jess pads across to Lippy and lays her head on her lap, eyes limpid, tail wagging hopefully. Lippy strokes the top of her head. 'What silky hair you have. Wish mine was as glossy.' Jess snuffles.

'She pays you more attention than she does Kat. She must like you.'

'I never had a pet — well, I had a goldfish once, but you can hardly call that a pet.'

'Are you up for a turn along the beach?'

'If I can borrow a jacket. I can't remember when I last walked on sand. Well, apart from...'

Jess pelts back and forward and her paws send sand spinning into the air. She is invigorated by space to cavort, the ground beneath her feet giving yet firm, and the myriad of scents to follow and run to origin. Up and down the beach she pelts as she splashes through puddles, and explores to the water's edge where she plays chicken with the waves. Her ears stick up but flop at the ends, her tail is held aloft, quivering, swaying slightly as she runs, sometimes reverting to full wag when she comes across a particular pleasure.

Lippy wears an old jacket of Ramsay's with the sleeves turned over, hugged around her by her arms or left to swing open. Ramsay picks up the stick that he leaves in a bush where track and grass merge with beach, and with a bit of searching in the undergrowth finds one suited to Lippy. So now they both meander along by the water's edge, sticks clutched in hands, ready to unearth or prod items they come across. The sand is grainy with crushed shells in different colours that catch the light

— it reminds Lippy of pointillist paintings she saw last year, perhaps the year before, at the Gallery of Modern Art in Edin. She, Ramsay and Jess are making their own marks on nature's pointillist work.

They huddle on the limpet-encrusted rocks, their surface dried by sun and breeze, though water still lingers in dips and crannies. With her stick Lippy whisks water in a pool near her feet. A tiny crab climbs out and scuttles off to a crack in the rock. Around them seaweed drapes itself. The receding tide has left much of it with a coating of sand that, as it dries, glitters like frosting. Fronds of the bulbous seaweed, yellow green in the light, remind her of olive branches laden with olives, the pointed variety with sharp stones. She picks up a strand to look closer at it.

'Lovely stuff, seaweed. I've become fascinated by it,' admits Ramsay.

'I suppose it's under-appreciated. We don't really think of it.'

'In fact...' Ramsay strokes his fingers over a frond that's gold shot with pink, a contemplative look on his face.'

'In fact?' Lippy prompts.

'I'm thinking of writing a book on seaweed.'

'What an interesting idea.'

'A million miles away from politics.'

'There's the environmental aspect, though. That's political.'

'True.'

'You'd need photographs.'

'Lots. I envisage a publication that's glossy, colourful, informative. A book that tells of the different seaweeds, how they grow, the habitats they provide, how we use them in cosmetics and for food. Sushi, of course. The other uses being investigated.'

'You sound as if you've given it thought.'

'Been mulling it over for a while. I need a rope to help me climb back into the world. Writing a book could be my rope.'

'Never thought of a book as a rope, but—'

'You'll help me, won't you? Give me advice.'

'I know nothing about seaweed.'

'On how to structure the book. Fit everything together.'

'I'd love to.'

'Good. I've already begun my research. I'll show you my material when we go back to the house.'

After a meal and poring over Ramsay's research and photographs already taken, they watch the news for updates on the man who fell or was pushed from the ferry to Amsterdam (the story hasn't changed merely been rehashed). The feeling of comfort experienced in each other's company makes it almost inevitable that Ramsay suggests Lippy stay the night.

'It's my bed, in case you're bothered by that', he rushes to assure her. 'The day the expenses saga broke Kat kicked me out. So I set up my own pad in another room.' As the words spill out he looks awkward, like a teenager not quite sure what he is letting himself in for yet who desperately wants to take the step. He looks with hope at Lippy, his eyes half pleading, half proud at his audacity at asking the question.

Lippy half laughs, though is clutched by embarrassment too. Her husband decamped years ago. Since then one or two men have shown interest, but nothing serious. It's a long time since she felt so at one with another person, and the desire to be with Ramsay, lend a hand in his journey back into the world, is strong. She wants to share his project and help smooth its road to success as she's gripped by a belief that it will succeed. She wants to be part of that, not to claim any of the kudos, just to feel a flicker of satisfaction that she has helped.

'It's fine...I'll understand if you don't...it's a big ask, but....' He touches her arms with his hands. 'Please.'

Lippy is mortified to find she is giggling like an inexperienced teenager instead of the woman-of-the-world that she is. She needs to propel words of reassurance out of her mouth as Ramsay's hopeful expression begins to turn to hurt. 'Let me get my bag,' is what she says.

'Your bag?'

Lippy nods, laughs a tad too loudly. 'I decided to take a leaf from Jasmine's book of life.'

'A fascinating book, I'm sure. But which leaf?'

'The be-prepared leaf.'

'Oh?' Like scouts.'

'Jasmine always carries everything she needs for an overnight stay in her outsize handbag. Just in case.'

'Wonder if Raisin has discovered that?'

'Her reasoning is that a journalist — in my case substitute author and playwright — never knows when an overnight stay might be necessary. Or enjoyable.'

'I like her style.'

'Good, because my overnight bag is in the car.'

'Does your staying rank as necessary? Or enjoyable?

'Necessary only inasmuch as I want to — very much want to.' She lets her fingers flutter over his hand. 'Enjoyable? Well, it's a while since...'

'We'll upskill together.'

Lippy giggles again. 'That conjures up wonderful images.'

'You thought I'd ask?'

'I must have known… Yes, I hoped you would.'

At the table Lippy sips her coffee, a Cheshire cat grin on her face, a fawn towelling bathrobe wrapped around her. She didn't ask who previously wore it. If it was Kat, then she is gone, but the robe remains so can be claimed by her. Today, for some reason, the world looks different. The kitchen is filled with bustle. Ramsay, looking carefree in tracksuit bottoms and a T-shirt, tosses hot toast between his hands while the coffee percolator chortles merrily as it makes a further brew. He talks of an omelette for lunch. They can walk to a nearby farm and buy fresh eggs to make it, and there are mushrooms in the fridge to add to it, along with a slice of brie. In the afternoon — what would she like to do this afternoon? He turns towards her.

Lippy leans her arms on the table. She can't remember when she last felt so comfortable, happy — so much at home she almost thinks. Good old Jasmine. She must remember and tell her of the efficacy of her overnight bag strategy. Though she suspects Jasmine already knows, otherwise she wouldn't be an advocate of it.

Jess dashes around the kitchen between Ramsay, Lippy and her water bowl. She expresses an interest in the toast and Ramsay tears a piece from his slice and feeds it to her before he wanders across to the door. 'Time you went out, Jess girl. The garden for now. A walk later.' Jess's feet scrabble and slide across the flagstones of the back hall as she dashes for the door.

Lippy studies the view through the window. The sky is as blue as a sapphire, the sun is shining and is almost overhead in the sky as they slept so late. She stretches contentedly. Before she takes any further decisions she's off for a shower.

The bathroom door is left unlocked — a bit of bravado on her part, she feels. An invitation, a message should Ramsay come exploring, though she's not sure what she'll do if he actually walks in with a view to sharing the shower. Best not to think about it, and just react when it happens — the way she played last night. And that worked out fine, better than fine. It took her to another place she has almost forgotten existed. Tentative beginnings was what she expected, but Ramsay had other ideas. Muttered he had much lost time to make up for. As she stands under the warm water and lets it run over her back, her breasts, her stomach, her arms, into every nook and cranny of her body, she closes her eyes, and the water is Ramsay's fingers and tongue, letting her relive the night that is firmly etched in her mind.

Today she feels twenty years younger than yesterday. As she dries herself she wipes the steam from the mirror to see whether years have indeed been shed. Her face glows, her eyes sparkle, her wrinkles — what wrinkles? Merely a few lines that confirm she smiles and laughs and occasionally cries. What she sees is a face full of life, a face that radiates happiness. She wishes she had other clothes to wear — the dress she wore when Derek and Gail came to dinner, or a frilly blouse — something colourful to reflect the way she feels. Instead she pulls on her jeans and a clean blue top from her overnight bag.

The farmer's wife has a stoical expression on her face and wears jeans that are turned up above her ankles, and a baggy T-shirt. The flip-flops on her feet slap her cracked heels as she goes off along a linoleum-floored passage to get their eggs. She knows Ramsay yet doesn't indulge in small talk, but briskly hands him a box of twelve new laid eggs and states the cost. Ramsay takes the eggs and hands over the correct money. All three of them nod and smile.

Instead of returning to make the omelette they head down the coast and end up in Berrick. The town is busy, with parking spaces as scarce as winning lottery numbers, but eventually after driving around they track one down. Ramsay goes off to buy a ticket from the machine while Lippy takes in her surroundings. She hasn't been in Berrick for years.

They find somewhere to eat before deciding to walk around the old town walls, peering down into the remains of buildings pierced by arches, window openings protected by heavy metal grilles, the stone remains of military life in previous centuries. They pass cannon, well cared for and elegant in design, that still point seawards through loopholes in the defensive walls. Lippy is amused by the seats provided for those who want to enjoy the sea view but are prevented from doing so by the height of the walls. Solution. A stepped wooden platform. She ascends the steps and sits down to see the Northerly Sea unfold before her.

The spring day has warmth in the sun, yet the sea is grey and forbidding, steely with a hint of menace. Perhaps it's her surroundings on this fortified wall, built to protect the town from ravaging Caledons, for around her she hears echoes of the sword clashes of vicious wars and the plotting of manipulative warlords, the barbed words of power struggles, the mean cries of retribution and greed. She almost imagines the waters still writhe with memories of centuries of hostility that stretch right up to the present day, and she feels a blade of ice slither up her spine and lunge at her heart.

To circle back to the car they go round by the main street. As they pass a small clothes boutique Lippy's attention is caught by a frilly red blouse. Her footsteps falter. She stops. Ramsay strolls back to see what has snagged her attention.

Lippy indicates the blouse with a dip of her head. 'Rather nice, isn't it.'

'It would suit you.'

'You think so?'

'Definitely. Go on, treat yourself.' She hesitates, before she steps towards the door.'

'I'll wait here.'

He had taken steaks from the freezer the previous evening and before he cooks them he opens a bottle of red wine. It was late by the time they returned so as they eat they watch the rerun of the news on the Plus One channel. Lippy pays little attention to the news reader. Her thoughts are elsewhere. She seems unable to stop them soaring with new possibilities.

The ferry incident has moved up the headlines and is now second to an item on Iraq. Confirmation is given that a man from Caledon went overboard early the previous morning, and despite a search involving the boat, a lifeboat and a helicopter, no body has yet been recovered. The news reader indicates the man and his wife travelled under false passports, but no names are mentioned. The film clips shown previously fade to an interview with the mother of a man whom the Dutch police hold for questioning on the incident.

The woman is dressed as if for a special occasion, wearing a peacock blue brocade suit with an eye-catching brooch. Jewellery is strung around her neck and bristles from her wrists. Her fingernails are black, and on most of her fingers she wears large rings that catch the light and toss it around. Her makeup, Lippy reckons, is centimetres deep — though is unable to cover the scowl that twists her face — while her long wavy hair is dyed a very red chestnut. She gesticulates wildly with her hands, which disconcertingly disappear then reappear within the picture frame. Her voice is shrill as she shouts a response to the interviewer, insisting the Dutch police are idiots, nincompoops, stupid bloody morons. No way could her son Jut have pushed a person overboard. No way could he have done such a thing. Idiotic Dutch bastards. Her son's a quiet, considerate person without a hostile bone in his body or a malevolent thought in his head. She draws breath and bestows on the television reporter a brittle smile, eyelashes fluttering over eyes as hard as granite.

'The man who fell overboard — whoever he is — must've been drunk, legless probably. These ferries are notorious for that. People go for a good time, a booze cruise. Out to enjoy themselves with no thought for others. Then when they go and do something stupid, poor, innocent bystanders get the blame.' She sniffs.

The reporter tries to break into the flow, cut her off, so he can probe deeper into her son, his identification by the dead man's wife.

'Vinegar sticks!' the woman shouts. 'I thought you wanted to bloody interview me.'

Lippy jumps in her seat. The tone of the voice, the hair... her mind picks up an echo of the past, plugs in the appropriate cables and makes the connection. 'I don't believe it! Good heavens! It can't possibly be.'

'Lippy?'

'Ramsay, who's that woman?' She raises her red blouse-clad arm to point to the screen. "Who did the caption say she was?'

'The shrieking redhead?'

'Yes.'

'Brankton's wife apparently. I've been told they stay not far from here, but I've never seen them.'

'It's her — I'm sure it's her.'

'Who?'

'Look. The caption. There's her name. Eilidh Brankton. Talk about being slapped in the face by the past!'

'You know her?'

'Wow and wow again! I just can't believe it. After all these years...'

'What?'

'Remember I mentioned a friend...an incident when I was young.'

Ramsay points the remote at the screen to turn down the sound. 'Is Eilidh Brankton the friend?'

Lippy nods, her eyes glittering. 'Small world. Dear heavens!'

'She's said to be a nasty piece of work.'

'I thought she'd ruined my life. For long enough afterwards it seemed like it.'

'I can understand that.'

Lippy stretches her hands across the table and grasps Ramsay's. 'Instead, she might just have had the opposite effect.'

37 - Fallout

Repercussions in the People's Union Party are swift — as decisive as an axe chop. As Lippy and Ramsay sit mulling over the television appearance of Eilidh, Brankton's ruthless red-haired wife and probable director of the Black Square faction, the call goes out, searing its way through phone lines, to spin doctors and MCPs. The parliamentary party is locked down, tighter than a clenched fist in a plaster cast. Immediate instructions are issued against any media contact or comment, uttered or on social media. Profiles are to be kept low, preferably out of sight but if that is not possible then definitely confined to the shadows.

Within the cage a palpable air of unease stalks amongst the imprisoned. The country is now in the run-up to an election and deep concern is muttered about the impact this debacle might have on the Party's chances of winning power, and on the ability of individuals to retain their seats and lifestyles should a fickle electorate waver in their support. Discontent rumbles, vitriol is poured over the perpetrators of the folly whilst scorn is expressed at the way the leadership has handled the situation. Defeat rests heavily on more than a few shoulders, and the Party hierarchy discerns a vicious gleam in certain eyes.

Old mantras are excavated and burnished: the Party must get its act together, rid itself of these factions, polish its appearance to allow the openness and transparency of its actions and organisation to shine through the political murk. Yet while heads nod in agreement to this strategy, others —scruples long since binned — believe this kind of soft, bouncy attitude achieves nothing. They are hell-bent on revenge — most likely against whoever disagrees with them — and on bringing much blacker arts into play. Voters might indicate they don't approve of, or like, negativity and slagging matches, downright lies and snide innuendoes, but the black arts stirrers have an unshakable belief in their effectiveness.

In the Party HQ, leaders and managers burn the post midnight oil. Lights seep from the edges of venetian blinds on the third floor windows of the room where members of the hierarchy, and a select few MCPs, slump over a long table and gaze into cups of cold coffee. Voices rise and fall, twist and turn, weaving denials and excuses into a multi-coloured, multi-textured blanket to cover their annoyance and ineptitude. They argue over phrases, words, nuances, as spin doctors stitch together and refashion a media release. Brankton, it will insist, is a lone wolf gone rogue due to the corrosive influence of the woman in his life, and her son whose reprobate background he insists he was unaware of. Further, it will assert, Brankton was forced into taking a position against colleagues — a position he now deeply regrets. As soon as the implications of his position became apparent, Brankton tendered his resignation to his Party leader who accepted it with some sorrow. The Leader, in the draft media release, touches fleetingly on Brankton's many years of devoted service to the Party while deploring the recent actions into which he was inveigled. Resignation, therefore, is the honourable action for Brankton, and the only option open to him.

Those who consorted closely with the dishonoured Member are not named, but as Mutt's eyes travel round the table they rest fleetingly on each one, in each piercing glance a conviction of their guilt, a warning about their future conduct. His glance lingers fractionally on the face of Ming who struggles to hide an uncertain emotion. Embarrassment perhaps. Or relief. In the late afternoon, with clarification in the news media of Jut's involvement, and the invective spewed on television by his mother, Party phone lines became red hot with traffic. Mutt had contacted Ming to nominate him as the Party's grey-suited man, bearer of tidings to Brankton that his resignation was expected on Mutt's desk, immediately, without delay, and without discussion. Or else. Ming had scowled down the phone, spluttered and stuttered at being shunted into such a position. However, it was made clear to him by his Party Leader, in a brusque and decisive voice, that this was the price for his readmission to the fold. With his position as an MCP on the line, Ming gritted his teeth. There was no contest. So, in a curt response he agreed to act as hatchet man.

Ming had felt a stirring akin to sorrow for Brankton. The man didn't seem to take in what he said to him, despite him laying it out clearly. The man floundered in a daze, unable to understand or accept what had happened. Jut had killed two people — that's what he was being told at any rate. But why? What had urged him to do it? Or perhaps he should ask himself who. But he didn't want to go there because he knew the answer, and the answer was inconceivable. The answer was...Eilidh, his wife. No, no. There was a mistake. This couldn't be true. Yet he knew it was, which was why he wasn't ready to think of it. Resignation? Whatever was required to let his mind focus on Eilidh — though he wasn't sure he liked the direction his thoughts were taking, questioning whether she had duped him, whether — deluded by her gushing admiration — he had been an idiot to lose head, heart, money and now career to her. He would sit down and dash off the letter Ming insisted he write, and then he could concentrate his thoughts on what had happened. And what to do about Eilidh.

Four hours before the early hours meeting at HQ was convened, Brankton's resignation lay on Mutt's Parliamentary desk.

Ming's mind swings back to the present. He lowers his head from Mutt's gaze and nods at the wording of the media release, though someone else has raised an objection that renews the sighs of exasperation, with the odd pen thrown onto the table. The wording is pushed through and weariness descends as chairs are shoved back and people scrabble for the door and home.

Ming squares his shoulders, and grabs the opportunity to insist to colleagues who mill around him that he saw through Brankton, saw right through him like an X-ray machine, and merely played halfheartedly along to gather intelligence on which avenues or down which alleys Pied Piper Brankton intended to lead the Party. He avers he always suspected Brankton was careering along a dangerous track to a dead end. And of course events have proved him right. Absolutely right. As can be seen by the backtracking that is taking place. But he was merely there for information, looking out for the Party, watching its back. Never, he repeats as he grasps passing arms with his hands, never did he have any intention of supporting that fool Brankton against Mutt. His outburst receives no response other than a few rolled eyes and cleared throats.

Released from the building, he lets his anger rip by kicking an Irn Bru can that lolls on the pavement. Mutt — what an ignorant, arrogant bastard he is. Pushing him around. Demeaning him like that. Who the hell does he think he is! Does he realise who he's tussling with? Ming. Mingally Dulse — ally and confident of the great Charlie Kintail. Sitting in his car, he thumps the steering wheel, then an idea forms in his mind. He digs his mobile from his pocket, switches it on (it had been silenced for the meeting), and presses Jasmine Stane's number. The time is after three in the morning, so no chance of her replying. He can leave a voicemail message, number withheld. An anonymous message will tip off Jasmine who will hopefully, in search of the low down, contact her Parliamentary friend — him — and show her gratitude in the best way journalists can. By giving him good, positive coverage — and plenty of it — to enhance his profile. And get back at that idiot Mutt.

With a tremble of his lips he remembers how well his interview with her went, though the piece has not yet appeared in the Callyman, and how she oozed warmth and understanding. Not like Mutt and those other bastards at the meeting. They'd have knifed him between the shoulder blades given half a chance. That deadbeat Mutt will have his work cut out to stifle this little episode. But Brankton has been an idiot too. So where does that leave him? He has no time to respond to his rhetorical question as the phone clicks and he hears a woman's voice.

'Shit!' He freezes, and hopes his exclamation hasn't been heard.

'Hello.' He doesn't respond, tries to mute his breathing. 'Hello. Who's calling?' She mentions no name but is certain it's Ming. Interesting! Jasmine is a journalist, used to speaking on the phone. She has developed a large database of voices she can recognise — an attribute useful for a woman in her position.

His first impulse is to disconnect the call, but then he shrugs and decides to brazen it out. 'Apologies, must have pressed your number by mistake. Eyes tired…like the rest of me. Not functioning up to speed.'

'Late on the go for you, Ming. It is Ming, isn't it?'

'Mmm.'

Jasmine had been phoned in the late evening by Lippy, astonished by the discovery the string-puller at the centre of the recent shenanigans is known to her. Aware a mobile is not the most secure vehicle for the imparting of such news and its dissection, Jasmine jumped into her red car and zoomed down the coast to be brought up to speed with events. She swithered over taking a couple of bottles of wine, but decided to leave them in the rack. Lippy and Ramsay would not welcome her visit being prolonged overnight. Besides, if the information is as good as suggested, she will want to return to write it up ready to lay before her editor first thing in the morning. If that means an all-nighter at the computer, then so be it. Sacrifices, she understands, need to be made to make the jump, over other hopefuls, from Lifestyle to Politics at the Callyman. Besides, the magnitude of this story and its ramifications could establish her as one of the most highly regarded political journalists in Caledon.

Before the phone rang, she had been sitting in front of her computer for an hour, arranging and rearranging the information Lippy provided with what she already knows. A rough draft taunts her from the screen. It needs more work. She thinks of Ming, wonders if she can pump him for information. Then, as if on cue, he phones. His phone call at such a late hour suggests unhappiness, in all probability with the implementation of stringent panic measures in the People's Union Party. Jasmine has a good idea of the defensive strategies that will be instigated, how wagons will be circled for Party protection. The distancing of MCPs in its barrel from the bad apple that is Brankton will be a top priority. So easy does it, a bit of small hours banter, lowering her voice into husky regions to make it more intimate, before she slides gently into the outskirts of the topic that consumes her mind. Under her tutelage, Ming, she is certain, will splash a few sweet droplets into her piece. All unattributed, of course — that goes without saying — but they will add authenticity and assurance that her finger is firmly clamped on the pulse of what is playing out. She tops up her glass of wine and leans back in her chair.

A post-it note is stuck to the corner of her computer screen. It reminds her to phone a friend who owns a house in Tenerife, in a little village near Costa Adeje. Attractive place, attractive climate, especially at this time of year. But can she attract Detective Inspector Raisin to spend a few days there with her? Of course she can. No problem. She'll phone him in the next couple of days. By then he should have shunted the Jut case off his desk.

The edict circulated to those in the Parliamentary group of the People's Union Party means most — though some unwillingly — will keep mouths zipped. Diary entries, and engagements that mention the name Brankton, are hastily deleted A number of meetings and social evenings are also scored through, pressure of work cited as an excuse. Attendance at a house party with fishing and clay pigeon shooting is on a number of cancellation lists, but there is no response from the inviter to telephone calls or emails.

Flanked by two hefty constables from Caledon, Jut Colcannon is flown back to Edin. Refused bail, he awaits his fate in a cell, but spurns the services of a lawyer. The only person with whom he will communicate is his mother, Eilidh. Her fate is still being debated by DI Raisin, who ponders on what grounds she can be charged, as she denies all knowledge of her son's crimes and other dubious activities. Though perhaps a search of the house will reveal the necessary evidence.

Mrs Elsie Ravenscrofte has reverted to her own identity and is shipped back to Neucastle where she is hustled into a police car and driven back to Edin. DI Raisin waits, fingers drumming on his desk, to interview her. She is the key to the entire case, as far as he is concerned. From Jut Colcannon (via Mrs Brankton) and Mrs Brankton herself, he has pieced together a train of events that corresponds to what others with an involvement in the case have indicated. Selina will hopefully have been told sufficient by her husband Schaw to provide the glue.

Then there is the matter of the package that Bluebell McDaid was perturbed about when he visited her in hospital. The DI purses his lips. His eyes scan the ceiling but see only a blur. The poor woman was devastated by the murder of Wilkie Smart. She was enjoying a fling with a fresh-faced guy half her age, but so what. In this shitty world you take pleasure where you can find it. No, the affair didn't raise his eyebrows. It was Bluebell's reaction when she learnt of Schaw's death that interested him. He was a friend she'd known for years, ever since Charlie Kintail had given her a leg up the candidate's ladder. She hadn't succeeded with Westmunster, but with another wee bit of magic from Schaw, she'd made it into the Caledon Parliament. So she and Schaw went way back, therefore her grief was understandable.

But what appeared to overwhelm her grief was the fact Schaw had stashed a package at her house. He asked her permission but, beyond a brief explanation of what was in the package, gave no indication as to why the contents were of such significance. Nor will Bluebell hazard a guess, though DI Raisin finds no difficulty in letting his mind sift through the possibilities and probabilities. Schaw had insisted it was best Bluebell didn't know where it was hidden. But she can guess, as does the Detective Inspector. Bluebell only knows that the package contains stuff that mustn't fall into the wrong hands.

With Schaw gone, the package is assuming enormous proportions in Bluebell's mind. The DI says he will return to the house to search for it, but Bluebell grows increasingly agitated, deciding she needs to speak to Schaw's wife, Selina, before she comes to a decision. She doesn't know Selina, but Schaw might have mentioned the package to her. DI Raisin hopes Selina is aware of the papers, their whereabouts and the reason for their importance. He needs Selina to persuade Bluebell that the safest place for the contents of the package is in his hands. Her co-operation will help determine the charges she faces, though he acknowledges that as she was unaware, until embarkation, of the false passports, there is little, if anything, can be pinned on her.

Ramsay's wife, Kat, has a man in tow — a man who is an extremely good catch, especially for a woman like her, no longer a young thing, lines like a spider's web are etched on her face, she is still — though she hopes not for much longer — married to a man she now considers a birdbrained dinosaur. Kat's new man is a businessman, divorced, hard-headed and ruthless when needs be with his workers and competitors, yet generous to Kat. Her hand has taken to stirring the air to show off the bracelet he recently bought her. She is preparing to jet off to one of his many properties for a holiday, though the man will fit in some business whilst there. So Kat has little interest in Ramsay and his cage break-out, or into whose arms he is happy to fall. Kat's mind is fixated on more exciting events and possibilities.

The evening of the People's Union Party's frantic activity at its HQ, Brian spends in a bar. In response to a number of pleading phone calls, a couple of friends he has almost lost touch with turn up out of curiosity to see what the Caledon Parliament has made of him, and receive a surprise. After enthusiastically welcoming them to his corner of the bar, Brian's attitude veers between fury, despondency and bravado. It doesn't take them long to decide all is not well in his world. One of his friend's has brought along a cousin, home for a holiday from Estonia where he works in the rapidly mushrooming electronics sector, and for a while Brian's gloom is lightened by burbling tales of a country about which he knows nothing yet has in the recent past flippantly dismissed as a midge in a beehive. Some of the information sticks to a part of his brain, and over the following days and weeks he investigates overseas opportunities. His parents are shocked. Brian himself is shocked. But when he mutters about the country's inherited democracy serving the few instead of the many, his father welcomes him to the real world and suggests now is the time for him to change Party as his own lot are headed for a big shock come the election.

Down by the coast Lippy and Ramsay take each day as it comes. They look no further ahead than the first night of Lippy's play. Each day they walk on the beach, with Jess capering around them. They watch the waves froth over sand and pebbles; sit, hand-in-hand, on purple rocks, staring out to the wide horizon — sometimes misty making differentiation between sea and sky almost impossible, sometimes sharply clear, a hard line drawn between water and air. They chat about whatever enters their minds, and on the way back along the shore pick up a strand of seaweed to add to the flowing bouquet that already hangs beside the front door to forecast sun or storms.

By the same author

DOROTHY BRUCE

On the WAKE OF THE COUP

A satirical political novel set in an offshore north-west European island

A coup. The civil service takes over government. Caledon, where a referendum vote favouring independence has been ignored, is given its autonomy, leaving Downsouth under a dictatorship.

In the wake of the coup Caledon born McTavish and Ludmilla, from an influential family in Downsouth, form a relationship whilst working together in Caledon where a colleague is mysteriously murdered.

They move to work for the Downsouth Government. Despite Ludmilla's assertions that life is good, it isn't long before rumoured manipulations and peculiar happenings cause concern. Conflicting loyalties are exposed, questions raised about colleagues. What are they plotting – the re-annexation of Caledon or the restoration of democracy in Downsouth? When Ludmilla disappears with the King's daughter the trail leads back to Caledon.

A political satire and a tale of two countries – are they really Scotland and England?

Plus ça change, plus c'est la même chose.
The more things change,
the more they remain the same.

Twinlaw
PUBLISHING
www.twinlawpublishing.co.uk

£9.99
€11.60
$14.99